The Æglet's Answer

BOOK TWO IN THE KINSMAN'S TREE SERIES

The Æglet's Answer

TIMOTHY MICHAEL HURST

ISBN-13: 978-1-9768523-7-4

Dedication & Appreciation

I Corinthians 1:27-28 & 31 (KJV) But God hath chosen the foolish things of the world to confound the wise; and God hath chosen the weak things of the world to confound the things which are mighty; And base things of the world, and things which are despised, hath God chosen, yea, and things which are not, to bring to nought things that are: That, according as it is written, He that glorieth, let him glory in the Lord.

To my lovely wife, Brandi— Here we are again, at the end of another book! Can you believe it? Thank you for your encouragement, faith, and support on this adventure. I am amazed at God's provision along the way, and I'm glad to have you walking this path alongside me.

To my mother—Your support and assistance were invaluable on this project. Thank you for your inspirational example of faith in pursuing your calling. I, too, am doing my best to follow Christ.

To my father—Your frequent encouragements gave me much-needed boosts on the many long, difficult days. Thank you.

To Bev, Brenda, Sandra, and Judy—I now fully believe everyone needs the kind of support you ladies have provided over the course of preparing this series. I cherish your prayers and exhortations.

To my greater family in Christ—I thank you once more for all your prayers and support in helping us arrive at the end of another project.

To the Rio Rancho Public Library system—Your study rooms, free Wi-Fi, and friendly assistance proved extremely beneficial when I needed a quiet place to work away from it all. Libraries are an important community resource, and I hope you continue to serve our city as well as you have served me.

Glossary

General Terms

Ægle (EH-gul)—A race of large raptorial birds

The Eben'kayah (EH-ben KAI-yah)—A group of Etom who preserve the prophecies of Elyon

Endego (EN-de-goh)—Nida and Nat's home town

Etom (EH-tom)—A race of small, semi-insectoid creatures

Etma (ET-ma)—A female Etom

Etém (eh-TEM)—A male Etom

Malakím (ma-la-KEEM)—The radiant servants of Lord Elyon

Nihúkolem (nee-HU-koh-lem)—The shadowy wraith army of the Empire

Sakkan—An Etom village far northeast of Endego

Shedím (shed-EEM)—Fallen, rebel Malakím

Sprig—A race of tree-like beings

Characters

Agatous—The Chief Counciletma of the Eben'kayah

Alcarid (AL-ca-reed)—A senior Counciletém of the Eben'kayah

Dempsey—A young etém highly involved with the Eben'kayah

Gael—An æglet; Sayah's sister

Kehren—The etma headmistress of Nat's school and Rae's mother

Makrïos (MACK-ree-ohs)—A Man, and Captain in the Empire of Chōl's army

Miyam—A Sprig who tends to the needs of new arrivals to Sanctuary

Nat—An etém; Nida's son

Nida (NEE-da)—An etma; Nat's mother

Pikrïa (PIK-ree-ah)—Nida's Great Aunt; a wealthy and solitary etma

Rae—An etma; Nat's best friend

Sayah (SAI-yah)—An æglet; Gael's brother

Shoym—An enigmatic and kindly gentletém

Tram—Rae's father; a wealthy merchant

Glossary (cont.)

The Supernatural
Astéri (as-TER-ee)—A messenger of Lord Elyon
Elyon (el-EE-awn)—The Creator of the universe and so much more
Gaal (GAWL)—The Kinsman
Helél (heh-LEL)—The villainous leader of the Shedím

The Nihúkolem
Belláphorus (bel-LAF-or-us)—A close comrade of Mūk-Mudón
Cloust—A close comrade of Mūk-Mudón
Imafel (EE-ma-fel)—A close comrade of Mūk-Mudón
Mūk-Mudón (MOOK muh-DAWN)—An ambitious, dashing Warlord

Epilogue:
The Kinsman's Tree

Nat awoke in sheltered darkness, at first aware of his encapsulation, then of stifling warmth. The severity of his confinement became increasingly apparent to him as he discovered that he was unable to move any of his extremities but for limited movement of his hands.

Spurred by momentary panic, he felt around the inside of his enclosure, and, encountering a woody texture, struck out in an attempt to shatter his breathy prison. Curiously, he sensed his enclosure sway as he contemplated his failed attempt to break free.

With all the strength he could muster, he rocked back and forth, pressing his hands against the walls in concert with his efforts as his swings grew in length and intensity. He swayed violently to one side, then the other, noting that he did not tumble, his head apparently affixed to the inside of his mysterious pod, before hearing a sharp "snap!" at the apex of his swing. For an instant, he experienced floating, which quickly became falling, as he plummeted in darkness, eyes wide and hands pressed out, braced against the inevitable . . .

Prologue:
The Æglet's Answer

Set amongst the thorns of strife,
A fractured egg brings forth new life
That wakes beneath a darkening sky
Without a hope or chance to fly.

Despondency awaits him there,
The weaker born between the pair.
A meager being for meager things
Subject to a sibling's sting.

Questions spoken from the air
Compel him to the broken edge,
A precipice beyond all cares
Or worries he might ever fledge.

Ready to sound his reply
He swallows now his throaty lump.
Trusting in new hope to fly
The æglet's answer is to jump!

Chapter One
The Ægles' Aerie

A lone, mottled orb remained intact among the remnants of fragmented shells that rested within a wicker cradle crowning leafy boughs. The keening cries of Sister first-born stirred the nascent life, and the rocking egg attracted Mother's interest in the afternoon heat of the summer sunlight.

Faint scratching emanated, distinct, yet quiet among the hungry din, and peeking through the port, the beak of one eager to meet his kin. The tiny nostrils drew deeply of the foreign air, the breath ending with a fitful sniff. Mother watched eagerly, anticipating her chick's emergence any moment.

Inexplicably, however, the chick turned within the shell to present instead soggy down through the jagged window, then fell still. Curious, Mother cocked her head, uncertain at the strange behavior as Father approached. Curled up nearby in the warmth of the falling afternoon sun, Sister's cries grew quiet as she settled down for a rest after a hearty first meal, leaving both parents to focus on their remaining unhatched chick.

With patient, gentle concern, Mother nudged the freckled egg with her hooked beak, hoping to elicit from the chick the burst of energetic activity necessary to break free from the incubatory prison. The child unresponsive to her more delicate persuasions, she pecked forcefully through the opening, expecting at least a squawk of protest, and at most a frustrated reprisal that might crack the egg open.

Not a peep.

Not a chirp.

Mother looked to Father in awareness that the Blight often struck those chicks too weak to hatch from egg into the world on their own. Nevertheless, a Blighted child was better than one stillborn. She raised a talon over the egg, intent on tearing her chick from the deathly capsule.

9

Father swept a walnut brown wing over the egg, placing himself between it and Mother. He looked up at her with imploring, golden orbs and shook his head back and forth in slow, gentle arcs. His eyes, able stare into the blazing, blinding brilliance of the sun, blanched under the fierce and fiery intensity of Mother's gaze.

Hesitant, he relented, backing away with bobbing steps to stand with wings furled and head downcast, on the edge of the nest, his back turned to Mother and the egg. Mother was displeased at Father's protest, yet reconsidered with talon upraised, worry and doubt a powerful undercurrent beneath the surface flow of her often menacing features. Conviction soon replaced misgiving, and ferocity furrowed her brow anew as her claw fell.

She split the shell wide open with a razor slash, her weary spawn spilling wetly onto the nest's thatched floor. With intent, Mother peered down to assess her son. His tongue lolled from his mouth as he lay sprawled on his back with moist, limp wings spread to either side and open eyes glassy. He did not look well.

Mother nudged his hollow breast once – no response. His loose and colorless tongue bothered her most, though she couldn't determine just why.

She nudged him again – no movement, though she perceived a subtle light dawn behind his eyes. His dratted tongue yet lay gray against the rough weave of the nest, and still her impotent frustration gnawed.

A final time, she prodded him – his chest rose in respiration as he blinked his chocolate eyes. His tongue grew pink, and he finally retracted the ghastly thing, much to Mother's elation. She frisked in an uncharacteristic and brief show of happiness, and sidled up to her son, who looked up at her with something like weak resentment. This was her first clutch of eggs, and as a new mother, she was not yet accustomed to the peculiarities of newborn chicks. Still, it seemed odd that her son seemed annoyed with her.

He yawned and, heavy against her side, he leaned, then tucked his head low into her feathers, prepared to sleep.

Oh no you don't! Mother thought, pecking her son gently to rouse him, then whipped her aquiline head around to glare at Father where he sulked at the nest's edge. He pretended not to notice her until she squawked in irritation. Grudgingly, he dipped down into the nest to tear a morsel of flesh from the fish that lay there. With a sullen, sidelong flick of the beak, he tossed the scaly meat to Mother, then returned to his perch. Mother stared, infuriated, as he turned his back. She caught the bit of fish with absentminded reflex trained in years of hunting, and did not break her piercing gaze, the sting of which Father felt as he hunkered away from her.

A soft press against her side reminded her to tend to her son, who once more nestled in her feathers in attempt to sleep. Mother swept the fish past her son's beak, hoping a whiff of the morsel would interest him enough to stay awake. Eyes closed, his questing beak sniffed the air, and Mother cheered within her heart. Her exultation was short-lived however, for after a moment, he lost interest, and laid his head low to bury his beak in her fringe.

Now Mother was not the most patient of creatures to begin with, and this development would simply not do. Her chick *must* eat. She would make sure of it. Winding her beak up and back, she carried the meat down across her son's face in a scaly slap.

With a fluffy, surprised shake, the chick awoke, eyes wide and beak spread in a squawk of protestation. Mother stuffed one end of the morsel into his mouth, stifling his complaints, which regardless ceased when the chick realized the food was pleasant. With greedy snaps, he gobbled up the rest, and at present resumed his squawking, though this time in demand for more.

Satisfied at having set her chick aright, Mother turned back toward Father, catching him as he snuck a low and timid peek around his wing. He straightened to look at her, his eyes glistening in supplication, and shameful head inclined in defeat. She softened, realizing him chastened, and cawed an invitation with a tilt of her head toward their son.

Brightening, Father shook his feathers in relief, then hopped down into the nest, snapping up the rest of the fish in his beak on the way to join Mother. There Mother and Father remained, doting over their son while Sister slept, and the sun fell in fire flaring across horizon's arc.

The chicks' first morning dawned, bringing with it discoveries for the entire family. Sister awoke first, rousing the rest with hungry demands. Brother, for his part, stretched and returned to dozing while Mother and Father scurried to tend to Sister. After a moment's debate, Mother elected to stay with the chicks while Father dove from the edge of the nest in relieved flight, happy to be clear of the noisy nest and in search of prey.

Mother did her best to console Sister, though none of her efforts proved effective. The æglet would not be satisfied with anything short of breakfast, and Mother grew increasingly panicked in the interim, unable as she was to please Sister. The commotion stirred Brother to peer with disdainful regard at his sibling, his contempt for the racket apparent in his gaze.

Only once before Father returned did Sister still herself, and that was the moment she noticed Brother staring. Without a sound, she looked Brother over. She sniffed and smiled slyly before resuming her cacophony. Mother, thinking Sister sated in the silence, had relaxed in the tranquil interim, but soon recommenced her alarmed fluttering about the nest in the dissonance.

Brother laid his head across his downy back once more, and observed Sister through sulky, slitted eyelids, annoyed at the interruption of his sleep. Father made a welcome entrance before long, the flap and gust of his wings announcing his return. Sister took one look at the mouse drooping from Father's beak, and locked eyes with him to give voice her keening insistence.

Seeking to assuage Sister's hunger and the accompanying ruckus as soon as possible, Father dropped the still-warm beast before her on the floor of the nest. Without so much as another glance at Father, Sister fell to with violent pecks, wetting her beak in blood.

Those unfamiliar with birds might be unaware the creatures can control the size of their pupils, which widened and shrunk with interest, happiness, anger, or fear. This expressive display is called pinning or flashing and indicates an emotional reaction to their environment. Today, and for the first time, Brother's eyes pinned with interest, the carnage before him whetting his appetite when he recalled his meal the day before.

Sated and plump from her meal, though a substantial portion of the carcass remained, Sister stretched her neck upward, tipping her head to one side and then the other. A single, piriform droplet of blood fell from her beak as she cocked her head toward Brother, who followed its grisly course with hungry anticipation. Sister spied him as he stared after the blood to its crimson splatter, and the sly smile returned.

Deliberately, meticulously, Sister jabbed at what remained of the mouse, picking at the bones until nearly nothing of substance remained as all the while Brother watched on in dismay, a plaintive chirp escaping him. When she had gratified her gluttony, she stood, a round puff of fluff atop spindly legs, and stretched her wings wide as she turned in a slow circle. She raked the nest with her talons in turn as she gyred, kicking loose bits of nest behind her, a few of which struck Brother nearby. Before finally settling, she cast a pointed look back over her shoulder, catching Brother's attention before she hooked the ragged skin of the scant carcass on a talon, and with an offhand toss, sent it flying at him.

The sticky, bony mess fell over him, blanketing him in gore. Crowing dourly, he trumpeted his displeasure while struggling out from under the fast-stiffening skin and bones. Sister paid him no further mind as he tore at her scraps, and choked down the tough fur, skin, and tendons left him.

Meanwhile, Father and Mother observed the interplay, but no warm affection existed among the ægles' instincts that might stir them to intervene. They were hunters. The strong ate the weak, and those too weak to fight for their portion may well die. Thus, was rivalry between Brother and Sister born.

It was customary among ægles to await the emergence of a dominant trait before naming their chicks. Often, this took several weeks, or even a few months while the chick developed. Ægles identified one another most often by sight, and weren't a particularly talkative bunch regardless, so the lack of names among the æglets didn't create confusion.

As was often the case between Sister and Brother, Sister was first to acquire a name, and did so with such aplomb and spectacle as usual. She was first to hatch, first to eat, first to talk, first to grow "real" feathers, which darkened as they grew strong and lost the downy softness of a chick. She was first in just about everything. Every thing but one. Brother was still the first to sleep every night, and he was unofficial nap champion of the nest.

The occasion for Sister's namesake came at the beginning of their tenth week, Sister having grown restless and impatient with strutting about the nest and intimidating Brother, whom she often bullied, pinning the smaller æglet beneath the ironclad grip of her talons and pecking at him with her beak. Mother and Father hunted together more often now the children had grown somewhat, leaving Brother at her mercy.

Even her favorite pastime of staring down from the branches adjacent to the nest had grown stale. At one time, she had only been able to manage peering over the edge of the nest, locating prey with the frightening visual acuity of their kind, and silently intimating the kill with hooked beak and slashing talon.

When first to speak, the words she whispered from her vengeful perch, "Kill, kill, kill *you*," she had spoken to none but herself, the baby-sweetness of tone belying the true, murderous intent of her statement. Mother and Father had, of course, beamed with pride not only at her facility of speech, but at its theme.

"Did you hear that, Father? Already talking!" Mother had chimed.

"What an excellent hunter she'll make!" Father had gushed, impressed with his daughter's innate aggression.

Sister had preened at the recognition, but it was a superficial response not indicative of what compelled the utterance. As if carrying another egg beneath her swelling breast, she felt a caged and frenzied energy 'scritch scritch' scratching within, questing to burst free from the shell that was her body. She instinctively sought the hunt in grim expectation that it would slake a restless bloodthirst that superseded natural hunger.

Brother had observed the interplay in the limited comprehension of his diminutive age and experience, aware that Mother and Father were yet again praising Sister for her accomplishments. He couldn't compete, nor did he care to. Least important among his concerns were the things that excited Mother and Father most. He cared first to sleep and then to eat. If his body hadn't required sustenance, he would have forsaken that as well in preference to the effortless dreaming that he best enjoyed.

Born frail through Mother's intervention, Brother was underdeveloped from the start. To make matters worse, Sister habitually hoarded the prey Mother and Father brought the æglets from their hunts, and many were the nights that sleep was a welcome respite from pangs of hunger. She grew yet larger and stronger than him, and any chance that he might challenge her, if ever there was one, disappeared. Even now, his feathers remained a pitiful reminder of his frailty, the drooping skin that covered his spindly wings visible through the piebald fluff that covered his body. Now that Sister had forsaken the infantile down of a chick for the true feathers of flight, Brother appeared half her size.

In addition to the physical flaws that diminished Brother's standing among ægles, his greatest disadvantage was a pessimistic, lackadaisical attitude. From egg to æglet, Brother lacked motivation to pursue anything but sleep, let alone prey. Father tried in vain to train his son in the art of tracking prey from the aerie but had given up after several attempts. To be sure, Brother's eyes worked well enough, but his lack of interest in the activity frustrated Father to the breaking point. Father had at last thrown up his wings in consternation before diving from the edge of their perch, rolling over mid-air to look back at Mother as he plunged.

"He's all yours!" Father had called to Mother, a disappointed frown contorting his features before he spun to right himself, opening his great wings to catch the updraft that sent him skyward without another look back. But that Sister now indulged in an uncommon late afternoon nap, Brother was certain she would have teased him at Father's displeasure.

The Æglet's Answer

Father resented Mother for salvaging Brother from his egg and perceived his son's weakness as a liability the æglet was unlikely to overcome. Whereas he reveled over Sister for all her fine ægle attributes, he brooded over Brother for all the child's lack thereof, none of which escaped Mother's notice.

It was perhaps due to her contention with Father that Mother was all the more patient with her son, the conflict drawing out a forbearance with his failings beyond that natural to the ægle. She came alongside her son at nest's edge, eyes narrowed in spite as she followed Father' speedy departure. Determined, she looked down at her son, and nodded with force down at the distant underbrush, desiring that he recommence the exercise of locating and following prey with his powerful ægle eyes.

Brother looked back up at Mother with reproach, beak agape and tongue hanging out a bit. In his estimation, the best use of his eyes at that moment was to roll them, a decision he at once regretted. At the apex of his disrespectful gesture, in that brief instant of visual impairment, Mother's head darted forth with a speed and force that stirred the impoverished fluff drooping from his cheeks. Brother opened his eyes to find himself beak-to-beak with his unflinching Mother. Intimidated by her advance, he craned backward until his head almost reached his rump.

Unable to escape when Mother again gave a pointed nod at the ground, Brother grudgingly set to task. He gazed out, languid at first until, in the shadow of a hollow log, he spotted the perking tail of a squirrel.

He cried out to draw Mother's attention, "Ki-ki-ki! Ki ki!"

She looked intently, following his gaze. After a few seconds, she, too, located the squirrel, which presently dashed under the cover of a nearby shrub as though instinct alerted the creature to their predatory focus.

Mother clucked her tongue. The squirrel was now lost to them in the dense foliage. She nodded at her son to begin again, then noticed that he yet stared in the direction of the squirrel. Well, he stared in its general direction, only now his eyes and head moved in coordinated ticks that sent his gaze subtly and steadily westward.

Mother tipped her head to look at him, a question in her mind, *Does he still see it?*

As if in response to her unspoken question, Brother cried out once more, "Ki-ki-ki! Ki ki ki-yi!"

Mother concentrated as she looked to confirm her son's acquisition of the target. There! A good distance from its initial location, a nut-brown figure peppered with grey streaked in the direction of the lowering sun. Incredulity was in the measured glance she shot her son, who yet remained engaged in tracking the squirrel, though now with zealous fervor that belied the apathy from which she'd goaded him.

What a strange one he is, she pondered, and for the first time, she praised him.

"Son, that was amazing!" she gushed. "How did you see it? Once it was in the shadows, I couldn't follow it anymore!"

He at first was uncertain how to receive Mother's affectionate compliments, ducking to one side and looking back up into her eyes, which shone with pride. The shock of favorable attention soon wore off, and he straightened his scraggly form to share a preening smile with Mother.

"Really, son!" she insisted. "How did you do it? I've never known an ægle to track prey in the deep shade like that. And at distance, too!"

He shrugged, unable to articulate how he'd accomplished the feat, and offered, "I'm not sure, Mother. I just *did* it."

A naïve lack of self-awareness made him ignorant of the singular gift he possessed. A superior perception of light and shadow made each the more distinct in his eyes, and the sharpened contrast enabled an acuity of vision that surpassed the ægle's already powerful eyesight. For all his other faults, he exceeded his kind in this one thing. Of course, he recognized none of this, thinking himself ever inferior to all ægles at large and Sister in particular.

Mother ground her beak thoughtfully as she considered her son's response. Unable to arrive at a definite conclusion, she prompted him to continue with the exercise. If he was able to consistently track prey thus, there might be hope for him yet, given he developed in other ways as well.

Sister awoke a short time later, spotting Mother and Brother side-by-side at nest's edge, heads bobbing and turning in concert while together they tracked another creature across the forest floor. She sneered, annoyed at the apparent pleasure the pair took in the activity. Between the æglets, the aerie was *hers*, and it followed that the attentions of Mother and Father were tribute due *her*, and only her. Besides, Brother was such a frail and feckless dullard. Why was Mother wasting time on *him*?

Irritation prompted Sister to investigate, and she strutted quietly up behind Mother, taking care not to draw their attention. She was familiar with the game, having played it with Father and Mother in weeks past until the pleased parents had decided she was competent to continue on her own. Over Mother's shoulder, Sister sought the object of their scrutiny, but found she was unable to locate the prey.

Consternated, she watched Mother with care, and discovered that Mother kept one eye on Brother to follow him for cues whenever the older ægle lost track of their target. Brother, on the other hand, appeared to have no difficulty whatsoever in spotting the quarry, which must have stopped for the moment, prompting the raptors to a patient stillness while they waited for movement to resume.

Sister crept around the other side to look over Brother's shoulder for a clue as to their mysterious prey's location. Following his intent gaze, she stared into the murk beneath the roots of a distant tree, puzzled still that she saw no creature resting in the darkened hollow.

Mother looked over at Brother after several long seconds and noticed Sister lurking behind him. She clucked her tongue for their attention, and Sister turned to her, while Brother yet remained engrossed in his surveillance. Sister noticed with distress that Mother, far from impatient at Brother's failure to come to attention, had instead smiled and shrugged before clucking again, this time more loudly.

Brother, looked up, an expression of dopy, contented surprise on his face when he swiveled to Mother. The happiness that bloomed there wilted as he realized Sister, too, was present. Sister was equally vexed at the joy, however fleeting, that she'd seen pass over Brother's countenance. This happy development she could not, would not abide.

Mother related to Sister Brother's new-found aptitude for locating and tracking prey, the excitement in her voice apparent, "Sister, you'd never guess what Brother can do! Why! It seems he's got even better eyes than I! You saw where we were looking. Did you see a rabbit hiding under the tree?"

Sister sniffed, unfazed, and replied, "Well, of *course* I saw it. It's no big deal. Clear as day I saw it." She lied with a ready confidence that convinced them both.

Mother gaped, then frisked with excitement, "Then we've *two* exceptional æglets in our nest! I can't wait to tell Father when he returns!"

Sister was satisfied that her act had taken them in, but within disquiet clamored its dissonant tune. She had *not* seen the rabbit, and Brother *had*. This was cause for some deliberation if she meant to compete with his inexplicable ability, and she wondered how long her sham might weather scrutiny.

It was just past sunset when Father returned to the aerie, the blazing jewel of the sun winking below the horizon as he fluttered down, a large salmon depending from his claws until he dropped it into the nest, where it flopped, weary and drowning in the evening air.

Sister struck at the fish in a flash of wing and claw, her beak ripping its scaly skin open to taste the nutritious flesh beneath. Mother, meanwhile, told Father how Brother and Sister had excelled in spotting and following prey from the nest. Though Mother emphasized how well Brother in particular had performed, Father yet eyed him with doubt before casting a more confident gaze on Sister, who had flipped the fish with a hooked talon to commence on its other side while Brother watched in hunger.

Father bid Mother depart on her evening hunt while he watched Sister devour the salmon. He had eaten his fill while out hunting, and their routine dictated he return with the meal for the æglets while Mother sought her own. Mother flitted away, well-fed by the accomplishments of her children while she careened toward the rabbit they'd found earlier.

According to her usual custom, Sister stripped the fish down to its bones, though this time she pitched any portion she deemed unsavory over the edge of the nest. No such charity remained in her this evening as to share with Brother, which became clear to Father and Brother when she began to purge the nest of the prey's remnants.

Perhaps it was new-found confidence derived from Mother's praise that inspired Brother to intercept the scraps, an exploit he'd never before attempted, and instantly regretted. Slipping sideways along the edge of the nest with quiet steps, Brother inched to the spot over which Sister was tossing most the remnants.

With a secretive, sharp upward snip of the beak, Brother snagged an arcing swatch of shiny skin from which depended the salmon's tail and a short section of spine. He shielded himself with a meager wing as beneath it, he bolted down the scraps with furtive bites. His eyes darted to Sister, who yet engorged herself in tantrum flailings. Relieved that she remained occupied, Brother sighed quietly and returned to his scant meal, hopeful he might finish this bit and perhaps garner another before Sister finished.

His meal and his relief were both short-lived. Sister's ears had caught his sigh on the air, though a moment passed before she'd comprehended it and located its source. The instant she had, her eyes locked on Brother huddled against the edge of the nest, his wing concealing in large part the food he worked to finish in frantic fashion. Sister's rage, before a diffuse and gusty flurry, focused on Brother with the tempestuous intensity of a cyclone, and she bore down on him, silent but for the flutter of her wings. The sudden assault caught Brother unawares, and he floundered to defend himself against Sister's barrage of talon and beak.

Her powerful talons pinioning Brother's meager wings to the nest beneath, Sister straddled her prone sibling, and shrieked, "Mine! Mine! Mine! Mine!"

With each shriek, she pecked and slashed at him, her beak etching fine, bloody lines across his head, wings, and body. Rearing back to tower over Brother's defeated form, Sister glowered down her wet, crimson beak at him, a keening swell growing within her heaving breast as if the inarticulate beast caged within raged against its imprisonment.

The mindless shriek resolved into words, which Sister spat staccato, spraying Brother with his own blood as each word struck him, "It's! All! MINE!!!"

The last word trailed off, returning to a mad, incomprehensible screech that shook Sister's visage with its fury, her eyes bulging in an unfocused and unseeing stare. Brother winced at the final shriek, and turned his head aside, looking up at her with one eye, guarded and ready to weave aside with what limited capacity he possessed. Sister stilled, and understanding seemed to return to her gaze, which grew reflective. Her apparent tranquility prompted Brother to turn and look up into her eyes plaintively, taking comfort that she no longer assailed him.

Comfort grew ever more distant, however, with the utterance of her remote response, a disquieting whisper chasing her rancor, "Those eyes, though. Those eyes. They are *not* mine."

She spoke as if only to herself, though terrifying suspicion crept through Brother's mind, a shambling ghoul bemoaning her consultation of the howling devil within for direction.

"Now what are we going to do about *those eyes*?" she asked, peering down with head cocked to one side, presumably listening for a response Brother could only guess at.

"Aha!" Sister exclaimed, her wild eyes brightening, and pinning as she looked up. "That's it! If I can't have them, then neither. can. he."

Her eyes narrowed with her last three words, and she recoiled, ready to strike. Brother gaped, shaking his head side to side in fearful protest. He recognized the seriousness of Sister's demeanor, and no longer believed he might escape without incurring serious harm.

Father must have also perceived Sister's grievous intent, and for the first time since the pair was born, he intervened. Father dashed at frightening speed, connecting under Sister's jaw with an upward sweep of his wing. As Sister's frame extended upward, Father arced the sweep of his wing back and then down, slamming Sister into the floor of the nest. The tip of his iron talon rested against Sister's throat as he looked down at her with unfeeling detachment. This was Father on the hunt, a stoic killer who didn't flinch to hazard his life in the wild, nor did he fret over the suffering of prey. He looked Sister over, as she remained beneath his claws, sense enough having returned to her that she recognized her life hung in the balance of Father's judgement.

"That's *enough*," Father growled, his beak gritted to a near-imperceptible seam. "You're well past the age for this."

He jerked his head at Brother, and continued, "Runt though he is, Brother may yet prove his worth. *You*, however, have already done so. You've an extraordinary share of the hunter's spirit, perhaps more than I've ever seen in an æglet, and you're strong. Very strong. But save it for the hunt. If you threaten Brother's life, or his *eyes* again, I'll break your wings and throw you in the river myself. And one last thing: this aerie, these hunting grounds, the honor of the family – they're. all. *ours*."

With these last, he stepped off what seemed a subdued Sister, who rolled upright, and addressed Father in monotone, "I understand, Father. I will do my best for the honor of the family."

Without so much as a glance at Brother or the decimated salmon, Sister went to the edge of the nest to stare into the forest gloom below. Brother reached forth a wing for Father's attention, wishing to express his gratitude, but Father either didn't notice the gesture or chose to ignore it. Accustomed to rejection, Brother didn't allow it to tinge his excitement at the remains of the fish, which he plowed into, filling his small belly beyond its capacity.

After the incident, Sister still picked on him, though less so than before, and she still took more than her share of the prey, but never overindulged out of overt spite as she had before. Thereafter, she looked ever more out from the nest in anticipation of the day she might take flight.

Thus, we return to the fateful day of Sister's namesake, a still and stale air smothering the fauna of the land beneath the dogged heat of the sun, which stood almost white overhead against the cloudless blue expanse. The breezeless air and oppressive heat kept most creatures at rest beneath the shade, which did nothing to assuage the dull ache of Sister's boredom. The tranquility of the forest below did not provide the typical diversion of tracking prey from the nest's edge, and tormenting Brother lacked the savor it once had, especially now Father watched for bloodletting.

Brother roosted at the western edge of the nest in anticipation of the pooling shadow that would grow along the edge as the sun ran in its course. He had propped his wings overhead in an awkward posture, determined to cool his head in their scant shade while he tried to rest. Perhaps he might just doze through the worst of the heat ...

The afternoon hours slouched onward, Sister's frustration with her restriction to the nest growing. It was infuriating to imagine Father and Mother slipping through the cool drafts and streams of air Sister knew flew overhead, or that they might be dipping head, beak, and claw into the flowing river nearby. She could not abide her confinement! But an æglet in her first of flights needed an updraft, a stirring of the air to carry the fledgling over the land lest she fall to the treacherous earth where injury or death might await.

The sun shone its slanting rays in the latening afternoon to cast lengthening shadows and indulge Brother his awaited sleep. Sister cast the blazing orb a spiteful eye, determined to match its baleful glare when, as if springing from nothing, a wisp of cloud appeared in the otherwise unmarred sky. The wisp coalesced into bulbous form, and bulged in haphazard, bloated growth until a darkening stormhead loomed in the western sky.

The growing bank of grey clouds approached at high speed, a grim flotilla advancing on shifting, formless sails to combat the sun's brilliance with drenching obscurity. The winds high above drove the storm onward, and soon deigned to visit their force upon the forest while lightning began to flash, crackling deep within the black heart of the cumuliform beast. The gusts blasted the forest, stirring trees until their whipping branches grudgingly relinquished tattered leaves.

Mother and Father had weathered several seasons in the nest, which remained interwoven in the crown of the great tree below, lodged there

23

in security but for a stirring of loose dust and detritus. Nevertheless, Brother huddled as flat as he was able against the windward edge, frightened at the storm's ferocity, and unwilling to test his sloughing plumage in the violence.

Despite the shredding winds, Sister stood steadfast in the center of the nest, talons hooked deep within the interlacing wicker while she stared, resolute, into the storm. A wild cackle flew from her beak to blow past her into the deepening, chaotic haze of the stormcurrent. This! This is what she'd been waiting for!

Leaning low beneath the limited shelter of the nest's edge, Sister spread her wings to calculate the power of the storm. Brother gawked when he realized her intention. She wanted to fly! In this!?!

Raising just the outer edges of her wings into the flow above, Sister let go the nest below. At once, the storm caught her, flinging her up and back toward the edge of the nest. She had anticipated this and folded her wings without delay to grasp for the upper edge of the nest when she flew past. It was a near thing, but she caught the nest with a straining claw, then fought to grip with the other while she strained forward to press her aerodynamic, aquiline head beneath the mighty current.

After an intense struggle, Sister stood horizontal, held parallel to the nest floor by the raging force of the storm. Her wings remained tucked as if in the full dive of the hunt, which Father and Mother had demonstrated for them innumerable times. She might stay here if she so chose, her sleek form undisturbed but for the most intense of gusts. If she so chose. But that was not what she desired.

The pelting onset of the approaching cloudburst forewarned her that her opportunity was limited. It was now, or never. With mad laughter, she sneered at Brother, then tipped her head upward, opened her wings, and soared aloft to disappear from his view into the dizzying murk.

Brother, now alone in the nest, considered Sister's fate. It was possible she might survive the buffeting of the gale, but he was dubious. The wet curtain of oncoming rain fell, draping the lone æglet in the cold fabric of moisture where he lay, pressed against the nest's edge and shivering in naked trepidation. The wind-borne showers abated and departed with the same speed with which they had arrived. The fleet of threatening clouds dashed against the sunray reef of sweltering heat high overhead, and parting shipwreck forms allowed piercing light to shine over the forest once more.

Brother arose when high and keening calls of greeting crossed the sapphire sky. Little more than specks in lesser eyes neared one another under sun's radiant beam. From the south, Brother perceived two figures, Mother and Father, and from the north, Sister, soaring triumphant.

Initial relief at Sister's well-being succumbed to the pursuit of swift dismay as he thought, *Ugh! She'll be insufferable now.*

Another followed, this more hopeful, *Well, at least she'll be away from the nest most of the day hunting. More time to myself.*

His mood changed again with the gloomy realization, *I'm sure there will be constant praise for Sister's accomplishment, which means more disappointment for me.*

He looked down at his odd, saggy body, doubtful it would ever develop into the robust ægle form that he so coveted. What would become of him now? Would he *ever* fly?

In his introspection, he failed to notice his family's approach, a celebratory convocation carrying the trophies of their hunt. They were only a short distance away when they hailed him in the nest, and Brother jerked his head up in surprise to observe their arrival. Mother and Father each had a large fish, which they dropped in the nest as they spiraled down to land. Even Sister had managed to collect two chevrotains and clutched one in each of her claws. She, too, released her prey before descending, a predatory grin on her face as she landed.

"Brother!" Mother began. "Did you see Sister? Flying! And in that beast of a storm, no less! She has become a full-fledged ægle today."

"Indeed, she has," Father intoned with pride. "I've never seen the like. I've never heard of a fledgling taking her first flight in winds like that. Mother, Sister, and I have discussed it, and we've decided on a name for Sister. From this day forward, she will be known as Gael. It's a good name and will remind us all of her strength and bravery during her first flight in the gale today."

Brother nodded, finding the name appropriate, for a number of reasons. He'd suffered many times under Sister's, no, Gael's capricious temper that the comparison to the unpredictable, shifting blasts of a gale seemed natural. Besides that, Brother nevertheless found Gael's feat today impressive, and worthy of her naming. She was indeed a force to be reckoned with, though exalting her to a force of nature was perhaps a tad conceited. A soft thud at his feet stirred Brother from his musings, and he gaped in uncertain pleasure when he saw a chevrotain lay there, whole and intact.

Gael allayed his confusion, addressing him in a loud voice for all to hear, "Dear Brother, please accept this as an invitation to feast with us in celebration of my first flight and my naming today. As a matter of fact, I have a proposal, should Mother and Father wish to hear it."

The petition apparent on her face, Gael looked to her parents, who both nodded their approval.

Gael inclined her head in deference before continuing, "I am so happy of heart today that I hope Mother and Father will not find me over-generous in proposing that I share the honor of the day with Brother, who, for all his failings, has but one exemplary gift by which he might bring glory to the family."

Mother, Father, and Brother all eyed Gael warily, uncertain of her intent. Gael took note of their skepticism and was not surprised.

She proceeded, "I understand that I've not been the best sister, but I assure you that this day has made me a new ægle. I feel just-molted and wish to extend a fresh feather in friendship to Brother, who I know now how badly I have mistreated. No! Abused! I am truly sorry, Brother."

Here she bowed her head and gave it a sad shake, spreading her wings in plaintive sorrow before Brother, who reared back in shock at the display. Mother and Father looked on in pleasure at how distinguished their Gael had become while Brother's awareness captured every disingenuous nuance of her conciliations. He didn't trust her for a second, but felt obliged to accept the apology, leery though he was.

"Thank you, Ga-Gael," Brother croaked. "I accept your apology."

"Splendid!" she gasped, her sinister eyes flashing at him. "Then I propose that we give Brother a name today as well."

Mother and Father stood aghast, in shock that Gael would confer such an honor on Brother the same day as her own namesake.

"We all know how wonderful he is at spotting those critters lurking in the shadows," Gael explained. "Why don't we name him Sayah? I heard from an owl that it means "shadow" in one of the old tongues."

Mother and Father contemplated Gael's recommendation, mulling it over while Brother fumed. He remembered the owl, too: an altogether unsavory windbag who approached their nest when Mother and Father had been absent on a late evening hunt. The puffed, wide-eyed bird had landed nearby on the crown of the tree under pretense of exhaustion and had sidled up to chat with the æglets.

Since the dispersion of the Stain, communication between different kinds of creatures had become difficult. The Stain had disrupted the harmony of Nature, and the muddling of the common language was yet another aspect of its inescapable perversion of the natural order. However, the disruption was incomplete, and as was usual among the various kinds of creatures, all birds shared a common tongue, though with varied accent and dialect. And it was in the strange and hooting accent of its strigiform dialect that the owl had hailed them as it circled on silent wings to land near their nest on a crowning branch of the tree.

The owl's large eyes had shone with strange light when he stared at the æglets, and oft his head would twitch nervously up, down, and side-to-side, even swiveling about altogether as he scanned the surroundings. At first, the owl had been keen to gain their confidence with tales of lands far abroad, and shared his vast knowledge with the æglets, who listened with rapt attention. The owl spoke in low tones, and the æglets had crossed the nest to draw near, interested to hear his hushed words.

They were almost to the owl's perch at the edge of the nest when the strange bird suddenly flew at the pair, eager to make off with an æglet supper (or was it breakfast for the owl?). He'd underestimated Gael, and she'd almost made a supper of him instead. After a brief scuffle, Gael had scared the owl off, and she'd screeched in bitter disappointment when the bird escaped.

Regardless, that was when Gael had garnered this tidbit about an ancient word for "shadow." The owl had mentioned at the time that it was often used as a name . . .for females. Brother was less than pleased at the prospect of carrying a female's name the rest of his already-miserable days and moved to make known his protest when Gael's beak slid alongside his head.

Speaking straight into his ear, Gael whispered, "That's right, *Brother*. You remember, don't you? And never mind what I told Mother and Father about my reason for picking the name. You should know the reasons I *really* picked it."

"Ah, yes. It's a name for a female, but that's being generous to such a useless thing as you, though I *know* you'll bear it as an indignity. What's worse is that you, Brother, will ever remain confined to this aerie, ever looking upward to see *me* circling overhead, casting my shadow over you. That's you. In *my* shadow. For the rest of your life. Now how do you like the name, my dear *Sayah*?"

Brother saw now how clever were her manipulations. Though Mother and Father might deem his new name appropriate, an honor, even, Gael had made certain that the name would always be cast in shame within his own heart.

He moved again to dispute the selection of his name, but Gael hissed a warning that made him freeze, "Stop! If you do other than accept your new name with the utmost joy that you ought, I. will. kill. you."

He shuddered, and turned in outrage to respond, "You wouldn't dare! Father said he'd dump you in the river!"

The sly smile returned, and she answered in mock distress, "Why! How tragic! You say he just disappeared from the nest while we were all out on the hunt? And he was just starting to come into his own . . . ."

She trailed off as Brother recognized the implications, the possibilities available Gael now she could fly. Wait until Mother and Father were both gone, and she could return to the nest to do whatever she pleased to him. She might just dump *him* in the river with broken wings. And just like that, he'd be gone without a trace.

Gael watched the sickened awareness play across his features, and at last interjected, "You see now, don't you? You've no choice here. Not unless you fancy dying. Or, you can choose to live as my everlasting pet, my trophy gimp. Now let's go see what Mother and Father have to say, shall we?"

Gael skipped merrily to where Mother and Father deliberated on the opposite side of the nest with an unenthusiastic Brother in tow.

Gael was close when they both straightened and Father spoke, "Gael, we think it's a fine idea to give Brother a name, and we're very proud that you would share this honor with him today. The family's honor is in our personal honor, and we believe that 'Sayah' is a suitable name to commend Brother's gift. Brother, what do you think? Will you accept the name, 'Sayah?'"

Uneasy, Brother gulped, then recalled Gael's threats, and did his best to pretend happiness at the suggestion, even capering about the nest in false jubilation. Mother and Father congratulated one another on the splendid job they'd done in raising their æglets, and the ægles spent the evening listening to Gael retell the tale of her first flight. Mother and Father interrupted the telling with eager questions, and Gael basked in their recognition while Sayah endured with chagrin. The day would mark the beginning of a whole new type of torture for him.

The remainder of the week passed with Sayah still pinned to the baking interior of the ægles' nest, and no respite from the heat arrived in form of another downpour. Gael, of course, hovered over the nest to drape her shadow over him while she hurled taunts to torment him. She delighted in his shame, and he raged in impotence at her.

Sayah grew more and more withdrawn, and Mother began to shoot worried looks at him between hunts, which Gael noticed. Gael confronted him, reminding him of the alternative to his feigned contentment. Goaded into the farce, Sayah played his role well, the dozy and elated son who was just happy to be welcomed into the fellowship of ægles, even though he didn't merit the invitation.

Somehow, this was the worst of Gael's tortures, and Sayah despaired in the counterfeit buoyancy that masked his crushed soul. Though his feather-bare wings wouldn't yet empower him to flight, Sayah took to venturing out along the tree's branches when the others were on the hunt. He found a fragile peace in peering down at the clear, trickling stream that ran below. He imagined himself standing in its flow, where he could hear its babble and feel its coolness pass over his scorching feet.

One day, early the following week, Sayah hurried to his special perch, an especially long branch that hung far over the southern edge of the tree's crown. The perch afforded him the clearest view of the stream below, though he had to pick his way sideways across its narrowing length with care to avoid falling.

This morning, Gael had been especially cruel, returning right after she, Mother, and Father had supposedly left for the day. As was common to Gael, her successes became an occasion to afflict Sayah, and her early success in securing prey had proven no exception. She dangled the hapless cony, still alive, over Sayah's head to tease her hungry sibling. Gael laughed with perverse glee as Sayah hopped about the nest in an attempt to hook his beak in the sumptuous hare. At last, Gael tired of her wicked game, and retired to a nearby tree to consume her meal in full view of Sayah. Though plenty remained of the hare, she kicked its remains to the forest floor and dashed away, cackling all the while.

Sayah's talons tore into the tree's bark in hateful remembrance, the recollection stoking the embers of his anger while he crossed to his perch. With some remorse, he viewed the exposed flesh of the branch as he scooted sideways to his place. He hadn't meant to harm the great tree, which in many ways was as much a home to him as his nest. Without its tall, powerful trunk and strong, spreading branches, he and his family wouldn't be able to live here, dead center in one of the best hunting grounds in the region.

He reached his perch and focused on the tranquil stir of moving waters below, entranced. A long time he remained there, unaware of the sun's beating, heated press, and still he stared, longing to dip his beak in the crystalline current.

A curious, small blue creature garnered his attention, its erect form seeming to study the tree from below. Oh! How he envied the strange being! To stand beneath the shade of the tree with the glorious stream a few steps away!

At the same time, Sayah, wondered, *If I shout, might he hear me?*

Curiosity and loneliness gripped him, its iron hand compelling him to lean out dangerously as he readied himself to call out to the alien figure. He raised his wings to either side to steady himself and took a deep breath. SNAP! He'd come out further than was usual, and the tip of the branch beneath him gave way. Sayah flapped his meager wings to no avail, and terror clamped its icy talons over his throat, silencing the cry there as he fell . . .

Chapter Two

Spring, Sprig, Sayah, and Spark

...like taffy, the seconds stretched long, and he forgot to breathe in the silent dread of his plunge. In blind anticipation, he imagined for an instant that he plummeted through a blue and infinite sky, the envisioned clouds producing within him a sense of peace.

With the abrupt irony of thwarted expectation, Nat met the ground, the shocking impact splitting wide his encapsulation. Peculiarly unfazed, he rolled forth, bouncing on the heathy earth, his corkscrewing vision describing a warped scroll of his surroundings unfurling within his mind.

Nat recalled his training in the Forge, and relaxed his body, rolling his forearms forward as his elbows met the ground to strike the earth with the palms of loose hands. He flopped to a stop in a limp sprawl on his back. Perceiving neither danger nor injury, he propped himself on his hands to sit up in wonderment, a curious, bright smile on his face.

Despite the substantial fall and subsequent tumble, Nat was clear-headed and oriented himself at once. Inspired by silly compulsion, he needlessly shook his head, causing tongue, lips and cheeks to flap and distort the monotone croak issuing from his mouth. His zalzal, which had grown long since leaving Endego, whipped side to side as he did. He chuckled lightly, amused with himself, and sprang up from the ground to dust himself off while he turned to clarify his blurred impression of the setting.

He was not surprised to find the Tree behind him, confirming the suspicion his memory had served him in conjunction with sensate clues discovered since awakening. Unsurprised though he was, he nonetheless stood awestruck, eclipsed in arboreal majesty. The desperate moments before discovering the Tree yesterday returned to him, as did his refreshment upon collapsing into its streams, and the ensuing joy that sped him toward the gnarled trunk and into oblivion.

It was a great distance to the first of the Tree's branches, which swayed in the gentle breeze. Nat luxuriated in the tranquility of the setting, and in the peaceable contentment that reigned his heart. The grief of having his friends and family torn from him remained, but now resided beneath the immense canopy of the Tree's glory, beneath that majesty rediscovered and familiar from his prior encounters with Elyon in Astéri's company.

He marveled, too, at the peculiar spring swelling from the principle crux of the great Tree. What had birthed such waters? He wandered to the edge of the pool where collected most of the sparkling spring and found a place of shimmering stillness where he might find his reflection in the surface.

Kneeling low along the pool's edge, he leaned out over the mirror sheen, and gasped. Gone were the grim, black tracks on his face he'd discovered as he fell into the waters at the outskirts of this place.

That was the Stain, wasn't it? He thought.

The sudden realization provoked confusion. He'd not found the Kinsman, the One foretold in His coming to eliminate the Stain and Blight, yet it seemed the waters here had accomplished the feat in His stead.

"*What* is going on here?" he thought aloud.

"Perhaps I might answer that question for you," a cheery voice called out from behind him.

The startled Nat spun so fast that he almost fell, but instead steadied himself with an extended hand as he crouched low and scanned the bower for the source of the voice.

At first, he was unable to spy who'd spoken, but the voice called again, giving him a clue, "Hello there! I think I can help. It's kinda my job, after all!"

Nat rubbed his eyes, hesitant to trust what they told him, for near the base of the Tree stood a tiny, treelike form that gestured to him. Though like a tree in trunk and branch, Nat clearly distinguished a face – eyes, nose, and smiling mouth – beneath the leafy mop that crowned the creature. Nat neared the stranger slowly, and discovered it only seemed tiny standing so close to the immense Tree. His new acquaintance in truth stood a bit taller than himself, was as slender and leafy as any sapling he'd ever seen and appeared to be female.

Timid, Nat waved, and offered a greeting, "Hello! My name is Nat. May I ask who you are, please?"

"Yes! Yes, you may!" came the reply, accompanied by gaping grin and twinkling eyes, but no name was forthcoming.

Nat bit his lower lip beneath the smile he wore and furrowed a perplexed brow until he figured it out – the sapling-girl-thing was joking!

He chuckled at the unexpected levity, then tried again, "Alright. Alright. What is your name, please?"

Suddenly grave, tiny tree-girl intoned, "I am Miyam, disciple of the Tree, and tender of new Fruit."

It was another tick before Nat, taken aback by her sudden, solemn shift, realized she was joking again. He laughed once more, this time with more freedom, and puzzled over the silly tree-girl's mood.

Breaking from her somber mode, Miyam winked at him, and explained brightly, "I'm a Sprig. There are only a few of us, and none of us are very old, but we *are* growing."

"And *yooouuu* – " She pointed a frond-like fingertip at Nat, circling it in the air around his face and narrowing her eyes before she finished, "You're an Etom! Am I right!?!"

She looked at Nat with an expectant smile until he saw she actually wanted an answer, which he provided at last, unable to suppress his grin, "Yes. Yes. That's right."

Miyam clapped her leafy hands together with a swish and didn't leap for joy so much as her trunk shot a space up out of the ground, exposing the tops of what looked to Nat like roots, the movement crumbling the rich earth around her.

Elated, Miyam exclaimed, "I knew it! I *knew* it! Nothing like an Etom in *this* world. And *you* are the first I've met!"

Nat blinked, nonplussed, then proffered a hand, "Well . . .then, nice to meet you!"

It was Miyam's turn at uncertainty, and, frozen, she stared at his hand.

From the side of his mouth, Nat offered confidentially, "Put yours out, too."

"Oh!" she exclaimed. "OK!"

Miyam extended a digit-covered branch to Nat, who with a gentle hand grasped her wooden fingers, careful not to crush the foliage that covered them. She stayed stock-still, amazed at his touch, and Nat pumped her hand once up and down before releasing it. Miyam retracted her splayed hand, staring down at the tender, yet hardy bark that covered it. Her other hand went to her mouth in astonishment, and Nat grew a bit concerned.

"Miyam? Are you alright?" he ventured. "I didn't hurt you, did I?"

She looked up at him, tears shining in her eyes, and his concern grew. In the same instant, her prior silliness came to mind, and he wondered if she was having another laugh.

"No," she whispered. "It's just...it's just incredible, isn't it?"

Nat was at a loss, and responded with his own question, "What? *What* is incredible? I'm afraid don't understand, Miyam."

He no longer believed she might be joking, but neither had she allayed his concerns.

"I'm sorry," she apologized. "I've never touched anyone besides my fellow Sprigs. The difference is...is...indescribable. But the incredible thing is that it's also so similar. You've come to the Tree. You've washed in its waters and have drunk of its springs. And I can *feel* your connection, same as mine. Same as the other Sprigs. It's simply amazing what He's done."

"He? Who?" Nat inquired, intrigued.

"Why, King Elyon, of course!" Miyam answered merrily. "Silly Etom! Who else could have done accomplished something this wonderful?"

"But, but..." Nat stammered his objection, "King Elyon abandoned our world ages ago! Has He returned to us? If so, then where is He now?"

"Dear Nat," Miyam consoled, "Elyon has not abandoned our world. We've ever had His promises, and in this Tree, we've seen the most important of them come to pass."

With canted head and cocked brow, Nat scrutinized the Tree, boring up the length of the trunk to the gushing font high above before responding, "And, what, exactly, has He accomplished here? I don't understand."

With a pensive finger, she tapped the side of her face while she searched her mind, until with a sudden bark, she answered, "Well, Nat! Do you remember the connection I mentioned?"

Nat nodded.

"That connection is what makes this conversation possible," she informed. "Didn't you wonder how we can understand each other? Have you ever talked to a tree-person before? Or even a non-Etom?"

Nat shook his head with a perplexed frown but saw her point. He remembered his mother's crude, limited interactions with Raaj, a beetle that lived near Endego. The etma and beetle had arrived at understanding through a smattering of words from each one's language coupled with extensive pantomime. Frustrating and *hilarious* pantomime, he recalled with a snicker.

The amiable Sprig continued, entertained by Nat's introspection, "Ooookay, then. If you haven't already guessed it, our connection through the Tree can help us understand one another, though we speak the distinct languages of our kind."

She held up a fronded finger, and finished, her eyes sparkling in wonder, "And that's just *one* of the gifts Elyon has given through the Tree. Pretty amazing, right?"

Nat didn't know what to say, but nodded, his eyelids open stiff and wide around the exposed, bright circles of his eyes.

Miyam offered a kind chuckle, a bright and sprightly thing that brought Nat's attention back to his new friend. She was peculiar, but Nat felt a growing kinship with her that compelled him to heed her words.

Miyam sobered, though her smile lingered, and she explained, "You may never understand fully what was done here. I cannot comprehend it, though I've studied the form of it since I sprouted, right here beneath these branches. However, I believe I can tell you the gist of it. The rest will be for you to discover through your own journeys. Come, sit with me."

Waving him to join her as she settled onto an upthrust twist of root, she continued, "First, you should know that the long-promised Kinsman has come at last. Second, since completing His mission in the world, He has departed to once more stand at the right hand of Lord Elyon. Third, this tree is the culmination of a great many of Elyon's promises and came at great cost to Him. For this, and for all His gifts, we should be grateful."

Nat sat beside her in perplexed silence, his eyes darting between her face and the towering trunk beside them.

Miyam empathized, "I can see that you are still confused, and reasonably so. Stay with me, and I think I can help. It *is* my job after all!"

She offered him another of her sunny smiles, and Nat responded to the warmth, finding comfort in Miyam's friendliness. He nodded for her to continue.

"Well, as you know, the greatest threat to any creature is the ever-present Stain and the deadly Blight that follows. The curse of our Stain awaits us all at the end. However, you may recall that the advent of the Kinsman promised freedom from the Stain, freedom from the death it causes. No other promises such a thing. Imagine! The world free of the Stain once more!"

Here she sighed, her verdant eyes shimmering with hope, then proceeded, "The first of the Kinsman's gifts are these waters, of which you may drink, and in which you may bathe for the cleansing from the Stain."

She stopped a moment to let her words sink in as rain penetrating the thirsty soil of Nat's soul. So, he *hadn't* imagined it! His Stain was gone! He gaped at Miyam as he realized the implications, and hope, finding purchase in the good soil there, sprouted within him.

Mom. Rae. Dempsey. Every Etom of the Eben'kayah, he thought. *No! Of Endego. All free of the Stain!*

Tears of thanksgiving fell from his golden eyes, watering the burgeoning hope as it blossomed into determination.

I must share this with them! With everyone!!!

Miyam clucked her tongue, and Nat met her eyes, surprised to find tears there, too.

Her leafy fingers swept the moisture away as she spoke, "I knew you were one of the good ones, Nat. Or at least that you could be. I bet you can't wait to bring everyone that you know, that you love, here?"

By now, Nat's mouth was dry from having hung open so long, but he finally worked his jaw, struggling to answer Miyam's insight.

"How . . .?" he trailed off.

"How did I know that?" Miyam asked. "Well, I *could* say that I've been doing this my whole life. This whole routine. Telling folks what this place means. How it changes things. How it changes *everything*. I *could* say that, but it wouldn't be true. Honestly, the reason I knew is because we are connected now. Connected through the Tree."

If Miyam anticipated a sudden burst of understanding from Nat, she was sorely disappointed. He sat beside her, head shaking, and distended lips pursed in a wry, befuddled frown.

"When we touched earlier, I said I felt our connection. Do you remember that?" she prodded.

Nat nodded, recalling her statement, but unsure what it had meant.

As if answering his unspoken question, Miyam answered, "What I meant is that you've washed in and drunk of these springs, and I've only ever known them. Through these waters, Elyon has made us free of the Stain, and has restored to us some semblance of the harmony of nature heretofore found in ancient Gan alone. Whosoever is connected to the Tree is joined to all others likewise connected. Do you see now?"

Nat did *not* see, at least not clearly, but he answered, "I think I'm beginning to see. I just wonder *how* . . .?"

He trailed off again, and looked down into his cupped, pale-blue hands, lost in his own thoughts. Miyam was content to wait in silence while Nat integrated the world-shifting information.

After several minutes, she startled Nat from his meditation, exclaiming, "I know! Maybe an old friend could explain it better?"

Nat was already a tangle of wonderment, but Miyam's latest suggestion added still a few more knots to the snarl.

With an overwhelmed sway of his head that said *why not?* he asked the question, "Old friend? None of my friends made it here. I came alone. Didn't I?"

Miyam was already speeding away, plowing through the rich soil to leave a thin, easy furrow as she traveled in the mode of her kind.

Between her branches, she called back to Nat, her face screened from view by her foliage, "You'll see!"

Nat heard her shout to herself as she drifted away, "I'm so EXCITED! Eeeeeeee!!!"

In baffled amusement, he smiled at his new friend, who no longer seemed a stranger. He couldn't help but like her and couldn't fault her enthusiasm. What he'd discovered thus far today was mind-boggling, and he struggled to cram what he'd learned into the framework of the knowledge he'd already possessed.

The promises of Elyon the Eben'kayah preserved have come true . . .the Kinsman has come and *gone, but left us this, this Tree . . .and somehow, this Tree grew a fountain that gets rid of the Stain? Ooookay . . .*with apprehension, he rested from the internal query.

He shook his harried head to clear it, ready to accommodate the strange and wonderful news, but uncertain just how for its immensity.

Peaceful moments passed in the relative silence, though Nat began to notice that the area was positively teeming with life. Butterflies flitted, and bees buzzed to and from the many flowers encircling the Tree's bower, while the distant songs of birds and croaks of bullfrogs filled the vibrant air. Beyond the thick, twining hedge that had almost prevented his approach, Nat heard the scamper of small, woodland feet and the swish of swift passage through the underbrush. Though it had proven difficult to infiltrate before his arrival, the thicket surrounding the space beneath the Tree's branches now filled Nat with a sense of security. It would be just as difficult for any predators to come near.

A strange thought occurred to Nat, *I wonder if the Tree would* let *them?*

Indeed, it was nonsense, but Nat was not able to dispose of it. The Tree was powerful, that much he knew, and Nat suspected the Tree could protect itself at need, perhaps even those nearby.

Another thought followed, *Predators carry the Stain, too. If Elyon intended all to be free of it, how else could they drink at the stream or bathe in the waters?*

He shuddered at the thought of kneeling along these banks, shoulder-to-shoulder with a fox or wildcat, and fear sent his tiny heart racing until yet another notion struck him, and his heart fell still, *What makes the Etom any better? We eat qábēs, and whip chevrotains to force them to pull our carts. Why should we be free of the Stain and not others, even those who might eat us?*

His train of thought produced a peculiar distress that at one time might have overwhelmed him. Instead, the peace that enveloped him seemed to shoulder much of the emotional load the line of inquiry evoked, though Nat bore enough to taste the burdensome grief of it.

He marveled once more at the Tree, staring up at its majesty in tender awe. In a short span, the Tree had revealed a rift between the world Nat knew and another that awaited beyond its spreading boughs. To one side of the Tree, Nat stood, beset by accumulating questions that made his little heart ache. To the other, he reclined in inexplicable certainty that his most fundamental concerns were settled. The sharp variation between two equally true realities tore at him, as a shining sword polished to mirror sheen, his soul caught in its reflection. In tears, Nat stood, eyes transfixed on the splendor of the coruscating flow as it cascaded down the Tree's mossy beard.

A fluttering commotion nearby commanded his attention, and out of the corner of his eye Nat caught sight of a dark, flapping missile streaking toward the ground when he swiveled his head to track the sound to its source. The plummeting figure met a dense clump of tall grasses with a puff of downy feathers and a wheezing caw. While drifting feathers yet hung over the stand of grass, Nat slipped over to investigate, employing every mode of concealment available him as he did.

He had honed his woodcraft over arduous months in the wild, and, coupled with his size, the skills rendered him near-invisible as he slunk behind a stony outcropping. Sliding down to his belly, Nat slithered forth slowly to peer from around the rocky base. Only the top of his head and his eyes, slitted in suspicion, peeked out from his hiding spot. The long stems of grass shook and rustled a bit, then stilled altogether. Nat's mind whirled as he deliberated whether he should go in for a closer look or continue watching from relative safety.

A sudden and prolonged sigh issued from behind the stalks, startling Nat, who flinched.

A pained, resigned voice followed, "I see you there, you know."

With care, Nat looked this way and that, uncertain if the voice addressed him, but likewise unaware of anyone else in the vicinity. Whatever it was, the creature was certainly not an Etom, yet Nat had understood it. Was it the gift of the Tree in operation?

Again, the strange form stirred behind the emerald blades, and the voice continued in a snarky drawl, "Yes, you. Your blue head kind of stands out around here. Not exactly the best camouflage in the forest."

Nat was on the one hand dismayed at his discovery but was on the other relieved that he needn't hide any longer. He was rather curious about the unexpected visitor. Trembling, but defiant of his fear, he stood and stepped out from concealment.

Hoping to be understood, Nat managed to still the quaking in his voice, and called, "Here I am! Now how about you?"

"Oh, you don't want to see *me*," the voice returned, sullen, then added, "I'm nothing special to look at."

"Well, that's just great!" Nat countered with a dry chortle, rejoicing within that the stranger had understood him. "Are we going to talk through the grass all day? Perhaps we should move over to the berry patch so at least I can have a snack while you protect your modesty, eh?"

"Wow!" the mysterious voice turned pleasant in response, "That sounds like a great idea! Why don't you turn away for a second while I . . .? Hey! Wait a minute!"

The stranger noticed Nat's half-lidded eyes and sardonic smirk, and finally grasped Nat's sarcasm.

"Was that supposed to be funny?" the stranger crowed, "It wasn't very funny."

Nat suppressed a laugh. It was obvious that the visitor was some kind of bird, and a large one at that. Such a large bird could make short work of an Etom, especially if it was a raptor of some kind. Regardless, the longer this interaction went on, the less anxious Nat became. The creature didn't seem threatening, and Nat grew more interested the longer it insisted on staying hidden.

Nat, his smile kind, offered an apology, "I'm sorry, friend. It's a tad strange that you're hiding like that. Could we maybe start with our names? My name is Nat. Now how about yours?"

"Uh, well, ummm," came the hesitant answer, and Nat wondered if his new acquaintance weren't somewhat *ashamed* to offer his name in return.

"Uh-well-um, huh?" Nat countered, using the universal, humorous chestnut of sadistic schoolteachers prodding nervous children to speak in public. "What kind of name is that? Sounds like a newt's name. Are you a newt, Uh-well-um?"

Nat was provoking him on purpose, hoping the bird's reaction might propel him into view. He was not disappointed. Nat was not a cruel Etém, and although he goaded the stranger impolitely, he did so to identify a potential threat to himself, Miyam, and the Tree.

The stranger burst into view, a comically under-dressed æglet covered in close, dark fluff and a few larger, wispy white feathers. Skin sagged from his lanky wings, and beneath his distended belly, a meager wattle flopped as he strode in angry steps over to Nat, who stood his ground though he wanted to fall on the ground in a fit of hysterical laughter. The æglet glowered as he loomed over Nat, his vicious beak almost touching Nat's forehead and his powerful, golden eyes glaring down into Nat's friendly face.

Nat blinked, and waved a hand in greeting, "*There* you are! Good to meet you! Like I told you before, my name is Nat!"

The æglet blinked, shocked by Nat's abrupt, amiable change in demeanor, and then recoiled, straightening to get a better look at the Etom. He'd never seen one before, and this one looked . . .dirty, his clothes a bedraggled, mud-encrusted mess, but his cheerful face and cordial tone were a welcome change to Gael's outright cruel treatment, or his parents' cold indifference. Amidst the barren, obsidian sky of Sayah's confidence arose a glimmer, evidence of a newborn star as Sayah extended a timid trust.

The æglet scooted back a step or two, then leaned his head low to put his eyes at Nat's level, to answer, "My name is...my name is Sayah."

"Sayah?" Nat responded. "I like it!"

Nat's compliment was genuine, but the æglet, unaccustomed to kindness, tucked his bashful head, and gave an awkward, "Thank you."

"Are you an ægle, Sayah?" Nat inquired. "I've never seen one up close, but you're not like any that I've seen."

Sayah winced, and Nat, seeing that he'd hurt the bird's feelings, apologized, "I'm sorry, Sayah. I really haven't seen many ægles. Ever."

Sayah registered surprise at Nat's tender apology, and managed, "It's OK, Nat. I know you didn't mean it. I *told* you I wasn't much to look at."

The level of care in the etém's voice shocked Sayah further when Nat responded, "Come on, now, Sayah. You really shouldn't talk about my friend like that. Besides, for what it's worth, I think you're a fine-looking ægle."

Sayah flipped his tail in pleasure at the compliment, and offered a gentle correction, "Æglet, actually. I'm nowhere near full-grown, and less so than most, as you can see."

Abashed, he held up a fluffy wing, still bare of fledging feathers.

Nat watched on a thoughtful moment, then offered his encouragement, "You're quite fearsome enough for me, good Sayah. Any more, and I might have run off. I mean, just look at those claws! That beak! To you, I'm just a snack!"

Sayah flipped his tail again but stared at Nat with eyes that shone wet with undecided sentiment. With a decisive sparkle in his eyes, Sayah slunk toward Nat, low to the ground and clicking his beak in hungry rhythm.

Alarmed, Nat protested and began backing away with care, "No! No! That snack bit, it was a joke! Look at me! Does *anything* blue taste good? Come on!"

Nat squawked, and Sayah's serious demeanor dissolved into an impish laugh. He slid his head along the ground before Nat's feet, flipping it over to stare up at Nat from the ground with eyes agog. Nat looked down at the æglet, face-to-upside-down-face, and tittered nervously. Sayah snapped his beak darkly, and Nat jumped back, tripping over a loose, round stone to sprawl on his backside. Sayah's body joined his head on the ground as he flopped over onto his back in a fit of laughter.

Everyone's a comic today, Nat thought, relieved.

"Ha ha, Sayah. You're too funny," Nat retorted, and stood to dust himself off. "You think maybe that could be the last time you pretend to eat me? Please?"

Sayah blinked up at Nat from the ground, then stood with an easy roll to one side and a happy curve to his beak. He'd never had a friend before. It was fun! But as he appraised his new acquaintance, he recognized legitimate distress in Nat's expression. Maybe he'd taken his joke too far?

"I'm sorry, Nat," he returned. "I promise I'll never *pretend* to eat you again."

Catching the inference, Nat chortled and shot back, "Gee. Thanks ever so much. You ægles must *love* your 'I'm going to eat you' jokes, don't you?"

Having warmed to his little blue friend, Sayah discovered he rather enjoyed trading barbs with Nat. His confidence in the etém grew with each moment, and he found the teasing delightful in stark contrast to Gael's deprecations.

Gael. He grimaced, considering what cruelties she might derive from his accidental plunge from the nest.

A desolate, happy thought crossed his mind, *Maybe they'll think I'm dead.*

Another followed, starving his already-famished joy, *No. They'll find me. They'll see me. That's what ægles do best. But . . .it'll be hours before they return. I'm going to enjoy my time down here.*

Shaking off his distraction, Sayah looked around for Nat, and spied him a short distance away, peering around the stony outcropping he'd hidden behind earlier. Nat cast a rueful look up at him when he approached, then looked down a moment in pensive silence, cupping his chin with a stubby hand.

He looked back up at Sayah, and said, "Sayah, I would like to introduce you to someone, but . . ."

He hesitated, " . . .but I wasn't lying earlier. You're honestly pretty terrifying at first."

Hearing it again made Sayah's ægle pride swell, but he understood now Nat's hesitation, and listened with rapt attention.

"Can you duck down behind the rocks here until I call you?" Nat implored, "I just want to make sure my friend is ready to meet you. Let her know that you're safe. OK?"

The æglet agreed, quite pleased with how intimidating he'd turned out to be, at least to Etom. Nat hiked back to where Miyam had left him, and Sayah nestled into some soft grass next to the rocks, very comfortable in his hiding spot. Here, beneath the span of shady boughs, so close to the crystal flow he'd coveted from afar, Sayah's sense of peace deepened, enriched somehow in the pristine surroundings.

He glanced up the mighty trunk before him, and encountered for the first time the water's source, the wellspring gushing thence eliciting from him a stricken, plain, "Well. *That's* interesting."

He gawked at the strange and wonderful sight, unable to reconcile it with the limited knowledge gleaned from his perch atop the tree. It didn't fit with what he knew, and he lingered, staring, while he wondered where the strange fount sprang from.

A surprised, happy shout broke the picturesque stillness, causing Sayah to start. He peeked out from his hiding spot, curious. Near the tree's mossy trunk, his powerful eyes homed in on Nat's form as the etém ran out of sight behind a screen of foliage. In mild concern, Sayah considered going after his new friend, but remembered Nat's request that he stay put until Nat had forewarned his other friend. For the time being, he stayed put, though curiosity gnawed away at his patience.

"Astéri!?!" Nat cried with joy when he recognized his sparky friend, who floated in tow behind Miyam upon her return.

Nat dashed to them, pleased to see Astéri, and happy to discover that the Sprig and Malakím were already acquainted. He had myriad questions for them both, and almost launched into interrogation when he recalled Sayah waiting hunched nearby.

"Miyam? Astéri?" he asked, looking to each in turn.

"Yes, Nat?" Miyam answered as Astéri issued a pitched whistle that echoed the Sprig within Nat's mind.

Nat giggled with pleasure at the familiar, yet long-missed sensation of hearing Astéri thus, then continued, "While you were gone, I met another friend."

"What?" Miyam asked in mild shock. "Who?"

The Sprig was familiar with all who resided near the Tree, and to have two new visitors within such a short span was unusual.

"Well . . ." Nat explained with a sheepish grin, "he just kind of . . .dropped in?"

A shrug capped his explanation, which left Miyam perplexed, provoking Nat to proceed, "He literally fell into a stand of grass over there."

He hooked a thumb in Sayah's general direction before warning, "But you should know, he's a little scary at first. Thought he was going to eat me!"

Nat's expressive eyes flew wide open, eliciting Miyam to mirror him while Astéri flashed in excited, variegated pulses.

A calmer Nat continued, "But he turned out be friendly, maybe a little sad, even."

He looked up at the Tree and wondered aloud, "I think the Tree might have brought him here somehow."

Miyam replied with a gentle smile, touched at Nat's tenderness, "And such it is with all who come. They must be drawn to the Tree, which speaks in mystery to a deep need within us all."

Miyam's favorable response encouraged Nat to ask, "Would you two like to meet him? He's close by, but I asked him to hide so he wouldn't scare you before I had a chance to warn you."

"Of course!" Miyam returned with cheer.

Absolutely! Astéri concurred with sunny, yellow light.

Nat took heart at their readiness to accept Sayah. With a wave, he bid them accompany him, and the little troupe marched single-file back to where Sayah hid.

One thing Nat had not considered was that Sayah might be hesitant to meet the strange, small company. Indeed, the æglet's eye's bulged in amazement when he spotted the trio emerge into view, and he pulled his fluffy head from view to lean back against the stony outcrop, wings spread wide and legs splayed before him on the ground.

Sayah's breath came in short, panicked gasps, as nervous consolations filled his mind, *It'll be fine. I trust Nat. He's a friend. A new friend who I barely know, but definitely a friend.*

His panic subsided to a tepid anxiety, and he risked another look. Nat and his *odd* friends were much closer now, the etém's brilliant smiling beaming forth before him as a lamp illuminating the way, though the sun shone overhead. Sayah had never witnessed such naked, innocent happiness in another, and the spectacle won him over.

How could I not trust him? He's just so, so . . . Sayah's mind struggled for the word, an unfamiliar, alien expression for a reality almost wholly unknown to him.

Kind! the word flew into Sayah's waking awareness, a beautiful stranger that Sayah longed to befriend but for the discomfort its foreignness evoked.

It was this very quality in Nat that at once attracted and repelled Sayah, who stood in awkward contrast to his charismatic new friend, unlovely and unloved.

47

The breathless panic returned with a press of harried logic, *How could I ever hope to be Nat's friend? Or friends with these others? And just what are they? A baby tree and a tiny sun? I'm a monster to them. A predator. They'll never trust me.*

His quivering hysteria might have compelled him to flee if not for Nat, who, suddenly close, uttered a single, gentle word, "Sayah?"

Sayah's quaking stopped, and, grasping the opportunity, he at last filled his lungs, relaxing more with each passing breath.

Nat called again, "Sayah? Friend æglet? I brought some folks who want to meet you. They're rather excited to, actually. Would you mind please coming out from there?"

On rubbery feet he arose, lifting his timid head over top the rocky outcrop, and making himself visible to the small gathering on the other side. Miyam gasped while Astéri spun and bobbed with excitement before the pair recovered themselves and looked to Nat.

The etém cleared his throat to introduce Sayah, "Miyam. Astéri. I'd like you to meet my friend, Sayah. Sayah, why don't you come out here, so they can properly greet you?"

Sayah gave a jerky nod, and ducked aside to come around while Nat whispered to the others, "Hey, I think he's sensitive about his feathers, so don't mention them, OK?"

Sayah came into full view of Nat and his friends, feeling exposed as he inched closer. Nat was glad he had cautioned Miyam and Astéri, for Sayah towered over them all, his dangerous, hooked beak gleaming in the sunshine, and his menacing talons digging into the soft earth for traction.

Miyam overcame her initial surprise to drop a short curtsy in her tree-like manner, and greeted the æglet, "I am Miyam. Very pleased to meet you, Sayah."

"Th-thank you," Sayah stammered, and although unused to the courtesies of such introductions, he lowered his head in respect.

Astéri had exchanged his yellow rays for a rosy glow, and he arose to near Sayah's beak, where he tipped forward with a pleasant chime, then scooted back to his place behind Miyam's shoulder. Sayah gave no indication he understood Astéri's salutation, which Nat had thought very polite, but the æglet seemed to perceive that the starlet was likewise expressing courtesy.

Sayah bowed again, and returned an uncertain, "Nice to meet you, too."

Miyam glanced at Nat, then turned a penetrating gaze on Sayah. If the æglet had felt exposed before, he now felt as if he'd been plucked bare, and his bashful countenance fell.

Miyam's clear eyes lingered on the æglet until she spoke to Nat, "I do believe you are correct, dear Nat. This æglet is a friend, though I've never seen his like before."

Astéri chirped and whirled his agreement in their midst, freckling the small gathering in a kaleidoscope of light. Sayah flipped his tail, happy to have met with the approval of the company. Nat smiled at Sayah, and the æglet experienced again the alluring warmth of friendship he would soon find indispensable.

Chapter Three
The Chat

Miyam addressed the others, "What do you say we continue our conversation somewhere a bit more comfortable?

Without waiting for an answer, she moved off toward the Tree, adding in singsong over a brown, barky shoulder, "I have snaaaaacks!"

Nat perked the instant Miyam mentioned food, and his stomach rumbled with eager anticipation. He jumped up, ready to follow until he noticed Sayah hanging back. For Sayah, it was his first time away from the aerie, and he hesitated to follow these three who had been strangers until mere moments ago.

Nat looked up at the æglet and reassured him, "Come on, Sayah. It'll be fine. Besides, didn't you hear? FOOD!!!"

The excited etém dashed a few steps in pursuit of Miyam, calling back to the dawdling æglet, "Come on, Sayah! Aren't you hungry? I'm *starving!*"

Nat pelted along behind Miyam, leaving Astéri with the indecisive Sayah. The star hummed with concern as he spun back and forth between the æglet and his other friends. Astéri turned back to orbit Sayah's head, surrounding the bird with indecipherable and melodic encouragement. Before long, Astéri's persistence proved goad enough to persuade Sayah to follow.

With a frustrated squawk, Sayah relented, "Alright! Alright! I'll come! Just stop with the noise already!!!"

Astéri sped a short way ahead, only to turn back, tilt, and darken altogether before flashing bright again.

A sulky Sayah followed, muttering, "Did that thing just wink at me?"

With an exasperated sigh, the æglet pursued, concealing his pleasure at knowing how badly his new friends wanted him to join them for a bite. It wasn't long before they arrived at a shelter of bowed grass, which was thatched together at the tips to form a low arch. It was large enough inside for Miyam, Nat, and Astéri, but fitting Sayah inside would be impossible. Instead, he lay on his side, poking just his head through the opening to join the discussion.

Inside, Nat sat on a crude chair of interwoven twigs, and Astéri floated lazily about the room while Miyam piled large, puffy, white flakes of something neither Nat nor Sayah had ever seen before onto a curl of smooth bark that served as a platter. She brought Nat a serving of a few wafers, then set the platter on the packed earth before Sayah. Sayah sniffed at the strange meal and detected no odor. None whatsoever. He extended his tongue carefully to taste the food, then saw something that made him freeze.

Nat sat with eyes closed, head down, and hands clasped over his food, whispering an inaudible prayer. Sayah had never seen such a thing, and he watched Nat with interest.

Miyam noted Sayah's curiosity, and offered, "It is always suitable to give thanks to Lord Elyon, especially in this place."

Sayah cocked his head, confused. *Who is Lord Elyon?*

Nat finished, oblivious to the exchange, and bit into one of the flakes, his eyes brightening at once. He tore through his remaining portion with greedy intensity, and eyed Sayah's untouched platter with concern.

"Sayah, aren't you hungry?" he asked. "The food is amazing!"

Sayah looked again at the odd, puffy wafers before him, and decided against it. He in truth wasn't hungry and didn't find much besides raw flesh appetizing. He said as much, politely as he was able, and Miyam nodded in understanding.

"You're an ægle, that much is certain, and your kind craves the flesh and blood of prey," she related before her eyes settled into an introspective stare. "There will be no further bloodshed upon this ground, however."

Though yet incapable of hunting himself, the æglet's pride swelled within him to retort, *No one tells an ægle where to hunt.*

Returning her gaze to Sayah, Miyam spoke as if in response to his unspoken rebuttal, her tone matter-of-fact, "If you get hungry, you'll have to hunt outside the bower. Beyond the hedge."

Sayah found much peculiar about his day thus far, and this was perhaps the most so, *No hunting near the tree? I might respect the boundary, but my family . . .*

He cocked a fluffy brow in question, and Miyam answered in a tired voice, "Later. We'll get to it later. Maybe."

Miyam stretched and yawned before excusing herself, "If you boys will just give me a few minutes, I'll be ready to chat with you. But first, I need to . . ."

She trailed off, and a confused look crossed her leaf-framed face while she appeared to search for the appropriate word, until she exclaimed, "Aaagh! I can't think of a word that fits. At least not just one. Eat? Drink? Rest? I just don't know! It doesn't matter. Just wait here, OK?"

With that, she swept out of the room, and Nat and Sayah tracked her progress as she crossed to the edge of the pool, above which dust and gnats swirled, revealing a broad shaft of sunlight. Miyam stopped in the pond's shallows and extended her branches upward into the falling rays. To Nat and Sayah, it seemed that every aspect of her frame raised itself into the light, and even the leaves mimicked her upturned and enraptured face. And there she transfixed, still but for the stir of the gentle breeze through her leaves, free of strain though all her being aspired upwards.

Nat and Sayah watched on in wonder until within Nat's soul spoke consideration of the privacy, the intimacy of the moment, though he didn't understand in full. Without a sound, he nudged Sayah to follow him back to the hut where they waited in thoughtful silence for Miyam to return. Astéri continued his meandering patrol within the grassy walls, glowing a contented golden-green and whistling a quiet tune.

It was a matter of minutes before Miyam called to them as she approached, "Hey! You guys didn't fall asleep, did you?"

Though they had not, in fact, fallen asleep, Nat and Sayah had relaxed into a meditative tranquility in her absence, the reflective beauty of the arbor lulling them. Miyam's voice brought them to, and they turned in concert to gape at a radiant, refreshed Miyam. It was if she were saturated with sunlight, and Nat could swear she was taller, if only a smidge.

But that's not possible. Is it? Nat speculated.

He shook his head clear of the thought and joined the conversation already in progress. From Miyam's exposition, Nat determined Sayah must have asked what she was doing at the water's edge.

"...so, as a Sprig, I'm closer to a tree than a Beast like yourself. I don't need to eat much, though I might from time to time, but I *must* drink of the spring here, and get plenty of sunlight, of course," she finished with a wink and a precise finger upheld for emphasis.

"But," Sayah countered, "I didn't see you drink at all. You were just standing there in the water, with your branches up, and –"

He cut himself off as he realized how invasive it might seem to her that they had been watching. Like they were spying, really.

Miyam sighed with understanding, "It's fine, Sayah. Honestly. Don't worry about it. And as far as my *drinking*, you didn't see it because you couldn't. I drink by soaking my roots, just like a tree, and they, dear sir æglet, are underground."

Overhearing the tail end of the conversation, Nat joined in, "You look well-rested, whatever you did. Refreshed."

"I *am*!" Miyam responded. "And I seem to remember saying I might explain more about this place. This Tree."

Her statement perked Sayah's curiosity, and he recalled her prohibition on hunting near the tree. Nat appeared just as interested, and he nodded his agreement that she should indeed tell them more.

Miyam gestured toward Astéri, and indicated, "I may need some help from our little friend here. He and I have already discussed at length the history of this place, and I believe he might best demonstrate what occurred."

Miyam addressed Nat directly, "You know what I mean, don't you, Nat?"

Nat gave a slow, knowing nod, well aware of Astéri's ability to transport others to observe the "flow" of past events.

Sayah looked to his new friends for some hint of what was in store, and Nat reassured him, "Don't worry, Sayah. Just stay close to us. I'll try to answer any questions you have."

"Oh!" Miyam interjected. "That reminds me! Sayah, you're the only one here who doesn't understand Astéri, right?"

"Er, yeah, I guess," the æglet replied.

Face fixed in a pensive frown and arms crossed in thought, Miyam pondered aloud, "I wonder why that is?"

Astéri flew into their midst, twittering and blinking in answer while Miyam and Nat listened, and Sayah just watched, oblivious.

"Huh. So that's why," Miyam murmured to herself. "That's interesting."

Nat, on the other hand, supplied Sayah with some useful information, "Astéri says you should be able to eventually understand him with some...mental calibration. I know it sounds strange, but I had to learn it myself, and it's not difficult. Just a little tricky. I'll try to show you how once we get where we're going."

"Going?" Sayah sniffed and recoiled with a sneer.

He liked his new friends but didn't want to go anywhere else with them. His adventures had brought him quite far enough today.

"No, no, no," Nat protested. "We won't actually be going anywhere, but Astéri can make it seem like it."

He shook his head in frustration, and lamented, "I'm not explaining it well. I promise it'll be safe."

Sayah shook his head in apprehension, unconvinced.

Astéri floated over to Sayah and hummed a lilting tune to soothe the wary æglet, who gave his glittering companion a doubtful, sidelong look.

"I don't think I should be going anywhere but back up to my nest at the top of the tree," Sayah insisted. "I've been gone a while now, and I need to make sure I'm home before my family gets back.

"Another thing . . ." his eyes darted to and fro from one patch of visible sky to another, "I'm worried about all of *you*. Ægles are hunters, and my family won't hesitate to snatch you up for a meal if they spot any of you.

"Especially Gael," he muttered to himself, and shuddered with revulsion, the feathers covering his neck and crest protruding as he did.

"Yeah. About that," Miyam drawled, eyes free of concern as they rolled up, and a frown of mock chagrin dragging down a corner of her mouth. "We should really talk over some of the ground rules of this place, just so you and Nat understand what's allowed here, and what's not."

There it was again! That insistence that even Sayah, an apex predator might be constrained by the authority of some, some twig. He scoffed, a quiet utterance that yet caught the attention of his companions, and he was embarrassed at the sentiment reflected in their glances. Nat's gaze, full of luminous, pure surprise, held the greatest reproach. No accusation was in the Etom's golden eyes, but the abundant innocence there provoked Sayah to shame.

"Sorry, Miyam," Sayah whispered, downcast. "Please. Go on."

She bowed her head and spread her branches wide, intoning, "It's quite alright, Master Æglet. All is forgiven."

Nat recognized her exaggerated solemnity for playfulness, and snorted a laugh, cueing Sayah to do the same. The æglet appreciated how ready his new friends were to forgive him and listened in fascinated gratitude while Miyam adopted an instructive mode, then began.

"First," Miyam enumerated, holding up a leafy digit, "You should know the name of this place, this bower beneath the Tree. It is called Sanctuary, for that is what it is – a place of safety, of refuge, and of unique, peculiar purpose."

Another finger flew up to accompany the first, "Second. And I'm looking at you, my æglet friend. Second. There shall be neither rooted contention nor bloodshed here. By rooted contention, I mean protracted and bitter. Sanctuary provides strict guidelines for conflict, though the aim thereof is ever reconciliation between all parties involved. Those unable to set aside their hostility must depart Sanctuary.

"As far as bloodshed is concerned," the Sprig put two furcated fronds to her eyes, then pointed them at æglet. "No eating *anyone!*"

A gentle smile touched her lips, but a stern determination stood firm behind her green eyes. With respect, Sayah nodded his agreement, eager to learn more about Sanctuary.

Miyam's thumb flipped out to join her upraised fingers, "Third, and this one's a doozy – Sanctuary may only be found by those to whom Elyon has revealed it."

Sayah's head spun with the implications, his raptorial brow drawing down in a confused frown. He snapped his head to fix Miyam in the sharp and penetrating gaze of an ægle on the hunt. While within Sayah's mind a thousand questions clamored, clambering for ascendancy from speculation to expression, in silence Nat pondered his journey to the gnarled and beautiful roots of the Tree. The pale blue etém nodded slowly, recollecting the settled determination that had driven him onward in his loneliness, the guttering flame of hope that had lit the way, and the humble surrender that had granted him passage into Sanctuary.

"I see it," Nat spoke in a quiet, firm voice that stilled the bubbling tumult that threatened to erupt from Sayah.

The æglet listened as Nat recounted his tale: The flight from Endego. Rae's injury and their subsequent diversion to Sakkan. The capture of his friends, and his mother. And, finally, his tearful return to the trail, after which he had found the Tree.

From the fringes of consciousness, a nebulous conclusion pricked him, until, at last, Nat groaned as the notion took definite form.

"Aaaagh!" he exclaimed, holding his head while pain pressed forth in tears. "So close! We were *so. close.*"

Miyam looked on in dismal knowledge while Astéri dropped an apologetic whistle and turned a familiar shade of orange. Sayah, concerned for Nat and more confused than ever, elected to stay quiet in hope all would come clear.

Nat perceived Astéri's apologetic trill and hue, then Miyam's sheepish expression, and, dumbfounded, whispered, "You knew. You both knew we were out there, and you didn't *do ANYTHING!*"

Nat couldn't think of another time he'd been so angry, and the loss of recent days stoked a furnace rage that burned in his blushing, violet cheeks. He didn't understand! Astéri was his friend. His guide since he had hatched. Somehow his sparkling friend had failed him, and that failure had cost Nat, well, everything.

Astéri flashed and twittered in rapid succession, but Nat didn't, couldn't hear him. The blood in Nat's head beat a dull and heavy rhythm that drown out his friend until his blood-bogged mind caught a single phrase *. . .tried to show you the stones. The stones outside Sanctuary.*

A curt reply died on Nat's lips when memory presented a moment filled with anxious consideration after Rae had fallen to injury. The wind blowing, a light shining on jagged stone standing as the tooth of some earthen beast. He and his mother standing together while his mind churned in a jumble of amplified concerns for Rae.

Nat stood in horrified realization, suddenly small and alone beneath the spreading Tree. Care for Rae had loomed paramount in the moment, and he had dismissed the signs Astéri sent him to follow. But, why hadn't his guide just spoken to his mind in the moment? Wouldn't that have been clearer?

Nat asked as much, and Astéri replied, his outward chiming subsumed by understanding inserted in Nat's mind, *Do you remember how you learned to hear me? You had to still yourself. Relax. Grow calm. Yes? You were so agitated when Rae was hurt that you* couldn't *hear me, so I tried to show you instead.*

Astéri turned an apologetic orange and dimmed sadly, *I tried, Nat. I really did. You were so focused on Rae's safety that you didn't* see, *either.*

Nat stumbled to a nearby stone, and sat down to chew on a knuckle, eyes wide and unblinking in his shocked disappointment.

"I can't believe it," he muttered, shaking his head. "It's my fault. All of it. They're all gone, and it's *my* fault."

"Now, now!" Miyam chided with merry consolation. "Don't go getting down on yourself. You and yours did the best you could, and no one could blame you for taking care of a friend, especially your best friend, right?

"Besides," she continued with a conspiratorial wink at Astéri, "we happen to know that there is hope for your captive company. But first things first, OK?"

"Well, as I was saying," Miyam proceeded, "only those to whom Elyon has revealed Sanctuary may find it. He alone stirs the longing of every heart for this place, and He alone directs the steps of those who seek it. Even if those steps bring them crashing to the ground, apparently."

Sayah looked up to find her smiling at him, and something in her smile made him bashful, so he looked down at the ground with blindly staring eyes.

Miyam returned to her instruction, "We know that some come with knowledge, with tales of the Kinsman, but all come with incomplete understanding that can only be made whole by partaking of these springs. Nat, we already know much of your tale, and your reasons for seeking the Kinsman, but you, Sayah, what drew you here?"

With one word, Sayah answered, "Thirst."

And it was true, but only in part. Thirst had compelled him to his perch overhead, as it always had, but today…today something had been different. He'd spied Nat, and a sudden awareness of his loneliness had seized him. The compulsion to reach out to the Etom had taken him farther out on the limb than he'd gone before, past the point of safety. Sayah shook his head, not quite ready to accept that this *Elyon* had orchestrated his fall to the forest floor, but likewise finding it hard to deny.

With a sage nod Miyam accepted Sayah's response, then resumed, "However you arrived at Sanctuary, you both followed a path laid before you, whether you knew it or not. I cannot overstate the value, the importance of Sanctuary, nor the price paid to restore these grounds, accursed from days long past."

More questions arose in Nat and Sayah's minds, and, recognizing their confusion, Miyam caught herself, "But I'm getting ahead of myself, or should I say ahead of our brilliant friend, Astéri."

At his mention, Astéri flitted about the trio, emanating an excited melody. Nat and Miyam listened with understanding while Sayah attended to Astéri with peripheral awareness. He'd yet to develop the knack for comprehending the strange being that Nat and Miyam possessed, though not for lack of desire.

"But can you manage all of us?" Miyam asked.

Astéri dropped an undulating whistle that Sayah interpreted as "who knows?"

Miyam inquired, "How about just two?"

Astéri rolled back and forth before her and tooted twice in the affirmative.

"Then I'll stay. The others can go. They *need* to go. I've been already once before, and . . ." pain twisted Miyam's face, a rare expression there, and she gasped, "and it was hard enough the first time."

The Sprig addressed Nat and Sayah, "What you two are about to witness will teach you much about Sanctuary, but you may find it difficult to watch. I challenge you not to turn from it."

Astéri led Nat and Sayah to a bare patch nearby with Miyam bringing up the rear to see them off.

The etém and æglet turned around to face her, and she asked, "Are you ready?"

Nat said, "yes," but Sayah shook his head, doubtful.

"Don't worry, Sayah. I've gone with Astéri before, and there's nothing to worry about," Nat reassured him. "We might not like what we see, but nothing can hurt us there."

"I just don't understand. Where are we going?" Sayah asked, confused.

"Just trust me," Nat implored. "Can you do that?"

Oh well. I've come this far, Sayah thought, and nodded.

With that, Miyam stood away from them, waving while Astéri blared what seemed a warning, and began to spin, faster and faster, his brilliant form glowing an ever-deepening shade of red. Sayah's eyes bore into the star's blazing core, and the world dimmed around them until all but Astéri fell to black.

Chapter Four
The Kinsman's Fate

Darkness enveloped them in slow, stifling seconds until overhead, a blue bolt sundered the midnight gloom, the crack of thunder chasing close behind the lightning. A downpour erupted around the trio, and Sayah held out a wing, mesmerized as the great drops passed through it to pound the ground. The wet bombardment soon turned the earth muddy, the sheen reflecting the moon's brightness to illuminate a broad, rough road. The road ran down to a crude bridge over a river raging with the added force of the torrential rain. The bridge and road were too large for Etom, and could only be the work of Man.

Nat blinked at the familiar scene, recognizing the bridge Company Jasper had crossed on their way to Sakkan, and they approached it from the west as before. Across its span, the road passed into the murk of the forest, which was that much more profound at night. Nat shuddered at the unbidden memory of the huge, lurking Nihúkolem they had dodged during their crossing. But for its clarity, the memory seemed distant, driven backward in time by the momentous events of the past several days.

So lost in thought was Nat that, without realizing, he still peered into yonder darkness when surprised by the appearance of many Men, a military column marching before a pair of mules pulling a cart. Two by two the soldiers approached, their faces grim in the heavy slog made yet heavier by weight of arms.

The mules struggled under the whips of their handlers, their work growing more arduous once the cart's wheels left the firm and level bridge to sink into the cloying mud. Sayah pitied the mules for the difficulty of their labor, made even more so now the road arced northward for the upward climb, and was alarmed to remain near the road, so close to Men.

Mother and Father had warned that Men were dangerous predators, so he whispered to Nat, "Don't you think we should hide, or at least move farther away?"

60

Keeping his eyes on the soldiers, Nat answered, "They can't see us. That's part of Astéri's ability."

Nat pointed at the ground with two blue digits, "We're not exactly *here*, if that makes sense. This is something like a dream, a vision."

Sayah's eyes bulged in doubt, but his friend's confidence emboldened him, so he stayed put, although in cautious readiness to flee should the need arise. Somewhat reassured, he joined Nat in watching the sodden procession while Astéri floated at his shoulder.

A cage of poles lashed together stood upright in the cart, and Nat detected the vague form of Man within its confines. The prisoner braced himself against the inside of the cage to keep his footing while the vehicle swayed and rocked over the uneven ground. Progress was slow, but soon the column reached the trio, and the cart, too, neared their position beside the roadway.

It was too dark to get a clear look at the prisoner in the sparse moonlight and fitful flashes of lightning, but Nat and Sayah strained to do so regardless. The card drew alongside them as it passed, causing Nat and Sayah to lose hope in satisfying their curiosity. At the last moment, the figure turned bright eyes on them, and the pair caught their collective breath.

Though aware that none might see them, the Man's eyes affixed Nat and Sayah there as though sending forth twin shafts to pin them to ground. He saw them! And then the moment was past, along with the column, leaving Nat and Sayah to watch the backs of the rearguard pair recede beyond the cascading screen of rainfall.

Astéri chirped for their attention, and Sayah imagined he heard the word, *Come!* resound among his thoughts. He dismissed the notion, following Nat and Astéri away from the road toward the precipice that loomed to the west.

They arrived at the foot of the cliffs, its rocky face stretching southward, in which direction lay Nat's memory of their descent with an unconscious Rae. Astéri fluted what seemed a warning before they all began to rise, the motion startling Sayah. Again, that strange and overlaid sense of meaning flitted through his mind, though he was too distracted by their unexpected ascent to ponder it. They soon surmounted the cliff's edge to survey a flat, rocky scrabble, and to the west, a thick forest. To the north, Sayah's ægle eyes caught the dread parade of soldiers limned against the flashing, electric sky as the soldiers arced westward at the top of the ramping road below.

Astéri called the others onward, and they glided effortlessly across the pebbled plain and through the tangled underbrush of the woods. Through the disconcerting blur of the foliage they passed, Sayah had a vague sense that their course would intercept the troops, perhaps at the column's destination.

Their sudden arrival at a vast clearing prompted Astéri to an abrupt halt. Nat and Sayah gasped at the devastation of the black, barren expanse, a shadowy blot in the midst of verdant growth barely visible in the scant light of the moon. The scene revealed in lighting flare held their breath captive yet a while longer, with Nat to receive the lengthier sentence at the evidence presented him.

I know this place, too, he thought, his eyes taking in the crooked, skeletal form of the dark and ragged tree hunched over the funereal plain.

Astéri whimpered a dismal reminder that echoed through Sayah's mind in parts, *. . .you . . .recognize . . .tree?*

"I do," Nat replied, his voice low and serious. "It's the Tree Ha Datovara, isn't it?"

Astéri droned in glum concurrence, *Yes, Nat. The Tree of the Knowledge of Good and Evil.*

Sayah gaped alongside them, his sharp gaze absorbing the dim and desolate landscape. Beneath the failing radiance of the moon, Sayah determined that neither stem nor blade arose from the chalky earth that spread beneath the tree. In the downpour, the land refused the water, which in beading runnels flowed away from the repellent tree.

From the north, the column of soldiers entered the clearing, the rhythmic splash of their heavy footfalls signaling their arrival. Out of the corner of his eye, Nat noticed a swirl of black grit blow in beside the ruinous tree and resolve into the looming form of a Man clad for war, his horned helm sprouting last atop a shadowy head. The Nihúkolem! Another swept in to join him, broader, then one slight and another lanky, all in the shape of Men. It seemed each moment was filled with the arrival of more sinister figures. To their places flanking the tree on either side, Men and fell Beasts strode in dimpled resolution made imperfect in the pelting rain.

Beside the trio, a faint oval impression appeared, a black outline displacing the water as it ran across the fallow ground. Then another, more distinct, and another, more substantial still. The ground around them quivered at first, then shook, and at last, with footfalls grown thunderous, the charging form of an elephant pulled up just short of the gathering, and, trunk wagging side to side, it sauntered to the end of the wing nearest the observers.

Upon noticing the appearance of the Nihúkolem, the soldiers had slowed their pace. Sayah saw alarm in their faces, and some servile obedience that yet dragged them onward. Nat watched on in concern for the soldiers, fearing what the Nihúkolem might do to them. He needn't have been anxious on their behalf, however.

From the front of the column broke forth a single Man, who Nat presumed must be their captain. The captain hailed the Nihúkolem, and gestured back toward the cart, where the prisoner still stood caged. The horned figure first to arrive stepped forward and raised a hand in greeting.

The buzzing rasp of the Nihúkolem's speech invaded their minds, and Sayah, having never before experienced this unpleasantness, squawked his surprise before recovering himself to listen.

Greetings, Captain Makrïos. I trust your prisoner is well, and intact?

Nat, familiar only with the aloof and dangerous Nihúkolem that prowled Endego, sensed a shade of the mysterious veil surrounding the wraiths brighten at the almost friendly salutation.

The captain, his discomfort apparent, cleared his throat and answered, "Um, er, yes, my lord. As ordered, one prisoner, the malcontent Gaal. We hope you will be pleased that he is unharmed. He did not resist, which made his arrest a simple matter."

Very well, came the grating response. *Bring Him before me.*

"Yes, sir!" Makrïos barked and hurried back to his troops.

"Bring the prisoner!" he commanded with a wave, and his troops sprang into action, the rearguard hurrying to lower the gate at the back of the cart while two others clambered over either side to open the cage.

The captain walked to the rear of the cart, calling to those opening the cage, "Careful! Not a scratch on Him, you lugs!"

With a hand beneath either of the captive's armpits, the two soldiers in the cart lowered him to the rearguard. The guards gripped either of the captive's arms above the elbow to conduct him around the side of the cart nearest the invisible watchers, where Nat and Sayah got their first good look at the prisoner.

His hands were bound behind him, and his wet hair hung in a lank mess about his face, which was yet obscured but for his eyes, which seemed to glow with a light of their own. Though flanked by captors, his steps were peaceable and unhurried, his gait noble and upright. He stood before the Nihúkolem unafraid, though it seemed they shrank back from him, if only so slightly.

The Nihúkolem leader of thorny helm evaluated his hostage, taking stock before he asked, *I am Mūk-Mudón, commander in chief over the Empire of Chōl, and you are Him? The Kinsman?*

Though he did not raise his voice, the prisoner's response was as clear to Nat and Sayah as if he stood beside them, "It is as you say."

Another flash of lightning lit the swirling maelstrom overhead, and Nat imagined he heard a malevolent cackle in the crackling peal that ensued. For a moment, Gaal's face was visible in the flickering light. Serene determination girded his humble features, and he once more turned his luminous gaze on the trio as if only to demonstrate his supernatural awareness of their presence.

As before, they were paralyzed before his countenance, though Nat now identified a familiar sensation, uncomfortable in its inception, but pleasant now he grew acquainted with it.

The fleeting moment passed, and the stunned observers were slow to note Mūk-Mudón's new orders, *Beat Him. We wish Him to suffer.*

The soldiers rushed to surround the Kinsman, who looked at them in turn, and it seemed each was hesitant to be the first to strike Him.

Do it! Mūk-Mudón menaced.

The captain's fear of the Nihúkolem overcame his reluctance, employing brute instinct to lash out at the tranquil figure. His looping fist caught the Kinsman on the cheek below His eye, splitting the flesh, and spilling blood in a gush that streaked down Gaal's face like tears. With an unsurprised frown, Gaal closed His eyes and furrowed His brow as His sorrowful tears joined with the flowing blood. The Kinsman opened his eyes to Captain Makrïos, then with a slow, deliberate turn of his head, He presented the other cheek.

Prompted by the gesture, a frenzy broke free within the captain, who, no longer constrained by reason, began in earnest to pummel the defenseless Kinsman. The others joined in the melee, slugging and kicking Gaal back and forth between them to keep their victim on His feet while they tormented Him.

The beating lasted several minutes until only the captain persisted, the others too winded from exertion to continue. Nat and Sayah watched, horrified at the blood-stained lump that staggered under the captain's blows. It seemed certain Gaal would collapse at any moment.

Enough! Mūk-Mudón growled.

The captain stepped back from the Kinsman, relieved at the respite, which he took with great, whooping breaths. Gaal, too, breathed heavily, and with each inhale, stood more erect. At last, He stood again upright, His spirit serene and unbroken, eyes bright as ever.

Mūk-Mudón interrogated Gaal again, *It is reported You fancy Yourself a king. Is this true? Are You a king?*

Once more the Kinsman answered with uncanny clarity, "It is as You say."

You must accept my apologies, Your Majesty, Mūk-Mudón mocked. *I know a thing or two of rulership and didn't recognized Your sovereignty. After all . . .*

The shadowy figure looked around, his hands spread to either side, *Where are Your subjects? And where is Your crown? Ah! I have it.*

Mūk-Mudón turned and shouted back into the dark and shifting ranks, *Corsucan! Bring the king here His crown!*

From among the wispy wraiths, a slinking figure sped. To Sayah, it seemed a weasel, carrying forth a band of some kind in its mouth to pass to the captain. Whilst the Kinsman endured His beating, some of the Nihúkolem had stripped a petrified and thorny vine from the trunk of Tree Ha Datovara and had woven it into the cruel circlet that the captain now gripped in meaty hands.

Come now, Mūk-Mudón entreated Captain Makrïos in merriment. *Let's give the king a crown. And we must make certain it is snug. We can't have it falling off now, can we?*

Gaal stared into the captain's eyes with understanding, and offered a near-imperceptible nod, then lowered His head to His antagonist. Makrïos' grim features hardened, and he placed the crown atop the Kinsman's head.

Nat, already distressed at the beating, sensed with foreboding that the worst was yet to come, and stifled a cry of protest he knew would be fruitless. They could observe only, and not intervene in these events fixed in the immutable past. The Kinsman smiled gently as He passed His eyes over the Etom, and Nat was again struck by Gaal's awareness of their presence.

How? the question rang forth within Nat's mind. *Just who is this Kinsman?*

He had heard the prophecies of the Kinsman, and of the mighty works the Eben'kayah expected of Him, but now that Nat had seen Him, He seemed something *more*.

Sayah, on the other hand, watched with some detachment. He was well-acquainted with cruelty and was just relieved it wasn't him. Until the captain's cudgel cracked down over Gaal's head, forcing the prongs of the crown deep into the Kinsman's scalp. The Kinsman stepped back, His face downcast as blood welled around each puncture, then ran in lazy, irregular streams down His face, head, and neck to form a crimson shroud.

The thorns likewise pierced even Sayah's indifference, and he echoed Nat, who now cried out without restraint in concern for Gaal. The Etom fell against the æglet's side, and Sayah welcomed the comfort of shared warmth in the face of cold cruelty. And it wasn't over. Not by a stretch.

Strip Him! barked Mūk-Mudón. *And bring the scourge.*

A soldier dashed back to the cart to collect the whip while the others removed the Kinsman's garments, leaving Him naked and bruised beneath the pouring rain. Nat experienced a sympathetic shame for the Man. Though no brother of Nat's kind, Gaal bore a resemblance of soul to all sapient creatures, perhaps more so than any other Nat had encountered.

The captain opened his hand for the scourge, a heartless implement of torture comprising several leather lashes. Starting about halfway down each lash's length, jagged bits of bone and metal were knotted into the lash, which terminated in a lead weight.

A soldier stood on either side of Gaal, gripping beneath His arms to support Him. The captain moved behind the Kinsman to stand on one side, the whip's long handle held in both hands. With a shout, Makrïos swung the scourge, which stuck in the skin over Gaal's shoulder-blade. The captain twisted the handle and wrenched downward. The scourge removed great, ragged ribbons of flesh, and left tracks that filled with blood as the whip again fell across Gaal's back.

Nat flinched, and tears poured down his young face while Sayah stared in silence, his sharp eyes reporting the violence to a numb mind with perfect clarity. Since the first beating had begun, Astéri remained quiet, and now he fell dim and grey as a thunderhead to express his sorrowful gloom.

The trio watched in quiet horror as the brutal whip fell again, and again, and again. At some point, the æglet had looked down, his eyes fixed on the flow at his feet that diminished as the rainfall tapered off and stopped. It seemed the torture would not end. Nat, however, watched through the dwindling veil of his tears, which also slowed as the wellspring within him emptied. Regardless, his sorrow remained alongside a determination to do as Miyam challenged and not look away.

Captain Makrïos at last stepped back to reveal in full the Kinsman's affliction. Gaal's flesh was riven to the bone and hung in shreds from His body while blood flowed in rivulets to pool on the ground beneath Him. The soldiers on either side stood the Kinsman up, then let go. He nearly swooned, swaying instead in vague circular motion to stay on His feet. Even in the relative murk, His once olive-tone skin reflected the moonlight in gaunt pallor.

You're still missing something, Mūk-Mudón considered, after again appraising his captive. *A robe! Hey there, captain! Have you a royal robe for our good king?*

Captain Makrïos sent a subordinate scurrying to the cart, whence he returned with a rich, purple robe to place over Gaal's shoulders.

See there? Mūk-Mudón quipped. *Now that's a king! None more stately have I ever seen. Come! Let us to Your throne.*

Nat thought Mūk-Mudón's jaunty, insincere praise most insulting, given the atrocious circumstances.

Captain, we will have need of mallet, nail, and ladder. Please have one of your men fetch them, Mūk-Mudón added.

With that, Mūk-Mudón spun about and strode toward the withered and bent tree. The Nihúkolem closed around their leader to form an alley leading up to the crooked trunk. Gaal blinked hard, His lips pursed flat in a bloodless line, then followed, wavering along the way, but pressing ever forward. Once He had entered the gauntlet, the silent forms began to jeer, mocking him as He passed, yet not once did He respond in kind. One staggering foot in front of the other, He trudged on, His eyes never leaving the tree.

Captain Makrïos directed his column to follow the Kinsman, and the troops complied, although their transit was an anxious affair accompanied by nervous looks to either side when they passed between the Nihúkolem. The captain led them, face stony and eyes distant as if he wished himself absent of this affair.

Gaal arrived at the dry and brittle roots of the tree, and stopped there before Mūk-Mudón, who turned to the dark assembly and raised his hands in magnanimity. The captain halted his troops and called them to attention.

Standing over the assembly on knurled roots, Mūk-Mudón waved a banishing hand over the Kinsman in request, *Captain, please.*

Captain Makrïos froze, uncertain what his commander desired until Mūk-Mudón spat in frustration, *The robe! Remove his robe!*

Spurred into action, Captain Makrïos waved a soldier to Gaal's left side while he gripped the robe at Gaal's right shoulder. With a heave, the two soldiers whipped the robe from the Kinsman's back. In the time since it had been placed on Him, the robe had sopped up much of Gaal's blood, which had begun to dry, affixing the cloth to His wounds. The robe's violent removal ripped His back open again and tugged at the shreds of flesh that clung to the garment, the new wounds etching their way around His torso until the scintillas of skin that yet held on at last let go.

Captain Makrïos and his cohort flung aside the robe, now scabrous and matted with ribbons of flesh, while Gaal cried out in pain, shivering in shock at the fresh, sudden agony. He fell to one knee and braced Himself with a hand as He fought to maintain consciousness. With shuddering intensity, He fought back up to stand before Mūk-Mudón, who stroked his chin in a pensive gesture.

The time has arrived for Your ascent, dear Kinsman! he announced, then looked to Captain Makrïos. *Let us make certain He is securely enthroned.*

A soldier near Gaal bid Him drink from the vessel he carried.

Brightening a shade, Astéri tolled, *At last, some small mercy. It is vinegar and contains an ingredient to dull this suffering.*

Nat and Sayah watched with interest as Gaal brought His split and bloody lips to the mouth of the jug. He tasted the concoction, then spat out the mouthful of liquid.

"What!?!" Nat exclaimed, then turned to Astéri, "Why?"

Glittering with pure, white light, Astéri answered, and Nat detected reverence in the tones, *He would not diminish the suffering He bears for the sake of Creation.*

A subordinate handed Captain Makrïos a mallet and nails while others again gripped Gaal on either side to conduct Him up to the tree. The tree's trunk bent sharply away, then, with a gnarled twist, came forward to form a rough 'L' in profile. Its first forking boughs loomed low and predatory as if some skeletal creature poised to snatch up anyone fool enough to come within reach.

Nat remembered the very moment of the tree's warping from long ago in Astéri's "flow," and was amazed at how little the tree had changed over the ages. It stood a fossilized reminder to all of the instant that Man had betrayed the harmony of the world for selfish ambition, and Nat guessed at some divine purpose in the corrupt monument.

The soldiers turned Gaal around, then hoisted Him several feet up the slanted trunk with legs draped down the tree's length. The Kinsman slouched forward so heavily in the contorted crook that Nat and Sayah were concerned He might pitch headlong from the awkward "throne." Captain Makrïos called for the ladder, and an underling scurried to place it beside the Kinsman, where the captain mounted it. The soldier who had brought the ladder took a few unsteady steps up the trunk, then with a shove, pressed Gaal's upper back against the rough bark of the tree where it bent forward.

Gaal cried out, and Nat winced with empathetic pain while Sayah hid his eyes beneath a downy wing. The captain nodded to his cohort, who yet held the Kinsman against the trunk, then brought Gaal's arm up to a drooping branch where his superior looped a short length of rope around the arm to keep it in place.

Another subordinate below the Captain passed up a mallet and nail. To call it a nail was an understatement, perhaps. The implement at hand was a twelve-inch spike, and thick at its base as a Man's finger.

The Captain placed the tip of the spike on Gaal's wrist, just below the hand, and raised the mallet in preparation, evoking a dread gasp from Nat, "Oh. No."

At Nat's exclamation, Sayah peeked out from behind his wing in time to see the mallet come down and drive the piercing nail through Gaal's wrist, pinning him to the bough. The Kinsman writhed in agony, the cords of His neck standing out while He beat His other fist in pain against the tree. So deficient in blood was He that instead of gushing from the puncture, the claret softly soughed forth as His tormentors moved to the other side to repeat the process with the other hand.

Sayah saw with ægle's eyes the Kinsman's lips moving in silence as the rope looped over the other arm, securing it to another branch. Gaal's face did not flinch at the touch of spike to skin, though His hand jerked in involuntary aversion, a futile effort. The second nail pierced the Kinsman, and His eyes went wide in pain, though not a sound did He make.

Last, Captain Makrïos descended the ladder and stood beside the Kinsman, where two soldiers had overlapped Gaal's feet. The Captain had removed the length of rope from the Kinsman's hands, and Gaal now depended face-down from the spikes that pinned Him to the tree.

Using the same length to tie Gaal's ankles in place, the Captain prepared the final spike, which he placed over the Kinsman's lapped feet, then swung the mallet. Nat and Sayah could hardly bear to watch Captain Makrïos as he struggled to see his task through. It took him many swings of the mallet to succeed in nailing Gaal's feet to the trunk, and he stepped back at last to examine his handiwork.

As Mūk-Mudón had requested, the Kinsman was secure in His throne upon the tree, where He remained in pained repose, a raw and regal sovereign over the bleak terrain. All present, Nat and Sayah included, appraised the Kinsman, who did not struggle against His fate, but looked down upon His ruthless audience with pity.

Gaal strained to lift His eyes to the sky, and implored, "Forgive them; for they know not what they do."

For better or worse, the words affected all gathered: the Nihúkolem and several soldiers scoffed, Sayah, Captain Makrïos and the remainder of his troops shook their heads in disbelief, and Astéri joined Nat in expression equivalent to the Etom's bittersweet tears.

Time passed, and it became apparent that Gaal's torment was taking its toll. He shifted to ease His breathing, pulling Himself up with His arms while pushing against the nail through His feet, which also served to increase His misery.

He cried out in agony, and shouted into the lowering heavens, "Elyon! Elyon! Why have you forsaken Me?"

Nat marveled that the Kinsman addressed Elyon thus, for to be abandoned meant that Gaal *knew* their Creator.

But that's impossible, isn't it? Nat considered. *Elyon left this world at the Sunder, and yet Gaal acts as though He has* seen *Lord Elyon, face to face.*

The Etom's circumspect mind walked about the question, approaching it from a variety of perspectives. Either Gaal was a fake, or crazy, or who He claimed to be. By every proof to which Nat could subject Gaal given the information available, He was indeed the Kinsman. But the list of qualities that the title Kinsman encompassed seemed to expand beyond the bounds established in Nat's mind through the prophecies of the Eben'kayah.

Gaal stirred, drawing Nat out of his reverie, His breath hitching as He looked to Captain Makrïos and beseeched, "I thirst."

With immediacy, the Captain called for another vessel of vinegar, this unpolluted by the narcotic offered earlier. Due to Gaal's raised and ungainly position, lifting the jug to His lips was not an option. Instead, Captain Makrïos sent for a sponge tied to a branch of hyssop, an implement whose common use was scrubbing the latrine, and soaked it in the sour liquid.

Of this, the Kinsman drank, and, sated of the bitter ferment, sighed with impossible contentment, "It is finished. Father, into Your hands I commit My spirit."

Gaal's final breath followed close behind His words, and He bowed His noble head, a ruinous figure depending from the accursed Tree Ha Datovara. Visible in the soft, surging light before dawn, His blood pooled at the foot of the tree, a regal red carpet proceeding from the site of Gaal's first humiliation to His last.

Nat's mind, still reeling from prior revelation, seized on Gaal's words, *He called Elyon Father? Just* Who *is this Kinsman?*

Mūk-Mudón commanded that Captain Makrïos ensure the Kinsman was dead. Still stationed to one side below the Kinsman, Captain Makrïos thrust a spear into Gaal's side. A gush of blood and water poured from the wound, and the Captain muttered something Nat was unable to hear.

Behind the clustered clouds overhead, the sky flashed a blinding white, and without delay thunder shook the earth. Where Gaal's blood had struck the fallow soil, it rent the impermeable earth, whence sighed a bracing gust. The breach opened from the foot of the tree into a shallow trench that ran between the ranks lingering in the aftermath of their murderous deed. Uneasy, the soldiers looked to Mūk-Mudón for reassurance as they staggered to maintain their balance.

The shaking ceased, and Mūk-Mudón clapped his sooted hands together, and proclaimed, *Well done! We have accomplished what we set out to do and have quashed the ambitions of this charlatan. Let all recognize the supremacy of the Empire of Chōl!*

He identified the misgiving present on the faces of the Men in his company and cheered them, *Congratulations are in order! Captain Makrïos, be certain you treat these men to a banquet befitting their accomplishment upon your return to the garrison!*

"Yes, my lord!" the Captain responded with counterfeit enthusiasm.

Though Mūk-Mudón didn't seem to notice, it was clear to Nat that Captain Makrïos and several of his troops were ill at ease with their "accomplishment."

With a guilty nod to where Gaal hung from the tree, Captain Makrïos inquired, "And Him, sir?"

With icy indifference, Mūk-Mudón answered, *What of Him? Leave Him to the birds and beasts of the wilderness. It's none of your concern.*

"Sir!" Captain Makrïos complied with a sharp, downward snap of the head.

At that, the captain departed with his soldiers and the cart, and the column moved off at a brisk pace across the level clearing. The Nihúkolem left as they had arrived, in dark grains that disappeared on an unnatural wind. Soon, only Mūk-Mudón remained, and he stood before the Kinsman in contemplation until at last, he waved a dismissive hand at the spent form.

Agh!

The trio discerned the Nihúkolem's disgusted utterance as he pivoted and swept away in an ebon flurry, leaving them alone with the Kinsman's lifeless body.

Chapter Five

Sanctuary

They stood in the bleak clearing, Nat and Sayah looking to Astéri for answers to their plentiful questions. Instead of offering explanation, Astéri called for quiet, and bid them watch the tree, but for what, he didn't offer.

As the sunlight touched the far end of the trench, where Gaal had received His beating, a curiosity arose. The rays spawned growth in the sunken soil, now made soft at the rending of its callous exterior. Green stem, then spreading leaf, and lengthening stalk arose at the bright and warming touch. The sun arose as ever, extending the reach of its luminous arms as they embraced the land.

Soon the once-barren channel teemed with verdant life, and with eager anticipation Nat and Sayah watched as the beams approached the tree. The first timid finger of light stroked a lowly root, moving Nat and Sayah to disappointment when the rays didn't produce the same effect in the tree as they had in the furrowed earth. The daylight scaled the haggard trunk to caress Gaal's pallid feet, illuminating His many afflictions as it climbed until at last the day had risen on His gentle head.

With rapt attention, they beheld the sunrise, which enveloped now the weary grey tree in full. In the daylight, it seemed even more disfigured, its many blemishes made visible under intense brightness, and for a while, it seemed nothing happened.

Then with a shout of, "Look there!" Sayah spied something of interest.

At the end of the trench farthest from the tree, where Gaal had begun His tortured procession, a single bud bloomed. The soft, velvet petals unfurled, a layered chalice of vivid crimson pouring forth heavenly perfume. The neighboring buds followed the first rose, blooming in rapid succession, as a royal runner unrolling to the tree's trunk.

Nat and Sayah followed the ruby carpet to its end beneath the Kinsman's feet. A faint 'clink' emanated from nearby, sending the pair's eyes darting to and fro to locate the noise's origin.

With a gasp, the sharp-eyed æglet extended a wingtip to point out a brutal spike where it lay upon the bleak and unyielding blanched earth. Following Sayah's wingtip, Nat likewise saw it, and together they raised their eyes to the hand it had once pierced.

The hand flexed and stretched, the wound at the wrist below a gaping, bloodless puncture through which Nat and Sayah saw the rotted, grey flesh of the tree. Gaal's head was down and His face not yet visible, though He turned slightly toward His liberated arm where still He held it aloft. He clenched the fist and brought it to His chest with slow deliberation, then at last raised His visage to the sky. The Kinsman's face was radiant, a brilliant star of the morning, of which it seemed the sun was a mere reflection.

Even Sayah's ægle's eyes could not countenance the sight, and he and Nat diverted their gazes to the ragged, empty hole in the branch whence had fallen the spike. Where once beneath the tree's crusting bark lay ashen, lifeless wood, now glowed forth a golden fiber. As though unburdened from some great and pressing gravity, the bough arose in leafing exultation.

In fascinated expectation, Nat and Sayah turned to where the Kinsman's other hand yet remained pinned to the tree. In soundless, persistent motion, the spike withdrew from wood and wound to fall beneath the tree. Gaal clutched both hands together as the enlivened branch, rid of invisible encumbrance, arose to join its counterpart, the pair aloft as two great arms embracing the heavens in thanksgiving.

Their eyes riveted to Gaal's feet, Nat and Sayah awaited the removal of Gaal's final fetter to the tree. The nail emerged with the same steady force as the other, as though a powerful, unseen hand were at work. Now free, the Kinsman stood, and with stately gait, descended the leaning length of the trunk, the wound in His side revealing the pulse of a beating heart. He dismounted the tree, the blossoms carpeting His path arising to carry each beautiful, scarred foot on lavish kisses to His sole. With every step, the crooked trunk of the tree uncoiled until it stood tall and straight as when it towered over Gan.

Reaching the end of the flowered lane, Gaal faced the tree, pausing beneath the vibrant canopy while the shifting screen of leaves cast shadows to play overhead. His back, too, bore the wounds of His affliction, though now emptied of their injurious power.

Nat nudged Sayah to point out the twining green that shot through the plait of thorns upon Gaal's head. The stiff vines forming the cruel crown softened, their stems returning to life. From the tip of each thorn, a small white flower bloomed, and in that instant, the roses at Gaal's feet turned the same pure white, releasing their petals in a gently drifting crush.

His living crown likewise shed its miniscule petals, which transformed into a shining garment as they cascaded over His shoulders. Green and woven stem upon His head became a diadem of intricate work, gold and silver conjoined in perfect symmetry to adorn Gaal's regal head.

Coronation complete and clad in purest white robes, the Kinsman raised a gentle hand, and addressed the tree with a sigh, "Ephphatha. Be opened."

At the crux of the boughs from which He had hung, crystal waters sprang, the flow growing to fill the trench below. The white petals floated atop the springwaters as they pooled, then ran across the Kinsman's feet to spread across the bleak and fallow plain, carrying the flowers' sweet perfume.

What the waters touched, they changed. All that they met grew somehow softer, and, for the first time since the Sunder, Nature was restored. From beneath the chalky soil, stem, leaf, and tendril sprouted with vigor to cover the resurrected plain with life. At the reaches of the clearing, a leafy hedge erupted to encircle the bower in protection.

The Kinsman looked about, satisfied, and with uncanny awareness, He again gazed into their souls. He favored each with a gentle smile, and looking again to the heavens, disappeared from their sight.

In the sheltered glow of the bower, the trio remained in contemplative silence until Astéri hummed and flickered. In perfect overlay, and in concert with each starlit flash, Nat and Sayah caught glimpses of the now-matured Sanctuary, Miyam's hand yet upraised in parting wave. The flickers quickened until Sanctuary and Sprig resolved in full, and they again stood before their leafy friend.

"Wow!" she exclaimed. "That *was* quick! You're getting good at this, Astéri."

The star blushed a rosy pink, and whistled, *Thank you.*

Nat, too, was impressed, recalling how his absence from the body to join Astéri in the flow had shaken both Rae and his mother. It seemed that in seamless revolution they had returned to the exact moment of their departure as if no time at all had passed.

Within his deepest being, however, he felt they had been gone for ages, the events he had witnessed impressing him with their profound import. The Kinsman slain, and now alive again! He perceived that he'd assimilated some secret, incomprehensible knowledge, too, through their proximity to Gaal. Just what it all meant, however, he hadn't even begun to work out, and suspected he might never fully understand its significance.

"I imagine you both have questions," Miyam began, "And I think I can help answer them."

Sayah crowed in concern, "Hold up! I *do* have questions, but only one I'm worried about right now is, 'How in the world do I get back up to my nest?'"

"Goodness, yes!" Miyam replied, "I believe I can help with that, too. But first, do you understand now why you may not hunt here?"

Sayah considered his response, and nodded his humble head, "Yes. I think I do."

The æglet's mind clamored, thought and memory colliding to produce two conclusions. First, to spill any blood on this hallowed ground would be to dishonor what the Kinsman had done. The blood of any other was unworthy and would be a profane insult to Gaal's work. Second, and this shook the æglet to his core, Sayah didn't *want* to. Somehow, what he'd seen, and the tranquility of Sanctuary had together blunted his killer instinct, though he wondered if it would be so outside the bower.

"Good!" Miyam answered, "Then I'd be willing to have you back. Now, are you ready to head home?"

Sayah begged a moment to say goodbye, then nodded to Miyam that he was ready.

Miyam instructed, "If you want to visit again, go to your perch in the morning and wait for us to bring you back down, *safely*. Astéri, would you do the honors, then?"

With a glimmer and a whistle, the starlet approached, and bobbed in front of Sayah before he began to spin, a wheel of blazing fire revolving with accelerating vigor. Cool sparks flew in multicolored spray as Astéri achieved target speed, then arose slowly, drawing a surprised and squawking Sayah upward. Nat and Miyam waved in farewell, and Sayah relaxed after the initial shock of sudden levitation, in truth quite pleased at the sensation, which he imagined akin to flight.

Soon, Astéri carried him amidst the flourishing limbs of the tree to pass through leafy layers and arise above the canopy. Sayah grew anxious at the dim and leaden light, fearing the hour later than anticipated, and turned his eyes westward, locating a silver-screened sun hiding behind clouds.

Strange, he pondered. *It seemed brighter below.*

By position of the burning orb, Sayah determined the time of day was mid-afternoon, although his internal rhythms told him it should be later. Of course, the day seemed prolonged for the hours spent in the vision, and Sayah was overcome with sudden fatigue.

Astéri set the æglet down in the nest, and Sayah thanked his odd friend for bringing him home. The star fluted with cheer, then darted away, leaving Sayah alone in the aerie. He was relieved to have a moment of solitude, and he spent it in rest, tucked under the growing shade of the nest's sunward edge. He dozed, entertaining dreams that both tormented and elated him with the replay of the Kinsman's suffering, death, and resurrection.

The cry of an ægle on approach awoke Sayah, and he shook his head in waking agitation. It seemed he couldn't escape the profound implications of his adventure today, even in sleep. Looking to the sky, he located Mother, who hailed him again in keening salutation while she descended in a wide and sweeping spiral to join him in the nest.

It was a little strange for one of his parents to arrive home before Gael, who often made time to torture her brother before Mother and Father returned from the hunt.

Mother pitched one of the mice amidst her clutches to Sayah, and inquired, "How was your day, son? Did you see anything interesting?"

His conscience pricked him as he lied, but he persevered out of concern for his friends, who might be in danger if revealed to Sayah's family. Not long after, Father also returned, and for once Sayah was relieved to be ignored, since he needn't dissemble any further. The sun was down, and a bruised twilight had settled over the forest before Gael returned, carrying a sizeable, white object.

Gael plopped her prey down onto the floor of the nest, and Sayah recognized the strange owl that had tried to eat them before Gael had fledged, his neck broken.

"Brought you a present, *Brother*," Gael taunted. "I waited until the sun was down and spotted this one not far from here. Do you recognize him?"

Sayah nodded, horrified.

Gael continued, "I thought you might want a bite after all day stuck in the nest. See? Aren't I a good sister?"

Sayah eyed her with distrust, his defenses coming up again after a day without need for them. He'd brought his appetite with him when he'd returned to the nest, and he'd eaten the mouse Mother had brought him. Nonetheless, his memory of the owl persisted, and he felt ill at the prospect of eating something, no some*one* with whom he'd held a conversation, notwithstanding the creature's attempt to eat *him*.

"Thank you, Gael," Sayah began, "but I've already eaten. Maybe Mother or Father would be interested?"

Gael seemed disappointed that he had eaten, but shifted tactics, undeterred, "Oh well. I guess I must make the sacrifice. You know I hate to see a good meal go to waste."

Gael locked eyes with him as she began tearing into the prone figure to partake of the owl's remains. She did not break her gaze as she ate, blood staining her beak and feathers until Sayah couldn't bear to watch anymore. The thought of eating another thinking, speaking creature like himself offended a sensibility newfound today at the foot of the Tree.

Sayah diverted his eyes and walked across the nest to stare into the starry night, feeling the heat of Gael's unrelenting glare. With a quiet wonder, he peered into the jeweled darkness, sensing the mute immensity spoke in concert with the events of the day.

Once Sayah had departed their company with Astéri, Nat and Miyam discussed what they had seen in Astéri's flow. It soon became clear to Nat that the Kinsman's fate had also left a marked impression on Miyam, despite it having been a while since her jaunt with Astéri.

Nat was privileged to possess knowledge of the beginnings of Gan and the Sunder that followed, for details thereof illuminated his understanding of what the Kinsman accomplished on the Tree, if only in a vague manner. It seemed that Gaal's primary purpose had been to reverse the death of the Tree Ha Datovara wrought by the Stain because of the disobedience of Kessel and Pethiy. This had also made possible cleansing of the Stain, as he himself had experienced just the day before. It was a great deal to contemplate, and Miyam was well aware of Nat's confusion.

As such, the pair returned to the thatched shelter, and took a seat, settling in for prolonged conversation as Miyam began, "We are fortunate you already know so much of the history of Gan, having experienced it alongside Astéri. I hope that will simplify our discussion. Let's see. Where to begin? Ah yes! Names!"

"Names are important, and some have special meaning, as you may know. Of chief importance now are the names of the Trees. You already know what they are called, but you may not be aware what their names mean. The first of the Trees that Elyon called forth from the earth was the Tree Ha Kayim, meaning the Tree of Life. It was a gift of our Lord

Elyon to bring eternal life and healing to Gan, and He removed the Tree to preserve it intact away from the corruption of the Stain.

"The second tree, the Tree Ha Datovara, was tethered in special connection to the Tree Ha Kayim, for it sprang from the waters of the first, and relied directly on the other for sustenance. Its name means the Tree of the Knowledge of Good and Evil, and it was this knowledge that Kessel and Pethiy sought in their temptation under the influence of Helél."

Miyam offered Nat a cup of steaming, fragrant tea, which he accepted a she continued, "The Man you saw was indeed the Kinsman, Gaal, but what exactly Elyon promised in the Kinsman is more than we could have imagined. Did you ever wonder why? Why He's called the Kinsman?"

Nat thought a moment, then offered his opinion, "I guess I always thought it meant He was the kinfolk of Man. Is that wrong?"

"No, no," Miyam answered, shaking her head, "but it's not the complete answer. The secret of the Kinsman is *not only* that He is, as you said, the kin of Man.

"What you might not know is," she added, then in a whisper, "He is also *the kin of Elyon*."

Nat's brow furrowed over shocked, round eyes as he leaned in to ask, "What was that?"

"You saw it, too, didn't you?" Miyam returned. "I don't know much of Men, but from what I saw, Gaal was clearly different than any of the Men who brought Him here, and, and . . ."

She trailed off, the liquid sheen of tears shining in her eyes, then she brightened, and offered with a smile, "Well, you saw what happened after, too. He was *dead*, but afterward, alive. And what about His clothes, His crown? He looked like a king to me, and what is Elyon if not the King over all kings?

"Oh! Oh! And look at this place! It was dead, too, and for a long time. Nothing could grow here after the Sunder, yet here we are."

She swept a hand around to point out the teeming, verdant life that surrounded them, the most notable of which was the Tree itself. Nat reviewed his memory of Gaal's execution and resurrection, nodding in

agreement as he recognized the truth of it. While he realized that one of
the reasons Astéri had shown him the beginnings of Gan was to educate
him on the origin of the Trees, he now considered that perhaps there
had been another purpose.

In the presence of Lord Elyon, he had experienced the King's
overwhelming goodness, a frightful sensation unique to Elyon until . .
.until . . . Well, until he'd arrived at Sanctuary, and again when the
Kinsman had turned His gaze on him with inexplicable perception. Nat
couldn't produce another explanation for the familiar, wonderful dread
that had struck him in each instance. The Kinsman was somehow alike
in essence to Lord Elyon, and that essence also resided in and around
the Tree.

At last, Nat asked, "What does it mean, Miyam?"

"I've had some time to figure that out, and Astéri has been very
helpful, though he doesn't know quite everything, either," she
answered. "Astéri told me of your journey with him to see the Sunder, a
journey I, too, have undertaken."

"It's true that the Stain overtook us in the catastrophe of Man's
conceit, but the real tragedy was in the Sunder of our connection with
Lord Elyon. Since then, a great gulf has remained affixed between us
that none in our world could span. What I have gathered, however, is
that the Kinsman came not only to rid us of the Stain, but also to restore
our connection to Lord Elyon. Gaal has become our bridge across the
Sunder!"

Nat asked, "How? How did He do it?"

"But, Nat!" Miyam retorted, "That's what Astéri showed you today!"

She swept her arm toward the Tree, and continued, "This is, *was* the
Tree Ha Datovara, the Tree of the Knowledge of Good and Evil.
Remember the words of Elyon, 'The price demanded to restore our
friendship pains me bitterly. As My Word stands eternal, One will come,
a Kinsman, to pay the price for the evil you have loosed this day. Justice
demands payment for this travesty even as My love for you compels Me
to ensure it is paid.'

"Don't you, see, Nat? The Kinsman paid the price, in His life's blood,
and has resurrected the Tree Ha Datovara. It has become an altogether

different Tree, the Kinsman's Tree. It is this Tree that stands with branches stretched across the gap between us and Elyon, and it is the waters of its spring that purify us of the Stain."

Nat absorbed the information best he could, and while he yet considered her words, Astéri returned with chipper chiming and happy flashes of bright cyan and magenta.

Miyam clapped her hands and squealed with delight at his arrival, "Eeeeeeee! Astéri, you're just the one I wanted to see! I need your help showing Nat the, you know . . ."

She drew her hands, a fore-frond to each leafy thumb, across her trunk in rough parallel to the ground as if clutching an invisible strand. Astéri blinked a sunny yellow, and with an enthusiastic tinkle in the affirmative, shot over to Nat's face. The etém blinked, hard and slow, as he drew back from the tiny star invading his space, his eyes crossing to focus on a very near Astéri.

Astéri recognized his rudeness, and backed away, apologizing, *I am sorry, Nat. In my excitement, I failed to ask permission to come so close. What Miyam is requesting requires it be so. An opening of the eyes, so to speak. Do you assent?*

Nat was in this now, for better or worse, and besides, his Malakím friend had yet to steer him wrong.

He nodded his blue head, "Sure, Astéri. What do I need to do?"

Just sit still and focus on my center, Astéri hummed in response. *You* must *keep your eyes open for it to be effective, no matter how bright I shine. Are you ready?*

Nat blinked several times and straightened in his seat, then said, "Yeah. I'm ready. Let's do it."

His golden eyes open wide, Nat stared straight ahead into Astéri's radiance, which alternated between brilliant yellow, sparking silver, and viridian green with an intensity and frequency that increased as he drew near. Tears forming in the corners of his eyes, Nat forced his lids to stay open in defiance of reflex. Astéri's display of colors now shifted so rapidly that the three shades blended into a familiar golden-green shot through with something new, a quickening silver energy. The radiance shimmered in the reflection of Nat's unblinking gaze as the star stopped directly before the etém's pale-blue face.

Nat was at the limits of his endurance when Astéri faded and withdrew, trumpeting, *Ok. All done. Why don't you rest your eyes a moment?*

With relieved gratitude, Nat complied, squeezing his eyes shut, then relaxing the bunched lids as cool, soothing tears flushed the dry and dazzled orbs. He welcomed, too, the relative darkness behind his lids, within which Astéri's sparkling form yet danced in unpredictable color. He passed several minutes thus, until Astéri's jittering mirage tired, then disappeared altogether from Nat's insular view.

"Why don't you open up your eyes, and take a look at me?" Miyam requested, her voice revealing her position close by. Nat slowly raised the shutters sheltering his sight, and beheld the Sprig, her form limned with golden-green light, and a silver flame resting upon her forehead. At the base of her trunk, the shining outline gathered into a cord of the same color, which ran through the grassy walls of her shelter.

Following his gaze, the now-brilliant Miyam beckoned he follow as she stepped outside the shelter, and called in gentle voice, "Come."

On unsteady feet, Nat joined her outside, and traced her glowing filament to the foot of the Tree. With growing awe, he identified innumerable golden-green strands extending in every direction, the Kinsman's Tree at their nexus. His curious gaze followed one such strand from the gnarled roots to his own feet.

"AAAGH!!!" he shouted, jumping back and falling on his rump.

With hesitant hands, he gathered the weightless filament, holding the length across spread palms.

"What? What is this?" he asked, eyes imploring Astéri and Miyam in a world once unseen.

Struggling to contain the elation in her smile, Miyam answered, "That, my Etom friend, is the Vine."

Chapter Six
The Vine

"The Vine?" Nat asked, his surprise evident.

Miyam answered, "In the Kinsman's death and resurrection, the Tree became the conduit of His essence, full of His life and power. Indeed, the Kinsman's Tree in many ways best represents His qualities, and that of His Father, King Elyon."

It was overwhelming, the novelty of everything Nat experienced, and he nearly forgot his earlier wonder at hearing Gaal commend Himself to His Father at the moment of His death. It disturbed something deep within to imagine that the immensity of Elyon's being might be contained within the Kinsman's fragile form, but he could not deny the weight of presence They shared. A weight Nat felt here in Sanctuary, too.

I can see your mind churning, Nat, Astéri chimed. *It's impossible to encounter the Lord Elyon or His Son without sensing Their unique substance. The strangeness you feel is Their holiness and the magnitude thereof is Their glory.*

Holiness is a characteristic unique to divinity and signals the primacy of the Self-Existent. The glory you experience communicates that as well, which is why you trembled before Lord Elyon, before the Kinsman Gaal, and...here.

Nat shook his head. So many great words conveying concepts uncontainable.

Miyam picked up where Astéri left off, "It's as if the Kinsman's blood flows through the Tree in place of the usual sap, and His Spirit connects us now through the Vine."

She lifted a loop of the strand, "This is but one manifestation of the Spirit Who guides us, directs us, and empowers us. He is the Vine, and we are the Branches. In Him we live, and move, and have our being. If we listen, we may yet hear the voice of Elyon in the pulse of the Vine."

She stopped as a gentle breeze stirred the bright, leafy canopy overhead, the branches waving in silent benediction while the three of them meditated on Miyam's words.

Tolling as a solemn bell, Astéri explained, *Earlier, Miyam stated that only those drawn to the Tree may find Sanctuary here, and as precise an explanation as that was, it was incomplete.*

For all intents and purposes, the work of the Kinsman transformed the Tree, and the clearing around it, Sanctuary, into timeless and unassailable fixtures. They occupy both this physical location and Eternity in concurrent existence.

The Kinsman's Tree stands ever in Sanctuary, an indestructible vessel of the Spirit, and a gateway, a portal linking us to the very throne room of Lord Elyon where the Kinsman advocates on our behalf. It is a powerful, living relic fashioned to bear the fruit of His masterpiece, namely, you, and any other in the Vine. Now do you understand, Nat?

Indeed, as helpful as Astéri's intent was, his exposition only served to further Nat's puzzlement. The scope of the mystery ballooned within Nat's mind, forcing aside trivialities as it occupied all thought. Seeing that the depths of the enigma were unfathomable, Nat made a decision.

"I don't know that I understand it all," he answered in a low, steady voice, "but I think I understand enough. I am grateful to Elyon that He fulfilled His promises and brought the Kinsman here."

"What it means to be connected to the Vine, I don't really know, but if it's part of Elyon's plan, I know I can trust it's good. And important."

"I think you're right!" Miyam replied with enthusiasm. "I don't get it, either, but as I soak my roots in this spring, and grow in the safety of this place, I *know* that this is good. That He is good."

I have spent a great deal of time in the flow, following the Kinsman as He walked this earth, and have witnessed miracles unlike any performed before, Astéri instructed.

In Gaal's own words, "Whoever abides in Me and I in him will bear much fruit. Apart from Me you can do nothing."

And also, "I and the Father are one." So, here you are, connected to the Vine, each one of you a branch that Elyon wishes to bear fruit.

You must *remain in the Vine to live, to grow, to bear fruit, for that is your connection to the Father, Elyon, by the Spirit and the work of the Kinsman.*

"You keep talking about 'fruit,' but what is it?" Nat asked.

Miyam jumped in, "That is a question with several answers, but the simplest are these: Fruit is the reproduced character of the Kinsman, traits inscribed on the soul in perfect relief.

"Fruit is also the introduction of another to this process, beginning with cleansing from the Stain, and continuing as one grows, as one abides in the Vine."

That is a very concise and clear explanation, Miyam, Astéri complimented. *I couldn't have said it better myself.*

Nat felt he was wrapped up in something much larger than he'd ever understand, and his mind boggled with every revelation. At the same time, his inner tranquility remained intact, the truth of their words resonating with him. He glanced at the Vine at his feet, and recoiled when he saw the strand indeed hummed, the vibration transmitting throughout the aspect that glowed about him. He felt an odd reassurance in the sensation, an affirmation that only grew as he focused on it.

He wondered, too, at the silver tongue of flame that rested on Miyam's forehead, which blazed higher as she spoke. With caution, he placed a hand to his own brow, feeling for a flame.

Miyam giggled with delight, and answered the question Nat had yet to voice, "No, no, no! You can't touch it."

Leaning in, she spoke low from the side of her mouth while covering the other side of her face, "Believe me, I've tried."

She backed up and winked at him, "It's definitely there, though, and burning bright."

"What *is* it?" Nat inquired.

If I may, Astéri inserted politely.

Miyam bowed her head and pointed with an open hand, "Go ahead. This one is tricky anyways."

What you see burning here is both a sign and a seal of the Spirit, Astéri offered, sweeping over Miyam's forehead. *Your eyes are open now to see what is unseen, but that will not always be so. The gift I have given in expanding your sight is instructive and will soon depart. However, in the meantime, we can teach you some important lessons.*

You have already experienced Resonance, a truth-sense given to all who have washed in the springs and have been joined to the Vine. This flame is the light of the Spirit and will guide you in the darkness of the world outside Sanctuary.

It is also a gauge of sorts and will burn brighter when you are on the right track, or are in the presence of your kind, communing with Elyon. Do not quench it. The brightly burning flame indicates the quickening of the Spirit.

You have joined now the Secret Kingdom, over which none but King Elyon has dominion, and this flame is a sign to you of your kind. You have also become part of a larger family, into which creatures of every kind are adopted. This fire is a seal of your adoption, your entry into Kinship with the Father.

"Because of what the *Kins*-man did?" Miyam interjected, nudging Nat with a woody elbow. "Eh? Eh?"

Blaring in a dry and sonorous tone that said, 'let's do keep things serious,' Astéri continued, *You will see this fire blazing in others, or you may see it failing. Celebrate with those who shine and encourage those who do not. They are your Kin, and you theirs. More so than your blood kin, for the blood that purchased your adoption is the more precious as derived from the Source of all life.*

"Uh, wow," Nat said at last, clutching his head. "This is a lot to take in."

Miyam sympathized, "I know, Nat. All you need to remember for now is that you are part of the only family that lasts forever. You are a child of Elyon, a brother to all other such children. The Kinsman was Firstborn, the singular Son of Lord Elyon, whose inheritance we now share at great cost to Him. Your identity in Him must supersede all other loyalties."

"But my mother, my friends, the Eben'kayah," Nat protested.

I understand your concern, Nat, Astéri rejoined. *Your love for your family and your friends is still of utmost importance, though your best expression of that love should ever point them to Kinship through the Tree. If you consider their eternal fate and current flourishing, then bringing them into Kinship is your desire for their best put into action.*

Nat huffed, releasing the growing tension within that had arisen to resist demoting those he cared for from his primary affections. He had a great deal of thinking to do but was happy to have Astéri and Miyam as his guides. In his heart, he uttered a prayer of thanksgiving to Elyon, and asked for help sorting this all out.

It seemed so complicated, especially for the clamoring emotions that revolted against Astéri and Miyam's words. Nevertheless, he suspected he might simplify the thoughts that argued for dominance within him. He envisioned a shining blade that could shear away the irrelevant, the unimportant, and the incorrect to leave only truth to guide his decision.

As if aware of Nat's thoughts, Astéri broke in, *You should remember from our time together in the flow that, at the moment of the Sunder, King Elyon struck the earth with a blazing sword, and thus separated Himself and His throne from the corruption of the Stain.*

That sword now stands at the gateway of your mind in form of silver flame, a power intended for your protection from the wickedness of this world. Indeed, as you mature, you will learn to wield this blade as a weapon, giving you wisdom and clarity in times of confusion.

Nat gawked at Astéri's answer, surprise evident on his face as he asked, "Can you see what I'm thinking?"

Ah! No, I cannot, Astéri replied. *However, the Spirit informs me, which is often disconcerting to the unprepared. Fear not! You will learn to perceive the Spirit and trust His voice. Before you know it, you'll be the one making others uncomfortable with your insight.*

Miyam detected Nat's bewilderment, and asked, "Would you like some time alone, Nat?"

"Yes, please," Nat answered.

Astéri and Miyam returned to her shelter, and Nat spotted an outcropping at the pool's edge. He walked to the edge, his head bent low in thought as he sat on the rocky overhang. The water coursed with supernatural energy beneath its serene surface, and everything in Sanctuary appeared to thrum in concert under harmonious dominion.

Images of Gan before the Sunder arose unbidden within his mind, and he wondered if the Spirit was at work within him. Unintelligible waves resonated through the Vine, and Nat's luminous shroud likewise reverberated in sympathy, directing them to the flame at his brow, where they were translated into lucid form.

A fluttering whisper came in response, *It's the same as Gan. Better, even.*

Nat shook his head, and looked about with skepticism, *Better? How? Outside this bower, death and danger are still everywhere.*

The still, small voice responded, *That's right. And outside Gan, it was the same — death and danger at every turn. But now I am inside. Before, I stood without. Now, I stand at the door, and knock. If anyone hears My voice, and opens the door, I will come into him.*

Inside each one, I make my home, a garden akin to Gan, and life abounds in it. Though death and danger may threaten the body, My life persists within, forever, and none may threaten it.

The etém looked around for a speaker, feeling self-conscious, and, truth be told, a bit mad. He found no one nearby, but his eyes found the Vine, which quivered again.

Anticipating another mysterious message, he closed his eyes in surrender and thought, *Speak. I am listening.*

The voice returned, surging with quiet power, *I have only one thing to tell you now, a promise that you can trust so long as you wish it. You are My son. Mine own. And I will never leave you or forsake you. This is My love for you.*

Nat was unable to contain his tears behind the unacknowledged dam within his soul. They broke forth as the words washed over Nat's fatherless heart, piercing the hidden barrier erected there over a lifetime of abandonment and disappointment. As pure, clear, and refreshing were the springwaters of the tree, these restrained in Nat were brackish, dark, and heavy. Regardless, as the saltwater flow met the fresh below, they comingled, and the pure overwhelmed the putrid to wash sorrow away. And across the etém's back, a ray of sunshine fell, a father's warm hand that Nat had ever missed.

Nat rested there in the unfamiliar, yet welcome warmth of the Father's love, soaking in the pool of radiance he'd long desired without his knowing. After a good while, a rustling drew his attention, and he lifted his head to discover Miyam nearby.

It seemed that Astéri's gift of augmented vision had departed in the meanwhile, as the star had forewarned, but nevertheless Nat sensed his Resonance with the Sprig in the wake of his experience. She greeted him with an awkward wave, her hesitance at invading the private moment apparent, though Nat could also sense her eagerness to speak with him, to share in the majesty of Elyon. He smiled at her and beckoned her over. Without a word, she joined him at the water's edge.

Miyam spoke with tears in her eyes. "With His own finger, Lord Elyon pressed the seed that contained my soul into the rich soil here, beside the waters. And here I have remained since, growing so I might serve those like yourself at their first encounter with the Kinsman's Tree. Astéri in the flow has helped increase my understanding, and no moment touched me more deeply than when Elyon left Gaal alone to die on this Tree. I knew that Lord Elyon ached with grief to forsake His Son, and that He flew to Him as soon as He was able. To comfort. To hold. To heal and to restore. To *love* again, for He *is* love."

She finished with Nat nodding in agreement. He felt refreshed, and stronger than before.

He recalled Miyam standing at the edge of the pool, her face upturned, and branches upraised into the sunlight, and wondered, *Will I be taller now, too?*

Given the context of sober reflection, the silliness of the question struck him. He laughed aloud and shared the odd thought with Miyam, who just looked at the blue Etom with a bemused grin. What a strange one he was!

Still, she laughed along when he insisted they stand up and measure, and Astéri arced his way over to where they stood to see what all the hubbub was about. Nat and Miyam were less than forthcoming about the joke, insisting Astéri 'just had to be there.'

Regardless, their levity also cheered the star, for whom witnessing the torture and execution of the Kinsman was difficult and grew no less so each time he escorted another. It was one of the Malakím's least favorite duties, but a necessary one nonetheless.

Nat dusted himself off, and looked to his friends, "Well, what comes next? I imagine we have some work to do?"

Indeed, we do, young Master Nat! Astéri trumpeted. *But first, perhaps a meal? And after, training!*

"Training?" Nat asked, his expression quizzical. "What kind of training?"

Why! Combat training, of course! Astéri responded. *How else do you intend to rescue your mother and friends?*

With that, the star zipped away, leaving a bewildered and excited Nat to accompany Miyam to her shelter for some supper.

Chapter Seven

Resonance

A drink from the waters and a portion of the puffed wafers Miyam had served earlier refreshed Nat, who had failed to realize how drained he had become in the course of the day's events. To say night fell beneath the Tree would be an overstatement, for it seemed that although the sun had set, a warm, pervasive luminescence yet provided light to the bower. The glow lacked the glaring intensity of sunlight, and was dimmer, providing a cozy ambience by which to rest.

In a corner of her shelter, Miyam provided Nat with a pillow fashioned from a folded leaf stuffed with soft, dry moss, and a cot overlaid with a mattress of similar design. They three said their "good nights" before Miyam and Astéri departed the shelter for whatever destination served them in rest.

Curious, Nat watched them as they went. Astéri stopped not far away, spun a few times in rotation and counter-rotation, then vanished with a flash. Miyam moseyed to the spot she'd occupied earlier when resting, eating…whatever it was. Her demeanor in this instance differed in that instead of stretching upward, she seemed to fold inward, resting her head against a shoulder. It reminded Nat of how some flowers would furl their blossoms at nightfall, only to bloom again at dawn.

Nat was keeping some strange company these days, and it. was. wonderful. He couldn't recall a more interesting time in his life and wondered how he might sleep with the steady stream of thought that rushed through his young mind.

Oh well, he mused as he lay down, resting his head on the crude pillow. *I should at least try to sleep. Seems like there's a lot to do tomorrow, and the sooner I complete my training, the sooner I can be on my way to get Mom, Rae, all of them. I can't wait to show them this place. I wonder if Astéri will take them to see the Kinsman. And the Vine, I hope…I hope they see…see the…*

In a turn that might have surprised the etém if he'd remained conscious, Nat fell asleep almost at once, and all about the bower, the firefly lights drifted and flickered in the safe and sleepy glow beneath the Tree.

"GOOOOD MOOORNING, SUNSHINE!!!" Miyam bellowed.

Her unexpected greeting startled Nat awake, spilling him from his rough bunk, which he was grateful stood only a short distance from the ground. His eyes open wide in shock, he looked up at the Sprig, who stood over him, smiling and brimming with enthusiastic energy.

"Agh!" Nat exclaimed as he shrank from her effervescence. He knew some morning folk, but this was ridiculous.

It's OK. It's OK, he told himself. *She's just excited, and I . . .I'm just not used to waking up to shouting. Or to someone standing right over me.*

Nat exhaled, blinking the sleep from his eyes, then returned Miyam's smile. She extended a hand to him, and he took it, surprised at the wiry strength in the Sprig's thin limbs when she helped him up.

He narrowed his eyes and took stock of Miyam, *Yup. She's gotten taller again.*

Spurred by his observation, Nat decided to ask, "So how tall will you get? Full-grown, that is?"

She lifted a hand to point to the Kinsman's Tree, "About that tall! I *think.*"

Nat's boggling eyes must have betrayed his misgivings, because Miyam felt it necessary to point out that she was just a sapling, and perhaps even younger than Nat.

"But what will you do if you get that big?" he inquired. "You won't fit in Sanctuary anymore."

With a conspiratorial glance to either side, Miyam leaned in close, and offered a sly whisper, "I hear we may be expanding soon. It's only a matter of time."

Expanding?!? Nat deliberated. *What does she mean?*

Before Nat was able to pursue the line of questioning, Astéri materialized inside the shelter with a 'pop.'

We need to get started right away! the star blared. *We've lots to do if we want Nat to be ready for his rescue mission in Sakkan!*

"Alright, alright, little spark," Miyam returned. "Let's simmer down, huh? Get some breakfast into this one before we begin?"

She hooked a spindly thumb at Nat, who salivated at the word "breakfast."

Very well, the sulky Astéri relented, *but let's make it quick.*

Miyam grabbed a squat and wide-mouthed earthenware vase, waving for Nat to follow, "Come on, then! Let's get you some breakfast!"

Without waiting, she proceeded from the shelter, and Nat scurried to catch up, finding the Sprig just outside the grassy home. Looking around, Nat gasped. It appeared that it had snowed overnight, for a shallow layer of white flakes blanketed the bower floor.

"Catch!" Miyam called, tossing one of the white flakes his way with a backhanded flick of her wrist.

Nat caught it, expecting the wet, cool press of a snowflake against his hands, but instead met the dry, crisp texture of one of the wafers he'd eaten the day before.

Strange, he thought. *Where did this come from?*

"And another!" Miyam shouted as she hurled a second wafer his way. "Get over here and help me gather some of these up, OK?"

Flakes still in hand, Nat rushed to Miyam's side, where she offered the vase, "Let's fill it up. Should be just enough to last you the whole day. Growing boy and all."

She winked, and Nat put his wafers into the vessel, then crouched down to gather a tall stack from the ground. Miyam placed a few of her own into the vase, then Nat lowered his heap into it, filling the vessel to the brim.

He bent down again to collect more, but Miyam cautioned, "No, no, Nat. Just enough for today. Any more, and it will spoil."

"Where does it come from?" he asked at last.

"What do you mean? Don't you have this outside the bower?" Miyam asked, perplexed.

"Not at all. I've never seen anything like it. It looks a bit like snow, but it's food," Nat answered.

"Snow?" Miyam inquired again. "What is snow?"

"Um, it falls from the sky? Like rain, but colder, frozen," Nat replied.

"Rain? We only get sunlight here . . ." she returned, confused.

It never rains here? Nat was flabbergasted, then considered the vital power of the Tree's springwaters. *There's no need of it.*

He switched tactics to explain better, "You went with Astéri to see the Kinsman the night He . . .well, *that* night. It was raining then. The water that fell from the sky?"

"Oh!" Miyam responded with genuine surprise, and . . .tears? *That happens a lot?* I thought that was the sky itself, weeping for the Kinsman. I didn't realize that was normal. And you say this 'snow' is like the rain, but frozen?"

Nat felt bad that he'd brought Miyam to tears again, even as empathy jarred a few from him, too.

He recovered to answer her question, "Yes. Rain might fall during any season, depending on how warm it is, but snow usually only falls in the winter, when it's cold."

"Season? Winter?" Miyam's round eyes blinked in confounded reflection.

Nat realized that his dear Sprig friend, for all her knowledge of the Tree and the Kinsman, understood very little of the world outside. His mild distress over her ignorance was overwhelmed by his love for her, and he smiled, bemused.

Love, though? he thought. *Really?*

However much he cared for others, love was not a word he applied lightly, and was a banner flown over just a select few long-time friends, and his mother, of course. But there it was. He loved his new friend, Miyam, and didn't even remember deciding to.

Maybe this is that Vine thing again? he considered, then returned to the conversation at hand.

"Miyam, I bet we have *a lot* to discuss, but maybe over breakfast?" Nat answered with a hungry hope.

Her curiosity whetted, Miyam nodded with fervency, and they ambled back to the shelter to partake.

Breakfast was a short ordeal, due to its simplicity, but also educational for the Sprig. Nat explained in concise statements the four seasons he'd known in Endego. Miyam thought it all very interesting, especially the varied forms of precipitation, but took frightened offense when Nat explained the fate of autumn's leaves.

"The trees are bare? *Naked*?" Miyam gasped, horrified.

In sympathy, Nat maintained the most serious expression he could manage, and nodded. He supposed he might find it just as disturbing if he were a Sprig but couldn't help finding some humor in it.

In a matter-of-fact tone, he responded, "The trees in Endego. Everywhere but here, really. They aren't *alive* the same way you are. The same way this place is."

"Not yet, anyhow," Miyam answered, a knowing look in her eyes. "'The creation waits with eager longing . . .'"

"Is that what you meant by 'expanding?'" he asked.

"I don't know the whole plan. Just bits here and there, but it's *good*," Miyam replied, then asked. "Now then, how do you get your food if you can't just collect it?

Considering her earlier horror at learning of autumnal defoliation, Nat predicted her dismay over the harvest of fruits, vegetables, and grains. He didn't dare to broach the subject of cooking, afraid the Sprig might perceive her natural kin among the kindling needed for the endeavor.

He changed the subject without delay, calling out, "Astéri?!? How about that training?"

Astéri, who had been waiting near at hand, responded, *I am ready to begin as soon as you are.*

"Great! Let's get to it, then!" Nat responded.

He was in truth very excited to train but felt bad to have ended his conversation with Miyam so abruptly.

"We'll talk more later, OK?" he offered in apology.

An unperturbed Miyam ushered Nat out of the shelter, urging him onward to training with the gentle press of her leafy hands.

Nat joined Astéri where the spark floated in the middle of a clear and level place nearby.

With a twitter, Astéri began, *You have experienced Resonance, and it is this Resonance by the Spirit and through the Vine that forms the basis of our training.*

Though you no longer have sight by which to discern it, I assure you that you may develop a more profound sense than sight by which to detect the movement of the Spirit.

To begin, I ask only that you search your memories of yesterday for the exact moment that you recognized your Resonance through the Vine. Let me know when you have it.

Nat closed his eyes, and prayed Elyon guide his memories, which came clear and crisp on the heels of his whispers. Yesterday's peaceable affirmation thrummed in the attuned vibration that had framed Miyam and Astéri's words. While the visible tremor in the Vine had alerted him to Resonance the day before, it was this unshakeable, inner confidence that had stood out. He nodded in grateful remembrance, and thanked Lord Elyon. Out of recollection, the sensation surged into the present, and Nat's smile spread wide upon his face.

"I think I have it," he whispered.

Good. Good. Astéri fluted. *Stay with it. With Him. What you are experiencing is proof of the Spirit's presence. One of many. Now prepare yourself for attack! This will be uncomfortable.*

Astéri's usual, pleasant tones took on a grating quality that Nat associated with the Nihúkolem, and within the Etom's mind screeched, *King Elyon would never love you! He could* never *love you!*

The sensation was jarring and proved a dissonant counterpoint to Nat's tranquility. Around him, Nat sensed the Vine shudder, and it seemed to tense and thicken, pressing outward. Before Nat's mind, a silver flame ignited in fury, leaping forth, and Nat grasped yesterday's memory from beside the pool as if in response to Astéri's attack. The still and powerful words echoed inside him, a quiet trickle of beloved remembrance that grew in swift coursings to breaking rapids that seemed to flood forth from within. The trembling flow reinforced Nat's resonant shell, washing outward to still the cacophony.

In shivering relief, Nat exhaled, "What *was* that?"

Well done, Nat! Astéri trumpeted encouragement, his voice again smooth and harmonious. *You have survived your first spiritual assault, albeit a simulated one.*

Miyam clapped in congratulations, cheering for Nat.

"A spiritual assault? It felt horrible. My skin is still crawling from it," he indicated, pointing to his tented knuckles, where the skin bunched around the ribbed, blue joints.

Ah, yes! Astéri chirped. *Many experience a physical response, especially the first time. However, most important is that you withstood the attack. Or, rather, that the Spirit within you withstood it. First rule — give credit where it is due, and all is due to our Lord Elyon.*

Astéri's words seemed to fan the flame inside Nat, and his elation grew as he reverberated with the star's statement.

Resonance, again, Nat concluded. *Curious.*

"I think I see the point of the exercise," Nat offered.

Indeed? Astéri whistled. *And what might that be?*

"You asked me to focus on my recollection of Resonance, so I would recognize the Spirit," Nat began. "Once I had identified the sensation, I began to feel it again. Then, you shocked me with the opposite for contrast. The whole point was to sharpen my sensitivity to the Spirit, to truth. Right?"

You are correct, Astéri replied. *That was the primary thrust of the lesson. The Spirit is known also as the Comforter and will ever provide comfort to the will not under coercion. Where the Spirit of the Lord is, there is freedom.*

The resonant surge overwhelmed Nat again, who reveled in it before answering, "Freedom, huh? I hadn't thought of it like that, but . . ."

In retrospect, the past couple days had been one liberating experience after another. His cleansing from the Stain, and its fellow, despair, upon his arrival at the Tree. And, yesterday, the Spirit had lifted the gaping, heavy burden Nat carried in ignorant disregard of his father's absence. Then, in final coup de grâce, the Spirit occupied emptiness with love, whole in its perfection, to guard his heart and banish all fear.

Nat? Astéri inquired out of concern. *Are you with us?*

His woolgathering came to an abrupt end, and Nat apologized, "Yes. Yes! I'm sorry, Astéri. It's a lot to take in. You said that was the lesson's *primary* thrust, but what else was there to it?"

Astéri tolled, an instructive bell, *I imagine you also sensed the Spirit come to your defense?*

In amazement, Nat nodded, "I *did*."

He is both armor and weapon to those in the Vine, Astéri explained. *Though you felt it, what you did not see was the reflexive hardening of the Vine to shield you, to hold you in comfort of the Spirit.*

"That sounds right. But there was more, right? Something to do with this?" Nat put a shy hand to his forehead, half-expecting the singe of the invisible flame.

Correct! Astéri bugled. *What you sensed was the sword of the Spirit and beware! It cuts both ways. At the moment the sword struck out, it pierced you as well, yes? I would guess that you returned to your memory of yesterday, when the Spirit came to you near the pool's edge?*

Nat nodded again, this time in awestruck silence, and Astéri continued, *The Spirit will combat deception with the most appropriate implement available but draws on the wielder.*

You were the one to wield the sword, and you don't have much in you. Yet. Every disciple of the Kingdom is like the master of a house, who brings out of his storeroom new treasures as well as old, and you must study to show yourself approved.

What is in you is seminal, however, and you mustn't ever forget it – your first love. If your growth in the Vine is upright, His love will be ever before you, and will supply the roots of your soul with nourishment and strength all the days of your life. It is from this wellspring that the Spirit surged, striking down the attack.

So powerful is His love, that I was unafraid to assail it, though you are yet immature in the Vine. I had no doubt you'd pass the test, Nat, and you did not disappoint. Stay in His love, and drink deep. You will never fail to bear good fruit.

Nat absorbed it all with relish, spurred by new strength, while Astéri drifted over to Miyam. For the most part, she had remained silent during the lesson, but leapt into action as Astéri approached.

"Finally!" she exclaimed, rubbing her wooden hands together with vigorous energy.

Nat's concern that she might set herself on fire passed as she began speaking, "The last point of the lesson is something you probably didn't notice and is something that the Spirit signals through the Vine. I might not be able to see what Astéri can, but when you were under attack, Nat, I *felt* it, and I stood with you in the Vine, praying Lord Elyon would strengthen you. And that is yet another secret of the Vine —we are stronger when we stand together.

As the morning progressed, Nat's training proved rigorous, and he begged of his instructors a brief recess in which he might reflect on his instruction and perhaps take some refreshment. Astéri agreed without hesitation while Miyam dashed to gather Nat a morsel. Astéri joined Nat as he wandered down to the edge of the pool where he'd seen Miyam resting, and with a cupped hand gathered a drink.

They had started early in the morning from what Nat could gather, though he didn't know what to make of time's flow in Sanctuary given Miyam's revelations about the place.

With a sudden dip and a crimson flash, Astéri honked, *Oh my! I nearly forgot! I will return posthaste!*

With that, Astéri shot up through the branches on what Nat presumed was an errand to collect Sayah. Nat chuckled. He enjoyed the company and support of his friends, but right now he needed to reflect on what he'd learned. Knowing his own meditations to be inadequate, Nat stared into the mirror shine of the pool, and sought Elyon's counsel instead.

Above the Tree where Sayah perched, Astéri met the impatient and disheartened æglet, who perked at the appearance of his brilliant escort.

"Astéri!" Sayah squawked. "I'm so glad you're here!"

Good morning! Astéri fluted.

The Sayah's beak flopped open and a surprised stare was all that the æglet could manage in response, until at last, he stammered, "I, I can understand you. You said, 'Good morning!'"

Astéri sparkled with pleasure, and returned, *That I did, young æglet! And you seem to have gotten the hang of hearing me. Perhaps you just needed to sleep on it?*

Sayah replied, "I don't know how it happened, but I'm happy we can speak now."

Indeed, Astéri offered. *It certainly makes being friends a much less complicated affair.*

"We're *friends*?" the æglet asked with hopeful eyes.

Absolutely! Astéri affirmed. *I wouldn't have it any other way!*

"And here I'd just about given up on you this morning!" Sayah exclaimed with relief.

Astéri tootled an apology, *I beg your pardon, Sayah. We have been preoccupied with Nat's training, and have only now taken our first break of the day.*

With an eye to the sun, Sayah allayed the star's anxieties, "It's not *so* late, Astéri. I just want to spend as much time as possible with you all. You know. Before my family gets back."

Astéri winked, *I understand, Sayah. We've missed you, too. Let's get down below so you can join us. Big things in the works today!*

Without warning, Astéri once more gripped the æglet with invisible force, and the pair descended to the forest floor near Miyam's shelter. She was just departing the bladed thatch and waved when she noticed them.

"Good morning, Sayah!" she called, raising one of the puffed flakes she was taking to Nat. "I'm taking a snack to Nat. Would you care for one?"

Sayah sniffed with revulsion, but recovered at once, "No, thank you, Miyam! Perhaps we can just walk with you?"

"Sure!" she agreed with a smile. "Come on, you two!"

It wasn't far to the edge of the pool where Nat sat, but those few steps together were a salve to Sayah's lonely soul. This craving for companionship was deeper than any hunger he'd felt, and the friendly words exchanged filled him with greater satisfaction than any meal.

"Sayah!" Nat exclaimed, jumping up to greet his friend. "Good to see you again!"

"Er, um, yeah," Sayah fumbled, taken aback by Nat's sincere excitement. "It's good to see you, too."

"We've had a pretty amazing morning so far," Nat shared with eyes wide and bright. "You wouldn't believe what we've been up to!"

"Nat?" Miyam interjected gently, "Maybe this would be a good time to ask Sayah if he'd like a drink and a dip in the pool here?"

"Whoa!" Nat blurted in shock. "I almost forgot that you hadn't, Sayah. Would you like to? You know what it means, right? You'll be cleansed of the Stain, and more. So much more."

Sayah inched to the water's edge and peered into the pool. The shine of the sun overhead poured its light down onto the surface, turning the pristine water into a great, crystal mirror. Sayah's reflection, clear and honest, stared back at the æglet, causing him to wince as no brilliance ever had. The truth of his reflection was unbearable, though he foresaw also transformation. It disturbed him such that he closed his eyes to it, turning his head aside.

How could that *ever deserve to be free of the Stain?* he reasoned. *I can understand why Nat would. I bet he's always been kind and brave. I'm just some vicious, useless beast.*

"No," Sayah rasped.

"No," again. Louder. "I can't. Not yet."

Miyam and Nat listened with concern, and Nat came close to pressing Sayah to reconsider, but a resonant tug told him not to.

Gentle. Gentle, now, the Spirit whispered.

Looking to Miyam, Nat saw his sentiment reflected in her face, and relented from his urge to persuade the æglet otherwise.

Instead, Nat turned to Astéri and asked, "Well, then should we get back to training? I think I'm re—"

An urgent shiver in the Vine interrupted, and Astéri, likewise sensing it, replied with seriousness, *It would seem the Spirit desires to engage us otherwise now. Please bear with me a moment while I seek clarification.*

Without awaiting their response, the star spun, shooting liquid darts of prismatic light, then disappeared with a 'pop.' Nat, Sayah, and Miyam felt the import of the matter in the burdensome weight of minutes passing. They hardly spoke as they waited, although Nat and Sayah paced near the water while Miyam took the opportunity to bask in the sun and soak her roots.

With the same sudden 'pop' of his disappearance, Astéri returned. Æglet, Sprig, and Etom gathered around the spark, who began to speak as they approached.

It appears that the Spirit has pressing need of your services, Nat. The time for your rescue mission has arrived.

Chapter Eight
Return to Sakkan

A blend of excitement and shock played across Nat's features before he could manage, "What? Now?!?"

Indeed, my young Etom friend, Astéri conveyed. *Received the orders from Nasi himself.*

It was all Nat could do to keep his bulging eyes in his head as he blurted, "Wait! Nasi?"

The thought of the Captain of the Malakím issuing commands in the present mystified the etém further, but the thought of the mission at hand sobered him.

"It's not important, Astéri," Nat apologized, "but am I really ready?"

I was asked to relay two messages to you, Nat, Astéri reported. *First, that you will succeed in your mission to rescue the prisoners of Sakkan, so long as you remain in Resonance of the Spirit. No true harm will befall you or those you liberate.*

Second, I will remain here in Sanctuary. You are to complete the mission without my help.

Nat, whose heart had leapt with joy at Astéri's first pronouncement, then plummeted with the second, squeaked, "I'm supposed to go *alone?*"

Ah! Astéri fluted. *Well that's not precisely what I said, is it?*

The starlet floated up to the level of Sayah's eyes, and beseeched, *Dear friend æglet, would you consider joining Nat on his mission?*

Horrified, Sayah recoiled at the thought of departing the safety and secrecy of Sanctuary, his near-perpetual ægle's frown deepening to convey his distress.

"How could I?" he protested, and held up a stringy wing, looking across his unwieldy form before returning his imploring gaze to Astéri, then to Nat and Miyam.

"Just look at me! I'm useless as a hunter, and just what sort of help would I be but maybe as a diversion for some predator to pounce on while he gets away?"

Astéri burned a pinkish-orange color that reminded Sayah of a salmon's flesh in the instant of Astéri's slow and deliberate approach. The ember glow of the star drew close until the spark hovered just in front of Sayah's beak, and the æglet stared cross-eyed in tremulous anticipation. Although Astéri had no eyes with which to stare, Sayah nevertheless detected a gaze both stern and understanding shining forth from the star.

The æglet felt he should look away, but could not, and remained pinned within the light as Astéri spoke, *Sayah, I know of your suffering, and of what you've been deprived – love, acceptance, comradery, to name just a few. But what remains will keep you. Courage and a steel hidden in you of which you're unaware.*

Recall my words to Nat. They extend to you if you should accompany him. No harm will befall you. What lies before you is a test of mettle, a test of your soul. While you need prove nothing to us, your need to prove yourself to yourself is foremost in your thoughts.

You are untested, and thus your ignorance of who you are and what you are made of cages you behind bars of despair. Go. And you may find that the one you rescue is yourself.

Nat and Miyam stood with jaws hanging low and eyes riveted to the other pair while Astéri slowly backed down from the æglet's beak. Without his knowledge, Sayah's breathing had halted altogether during Astéri's sermon, and his breast now swelled with a great whooping gasp, followed by a heavy sigh. The æglet looked down at the ground in thought, the others surrounding him in silence while they awaited his response.

At last, he looked up at Astéri, a shining fire behind his gaze even as a great tear fell from one golden eye, and he spoke, "I will go. You're right. I *want* to go. As much for me as for him."

He jerked his beak at Nat with eyes yet locked on the star, "He is my first true friend. One of a few, now. But I have to ask again, because I don't see it. *How* do you expect me to help? A flightless æglet runt?"

As Sayah had started speaking, Astéri's aspect had changed, his hue turning silver and flaring ever brighter with the æglet's every word. In

Nat's eyes, the Malakím became a minister of silver flame and sensed the blaze growing before his mind shining also from Miyam.

In truth, the spark grew to such brilliance that he seemed to increase in size, and when he spoke in response to Sayah, it was with a crackling intensity that reminded the others of lightning.

It was no longer the voice of the advisor, teacher, and friend they'd come to know, but that of a commander on the battlefield, confident and resolute, *The mission before you is that of infiltration and extraction. With all stealth, you two must infiltrate the village of Sakkan, avoiding detection if possible, and engaging in combat if you must. Let us pray that you don't, for the twisted Doctor Scarsburrow is in league with the Nihúkolem and may call them down upon you if he's alerted to your presence or operation.*

Once at the Doctor's so-called 'clinic,' you must release the prisoners for extraction from hostile territory. All of them. You are not to leave a single captive to the Doctor for his perverse experiments. Lead them from captivity up the road north of the bridge and bring them here. Miyam and I will make preparations to receive and care for your charges here.

To answer your question, Sayah, your role will be to provide reconnaissance support to Nat here, who will be the advance scout. I suggest the two of you work out a system of signals you can use at distance during your trek to Sakkan. It is likely you will have need of them sooner, rather than later.

Also, Sayah, you may not feel it, but there is a warrior within you, and it's my hope you discover him on this mission. Use beak and talon in defense of your friend and of those he risks everything to rescue, and you may yet locate the courage you possess.

Nat, you are the lead on this mission, and must pay special attention to your Resonance with the Spirit. He will guide you through to the safe success of the rescue and your exodus from Sakkan. You know much already, and more than you are yet aware.

Don't ever be afraid to trust the Spirit, and you will learn even more. To draw on the power and wisdom of the Spirit is to draw on a well unfathomable. Remember that you fight for those you love, and that it is better to be still and have surety in the Spirit than to rush in. You are well-prepared for leadership of this mission, and I am honored to have had a hand in your development.

Having thus dispensed to Nat and Sayah their orders, Astéri diminished once more to his former frame. Within their deepest beings, it seemed Astéri had passed his quickening flame as a torch in relay igniting crucible embers hidden in their souls. Astéri's words had bracing effect on the pair of youths, and they stood at sharp attention while Astéri and Miyam convened to discuss final preparations.

After a few short words, Miyam departed for her shelter, and Astéri returned to address Etom and æglet, *Miyam has gone to collect a few provisions for your journey, after which you shall leave at once. Nasi stated a need for urgency in your departure, but you should both be aware that is no cause to hasten in excess contrary to my earlier advice.*

Nat, you must set the pace, and allow the Spirit to lead. Anything contrary to His leading may prove disastrous, so stay focused. This mission, too, is part of your training, and I expect you to return a more capable disciple than you are now.

Miyam was not long in returning, and she approached them with a glint in her eye and her leafy limbs concealing something behind her trunk.

"Dearest Nat," she said, standing a few steps from the etém.

"You and Sayah will need to find most of your meals yourselves, but . . ." she produced a leafy bundle from behind her trunk, "I've packed some of our 'snowflakes,' and a flask of the water from the spring for your journey. I hope you find them welcome nourishment in the wilderness outside Sanctuary."

Nat received the bundle, and was about to thank the Sprig, when she interrupted him, "Every warrior has need of a blade, and I discovered one tangled in the hedge while you slept. I hope you can make good use of it."

Across her leafy palms rested the machete he'd wielded in his journey from Sakkan to Sanctuary. The sappy muck that had covered blade and grip before he lost it was now gone. Gone, too, were the many notches in the edge, which no longer bore the dint of use, but gleamed sharply in the sun.

He accepted, too, the machete, with gratitude, "Thank you, Miyam. But how did you repair—?"

"Oh, we have our ways," she interrupted again with a mischievous sparkle in her eyes.

Nat couldn't help but wonder else remained hidden from his awareness in this place as Miyam stood before Sayah, who stooped low to meet her eyes.

"Master æglet," she began, "I have no such gifts for you today.

"You've no appetite for our refreshments, and no hands with which to grip a weapon," she offered, eyeing his steely claws, "though I imagine you'll fare well enough.

"What I do have, I give freely," she added, and stretched up to plant a kiss on Sayah's beak. "You have my affection, and friendship. I hope you find them meaningful reasons to despair no longer. Find your courage. I, too, see it within you."

Sayah lowered his head to conceal the shattering play of emotion visible there, determined with all this talk of courage to shed no further tears.

Astéri swept in to his rescue, sounding a demanding klaxon, *And now, you must be off without delay!*

Savoring the tender moment, Miyam clucked in feigned disapproval, but shooed the pair toward the hedge. Nat was concerned with how they might pass through the thicket but needn't have worried. When they drew near the verdant barrier, it opened to either side with a gentle sigh.

Through the narrow gap, Nat and Sayah surveyed the landscape, the relative gloom of the wild underbrush evoking shared, unspoken reservations in the pair. Glancing back at Astéri and Miyam standing in the golden glow of Sanctuary, Nat waved one last goodbye, then stepped out into the wild. Sayah fell in behind him, his large, dark frame blocking the pale blue Etom before the hedge closed behind them with a whisper.

Nat and Sayah were only a few steps outside Sanctuary when Nat stopped to orient himself. His eyelids felt leaden and sticky in the oppressive humidity, and he blinked in slow deliberation while he considered their position. From what he could tell, they had departed through the hedge's eastern side.

After a short parley with Sayah to confirm their heading, Nat set out due east with confident strides. With each step, however, an indistinct reminder tugged for his attention with gentle insistence. It was annoying, and he ignored it for a short time, attempting to thrust the sensation into a distant corner of his awareness. But it was slippery *and* annoying, in addition to unrelenting, and at last, Nat halted their short-lived march to puzzle over what might be bothering him.

Did I leave something in Sanctuary? he pondered, reviewing their last moments.

Hmmm, no. That's not it. He rejected the thought after reviewing their brief inventory of goods.

He scratched his head with a pensive finger, *What* is *it?*

Several moments passed, and a bored and hungry Sayah began to look for potential prey in the surrounding murk. While the plain truth of Nat's oversight yet evaded the Etom, the irritating prickle had ceased. Not satisfied, Nat racked his brain.

"Ah!" he exclaimed. "Is *that* it?"

Sayah watched Nat with dubious surprise as Nat closed his eyes in concentration. The Etom cocked his head to one side as if listening, his face serene. In his heart, Nat petitioned Elyon for guidance, and clamped onto the few powerful memories he possessed of Resonance. It came in an instant, the recollection and presence of the Spirit permeating, enveloping, and surging through him.

The burgeoning contact was brief, yet lingered in abated form, and Nat had the sense that he'd need only have sought guidance to satisfy the wishes of the Spirit. He called to Sayah, who peered without success into the shadowy foliage nearby, and with tentative steps they set out eastward again, Nat now better attuned to his role as leader.

It was a strange experience, not only the constant presence that Nat sensed, but the knowledge that he now answered directly to Lord Elyon through His Spirit. He could see the potential for amazing things, and the gravity in the responsibility. The combination humbled him, and he was honored at the sense of being selected, chosen to commune with the Creator.

It was exhilarating and frightening, and he looked forward to sharing it with those he cared about. His eyes darted to his large escort, and he wondered if Sayah might ever be open to it. He had hopes that the mission they shared would help Sayah in his decision, and suspected that Astéri had the same in mind when he invited Sayah.

It was early afternoon when they exited the forest, and Nat looked across the now-familiar, stony scrabble, the faint rush of water in his ears. For his part, Sayah felt exposed, and was apprehensive in the knowledge that his farsighted kin often hunted the skies overhead. With sharp twitches of his head, the æglet scanned the firmament, but did not detect the dark, wheeling forms of raptors against the azure background.

Already aware they were north of Company Jasper's prior point of descent from the cliffs, Nat nevertheless took another moment to seek their direction. He remembered Astéri's provisional promise of a safe and successful rescue and didn't want to endanger anyone due to his carelessness.

Nat's natural instinct was to return to his prior route, but the reverberant press of the Spirit was to the north, where Nat knew lay the road by which Gaal had arrived on the way to His death on the Tree. There was comfort in familiarity, however, and Nat struggled before deciding to submit to the guidance. It *was*, after all, an adventure, and those were most often through unexplored territory.

With a soft punch to a dark and downy wing, Nat drew Sayah's attention, "My friend, let's head north. I sense our leading in that direction, and I'm curious to see the road that Gaal traveled."

With a quiet nod, Sayah agreed, and the pair hugged the tree line, which provided them a welcome, westward shield from prying eyes as they journeyed north. Sayah walked in wonder as the diversity of the landscape filled his powerful vision. To hike along the ground in lands he'd longed to explore was an unexpected treat, and the æglet strode in silence behind his dogged Etom friend.

Ægles, by design, are ill-equipped to walking, and the underdeveloped Sayah was even more so, his legs shorter than most others his age. Regardless, he'd thought his pace would far outstrip the much smaller Etom, who might take five steps for every one of Sayah's. Conditioned by his many months in the wild and refreshed by the new strength and nourishment he'd received beneath the Tree, Nat surprised the æglet. Once the Etom hit his stride, he set a challenging pace for the æglet, who discovered his spry, blue friend had a knack for woodcraft.

Over, under, around and through the various obstacles they encountered, Nat clambered, slipped, wriggled, and leapt while Sayah trundled along in clumsy pursuit. By the time they reached the road, Sayah was huffing and puffing with exertion. Nat's cheeks glowed a burnished violet to bracket an exhilarated smile, and the Etom took deep, controlled breaths in contrast to Sayah's ragged ones.

The æglet viewed his tiny friend with newfound respect, and resolved to discipline himself best he was able in support of Nat. He might never match the Etom's agility, but he would use his own unique strengths to ensure the success of the rescue. Sayah celebrated his good fortune in finding such wonderful friends and would not take Nat for granted. If the people Nat cared about were imprisoned, then Sayah could be certain they were worth the trouble of liberating.

"Sayah!" Nat called from the edge of the road, beckoning the æglet to join him where the road hooked southward to descend alongside the sheer cliffs.

Break time's over! Sayah thought, then shuffled up to Nat.

Nat pointed down the rugged lane, and exclaimed, "Look! The Kinsman left a trail!"

And, indeed, it seemed Gaal had. In the ruts Gaal's cart had left in the soft, wet mud the night of his execution, crimson blossoms bloomed. Sayah and Nat recognized them as those that had carpeted the floor beneath the Tree to conduct Gaal from His place of suffering.

"Amazing," Nat whispered.

It seemed wherever the Kinsman had been, life sprung up now in the wake of His resurrection, and Nat wondered if more clues awaited them along the road. The Spirit trembled in confirmation, leaving Nat astonished at the reply to his unspoken question. He now comprehended why the Spirit had led them here, and with joy began looking forward to the promise of revelations that lay before.

Nat's desire to share these remarkable events with everyone he could swelled within him, and he looked up into Sayah's golden eyes, so much like his own. The æglet noticed Nat's stare, and perceived the persuasive argument there, but looked away in refutation.

Sayah sensed that sacrifice lay along the path that Nat had chosen and feared his own courage would prove insufficient to walk it. The æglet shuddered as memories of the Kinsman's final moments arose unbidden within his mind like ghastly spectres of death, and Sayah's feathers stood out from his pimpled flesh, giving him a fluffed and ruffled appearance.

A small, firm hand pressed against Sayah's wing, and he glanced over to where Nat stood beside him, hope on his small, blue face. Sayah remembered the Kinsman's resurrection, and that He might yet walk their world, and relaxed at the thought, taking comfort in it and in the presence of his friend.

He presented an open wing, pointing down the rutted road while looking to Nat, "Shall we?"

With a broad grin, Nat replied, "Yes. Let's go."

Since departing Sanctuary, they had begun working out some of the necessary signals as Astéri had suggested before they left. They continued the process as they hiked down the rough lane in the shadow of the cliffs. The scenario they envisioned would have Nat performing the infiltration and rescue with Sayah on the perimeter providing support and intelligence with his powerful vision.

The mission requirements dictated that Nat's communication be altogether silent and would consist of distinct hand signals that Sayah could make out at distance. Sayah would provide direction and alert Nat to danger through a variety of calls, which they both hoped would go unnoticed amidst the natural sounds of the forest.

In general, the eyesight of ægles was not good at night, but Sayah possessed remarkable acuity of vision, even in darkness. Nat knew next to nothing of ægles and accepted the æglet's confident word that he would be able to cover Nat's infiltration after nightfall.

The road curved to the east near the base of the cliffs to meet the bridge of Men where the land leveled out. In the dwindling light preceding sunset, the shadowed road that led away on the far side of the river seemed to Nat more ominous than it had before. Sayah, however, detected neither form nor movement among the shadows under the thick forest that loomed over the lane, and assured Nat that they had not been spotted.

Nevertheless, before they attempted a crossing, Nat insisted they duck into the wooded glade south of the road to consult with the Spirit. Nat did not want to presume again that the obvious course was what Elyon desired, and took a seat on a low, flat stone to rest while he awaited guidance.

Sayah was hungry, regardless, and wandered off to hunt in the shady thickets and woodlands as he waited on Nat. While he was unable to pin down anything substantial, he instead made a meal of beetles, crickets, and the like. They were not his preferred fare, but he'd snapped up snacks of moths and such fluttering near the nest when at his hungriest and had acquired a taste for them.

A masculine voice rumbled near Nat, prompting him to whirl around in reaction, "You and your friend come here often, little one?"

A Man! Nat thought, spying a seated form resting against a tree with a hand upraised in salute.

The Man's clothing, covered in earth, had camouflaged him from Nat and Sayah when they entered the woods, and he had remained still until speaking. That the Man had chosen to reveal himself thus gave Nat some hope that the stranger might not be hostile, yet he stayed on his guard until he could be certain.

"Who are you?" Nat piped in hopes his voice would carry the words to the lofty ears of the Man.

"Alright, I'll answer first, though I *was* the first to ask," chided the Man. "My name is Makrïos, formerly Lokagós Makrïos Toudóratos of the Imperial Forces of Chōl, a Captain in the common tongue. But no more."

Makrïos spat, a gesture of disgust at his prior association with the Empire, and Nat recognized the Man's name and features from his vision of the Kinsman.

This is the Man who nailed Gaal to the Tree! Nat thought, horrified.

"Don't be afraid, little one. I've no harm left in me. Not after what I've seen. Not after what I've *done*," Makrïos offered in a resigned voice. "I've slain my best friend, a Man better than any I ever knew. I haven't the heart now to hurt another being."

Nat identified the Man's remorse, the burden of his shame at what he'd done to Gaal. The Etom was mystified that Makrïos, so callous in his administration of the Kinsman's punishment, would be so regretful now.

With timid lips, Nat ventured, "Who was he? The Man you killed?"

"His name was Gaal, and he lived an amazing life. Unparalleled, in fact," Makrïos answered. "But he was too extraordinary, too truthful. He made enemies of many by his words and deeds, the Empire counted among them. And I was his friend. Well, supposed to have been."

"What happened?" Nat inquired. "Why did y—Why did the Empire kill him?"

"The powers that be had it in for him, that's what," Makrïos replied with chagrin, "His own people, subjects of Chōl, expected him to liberate them from the Empire, but for all his greatness, he refused to take a crown. Well, until the very end, when he gladly wore a crown of suffering.

"When he refused to rule in defiance of the Empire, his people turned on him. Out of jealousy, their leaders pressed the Empire to do their dirty work, and the Empire more than happily obliged. The Nihúkolem wanted him dead as well, though it seemed they didn't know exactly why. Even those grim shades of once-living creatures take orders from unseen forces.

"Long before all that, though, Gaal had befriended me, and I marveled at his miraculous wisdom and power. I'd never seen anything like him! And neither had anyone else. I promised him . . ."

Here Makrïos' speech grew ragged with tears as he struggled to continue, " . . .I promised him I'd follow him wherever he led me. And he told me I'd deny him. Three times."

Makrïos held up three thick fingers, "Three times! And I did, with each nail I pounded into him. I denied our friendship, but even as he hung dying at *my* hand, he whispered forgiveness to me. And declared it to all Creation from that accursed Tree.

"I never deserved such a friend. And I never will, but I tell you now, I *refuse* to aid the Empire another moment!" Makrïos held a single, trembling finger before him as he spat his declaration.

Nat listened with awe, uncertain how he should respond, but struck by the transformation this Man had undergone. He'd forsaken the prestige and wealth of an Imperial captain, trading them in for rags and purpose. The Etom considered revealing his knowledge of the Kinsman, for it seemed Makrïos yet languished under the perception that the Kinsman remained dead. Nat might provide some relief to the Man's afflicted soul if he shared what he knew. It was a risk, but it seemed the kind worth taking, the very kind that Gaal had taken in submitting to abuse and execution.

"I've seen Him, you know," Nat stated, a hopeful look in his eyes.

"Who?" Makrïos replied with a confused scowl.

"Your friend, Gaal. I saw Him. And you," Nat rejoined. "The night He went to the Tree. I was there."

"Impossible!" Makrïos retorted. "We would have seen you. Do you take me for a fool?"

Nat took a breath to calm himself and to collect his thoughts, then continued, "Do you remember when Mūk-Mudón ordered Corsucan to bring the crown?"

The blood drained from Makrïos' face, turning his olive-toned skin a sickly green, as he whispered, "How do you know that?"

"I told you. I was there. I saw it all," Nat returned, then in a lower voice, "Even your part in it. The beating, the scourging, the mall—"

"Stop!" Makrïos barked, then broke down into weeping, "Please. Stop."

"Ok," Nat complied, then in a gentle, firm tone, "But you don't know what happened *after*."

The sobbing Makrïos stilled at once, looking at the Etom with a pained and desperate hope on his face, and asked, "Why? What happened?"

"After you and the Nihúkolem left, all was quiet for a while," Nat described, "Then the place started to come alive. Grass and flowers sprouted up from the dead land around the Tree, and the nails holding Gaal to the Tree came out. Gaal stood up, alive, and then the Tree came back to life, too. A few seconds later, he looked at me and my friends, and disappeared. I've never seen anything like it."

Makrïos stared at Nat, bearded jaw hanging low on his shocked face, and mouth working in slow, soundless movements until, at last, he managed, "You're saying he's alive? Gaal is alive?"

Nat nodded as he answered, "I don't know how else to put it. He got up looking more alive than anyone I've ever seen, and then just vanished. I have no idea where He went, though."

Makrïos sat back hard against the tree, his gaze long yet introspective as he muttered, "I can't believe it. I just *can't* believe it."

"Well, believe it, Mister Captain Man," Nat quipped, "I saw it with my own eyes, and so did my friends, Sayah, Astéri, and Miyam. He's alive, and I think you'll find the truth at the Tree. I'm on an important mission right now. Lives are at stake. Otherwise, I'd take you there myself, but . . . you know the way, right?"

Makrïos nodded in silence, then stood to leave, his expression distant as he gazed in the direction of the Tree.

A sudden smile broke across the Man's face, and Makrïos turned to crouch low and offer a thick finger to Nat, "You never did give me your name, little one. Would you do me the honor now?"

Taking Makrïos' calloused finger in both hands, Nat shook it and answered, "Why, of course, sir. My name's Nat. Nice to meet you!"

Sayah returned from hunting down a meal to discover Nat lost in thought. It wasn't long after Makrïos left that Nat sensed their direction, but night had fallen almost in full before they were underway again. The Etom took a nibble or two of the wafers Miyam had packed, and a sip the water from the flask. It wasn't much, but the nourishment had an invigorating effect, and Sayah was also pleased to have something in his stomach, even if it was just insects.

Nat felt the Spirit leading them to cross the bridge and cut down the bank at its far side as he and Company Jasper had done before. Notwithstanding, the tug of Resonance compelled him to stop at the far end of the bride, and to peer into the deep gloom that covered the road as it led away into the woods. He sensed something important in tracing Gaal's route back along this road, but also that this would be a quest for a later date. While confident in his own assessment that nothing lurked in the woods, Sayah couldn't shake the anxiety of their exposure near the bridge and waited in nervous hope that Nat wouldn't remain long on the road.

The moment passed, and Nat started down the bank, a relieved Sayah in tow as the Etom took them into the woods and due east toward Sakkan. It wouldn't be far to the village where Nat's loved ones were held, and he continued in harmonious Resonance to the camp they had struck near the village what seemed now like long ago. Nat located their packs, which had remained undisturbed, and rummaged through them for a cold morsel while Sayah sought a warmer meal.

Sayah developed a means of quietly stalking his prey, a woodland mouse, and lay in wait downwind after spotting the creature quivering amongst the tall grass. The unfortunate beast drew near, and Sayah struck out with his beak to snatch the beast up and carry it back to camp to devour.

The æglet made short work of the mouse, eating every bit of the creature while Nat looked out from the tree line and across the meadow to where Sakkan lay. The lights of homes glowed a dim and warm invitation, and Nat was struck by a sudden homesickness. To be with his mother, his friends, or among the Eben'kayah in Endego – he longed for the distant warmth of community.

No! he chastised himself. *I can't afford self-pity now. Besides, if all goes well tonight, it'll be enough to be back with Company Jasper. If I don't focus, though, we might* never *see each other again.*

The thought sobered Nat, and he looked back to see if Sayah had finished with his meal. That the æglet had polished off something larger than Nat disturbed the Etom a bit, but he reminded himself that Sayah had become a good friend and a powerful ally. He called the æglet to his side, hoping to gain some insight from the far-sighted raptor regarding the mission.

Sayah joined Nat at his vantage, and Nat described the location of Scarsburrow's clinic within Sakkan. After Nat's explanation, they stared together in silence across the clearing into the village. It seemed as though Sayah might ask a question of Nat, but he instead stilled himself, cocking his head to listen.

After a brief moment, he rasped an urgent whisper, "Nat! Get back! Now!"

The æglet slunk back into the shadows and around the far side of the tree where they had struck camp, Nat crawling after to meet him there.

"What?" Nat asked with concern. "What is it, Sayah?"

"Shhh," Sayah shushed. "Just listen."

From the direction of the village, Nat detected the hooting of owls. With dismay, he recognized the danger, and his dread grew when another hoot sounded straight overhead. A soft flutter of wings reached their ears through the branches, followed by another distinctive strigiform cry. Pressed up against tree's trunk, Nat and Sayah froze in place even as they prepared themselves for flight.

In minute ticks, Sayah's head twitched as he sought the predator in the dark. Nat watched, breathless, until the æglet stopped moving altogether, and followed the direction of his gaze to a clump of leaves on a branch to the right of their hiding place. He strained his inferior eyes to make out what Sayah had ascertained, and the flat, oval flash of the owl's questing eyes greeted him as it looked out from its perch in their tree.

Well, so much for a nighttime infiltration, Nat conceded with chagrin. *With these owls on sentry duty, we'll never enter Sakkan without being seen.*

The thought struck a sympathetic chord in harmony with his new internal perception. Neither Sayah nor Nat dared move more than breathing required while they awaited the owl's departure with anticipation. With a final hoot and a flapping flurry, the nocturnal hunter departed, and Sayah snuck his head around the trunk to follow its course back to the tops of the trees surrounding Sakkan.

With a sigh of relief, Sayah withdrew his head to inform Nat, "They must have only *thought* they saw something. It's a good thing you're so small, and my feathers so dark. We could have been in real trouble. We had better stay put, at least for a while. They may pay attention to this spot now they're on alert."

"Sayah," Nat began, "I think the rescue may need to be a daytime mission. Anything moving around out here at night will draw the owls' attention, but I might be able to slip in unnoticed during the day. With your help, of course."

"What does your, um, you know, tell you?" Sayah gestured in awkward reference to Nat's resonant guidance.

Nat chuckled, and answered, "I know it can't be at night, so that really only leaves us the day, right?"

"Right," Sayah agreed.

Nat continued, "Either way, I'll spend some time on it tonight before I sleep, and let you know what the plan is, OK?"

"That sounds . . ." with a yawn the æglet interrupted himself. "That sounds . . .good."

Nat couldn't blame Sayah for being tired. It had been a long day, and he figured the æglet had never traveled as far as he had today, cooped up in the nest as he'd been. It was time to rest.

"Let's get some sleep, huh?" Nat asked.

Sayah nodded with drowsy approval, and the duo nestled up in a nook between the tree's spreading roots. Sayah fell asleep in an instant, and Nat leaned against the æglet's warm, downy side, wondering if his friend thought it odd to be sleeping outside of his nest for the first time in his life.

Nat snorted a laugh, *What a pair we are! I wonder what Mom and Rae will think of him?*

He was happy to reflect on the hopeful results of tomorrow's efforts, held in promise of triumph. His reflection brought him back to Sayah's questions about the rescue, and Nat turned his focus to consultation with the Spirit on tomorrow's task.

In place of direction, Nat received gentle assurance, and though he submitted his repeated plea for illumination of the plan, he gained no such lucidity. Tranquil thought inundated his mind, caressing him into a restful sleep.

In sleep, Nat's dreams awakened, his vision clear within a corridor encased in the swirling blur of indistinct surroundings. He recognized the setting somehow, and the lane of clarity running straight across the meadow and into Sakkan. He followed its course in confidence, unafraid though it weaved in unpredictable turns to either side, and he recognized Sayah's muffled call, signaling him. Beneath him, his feet beat the ground in step with an abiding and familiar pulse.

The shifting haze encompassing his path seemed to beckon his hand to its borders, and he stopped to stretch forth curious fingers and tease the swirling wisps. Upon contact with the fog, the ever-present pulse seemed to skip in irregular, tripping rhythm, jarring Nat from his confident fearlessness. As from a searing stovetop, Nat retracted his hand, and found again the pulse, its beat once more steady in his ears. He stared down at his hand, confident he should learn something from the phenomenon as Sayah squawked again in the distance.

"Wha—? Is this some new kind of Resonance?" he inquired of the Spirit, and, in his dream, did not anticipate an answer.

Answers are easy, my son, the Spirit whispered. *What you don't expect is a relationship, but how is it you have seen Father and Son, but don't recognize My heartbeat?*

Nat fumbled for a response, but the Spirit quelled him, *There is no need to respond, but you must learn to know Me, and you will recognize my manifestations. For now, though, just remember. And awaken.*

Sayah's squawking yet resounded in Nat's ears as he sat up, his face meeting the æglet's beak when he arose.

Sayah stood over him, worry in his eyes, as he exclaimed, "Finally! I've been trying to wake you for a while, but you were dead to the world."

Chapter Nine

The Rescue

A relieved Sayah explained that he'd been calling Nat for several minutes and had even tried to shake him awake. Nothing had worked, so he'd begun to squawk as a final, panicked resort. Nat looked around, anxious that Sayah might have alerted the denizens of Sakkan to their presence.

It was early, and though dawn had yet to arrive in full, the owls had already retreated to their nests for the day while in large part the Etom of Sakkan had yet to rise. Sayah had still to finish expressing how worried he'd been, but Nat ignored him as his focus was drawn to the edge of the meadow. A low and meager mist swirled about the wildflowers, reminding him of his dream. Sayah, although exasperated when he noticed Nat wasn't paying him any mind, quieted when he saw Nat close his eyes. Nat sought the pulse he'd come to recognize in the dream and was not disappointed.

A heartbeat, the Spirit had said, Nat contemplated, and in the stillness, he sensed the pulse, his own heart leaping with every beat.

"Now," he said, his tone commanding, as he turned to Sayah. "We go now."

Sayah blinked, then nodded, "Alright, then. Where do you need me?"

Nat instructed Sayah to stay out of sight in the woods, but to reposition himself to the south as he followed Nat into Sakkan. In general, the route of Nat's infiltration would follow the directions Doctor Scarsburrow had provided Dempsey when they'd taken Rae for treatment.

While Nat didn't like the idea of retracing the steps of their previous folly, he sensed the urging of the Spirit to enter town from the south as before. Barring a linear infiltration from the west through yards and past windows, Nat realized that their prior avenue was the most direct. Besides, this time, the good Doctor shouldn't be expecting him.

The Æglet's Answer

With the awareness that Sayah stood at the ready to signal him should danger of discovery arise, Nat crept through the meadow, aiming straight for Sakkan from the place he'd seen the mist gathering. The tall stalks surrounding him reinforced his vision from the prior night, and mirrored the sense of safe encapsulation he'd experienced, that he still experienced as he concentrated on the reverberant thrum that guided him through to the far edge of the meadow.

From a perimeter stand of wildflowers, he peered at the grove of trees comprising Sakkan's southwest border. No homes stood on the side nearest Nat beyond the sturdy oak that stood at the southwestern corner of the village, though a number filled the gap between it and the next tree north. From these came neither sound nor smoke in the morning stillness, and Nat pressed on to the corner oak's south side, hopeful Sayah had already circled to the south for a better view.

Back pressed against the tree's trunk, Nat looked for a sign of his friend without success and sighed. Oh well, the whole point was that Sayah's eyes were much sharper than his. He fell back on their system of signals, angling one hand up and to the side and the other bent at the elbow across his face in parallel to the first.

Do you see me? the signal asked.

Across the expanse to the south came a single screech as response in the affirmative. With the assurance that Sayah could see him, he signaled again, raising both arms skyward.

Is the way clear?

The solitary screech again sounded in reply.

In the pulsing flow of Resonance, Nat's already firm certainty was bolstered by Sayah's communication. The simple truth is that it just felt good to know Sayah waited in support of the mission, and Nat moved with quiet ease from behind the tree to cross the lane into Sakkan. Once across, he proceeded with simulated nonchalance up the northbound road, ready to duck or dart out of view until a notice posted to the gate of a home he was passing brought him to a halt.

It was a sketch of him, or a very near facsimile over which in bold letters was written the word, "WANTED."

Nat read the script below his likeness with interest, "Wanted for questioning in connection with actions taken contrary to the public good. If spotted, inform the constabulary or Doctor Scarsburrow at once."

Looking down the street, he saw a number of the notices posted at regular intervals. Not long ago, the sight of the posters would have filled him with dread, but now he found it somewhat entertaining. The knowledge didn't change his mission at all, and the notices were an open manifestation of his need for stealth. An amused grin on his face, he sighed and returned to the business at hand.

It's the third street on the right, he recalled. *I should be able to see it from the intersection.*

From outside the village came Sayah's cry, one short, then one long, followed by another two short bursts.

On the left! Nat thought, dropping to a crouch on one knee while he scanned the other side of the street.

There!

An elderly lemon-colored etma a few houses down came outside to empty a pot of dishwater into the flower bed beside her porch. She shook the pot upside down from the porch and turned around to head back inside without so much as looking up. Nat breathed more easily, but recognized that the village was waking up, and it was likely he'd encounter more Etom on the road if he didn't hurry.

He stood in haste, ready to march forward when he felt that persistent, gentle tug that had first beleaguered him outside Sanctuary. The anxiety of the mission pressed on him, and it was with some irritation that he stopped and fell again to one knee to assess his focus on the Spirit.

He sensed again the comforting beat, though it seemed a bit distant. The etma from earlier exited her home again, this time surveying the street in both directions before stepping from the porch. Nat realized she now wore a jacket and looked as though she were leaving for the day. With the realization, his anxiety spiked, and he prayed she wasn't headed his direction. He was just out of sight now behind the low fence surrounding one of her neighbor's homes, but he wouldn't remain so for long if she came his way.

The yellow etma teetered down her walk to edge of the lane, and again looked both directions, her gaze lingering southward as Nat crouched in stock-still petrification. At last, she turned and started her journey north along the road. Nat's earlier frustration had fled him in the terror of his potential exposure, and he uttered a prayer of gratitude to Lord Elyon as the aging etma departed.

If I had rushed ahead . . . he pondered, amazed at how the Spirit had kept him from discovery.

Now free of worry and vexation, Nat sensed the guiding thrum with clarity, and it dawned on him that his poor attitude had been responsible for his earlier difficulty in detecting the Spirit. He marveled at the thought as he arose to proceed in the confident ease he remembered from his dream. Attuned to the Spirit's leading, he neither rushed nor delayed as he proceeded.

Just another Etom enjoying a morning stroll through town, he thought with a quiet chortle.

He passed the first road on the right and was about halfway to the second when an officious etém the color of coffee rounded the corner from the right at a brisk pace. Nat almost froze again, then reconsidered when he noticed the etém had turned north without a glance in Nat's direction.

Nat didn't break stride and his smile broadened as he considered, *The delay saved me here, too, didn't it?*

He asked the question, not of himself, but of the Spirit that had thus far proven the strength of the promise Astéri extended before they left Sanctuary. No answer did he receive but the continued affirmation in his soul, and that was sufficient to buoy him to his turn at the third street.

Nat's instincts screamed that he should just peek around the bend before taking it, but the whisper within steadied him along the way. Rather, he slowed himself to a leisurely pace when the thick, black pillar of the clinic came into view. Nat imagined Sayah's imagination running wild since he passed out of view and knew the æglet wouldn't catch sight of him until he returned with the prisoners. Hopefully. The length of road between him and his destination was deserted, but Nat remembered the pair of guards stationed at the clinic doors, and he sought an alternate entrance as he neared.

No such avenue was forthcoming, and Nat reconsidered his approached, out of reflex seeking the will of the Spirit while he proceeded. The plots to either side of the obsidian prison were bare, and Nat noticed a simple network of pathways running around and behind the clinic. One leg of trails shot off parallel to the road, and Nat sidestepped through the scrub to join the path.

Once on the trail, Nat felt a greater security than he'd had exposed on the road. A gentle rise between the trail and the road lowered his profile, and he knew the angle of his approach put the tower between him and the guards stationed at the door to obscure him from their sight. He also knew he'd be unable to sneak past the guards to enter through the front doors, and the plan remained fluid within his mind, submitted to the will of the Spirit.

Nat was almost to the cylindrical structure when he sensed the tug of the Spirit to follow the spur of trail that skirted the backside of the clinic. He circumnavigated the building, hugging the black wall as he drew close to the entrance. He didn't dare peek around the edge to confirm the guards' presence, but stood in the shadows nearby, listening.

He'd all but given up on eavesdropping, and was about to venture a glance when he heard the rough clearing of a masculine throat, a gruff voice following, "How do suppose the Doctor is faring with our new guests?"

The steely voice conveyed irony in its enunciation of the word 'guests,' and at once Nat knew his mother and friends were the subjects of conversation. His attention piqued, he attended the discussion with all the more care.

The other guard responded with a cruel snicker, "I imagine he's enjoying himself. I've supposed as much before, though, and the Doctor has surprised me."

"He's an odd one, no doubt of that," the first answered. "Just when I think I have him pegged as a sadist, he's beside himself with worry over a patient."

"And the gloves, eh?" came the reply. "What's with them?"

"You've noticed, too, then," returned guard number one. "Like flipping a lever when he puts them on."

Despite Nat's interest in learning more of the Doctor's disturbing pathology, the import of rescuing his friends far outweighed the desire to continue listening in on the goons' conversation. The dilemma they presented, however, required a level of resourcefulness he was unsure he possessed. In diverting the sentries' attention to slip past them, he would likely draw their attention to himself, thus defeating the purpose and alerting them to his presence. His greatest advantage would be lost, and his enemies might sound the alarm to call for reinforcements.

At his wit's end, Nat turned to the One who had guided him thus far with success and whispered his need to the Creator. In his desperation, he had grown impatient, but his prayers were a ladle drawing the waters of that peaceable flow beneath the Tree to calm his agitated soul. The reservoir within quelled his worries, and beside the still waters, echoed the implausible answer that otherwise might have brought him further distress.

Stand up, and enter the building, came the response to his petition.

Nat detected the Resonance of the command with uncommon sense, even as that which was common protested its advisability.

But, they'll see me, Nat contended.

Do not fear, but trust in Me, answered the Spirit.

With trepidation, but determined to see his mission through, the etém stood. His steps halting, he forced himself from concealment to step into full view of the guards. The brutes continued their conversation without taking any notice of Nat, who stood before them in frozen surprise when he realized they could not see him.

Do not delay, Nat.

Nat pressed on, careful not to touch either guard as he passed between them, and was almost past when the voice directed, *The keys.*

From the belt of one of sentries hung a large ring of keys, clipped there with a simple mechanism much like a carabiner. Nat was well-acquainted with the device from all his experience climbing but was nonetheless hesitant. With great care to avoid the gesturing arms of the guard, Nat reached for the clip and collected the keys without so much as a tinkle.

He turned to the double doors of the clinic, and slipped inside, uttering a great sigh of relief once he'd determined the immediate interior free of occupants. Amazed and grateful at his miraculous and undetected infiltration of the tower, he offered his thanks to Elyon before looking around.

The clinic was dark and hushed as he remembered, but his awakening to its secondary purpose as a dungeon rendered it sinister in his mind. Within its dim confines were his captive company, and he wasted no time in beginning his search.

Narrow corridors curved away to either side of the main one leading straight forward to the central atrium of the structure. While they had discovered no cells on the ground floor when they arrived before at the dank penitentiary, Nat took care to check every door regardless while Resonance provided an unhurried counterpoint to his search. It was an opportunity for Nat to familiarize himself with the ring of keys as well, and he soon learned the pattern of their use while he navigated the numerous rooms encircling the building.

The keys were each etched with a single number and character, which corresponded to a small panel mounted on the wall next to each door. For example, all keys marked with the number one and the character 'samekth' were storage areas, of which there were many on the first floor. Most of the storage rooms Nat entered held cleaning supplies or medical equipment he couldn't identify, although the one nearest the stairway to the second floor held wheeled stretchers, an item he at least recognized.

Only three doors opened off the central atrium, where the dwarf tree stood far below the now-open skylight. The tree appeared a bit tattered, which Nat concluded was a consequence of the falling glass of the shattered skylight. Doctor Scarsburrow had yet to replace the skylight, and the open space overhead admitted a slight breeze that Nat felt as he crossed the space. The crunch of leaves beneath his feet alerted him to the many that had fallen from the ragged tree. Nat suspected the little tree had in its sheltered life little tolerance for even the nighttime cold.

The thought passed as he scanned the wall for the coded panel next to the first door he arrived at. The inscription read the number one, as he predicted, and the character 'eepe.' Nat sifted through the keys, which he had been grateful to discover were organized on the ring by floor, making it a simple matter of flipping through the several marked for ground floor use before he found the one he needed. He inserted the key into the lock, and opened the door onto the vacant white examination room Scarsburrow had examined Rae in. Predictably, he found the remaining two rooms identical in style and function, and likewise empty.

Nat looked toward the staircase to the second floor, and the emotional press of recollection almost overwhelmed him. Their prior ascent of the stair had marked the beginning of their flight from Scarsburrow and his goons. The discovery of the asylum cells on the upper floors had been disturbing, as had been the haunting features of captive Etom watching Company Jasper's doomed pursuit around the circular chamber.

Nat steeled himself in preparation for the macabre encounter and set to the work of locating the members of his company. Astéri had ordered in no uncertain terms to free all the prisoners here, but Nat intended to collect those he knew first. He would need trustworthy and reliable help in rescuing everyone else.

He climbed the stairs with steady strides, and approached the tiny window inset in the first door on the second storey. He lifted a hand, paused for an instant, then rapped on the glass with tense knuckles. Nothing was visible through the murky portal, but Nat waited with anticipation of the patient's sudden appearance, recalling his mother's shocking experience.

After long and disappointing moments, the etém who had surprised Nida just before company Jasper's capture failed to appear. Nat wondered if the Doctor had moved the patient, and worry struck him as he considered the possibility Company Jasper might also have been moved.

No! he thought. *I don't believe the Spirit would bring me here just to find out everyone has been moved.*

Nat moved to the next door and repeated the procedure with diminishing reluctance, recognizing the need for efficiency if he ever hoped to check the dozens of rooms encircling the tower. A drab and weary etma cupped her hands around wincing eyes to peer down at Nat, and her sorrowful expression compelled Nat to release her at once.

He resisted the impulse, however, and lifted a hopeful hand as he told her to wait. He hadn't been looking for it next to the first door, but now he examined the wall for a designation like those below. He was pleased to locate the panel and inscription beside the door, though the markings varied somewhat from others he'd yet to encounter.

This one was marked as follows: 2-002. Like downstairs, the first part represented the floor, but the second corresponded which the specific room. Unsure if she could even hear him, Nat reassured the captive etma as he backed up. The prisoner's distress was apparent when Nat pulled himself away, but he made a mental note that room 2-002 was occupied.

Nat wasn't surprised that the next room he arrived at was designated 2-003, which he read on the panel next to the door while he pounded for the attention of the resident. Another bleak countenance filled the darkened frame, and Nat marveled that each Etom seemed discolored, perhaps from long imprisonment away from the sun. He continued around the chamber on the second floor, finding every room occupied but for a single storage closet, but did not encounter anyone from Company Jasper.

He mounted the steps to the third storey and worked most of the way around the level to again discover each room full. From where he stood awaiting the appearance of another pallid Etom at the door, he could see the ladder they had used in attempt to escape this horrid place. Only three doors remained on the third floor, and the despair of the memory fell on him, its weight attempting to smother his dwindling hope, grown heavier in the revelation of yet another unfamiliar face in the window.

The gravity of Nat's disappointment confronted a novel resilience that shrugged off the crushing weight in favor of perseverance, and the etém in slow, deliberate strides went to the next door. As the struggle crystallized, Nat turned to Elyon for strength, his heart and lips fluttering in search of His presence. Despondency was a grasping claw struggling to find purchase in Nat's soul as beneath the press, he grew stronger with each step. And at the black portal, Nat raised his hand to knock, his fist falling leaden against the metal surface.

Within the shaded chamber beyond the window, a faint figure stirred to draw near, and from the shadows broke forth a familiar yellow face to press against the glass.

The dark and questing grip on Nat broke altogether, and his heart leapt as he shouted, "Kehren!"

Tears streamed down the etma's face while Nat flipped in a frenzy through the ring of keys to unlock the cell. At last, he came upon a key marked 3-XXX, which he hoped was the master key for all the cells on the third floor. He rammed the key home and turned it with a satisfying 'click.'

With excitement, he pulled the heavy door open, and Kehren fell on him in embrace as she exclaimed, "Nat! Dear Nat! I can't believe you came back! Your mother is going to be *very* upset with you!!!"

"She's here?" Nat inquired, his hope buoyed at the news.

"Yes! Yes, Nat!" Kehren replied. "She and Dempsey are in the next two rooms. I guess Scarsburrow didn't want to chance our escape, so he put all of us as far from the exit as possible."

The open door admitted a broad blade of light into the gloomy cell, and from its depths came scuffling steps, slow in the murk until they brought two pink and dirty feet into view.

"Nat?" came a forlorn and hopeful cry.

Rae lurched into view, illuminated by the falling light, and Nat hurried to steady her. The two friends shared an embrace as Kehren laid a hand on each of their shoulders. In the savor of their reunion, neither spoke a word until Nat stepped back, his mission returning to mind. The last he knew, Rae had been for the most part immobile, and her recovery from the concussion yet incomplete.

"Are you well?" he asked with concern.

"Yeah. *I* am," she responded with dismay. "But something else happened while you were away, Nat."

With dread, Nat realized that neither etma had made mention of Tram, and he asked, "Is your father alright? Where is he?"

"He's here," Kehren answered with sadness, "but he, he's not *well*, Nat. I don't know what we can do for him."

Her sorrow broke Nat's heart, but his commiseration lasted but an instant as their circumstance galvanized his resolve.

"I know what we can do," he replied, the fires of indignation at this injustice alight in his eyes. "We can get him and all of you out of here."

"But Nat," Kehren protested, "Tram can't walk, and Rae is . . .well, she's just not very strong yet."

"We need help," Nat replied. "I'm going to get Dempsey and my Mom. We're going to get you out of here if we have to carry you."

At that, Nat dashed from the cell to the next door. He didn't bother to knock and slid the key in place to open the door without delay. The light fell at once on Dempsey, who sat against the wall, blinking, and hand upraised as he tried with eyes acclimated to darkness to make out who had opened the door.

"Dempsey!" Nat called. "It's Nat! I've come to free you, and I need your help with Tram. Can you walk?"

Dempsey's face peeked out from under the visor of his hand in disbelief as he responded, "Nat!?! Is it really you?"

"Yes! Yes, it is!" Nat exclaimed in a mixture of impatience and excitement. "We need to hurry if we are going to escape. Can you move?"

Nat was relieved when Dempsey sprung up from the floor, "Absolutely! Have you freed your mother yet?"

"No, but I'm headed there next," Nat replied. "Can you go next door to help Kehren with Tram? He can't walk on his own."

"Right away!" Dempsey responded, patting Nat on the shoulder as he passed. "Let's go!"

With that, Nat exited Dempsey's cell, and sprinted to the next door, behind which his mother awaited. Afraid how he might find his mother, it was with a trembling hand that Nat pushed the key into the lock and turned it. He swung the door open to reveal Nida, who stood just inside the cell with tears in her eyes.

"Mom!" Nat cried, running to her.

"Nat?" she asked, her doubts dissolving as her son's arms encircled her. "I can't believe you came back!"

They passed the moment of their reunion in silence until Nida gripped her son by the shoulders, and held him at arms' length as she looked him in the eye and asked, "What were you thinking, Nat? You got away safe, but you risked it all on this rescue attempt. Why would you do such a thing?"

Nida spoke from the fierce, protective heart of a mother, even as she admired her son's bravery.

It was hard to remain upset at Nat, his eyes bright and clear as he answered, "I can't explain it all, but just know this: I've seen the Kinsman, and it was Lord Elyon's wish that I rescue you. Not just you, though. I am to release *all* the captives here and lead everyone back to safety."

Something in Nat's settled confidence took Nida aback. He acted as though the rescue was as good as done, and she was curious at his reassurance.

"Mom," he began, "do you think we can get moving now? We have a lot to do before we leave."

Nida set aside her curiosity to engage in the task at hand, "Yes, Nat. How can I help?"

He waved for her to follow as he stepped from the room, and said, "I need you to help me open all the cells, but first, I want to make sure that the others are ready to move."

Dempsey and Kehren stood on either side of Tram, whom they had propped against the rail, his head lolling wearily. Something in Tram's manner reminded Nida of Cairn, their neighbor in Endego, after he'd been returned to his wife following a Nihúkolem interrogation. In her heart, she damned Scarsburrow for his complicity with the Empire. She couldn't understand how the etém justified working with Chōl and the Nihúkolem but recognized the rescue would deprive the Doctor of his fodder.

They gathered there on the third-storey walkway, Company Jasper restored in membership, if not health, once more.

With an air of command, Nat explained his plan, and Nida marveled again at his confidence as he began, "I have the keys to the cells on each floor, and we need to split up to make sure each is opened. Only the first room at the top of the first flight of stairs is empty. That means we have dozens of doors to open and at least that many Etom to release and lead out of here."

Nat slipped a key from the ring and held it out to Nida, "Mom, you and I are the only ones who can move fast enough to get it done. Can you take the second floor?"

"Yes, Nat. Of course," she agreed with pride in her growing son.

Nat pressed the key into his mother's hand, and looked to the rest with concern, "I know you can't move very quickly, so just do your best to get down to the ground floor. Can you do that?"

Dempsey, Kehren, Tram, and Rae all nodded, resolute in their commitment, before Dempsey piped up, "I doubt Rae and Tram will be the only ones we encounter with mobility issues. How are you and Nida going to handle the folks who can't walk?"

Nat looked down, his face screwed in thought, then responded, "I think we'll find enough of the prisoners are well enough that they can help the others out. If not, then I might have another idea. Now, are we ready to move?"

From among the company arose agreement, and Nida dashed away toward the stairs while all but Nat began their ponderous, shuffling journey along the walkway to the stairs. Nat followed them to the first closed door they came to, then turned aside to collect the captive there.

He knocked at the door for the second time that day, and at once a grizzled etém face appeared in the window to grumble, "Yeah? What do you want? About the only good thing about this place is I get to sleep most the day, and you're interrupting."

Nat shook off his initial surprise to answer, "Well, sir, I was wondering if you'd like to leave?"

Nat held up the keys and shook them with a rattle, drawing the eyes of the prisoner, who considered then a moment before returning his gaze to Nat, "No, I don't believe I'd be interested in that. Likely get caught in the escape, and I know how the Doctor likes to punish those who step out of line. I think I'll just take my chances here, if it's all the same to you."

With eyes wide and brow tightened in perplexity, Nat stared at the stranger. An internal tug of the Spirit warned him of compelling the captive into freedom.

Eyes still on the prisoner, Nat unlocked the door, and offered, "If you change your mind, the door is open. We have to gather the rest, so you might meet us at the bottom before we leave, and if you don't, I hope you won't alert Scarsburrow of our escape."

The captive winked, "What escape? You've no worry of that, young one. I was napping all afternoon and didn't see a thing. Now on your way! You're disturbing my rest."

With a mystified shake of his head, Nat backed away from the door, then went to the next, where he found a much more willing escapee. Nat gathered a number of prisoners, most of whom could walk, while those who couldn't the others were happy to help.

Before long, the teeming crowd ahead of Nat was streaming down the steps and around the second storey walkway, and he could see a throng amassing around the dwarf tree below. Near the end of the third-floor walkway, Nat found another unwilling to depart the dungeon's confines, but pushed onward to release those who desired freedom.

With satisfaction, he opened the last cell on the third storey, the occupant awaiting rescue with an eagerness provoked by the passing crowd. In a strange twist, the exodus took on a celebratory festivity, and many fugitives called to one another in hushed excitement, their preexistent acquaintance becoming apparent in the process. Nat smiled at their happiness in the moment, taking pleasure in the fact he'd had a hand in the liberation of so many Etom.

With whispers of encouragement and reassurance, Nat pressed past the hobbling crowd to reach the bottom floor. He looked around at the many encumbered by injury or disability and hoped his plan would work. Wending his way through the milling press of bodies, Nat arrived at the nearby storage closet, and opened it after a brief search of the keys.

Tucked inside were the many gurneys he'd found earlier, and he whistled for attention as he addressed the crowd, "Everyone, my name is Nat, and I've been sent by Elyon to deliver you from this place! In this room behind me are stretchers for those unable to walk. If you are one of those who can't walk, please raise a hand!"

Hands shot up throughout the crowd, and Nat continued, "Ok, then those of you who aren't already assisting someone, collect a stretcher and take it to the Etom with their hands raised. Elyon is with us, and we should have enough to carry everyone. A few of you should stand at the bottom of the stairs with stretchers for those still descending. Now, let's move!"

Nat ducked into the closet and began pushing the gurneys to the waiting hands outside. A tall, thick etém joined him in the closet once there was room for another body, and the pair worked together to deliver the stretchers through the doorway.

They worked hard for several minutes until the last stretcher left the storage room. There had been far more packed into the closet than Nat had at first estimated, and he hoped it was enough. Sweat beading on their foreheads, the pair stepped back into the atrium to find an orderly procession prepared for exit from the clinic.

Nida approached Nat to explain, "There were just enough stretchers, Nat. Everyone who needed one got one, and we figured we had better line up. As you can see, everyone is just about ready."

Nat was relieved at their initiative, and once more addressed the assembly, "If I may, I would like to ask for your patience. Please remain where you are as we execute the next part of our plan."

The crowd murmured with anticipation but stayed put while Nat consulted with Dempsey and his mother. They knew the next obstacle to their escape was the pair of sentries posted outside the doors, followed by the jaunt through Sakkan, during which their exodus might be exposed. They peered around the corner and through the glass doors at the backs of the hulking guards.

"We need to get rid of those two if we're to have a chance," Nida asserted.

"Agreed," returned Dempsey. "I could gather a few of the other fellows here. If we were quiet, we could take them without much of a scuffle."

"Nat?" Nida asked. "What do you think?"

Nat listened to their plan with interest, though a portion of his awareness reminded him to consult the Spirit for the answer. Within the mellow folds of his tranquility, he sensed good pleasure, and an exhortation to boldness.

With decisiveness, Nat agreed, "Let's do it. Dempsey, look for three etém strong and fit enough to snatch the guards from their post. Remind them that silence is better than speed, though we have need of both."

Recognizing the commanding character as it emerged from him, Nida looked at her son with some sorrow at how much he'd grown in her absence. He seemed distant from his former self, a dependent and child-like being, though his sudden maturity was to their advantage in the moment. It wasn't the time for this reflection, she knew, and relinquished the thought in submission to the urgent. Dempsey had sped away while Nida gathered the sad wool of loss, though Nat observed her with some concern.

"What is it?" he asked.

Nida offered a wan smile, and replied, ruffling his long, unkempt zalzal, "It's nothing. You just seem so much older than before. You're not so little anymore."

"You're right," he said with resignation, "Everything has changed so much, even in the past few days. But I promise you it's for the best, and I'll try to explain everything once we are on our way, OK?"

Nida nodded as Dempsey returned with the three etém he'd hand-picked from the crowd, one of whom was the responsive fellow who'd helped Nat pull the gurneys from the closet. During introductions, Nat learned his name was Muta, and the others Kabir and Kaasi. Pleased at the selection, Nat nodded his approval, and the quartet wasted no time in taking up their positions at the doors.

They separated into pairs, Dempsey gripping the left-hand door handle with Kaasi behind, and Muta stood at the right-hand door with Kabir in tow. Dempsey nodded to Muta, and together they opened the doors, which swung in silence to permit a stealthy exit. Kaasi and Kabir reached back with gentle hands to slow the doors as they closed while Dempsey and Muta kept a watchful eye on the goons ahead. Neither sentry turned but remained focused on their conversation and the roadway before them.

So far, so good. Dempsey stood up, bracing himself against the wall in preparation to pounce while Kaasi crouched behind the left-hand guard's knees and Muta and Kabir mirrored them. Once the four etém were in position, Dempsey gave another silent nod and they sprung into simultaneous assault, Dempsey and Muta wrapping their arms around each guard's neck up top while Kaasi and Kabir enveloped them at the knees below. The goons were taken by complete surprise. They submitted readily as Muta and Dempsey applied brute pressure to their chokeholds, and Kaasi and Kabir toppled their forms toward one another.

The four etém at once dragged the pair of guards inside, where Nida and Nat had collected long strips of heavy gauze to bind them. Once the guards were restrained and gagged, they were taken to the closet for the stretchers and locked inside.

"There!" Dempsey exclaimed, "That should keep them a while! Shall we be on our way?"

Nat, Nida, and the others had made good use of the time spent binding the guards, and had meanwhile raided the closets for crutches, canes, and whatever else they could find and fashion into weapons. If they met resistance, they would do so armed.

Nat felt the reverberant pulse urging their departure, and without delay asked for the group to ready themselves to leave. As many as were able stood on either side of the stretchers to push them or to carry them, whichever the situation demanded. Nat asked Dempsey and Muta to stand as rearguard while Kaasi and Kabir acted as escorts to Nat and Nida at the head of the column. At last, they were prepared to escape their prison.

Chapter Ten
Exodus

In readiness, Nat and his mother stood just inside the clinic looking out, and with a deep breath pushed open the doors to their prison, striding forth to the main road. A pair of able-bodied Etom peeled off the column to hold the doors open as their procession poured out, an invalid parade in exodus from the horrors of Sakkan.

With an eye to the pace of those behind, Nat guided them down the road to their first and only turn, which would take them, Elyon willing, out of the village and under cover of the surrounding wilderness. Far at the rear of the list, Nat spotted Dempsey's yellow form dashing to the road to take his place at the tail of the ragtag formation. He smiled with mellow satisfaction that they were yet unnoticed, and that their company, now grown beyond all expectations, was reunited.

They approached their turn, and Nat ceded his place at the head of the column to Nida, so he could stand in the middle of the road and signal those behind to follow his mother to the left. With the susurrating hush of many moving bodies, the front half of the line passed from the lane in relative silence, and Nat was just about to sprint back up to the front when a distant cry alerted him to danger.

Standing in the road before the clinic was a red-faced figure clad in white, Doctor Scarsburrow. An unintelligible, frustrated curse resounded from his lips while he pursued in as speedy a shuffle as he could manage. Nearer to Nat, Dempsey waved the procession forward from the rear, urging them onward to freedom, the flag of his yellow hand flailing a signal to charge.

Nat jogged alongside the line toward the front, doing the same as Dempsey as he passed to the head, his hopes pinned on Sayah that the æglet remained in surveillant position outside the village. Once at the front, he in a rush informed his mother that they had been detected and began gesticulating toward the far forest line where he expected Sayah yet stood. The operation thus far had taken a few short hours, and while

Nat doubted Sayah would ever desert him, he worried the æglet may have gotten distracted in the boredom of the wait.

Nat need not have worried, though his assessment of Sayah's condition was correct. The æglet did not abandon his post, but over time he had become quite famished. In his hunger and disinterest, he had stalked several large insects to a satisfying end in his stomach, but he ever kept an eye toward the village and on the street where Nat had turned in particular.

Sayah was just crunching on a large beetle when he spotted a flash of movement on the road into Sakkan, almost choking on his meal when he saw the size of the formation. He sharpened his gaze, focusing on the mass of Etom charging down the road, and found Nat running to the front of the line, where he fell in to speak with a bright pink Etom.

Nat raised his arms in repeated signal to request confirmation that Sayah could see him. The æglet screeched once in the affirmative and saw Nat's features flood with relief at the answer. The blue Etom raised his arms straight up to ask if the way out was clear. Sayah scanned the broad boulevard for a few seconds, and determined that none obstructed the way, then again emitted the solitary squawk in response.

Nat waved the group onward, compelling them to hurry, which they did to their best ability, though encumbered by the number of those unable to walk. The stretchers were not meant for the rough, uneven roads they traversed, and their small, hard wheels stuttered along the bumpy surface as those pushing them forward did so by main force. Nat wondered if it might prove easier to just carry the gurneys and stepped back to where Tram reclined on the first of the stretchers in the column.

"I'd like to try lifting him," Nat told the pair handling the gurney, "but let me get another hand first."

Nat called his mother back and explained the plan. The four of them spread to the various corners of the stretcher and each grasped a sturdy rail.

Counting down, Nat gave the signal, "Three . . .two . . .one . . .now!"

The four of them lifted the stretcher, which was light and sturdy, and discovered their efforts in moving Tram reduced.

"Let's try one more thing," Nat suggested. "We don't have enough Etom to put four on each gurney, but we might be able to do three. Set him down for a moment, OK?"

They eased Tram's stretcher back down and Nat asked one of the two who had been pushing it to go to the head of the frame. Nida and the other Etom Nat directed to the sides, near the feet, but not quite at the end. At his signal, they lifted again with success. The Etom at the head of the stretcher helped balance the weight and the two at the feet carried the majority of it.

"How is it?" Nat asked his mother.

"It'll work," Nida puffed, "We might need to switch back and forth between pushing and carrying if we intend to go very far."

Satisfied, Nat went back along the column to explain their new strategy, which would permit them to move faster in the short term. At the rear, he learned they did not have quite enough mobile Etom to put three on the final gurney.

Dempsey, anxious to expedite their retreat, told Nat, "I think Muta and I can handle this last one, just the two of us. Let's give it a try at least."

"Absolutely!" Nat concurred. "Do it!"

Muta reached behind to grasp the rails at the front of the gurney while Dempsey ran up behind it. The pair grunted in concert to lift the elderly etma on the stretcher and dashed forward in pursuit of the others. Nat cast a look back over his shoulder to where the Doctor hunched over in the street, his hands on his knees and his face redder than usual as he huffed from exertion.

Good, Nat thought. *Maybe we'll escape without a fight after all.*

Nat dashed away to the front of the line, checking on those he passed as he sped by. He arrived at his mother's side in a few minutes, and it seemed that everyone was holding up pretty well. Their escape had yet to bring down any meaningful pursuit upon them, and Nat was hopeful they might reach the woods uncontested.

The wide road leading out of Sakkan still stretched long before them, however, and the group of escapees had barely reached the second intersection after the turn when Sayah's coded signal reached Nat's ears, a long shriek followed by three shorter ones.

Behind you! it said.

From the lane down which the clinic stood issued a dozen hulking etém with the two waylaid guards at the front. One of them pushed the sneering Doctor Scarsburrow in a wheeled chair of sorts. The Doctor was a pitiless figure hectoring his troops to hurry from his bobbling throne.

Stepping out into the middle of the road to wave his arms, Nat shouted, "Dempsey! Look out!"

"Hurry! Hurry!" Dempsey urged those in front of him. "They're coming!"

Dempsey and Muta broke formation to sprint forward, pulling even with the Etom in front of them, then passed them. As the realization that the Doctor and his minions pursued them filtered through the crowd, the column spread itself across the road to allow for greater speed.

Thought their overall pace increased, Nat noted with dismay that their pursuers were gaining ground and might overtake them before they left the village. He pressed the flagging escapees to give everything they had, reminding them of the freedom that awaited. With cries and groans of exertion, the weary procession found new strength to struggle on, and they passed the outer limits of Sakkan with the Doctor and his forces on their heels.

A shriek from behind warned Nat that one of their number was in immediate danger. He spun around to see a meaty hand groping for the gurney that carried Rae, and his protective instincts took over. He snatched up a cane from where it lay on a stretcher as he streaked by, intent on braining the brute that would abduct his friend.

At a full run, he leapt toward his foe with the makeshift club raised high overhead. Rae's attacker noticed Nat's attack at the last moment and attempted to raise a thick forearm in defense. Too late. The heavy handle of the cane crashed down across the brute's face, and he fell back, crumpling to the ground in pain.

"Go! Keep moving!" Nat barked at the stunned trio who carried Rae.

They departed with renewed urgency as Nat turned to face the forces closing in and recognized his own inadequacy in meeting them.

Three of Scarsburrow's enforcers drew near to surround him as the Doctor commanded them from behind, "That's him! He's the one who let them out! Get him first!"

The goons were an arm's-length away from Nat when an iron claw clamped down on the one nearest the Etom. Sayah stood atop the brute in his grasp and kicked out with the other talon to slash another while the third backed away in trembling fear.

"An æglet? Here?" cried the Doctor in confused incredulity.

With an offhanded flip, Sayah bowled the enemy in his grip into a crowd of goons and lunged forward to screech in the final attacker's face, a forceful sonic assault that made the hefty etém's jowls quiver. His foe decided he'd had enough and turned tail in clumsy retreat.

None but Scarsburrow remained nearby, and the Doctor looked up in melting abdication to squeak, "Oh dear."

With indelicate precision, Sayah tweezed the Doctor's jacket in his beak, and whipped his head sideways, hurling Scarsburrow high over the row of houses down the boulevard. The Doctor hollered in fear, and his gritting outcry stopped when he struck a roof, sticking headfirst and upside-down through the thatch.

Nat beamed at his æglet friend, and exclaimed, "Sayah! That was amazing!"

The oft-bashful Sayah swelled with pride at the praise, rather pleased with himself. He did not revel in the moment long, however. His eyes caught the numerous skirmishes unfolding in the vicinity and swung back into action, pecking, slashing, and flinging the foes of the freed wherever he found them.

Nat was unable to assist the æglet in any meaningful manner, and thus trotted up to where the scattered escapees gathered near the meadow to watch in awe at Sayah's terrible might. It put the world in perspective to understand such powerful forces and those even greater existed. That the Etom survived at all was a miracle for which Nat was grateful.

Their enemies dispatched, the remainder streamed to join the others with Sayah bringing up the rear. As the æglet neared, the throng turned to look up at him, uncertain of his intentions.

Nat walked up next to Sayah, laid a hand on his friend's wing, and offered an introduction, "This is my friend, Sayah. As you can see, he is an æglet, and has promised to help us escape. Sayah, these are the former prisoners of Sakkan."

Sayah provided a hearty, "Hello!" though all everyone but Nat heard was a mighty shriek, and they shrank back.

Nida crept forward to Nat's side to ask, "Can you understand him?"

Stunned, Nat recalled Miyam's explanation that the Tree enabled understanding between different kinds of creatures and realized that the Vine had been interpreting Sayah's speech since he'd met the æglet.

"I can," Nat replied, then informed Sayah that the other Etom couldn't understand him.

Rae had joined Nida nearby, and Nat turned to them to find their features frozen in bewilderment.

Rae pointed at Nat's mouth in shock to proclaim, "You speak bird!"

The statement hung in the air, the ludicrousness thereof almost driving Nat to hysterical laughter but for the apparent truth of it.

Nat could but answer, "Yes. I suppose I can."

Unable to resist the opportunity, he cocked a superior brow and gripped his chin in a pretentious hand to banter, "Why? Can't you?"

Rae and Nida sputtered laughter in response to Nat's preposterous question. Kehren held Tram's hand where he reclined on a stretcher close by while Dempsey approached in amazement. They were back together, and it felt good. Right.

Nat chirped something to Sayah about giving him a moment, and he addressed the crowd once more, "This æglet here is a friend. His name is Sayah, and he left his home to help me rescue you. Please treat him well as you get to know him better.

"Now! We are not out of the woods yet. To be frank, we need to get back into them as soon as possible. We must cut across this meadow to the woods west of us right away. We have much of the day to travel, but Scarsburrow's owls will be out tonight in search of us, and who knows what kind of help he might have from the Nihúkolem? We cannot spare a moment to rest just yet. So, I ask you – are you with me?"

With a resounding shout, the liberated captives cheered, "YES!!!"

They passed what was left of the day in fitful travel, and frequent stops slowed their overall pace to a near-crawl. The woods were less accommodating to travel by litter, and most of the Etom healthy enough to carry one were exhausted by their hurried exit from Sakkan. Nat recognized their need for rest, and thus provided many breaks once they had entered the shaded shelter of the trees.

At times, the journey slowed such that those able to walk, albeit with difficulty, disembarked their gurneys to proceed on foot. The Etom carrying or pushing the stretchers found these periods a welcome respite, and it was a challenge through which the debilitated strengthened themselves.

They pushed as deep into the woods as they were able, and it was almost evening before Nat perceived that those who bore the burden of the stretchers would need one themselves if they didn't stop soon. The trickle of a stream reached his ears, a distributary of the nearby river, and he called the grim parade to its graveled shore.

A spreading depression in the amalgam of smooth stones and rich soil near the brook made an ideal campsite for the group. Nat bid everyone refresh themselves while he consulted the Spirit for direction. He sensed the confirmation of his decision and informed the group they would set camp there for the night.

A ripple of relief spread through the crowd, a wandering wave of relaxation that caused everyone to slump where they stood. An insistent tapping rapped against Nat's consciousness, an objection of the Spirit that drew his attention once more. As he looked around the encampment, the issue became clear. They had no provisions, nor had they set a watch. If they didn't secure food, they would still be too weary in the morning to continue, and if they failed to be vigilant of pursuit, the likelihood of capture was high.

Nat called his mother, Dempsey, and Muta together to explain his concerns. They still had some daylight by which to gather food, and they needed to take advantage of it. Muta took on the task of collecting food and sped away to recruit help.

Nida volunteered to organize the campsite. The majority had collapsed wherever they had stopped, leaving the group spread out and exposed. Nida set out to determine where the throng would be best concealed, then enlisted assistance in relocating those who couldn't move themselves.

Nat worked as intermediary between Dempsey and Sayah to set a watch, explaining that the æglet's sharp eyes would prove valuable. After a brief discussion, they all decided that Sayah would be most effective at night and sent him to get some rest, so he would be fresh for a later watch. As sentry was a stationary duty, a number of the immobile were able and eager to help. Dempsey, Kaasi, and Kabir wheeled these to locations at the perimeter of the camp and directed the other volunteers to nap.

With preparations made for the night, Nat detected the return of smooth harmony within his being and allowed himself a moment to thank Elyon for all they had accomplished. Just as Astéri had said, the rescue had been successful, and they were well on their way back to Sanctuary.

They passed the night in relative ease, though the hooting of owls was in the distant air. Sayah and the other late-night sentries arose an hour or two past midnight to fulfill their duties. The genius of using the bed-ridden on watch was that they would need to be carried whether or not they were awake for the following day's journey.

Nat was somewhat concerned that Sayah would not get enough rest and said as much to the æglet. Sayah insisted he would be alert, and the keen brightness of the æglet's eyes convinced Nat, who went to rest as Sayah headed to his post.

The dawn greeted them with the dubious delight of a bright morning. An overcast day would have suited the swelling company better than the stark illumination that bore down through the canopy. Nonetheless, they set out as early as they could manage, pressing ever westward toward the river, whose pounding rush grew louder throughout the morning.

It wasn't yet noon when they arrived at its banks, the rough-hewn bridge across standing a good distance to their north. They hugged the sylvan foliage to reduce their visibility as they strove onward in hopes of reaching the bridge before midday and were not disappointed.

Nat snuck up the steep bank rising to meet the road and slipped down the murky lane east of the road to ensure no enemy lurked there. He perceived no threat and returned at once to urge the procession over the bridge. Sayah stationed himself at the edge of the road, ever watching the shadows while the others crossed, the relatively smooth and level plane of the bridge lending itself to the speed of the stretchers' passage.

At the far side, Nat saw the last of the Etom over, and whistled for Sayah to join them. The æglet's solitary form left a lonely impression on Nat, and the Etom hoped they'd be able to stay friends once the mission was over. It was hard to be alone, as Nat had learned in his earliest days.

With wings and tail feathers tucked and head low, Sayah loped toward the Etom at easy speed, each long talon unfurling and catching propulsive purchase in the rough grain with each step. He measured himself with increasing worth in Nat's company, especially after proving his value to the mission when he'd defended the smaller creatures outside Sakkan. It was strange to consider himself a protector of these tiny beings, rather than a predator, but it gave him wholesome pleasure to accept the role.

Nat had started on the road once he ascertained Sayah was coming, his steps swift and his mind set on catching up to the rest of the column, the head of which had already passed the northbound arc to begin climbing the grade. With a contented smile, he turned to check on Sayah again, and what he saw there made the corners of his mouth plunge into a grimace.

Sayah was more than halfway across, but beyond him, the woods seethed with sooted menace. A quaking force snapped branches and shredded leaves as it charged unchecked toward the bridge, and through the canopy a blast of blackened grit shot skyward to accompany an unnatural trumpeting.

"Sayah!" Nat shouted with dread, but he might have saved his breath.

The æglet had sensed the threat at once and increased his pace until his lanky legs were a blur beneath him. He had a good lead on whatever darkness bounded from the far-side cover, but he perceived the swiftness of his pursuer's catastrophic advance through the shivering timbers of the bridge.

An ebon and indistinct quadruped burst at last from the trees for Nat to see, its massive form now resolving in pachydermal outline once clear of obstruction. It was a great elephantine Nihúkolem, likely the same as joined the dark gallery the night the Kinsman perished, and its immense weight caused the bridge to shudder as it tramped across the crude frame.

Nat observed with some comfort that Sayah was nearly across the bridge, though he wondered how the æglet or the Etom, for that matter, would fare in a chase with such a frightful juggernaut.

It was never to be, however. The bridge quaked beneath the enormous force of the Nihúkolem's progress, and a whining creak preceded the thunderous snap of a primary lengthwise beam, the felled trunk of a tall, straight pine. The bridge slewed, pitching the Nihúkolem to the downstream edge at once while the underpinnings buried in the banks at either side of the river were uprooted.

Sayah dove in a helter-skelter dash for safety, skipping from one twisting plank to another as the bridge dissolved beneath him and he scrambled to survive its demolition. With heroic effort, he gripped the contorted rail with both claws and flung himself into the westward shore.

It was an all-out, uncontrolled lunge, and the æglet met the earth in a messy, headlong roll. He sprawled to a stop on his back and spat grit from his beak before forcing himself to slow his breathing and still his pounding heart. Dust was ingrained in his every fluffy nook and cranny, and he sat up to shake himself off while Nat rushed down the road toward him.

"Sayah! Are you alright?" the Etom asked, worry straining his face.

"I'll be fine," Sayah muttered, a little embarrassed at his friend's concern. Sure, he'd almost drowned, but he felt pretty good, all things considered.

Then a penetrating, skyward cry met his ears, and eliciting a groan of complaint.

"You have *got* to be kidding me!" the æglet squawked, whipping his head toward the sound.

Nat thought he spotted a low and level sequence of five dashes undulating over the distant tree line, and Sayah confirmed it with a cry, "Kestrels!"

The æglet swept Nat up, pinning the Etom between wing and body to race up the curving lane.

"What's a kestrel?" Nat asked, shouting to be heard over the din of Sayah's locomotion.

"They're birds, raptors like me, but smaller. Bothersome creatures," came the winded reply, "Nat, you need to tell everyone to hide."

"Where, though?" Nat asked. "We're in the open here on the road, and don't have time to get back down into the forest."

"Of course!" Sayah shouted. "The wheel ruts!"

Nat looked up the road to the furrows, still full of crimson blossoms that had sprouted in the Kinsman's wake and recognized at once Elyon's provision even in this seemingly small thing. Sayah caught up to the rest in a few moments and dropped Nat off at the end of the formation.

Nat at once began to direct them, "Hide! Quickly now! Get beneath the flowers and be still!"

Nat dashed up the line to repeat the message, which traveled faster on the lips of those in the procession than his legs might have carried it. Up ahead, he watched the Etom slip with care into the lush growth that filled the ruts, and within seconds, every last one was out of sight. Satisfied, Nat too dove under cover, and prayed in hope that the dense stalks and spreading petals would be sufficient to hide them.

Peering up through the rouge screen, Nat passed the moments awaiting the kestrels' arrival in tense reflection, *Is the cover thick enough? Will everyone stay quiet? What should we do if we are spotted?*

A disquieting though jarred Nat from dismal meditation, *Sayah! He's too big to hide here. He'll be spotted for sure!*

He crept to the edge of the stalks and parted them to glance back down the road where last he'd seen the æglet. Sayah was nowhere to be found, and Nat hoped he'd been able to get down into the woods before the kestrels spotted him.

Nat's concerns were well warranted, as the kestrels had indeed spotted the æglet when he tore down the lane to duck into the cover of the woods. Two of the kestrels peeled away from their formation in pursuit, drawing up over the forest's dark edge to seek out their quarry.

They were quite a bit smaller than a full-grown ægle, though not much so in comparison to young Sayah, and were plenty eager to perform the duty assigned them. Scarsburrow had provided great detail in the report he'd sent once goons had recovered him from his ensnarement in the roof. The Doctor had made certain to warn of the æglet that seemed to be in league with the escapees.

The pair of kestrels dropped down into the woods, determined to proceed with thorough caution. An ægle of any age might prove a dangerous foe, and they would stalk their prey with that in mind. With coordinated, fluttering hops from branch to branch, they swept through the woody tract running between the river and the cliffs. It was tedious work, but they continued in diligence, their senses alert to any movement. And from the shadows where he nestled in darkness, Sayah tracked them with bright eyes.

The three remaining raptors descended over the road, aware the æglet had not been alone, but unable to determine his companions' location. They had not seen the Etom, but followed the leads the Doctor had given them, and presumed their prey's presence on the grade once they had spotted Sayah.

The Æglet's Answer

The kestrels hovered over the uneven lane as they surveyed the area but detected no sign of the Etom they sought. Their leader narrowed her gaze, focusing on the red blooms filling the ruts in the road in hopes her ultraviolet vision would reveal their trail, but Etom were hygienic creatures, unlike many of the vermin her kind were wont to devour. A succulent vole might leave a trail of feces or prints contaminated by urine, which shone like fire in the eyes of kestrels and their kin.

No such spoor greeted the trio of raptors today, however, and after several long minutes hovering over the road, the kestrel in the lead squawked a command. From his vantage in the stalks below, Nat caught a garbled understanding, amazed again at the translational function of the Spirit speaking into his mind. His wonder was short-lived, for though he was relieved that the kestrels had abandoned their search for the Etom, they intended to redouble their efforts in finding Sayah.

Chapter Eleven
Separation

In the still aftermath of the kestrels' departure from the road, Nat vacillated between his loyalty to Sayah and his greater responsibility to the Etom in his care. He was the only one among them who knew the way to Sanctuary now they were separated from Sayah. He prayed for clarity, though he felt certain what the Spirit's answer would be. Nat's prediction proved accurate, and he wrestled with the grief of leaving his friend behind even as he began in silence to beckon the Etom onward up the hill.

They were well underway again when Nida found Nat at the rear of the formation, his face set in sad and stony determination. She recognized something was wrong and sought the cause of Nat's distress.

After a long look around, she gasped, "Nat? Where's Sayah?"

Nat's frown deepened, and he answered, "I think he hid in the forest at the bottom of the hill. There was nowhere for him to hide on the road, and he wouldn't have wanted to draw the kestrels to us."

"Oh, Nat," Nida responded with empathy. "I'm sorry."

She hadn't known the æglet long but understood that Nat regarded him a friend. It couldn't be easy for Nat, who probably would have rather gone after Sayah, if not for his duty in getting everyone else to safety. They continued along in silence, Nida's presence lending Nat some comfort while she prayed Elyon give him strength, what was left of hers if need be, to persevere under such heart-wrenching circumstance.

Without further event, they arrived at the top of the grade at sunset and turned westward into the forest, where the road became overgrown and impossible to distinguish among the thickening foliage. Darkness fell quickly in the shaded wood, and Nat called their procession to a halt once he deemed them well enough concealed.

Nat asked Nida, Dempsey, and Muta to help set up camp again, and then sought solace at a distance from the others. Nida watched him as he walked away with head down and shoulders bowed under a weight her mother's heart longed to bear for him. She recognized the thought as dangerous and reprimanded herself for it. Nat needed to learn how to handle these kinds of burdens, and she knew him to be resilient enough to grow stronger through the difficulty. She set to the task of organizing the camp and left her son to his thoughts while in silence entrusting him once more to the care of Lord Elyon.

It wasn't long before he returned from his reflection, his smile bright as he approached Nida, Dempsey, and Muta where they convened near the center of the encampment.

"You look like you're feeling better," offered Dempsey as he put an arm around Nat's shoulder.

"I do," Nat agreed, then looked to Nida. "I've decided to go back for Sayah. Tonight."

Nat's expression did not seek Nida's approval, but communicated instead his resolve. His mind was made up, and though it pained his mother to relinquish him, she did so with some appreciation for his maturity.

"What if you can't find him, son?" she asked.

"I'll look as long as I can, but I'll be back here in the morning," he replied, "no matter what I find."

Dempsey, too, saw how determined Nat was, and inquired, "Would you mind some company?"

Nat nodded, pleased at the prospect of help, and Dempsey went to arrange for a sentry to replace him during the night. There were plenty of Etom still too weak to help any other way, and Dempsey had no trouble finding a volunteer. He returned to Nat within a few minutes, and the pair discussed the plan to locate and retrieve Sayah.

"I didn't see where he went," Nat began. "Did you?"

Dempsey shook his head but put a hand to his face in thought and asked, "But I wonder if anyone else did. Have you asked around yet?"

Nat had been so focused on finding a safe place to camp for the night that he hadn't considered asking the rest of the Etom. With a little help from Nida, they gathered the whole group together.

The warm light of the campfire illuminated the willing faces of those at the front of the throng as Nat addressed them, "I'm sure you've all noticed our æglet went missing today. Did any of you happen to see where he went? It would've been when the kestrels came looking for us."

The crowd murmured in consideration until an aged voice at the back called out, "I saw 'im!"

"Who's there?" Dempsey asked, the crowd parting to reveal the source of the exclamation.

An elderly etém lay prone on a gurney, one hand pulling on the rail to raise himself up and face Dempsey, while the other held a cane.

"I'm Hezi," he grunted. "I saw that æglet feller go running down the road and disappear into the woods."

"So, I was right," Nat mused to himself, then, "Did you see anything else?"

"Nope," Hezi replied, "but I tell you that those kestrels likely have more to fear from your friend than he does from them."

Hezi brandished his cane in defiance, "I saw what he could do when we were leaving Sakkan. I tell ya, if I could, I'd go after him myself!"

Hezi pointed the cane at Nat and continued, "You've got yourself a true friend there, sonny, and those are hard to come by. I was glad to have him with us."

Nat pondered with pleasure the coarse honor Hezi bestowed on Sayah and wished the æglet were there to hear agreement sweep through the throng.

"You be sure to tell him yourself when we get back, eh, Hezi?" Nat responded. "Dempsey and I are going back for him."

Agreement turned to approval among the Etom, and they wished the pair success in the adventure. Indeed, a great many asked if they might join them or help in some way, but Nat declined out of concern for their safety. The risk was already great enough.

Though Nat and Dempsey didn't leave the gathering with much more information, the confirmation of Nat's suspicions gave them a definite starting point for their search, and they both were encouraged by the response of the others. They, too, saw Sayah as instrumental in their escape, and were grateful for his help. Nat looked forward to telling Sayah about it when they found him.

Nat and Dempsey gathered a few morsels of food from Muta and headed out right away, Nat armed with his machete and Dempsey with a club he'd modified from the same type of cane as Hezi's. Both ate in silence as they exited the forest to make their way back east, the stars twinkling in the night sky overhead.

The pair made good time, both free to exercise the abilities and conditioning they had gained in their long journey from Endego. Before long, they were trekking down the road, the indistinct darkness of the woods below looming as they neared. They kept their eyes sharp for movement in the sky and the treetops, and their ears perked for any strange noise, especially the hoot of an owl.

They sensed neither on their approach and hoped that the absence thereof didn't indicate Sayah had been captured, a thought on their minds they didn't dare let touch their lips. The forest seemed a dank, amorphous mass with only its outline in vague distinction against the spangled midnight sky. It was daunting and filled with the unknown, but they didn't hesitate to march into its murk in search of Sayah.

The dark wood closed its timber teeth around them, swallowing them in gloom. Nat and Dempsey stood still within its dark perimeter to permit their eyes to adjust. With minimal improvement to their vision, they crept forward, taking care not to stumble or to make noise. Whether or not kestrels or owls might be present, other things hunted in the dark, and they didn't want to alert any potential predators to their presence.

Nat had spent some time with Sayah and knew the æglet preferred to rest in nooks under the roots of trees. He and Dempsey sought Sayah in such inky hollows, feeling for his downy form with distaste for what they might encounter in his stead. It was dangerous work for an Etom since their small size put them near the bottom of the food chain, yet Nat and Dempsey didn't allow this reality to discourage them in their quest for the æglet.

After searching around perhaps a dozen trees, Nat perceived a yawning pit beneath the curled roots of a large tree. It would make an excellent hiding place, and thus would have appealed to an æglet fearful of discovery. Nat extended a hand back for Dempsey to grasp as he stepped down into the hole, unsure in the darkness of where his foot might find purchase.

With the timid dabs of a pointed toe, Nat stretched out over the void as he searched in vain for a place to land. Behind him, Dempsey strained to keep his grip, and soon his other hand joined the first to maintain Nat's anchor on solid ground.

"My feet," Dempsey whispered. "I'm slipping."

"Just a bit more," Nat returned, absent-minded in his focus on locating Sayah.

"No, really," Dempsey warned. "I can't keep hold of you like this. You're too far out."

The alarm in Dempsey's voice at last caught Nat's attention, and he pivoted back toward the edge. Too late. The fragile verge crumbled under the concentrated weight of both Etom, and with a hitching cry, Nat plunged into the darkness.

Dempsey hung along the fringe in breathless paralysis, having caught a scant handhold in the infirm earth as he fell. His strength failing, he extended a wary hand to either side until he found a hold more secure.

He scrambled up from the treacherous pit, then lay on his belly with elbows extended over the edge as he pitched his voice through cupped hands to call out, "Nat! Nat? Are you there?"

A dismal flow of scenarios spilled through his mind, his imagination producing myriad nightmares in which he told Nida her son was lost.

No! the staunch refusal braced Dempsey against a slide into dark oblivion of a different sort, and he called again for Nat.

"Nat! Nat! If you can hear me, answer!"

The near-imperceptible sound of movement below gave Dempsey heart, and the air around him stirred ever so slightly.

"Uuuuuuhhhh . . ." Nat groaned.

He doesn't sound very far away, Dempsey guessed. *Maybe I can reach him?*

Again, Dempsey felt the gentle caress of air in motion, and he imagined Nat hurt and struggling in unconscious pain on the floor of the pit. The vision spurred Dempsey into action, and, instinct screaming against the decision, he lowered himself down into the hole once more. He took his time finding stones embedded in the clumpy earth, and with measured patience, descended into the unknown.

He was well into his descent when he heard again Nat's moans of distress. Nat's voice didn't come from far below but echoed in a hollow manner that disoriented Dempsey. Another breezy wisp tickled the back of his neck as Dempsey continued downward, certain he'd encounter the floor at any moment. As Nat had done before at the edge of the pit, he searched the darkness with an extended foot, and discovered . . . nothing?

Dempsey growled and lifted his head skyward out of a frustration that turned at once to molten fear when he recognized the arachnid outline that hovered against the starlit background. The spider was close, and its presence explained why Dempsey had failed to find solid footing. Nat was suspended over the hole in the dangling creature's web.

Dempsey tensed and, in his fright, misplaced his foot in the wall. The foothold crumbled underfoot, and the sudden shift of Dempsey's weight was too much for the other holds. Dempsey fell back into the spider's lair, slipping between the strands that held Nat in place.

"AAAAAAAGH!!!" Dempsey cried with a voice no longer checked by the need for stealth.

The elastic boundary of a lower web caught him in its sticky embrace, and Dempsey struggled in horrified impotence as the creeping silhouette slowly descended to where Nat sprawled above. The working of the spider's spinnerets was limned in clarity against the sky, and its many jointed legs turned Nat over and over with a disturbing grace to wrap him in silk.

It must have stung him earlier, Dempsey concluded. *That's why he couldn't warn me.*

With dread, Dempsey foresaw the spider's sting in his future, and resumed his struggle against the gossamer that bound him, hanging over the void. The spider finished enveloping Nat and dragged his cocooned form to the treeward edge of the web to hang the etém there by a twisting strand.

With interest, Dempsey noted a larger form blotting out the midnight tapestry, and two golden orbs glinting down into the hole. The spider likewise attended its new guest and recoiled too late from the snip of Sayah's beak as the æglet took the creature for a snack.

With an inquisitive squawk, Sayah called down into the hole, and Dempsey responded, "Sayah! It's Dempsey! Can you see me?"

An unintelligible chirp made Dempsey long for Nat's uncanny ability to communicate with the bird, though he was confident they would figure something out. Sayah sunk his lengthy talons deep into the earth and leaned down into the pit to hook the strand Nat hung from in his beak with delicate precision.

Sayah leaned back out of the hole, and Dempsey assumed the æglet was putting Nat down, then would return for him. Seconds passed, and still Dempsey waited, shackled in the dark expanse while worry stole over him as surely as the spider had earlier.

When he could bear the wait no longer, he hollered again, "Sayah! SAYAH!!!"

Sayah's outline appeared again, his head cocked to one side as he clucked at Dempsey.

"I would *very much* like it if you would get me out of here," Dempsey petitioned in as polite a tone as he could manage.

"Please!" he barked in desperation.

With a sort of maddening nonchalance, the æglet crawled down into the hole and collected Dempsey, who dangled from Sayah's beak by one leg until he was laid beside Nat on the forest floor. Dempsey understood now what had taken Sayah so long – he'd freed Nat from his sticky shroud, and the young etém lay limp and unmoving under the effects of the spider's venom.

Sayah uttered a low, sad squawk as Dempsey moved closer to check on Nat. He placed a hand on the Nat's chest and an ear to his mouth. Through his hand he felt a shallow beating, and against his face the faint, warm moisture of Nat's breath.

Dempsey turned to Sayah and, against the hope of being understood, implored, "He's alive, but only just. We need to get him help. Can you carry him?"

159

Sayah cocked his head to one side, and then the other as Dempsey spoke, and it was apparent the æglet wished to understand. Determined not to let Nat die, Dempsey tried something else. He pointed at Nat and then in the direction of the road. Sayah nodded. Good. They may save the youngster yet.

Dempsey picked Nat up, then began walking around to place him on Sayah's back, but the æglet wouldn't allow it. Sayah shook his aquiline head and pointed under a lifted wing.

"Aha!" Dempsey exclaimed with understanding. "I see."

He lifted Nat's slack form up to Sayah's extended wing where the æglet enveloped him at once. Sayah turned around to present his back to Dempsey and nodded again. With a chuckle, Dempsey climbed the æglet, careful not to pluck any of the downy fluff from his back.

Sayah kept a close eye on Dempsey until the Etom's arms encircled his neck, then darted off without delay, pelting as quickly as he could manage up the uneven roadway. The added burden slowed him somewhat, and his wing ached from clutching Nat against his breast, but Sayah hurried onward, determined to save his friend as the first rays of day fell over the land.

With gentle pressure against either side of Sayah's neck, Dempsey guided the æglet to their encampment, where most of the Etom awaited their arrival. Sentries had passed word of Sayah's approach throughout the camp, and the remainder streamed to the gathering until all were present.

Dempsey slid down from Sayah's back and held out his arms for the æglet to release Nat to him. Nat's skin was deathly pale, and his head lolled over Dempsey's arm when the older etém caught the younger's body, puffed and swollen from the spider's poison. The crowd let out a collective gasp, and Nida ran to her son when she saw his state, a hobbling Rae close behind.

"What happened to him?" Nida asked with eyes full of tears.

Dempsey looked away as he answered, ashamed he'd let harm come to the youth, "A spider. A large one."

Sayah tweeted what seemed a question as he looked first down at Nat, and then at Dempsey.

Dempsey deduced the æglet's intent, and asked aloud for all to hear, "Do we have any kind of medicine for this? Can anyone help him?"

The glum mutterings of the throng surrounded them with despair as they looked about for a glimmer of hope in the crowd. None knew of any medicine that might help Nat, though their desire to do so was apparent.

Head bent low and eyes closed, Sayah stewed in blame, *If I had just left my hiding place sooner . . .but I fell asleep! I was just so tired from not sleeping last night. Agh!*

The æglet shrieked in frustration, and in the distance, heard a cry in answer from his nest atop the Tree.

Of course! The Tree! Miyam and Astéri can help him!

Sayah chirped at Dempsey, nodding to his lifted wing again.

"What?" Dempsey asked. "What is it Sayah?"

With his beak, Sayah pointed again under his wing, then toward the Tree in hopes Dempsey would gather meaning from his gestures.

"I think he wants to carry Nat again," Rae ventured in a forlorn voice.

"Do you think that you can find him help?" Dempsey asked, promise returning to his eyes.

Sayah guessed at Dempsey's meaning, nodding with fervency in hope the motion conveyed his urgency.

Dempsey looked to Nida and affirmed, "This æglet's already proven he's trustworthy. If he thinks he can help, then we should trust him."

Nida looked up into Sayah's anxious eyes and extended a hand to his lowered beak, caressing him with a mother's care as she charged him, "I know that you're a good friend to my son. Please look after him."

Though Sayah could not understand Nida's words, her affection conveyed a primal message to the æglet, and he gestured again to his upraised wing. Nida nodded to Dempsey, who raised Nat once more into Sayah's care. Without a sound, the æglet dashed off in direction of the ægle's cry, hopeful he would find the Tree, and with it, healing for his friend.

Chapter Twelve
The Refuge of Bower and Stream

The æglet's legs, grown strong under the duress of the past few days, carried him and his friend across the overgrown forest floor. With a renewed vigor that belied his earlier exertion in transporting Dempsey and Nat, the unfledged æglet charged through the woods with abandon in his desperation to save Nat. Nothing impeded him, and his fight through branch and vine was a credit to the ferocity of his hunter's lineage.

Sayah leapt over, wove through, and ducked under anything his sharp eyes determined impenetrable in the split-second afforded him before arriving at the obstacle in his reckless rush for Sanctuary. It wasn't far, but the swiftness of Sayah's advance put an enormous burden on his being. Instead of pain, however, the consequence of the mission filled Sayah with exhilaration, and for the first time in the æglet's heart, he felt his call to soar.

They had to be close now, he knew it. A dark thought passed over his mind like storm clouds shuttling across the sky to the blot out the sun.

What if I can't find it? Miyam said Elyon only makes Sanctuary visible to certain creatures, and why would He show it to me?

He came to a ponderous halt, and opened his wing a bit to peek at his friend before whispering, "If not to me, then certainly He'll show the way to Nat. *For* Nat."

Though winded, Sayah now spoke aloud with boldness as his love for Nat gave him courage, "Elyon, I know You don't know me, and You might not want to, but You know my friend, Nat. He's hurt. Bad. And he will probably die if I don't find Sanctuary soon. Only You can help him. Help *us*. So, please, *please*, show me the way."

In tears, he looked down at Nat again, then gasped, "I don't want my friend to die."

A reverberant whistle rebounded through the trees, chased by the arcing form of a tiny comet on collision course with Sayah. Astéri stopped just shy of the recoiling æglet with an eerie instantaneity, then floated over top his wing's edge to peer down at the gaunt Nat.

Flashing and twittering with urgency, the star set off for Sanctuary with Sayah in close pursuit. It was mere moments before they arrived at Sanctuary's gates, spread open wide before hopes of healing. Astéri and Sayah darted through into the brilliant bower, its light alone bringing some color back to Nat's cheeks as they hurried to where Miyam stood in the pool off its gentle shore. Miyam's posture in the water reminded Sayah of when he'd observed her there, her being upraised in exultation before the Tree.

Her eyes remained closed as they approached, yet she reached with wooden hands and spoke, "Lay Nat across my arms, please, Sayah."

Sayah complied at once, releasing Nat's slack, distended form into the Sprig's care before stepping back to watch on with hopeful concern. Holding Nat face up, Miyam waded into the waters until deep enough that she held Nat just over the liquid surface.

She raised her face once more into the golden light, and whispered something Sayah couldn't make out, then lowered Nat into the water. Resting on Miyam's arms, Nat floated there with only face, thumbs, and toes poking up out of the water. His body shook once, then again, to send forth ripples that quivered around Miyam's submersed arms and trunk.

Miyam stood still but for the quiet flutter of petitioning lips, her form bent to lay Nat in the water. Sayah's keen eyes perceived in the clear waters the inky streams of venom leeching from his friend. The æglet was revolted to see the murk invade the purity of the pool, even as he glanced to Nat, who convulsed a third time and vomited a gush of black filth to join the foul cloud swirling around him.

Though distressed at the defilement of the waters, Sayah was relieved when he noted in Nat's face the absence of swelling and the return of the Etom's lively blue color there. Satisfied at his friend's recovery, Sayah returned his attention the poison's black desecration of the waters in time to observe something curious. While he watched, the darkness spread through the flow, its tendrils reaching for the open shore. Sayah feared its transmission, its contamination of this place, but before his eyes, the wandering tendrils became withering wisps, then

163

along with the rest of the stain, they disappeared from the crystal flow altogether.

The æglet blinked, unsure of what he'd seen, but more interested at the moment in Nat's recuperation as Miyam turned to carry Nat to shore. Nat's eyes fluttered open to look about in confusion, the golden orbs flitting over his surroundings until at last they fell on Miyam.

"Am I in Sanctuary?" he asked in a firm and steady voice. "How did I get here?"

Miyam looked down and favored the Etom with a smile, "You were badly injured, Nat. On the brink of death. Your good friend, Sayah, brought you here. Can you stand?"

Nat nodded, and Miyam raised the arm supporting his head so the Etom could plant his feet beneath the water to stand. He straightened, smiling as though deathly harm had not befallen him, and embraced the Sprig, who at first balked at the unexpected affection, then received it with understanding at Nat's gratitude.

Astéri bobbed at Sayah's shoulder, gleaming with warm, sunny satisfaction as Nat strode from the pool to where they waited. The frightened, indifferent hatchling within Sayah sought to run from anticipated affection, his torn and lonely soul undecided on the matter of an intimacy from which he was so estranged. It took more courage for him to remain than had any prior endeavor in his experience.

"Looks like I owe you one," Nat began, genuine warmth in his tone and in his smile.

He extended open arms to the æglet, and asked, "May I?"

Sayah flinched when Nat reached for him, but nodded, perplexed at his own exposed vulnerability – that an æglet should fall before the gesture of a tiny Etom.

Nat fell against him, his short arms incapable of wrapping around Sayah's fluffy midsection though the Etom's affection enveloped the æglet from head to toe. Sayah was a stiff and awkward headland withstanding gently breaking waves of friendship in his incomprehension. Miyam came alongside Nat to join him in embracing Sayah, and beneath the rising tide, Sayah's composure broke. His lower beak quivered, and his shining eyes produced great tears that somehow escaped even though he squeezed his lids shut. Unbeknownst to the æglet, he'd fallen victim to the "group hug" formation, from which no escape was known, and without further resistance he surrendered, wrapping warm wings around his friends in response.

How long they stood there, Sayah couldn't say, nor did he much care. In many ways, this was his first true experience of family, and he savored their loving embrace, his soul incubated in its warmth to hatch anew. His care for Nat, Miyam, and even Astéri, grew within him to mark them encircled in his heart as something deeper than friends, with those he'd left on the road likewise flagged for potential inclusion therein.

The æglet looked up in wonder at the Tree, a breeze stirring the branches, which bowed under the gentle press as though arms longing to sweep them up in embrace. In his heart, Sayah ached with longing for Mother to hold him close, for she had never clutched him so. The affections of ægles were limited to proud praise and rough play, both intended to inspire their æglets to bring the family honor. While Sayah appreciated the little he'd received of each, the deficiency of warmth had left a yawning void that Nat and the others had stepped into to fill, though incompletely.

All because of the Tree, Sayah realized, turning his gaze to the water's mirror edge.

With slow deliberation, Sayah released his friends, who watched as he toddled to the shore. The water lapped in gentle waves at his feet as he leaned out to look at his reflection. The æglet staring back was yet an immature mess, but Sayah no longer harbored the hatred he'd once held for himself, aware of the development he'd undergone in recent days.

Out of the gaze reciprocated from the fluid mirror, a reminder of the Kinsman's wise and caring eyes arose to provoke a healthy desire in the æglet. The power of Sayah's sight, which exceeded even that of other ægles, was incomparable to the Kinsman's insight, and the æglet craved the same capacity, sensing profound purpose in the ability to see the unseen. Gaal's eyes had seen deep into Sayah to expose the unspoken desires there and answer them with community, friendship, and, at last, family.

He augmented his earlier thought, *No. Not just because of the Tree. But because of what the Kinsman did on it.*

Sayah raised a talon over the water, pausing again to look into his reflected countenance, in part obscured by the upraised claw.

I'll never be the same, he thought, *but that might be a good thing.*

With finality, he brought the talon down onto the mirror of his visage, stepping down into the water, his tail sweeping the water side to side gracefully as he swayed forth into the pool's depths. The water was to the middle of his breast when he dipped altogether beneath its surface, covering in full his wings and head.

He arose from the waters a changed æglet, and desired at once a drink of the springs, indulging himself in the flow before turning to face his friends. Nat and Miyam looked at him with tenderness and an excitement that Sayah sensed bubbling beneath their expressions.

Alongside his thirst, a hunger had likewise arisen, and while wading to the shore, he asked, "Miyam, do you have anything to eat?"

With a wincing, lopsided grimace, Miyam answered through gritted teeth, "I doooo . . .but I don't think you're going to like it."

"It's those white, puffy flakes, isn't it?" Sayah asked with doubt.

At the thought of the wafers, however, his stomach growled with appreciation, prompting him to ask, "That's alright. I think I'd like to try it, if you wouldn't mind, please?"

Pleased at Sayah's request, Miyam brightened and replied, "Of course! I'll be right back!"

She hurried to collect the food from her shelter where she had gathered and stored a portion earlier in the day. Before long, she returned with a stack of the irregular wafers in her arms and set one on the ground before the æglet.

Sayah thanked her and stared a long while at the strange food at his feet before asking, "What do you call this?"

"That, my friend, is rhema," Miyam answered, "and I recommend that you eat at least one portion every day. It's very satisfying, but you may find you crave more once you've tried it."

She offered one to Nat as well, and he received it with gratitude, but waited for Sayah to begin before eating. At last, the æglet snapped up the wafer in his beak, bolting it down before he could change his mind.

"What do you think?" Miyam enquired.

"It's sweet," Sayah reacted, "but not *too* sweet. I like it."

"I think they taste like honey," Nat offered.

"Huh. Honey?" Sayah wondered aloud. "I've never had honey before, but Miyam you were right. I'm already full."

"Great!" she answered with a smile.

Sayah's appetite sated, his mind turned at once to the encampment that yet awaited his return. Doubtless, news of Nat's welfare and of their own trek to Sanctuary were foremost in the escapees' minds. The rescued yet needed rescuing from vulnerability in the wilderness, if no longer from captivity in Sakkan.

Nat spoke Sayah's mind before the æglet had put thought into word, "What of the others? Where is everyone?"

"They're just inside the woods to the north. Your mother and Dempsey sent me ahead in hopes I would find you help," Sayah informed.

"Are you well enough to travel, Nat?" Miyam asked.

Nat swung his arms about and bounced up and down a few times on his toes before answering, "I've never felt better!"

The Etom looked to Sayah with a dauntless gleam in his eyes, and asked, "Shall we?"

Sayah took a deep breath as he assessed his own preparedness before replying, "Yes. Let's go get them."

The pair set out at once with quick goodbyes and hopeful promises that they'd be back soon, their forms receding into the underbrush a short distance beyond the hedge as Miyam and Astéri watched. Once Nat and Sayah had left their sight, Sprig and star leapt into action in preparation for their friends' return with several dozen guests.

Meanwhile, Nat and Sayah scurried to backtrack the æglet's trail, Nat marveling at the sign of Sayah's desperate transit to Sanctuary in the torn leaves, broken twigs, and etched branches they passed.

He really came through for me, Nat realized, casting an appreciative look at Sayah.

The Etom followed Sayah, who trusted to his earlier course to guide them back to the refugee camp, though in the end they didn't have to travel the entire leg back. In just under an hour, Sayah spotted the multicolored motion of the Etom exodus through the foliage ahead. A few seconds later, Dempsey's form burst through the screening brush, his butter-yellow face the first to register surprise at encountering them on the trail.

"Nat!" he cried, running to embrace the youngster.

Nat still in his arms, Dempsey looked at Sayah with grateful eyes, "You did it, Sayah. Thank you."

From behind Dempsey, Nida's voice rang out, "I don't believe it! Nat?!?"

Short seconds later, Nida joined Dempsey to envelop her son as awed voices sprang from the trailing procession.

Rae, too, added her arms to encircle Nat, and then Kehren, until Nat yelped from beneath the crush, "Help! Can't breathe!"

The glad quartet relinquished their hold on him, though Nida yet gripped him by the shoulders to convey with tears, "I thought you were dying, son, but here you are. Like nothing was wrong."

Nat looked back over his shoulder at Sayah to share, "Sayah saved my life. He tore through the forest to carry me to another good friend, Miyam. She did the rest."

Nida stepped aside and stood before Sayah, beckoning him to lower his head. With some hesitation, the æglet complied, and Nida looked him square in the eyes as she cupped his beak with tender hands.

"Thank you, Sayah," she wept. "Thank you for being such a good friend to my son. To all of us. Thank you."

Sayah crouched before Nida in stunned silence, for though Nida's gestures alone spoke volumes, her words had likewise acquired sudden significance.

Sayah's golden eyes grew wide as he squawked his surprise, "I can understand you!"

In concert, the crowd whipped their heads to stare at him as Nida replied in shock, "I understand *you*."

In delight, Nat guffawed, "Ha! Look at that. You can do it now, too, Sayah!"

His surprise equal to that of the others, Dempsey nevertheless recognized their need to keep moving, and so broke in to interject his concern. Nat agreed, aware in full that his explanation of the strange phenomenon would only serve to distract. If they arrived at Sanctuary before nightfall as planned, no explanation would be necessary after all.

They elected to get back underway, and soon were making fair time on the trail Sayah had broken hours before. The final leg of their journey presented some challenges, but they surmounted them together without much difficulty.

The falling sun glowed amber to cast long, eastward shadows when they approached the Sanctuary hedge. The verdant wall stayed in place as they neared, and Nat wondered if it might not open to them. He placed his hand against the leafy obstacle and reached for insight from the Spirit. As he did, the wall fell away to either side to reveal the Tree, luminous as it presided over the spring. A triumphant grin spread across Nat's face, and he turned around to wave the others onward as he led them into Sanctuary.

Chapter Thirteen
. . .and the Branches

Sanctuary opened before the weary refugees of Sakkan, their haggard forms spilling into the sacred bower to receive aid and succor from Miyam. At once, Nat and Sayah recognized some developing peculiarities among the Etom and wondered at their significance.

The first such peculiarity was the initial reaction of many to Miyam herself. Nearly every Etom balked when they met the Sprig, though most overcame their shock at once when she served them, supplying them with food, drink and a place to rest. Some, however, continued to eye her with suspicion, and were careful in receiving refreshment from her hands.

Even among those who received her offerings with joy, a great many cared neither for the rhema nor the water Miyam brought them from the spring. Sayah recalled his aversion as he watched the Etom set the provisions aside to partake of what they had carried in from outside Sanctuary. The suspicious Etom threw Miyam's food and drink to the ground with contempt, and in bitterness snuck bites of food they kept concealed.

It was also these, the hostile ones, who seemed ill at ease in Sanctuary, their eyes roving along the protective hedge that had closed behind them in search of some escape. The majority of the Etom took respite among the tranquil security of the bower while these others held themselves apart in distrust. After some time, their disquiet grew, and they spread out along the hedge to look for an exit.

Nat and Sayah watched them, incredulous at their wariness in the secure and peaceful confines of Sanctuary. They both found it difficult to understand the apparent discomfort of these few, who gathered in a sheltered, conspiratorial knot after an unsuccessful search.

Dempsey came alongside them, pointing with an open hand at the huddle to postulate, "No doubt Iver's at the center of this."

Nida joined them to agree, "I wouldn't be surprised. He was the first to complain after we left Sakkan and hasn't stopped since."

Nat had been so focused on their escape and the journey to Sanctuary, he hadn't given much consideration to camp morale. Notwithstanding, it seemed odd that anyone might gripe after being freed from the perverse grasp of Doctor Scarsburrow.

"What do we know about him?" Nat asked, curious if Iver's background might deepen his understanding of the strange etém.

"We don't know much of anything about the Etom we broke out of Sakkan," Dempsey explained. "The Nihúkolem delivered them to Scarsburrow from all over the Empire. Most of them didn't know each other before they were captured, though there are a few exceptions, and we've confirmed many of them are Eben'kayah from other villages."

"What do you make of Iver, mom?" Nat asked.

Nida collected her thoughts, then responded, "I doubt he's an Eben'kayah. Even among the those we've met from other villages, we share common values, and our faith in Lord Elyon."

She shook her head before continuing, "It wouldn't surprise me if Iver got himself into an altogether different kind of trouble with the Empire. Something criminal, maybe violent."

Nat nodded in quiet agreement as he watched the cluster of dissidents. A solitary face, the deep orange of turning leaves, arose from the far side of the huddle to look their way.

Dempsey, too, noticed the Etom watching them, and muttered to Nat, "That'd be Iver there."

Iver recognized their conference was under surveillance, his visage growing pinched, and eyes narrowing before he submerged again into the scrum. With sudden urgency, the cluster of Etom broke apart, its members strolling away in affected nonchalance, though the sullen, sidelong glances sent their way belied it. Nat waved at several as he noticed the looks, his sunny smile winning him no new friends among them.

"What do you think we should do?" Nat asked aloud.

His tone dry and serious, Sayah offered, "I *could* eat them."

The trio of Etom failed to contain an outburst of laughter, and Nat waggled a finger as he chuckled, "Sayah! What did I tell you about your jokes?"

Sayah's eyes twinkled with mischief, and he sent a wink his friend's way along with his answer, "It must be that you thought them funny, because you're laughing now."

The levity lightened the serious mood, and they agreed just to keep an eye on the unhappy Etom from time to time. It was getting late, and Nat hadn't yet the opportunity to share with Company Jasper his most important discovery since their separation in Sakkan. The majority of their charges now resting in comfort under the security of the bower, Nat led his mother, Dempsey and Sayah to Miyam's shelter, collecting Rae, Kehren, and Tram along the way. It was finally time to tell them of the Kinsman's fate.

As Nat had hoped, he found Miyam and Astéri near the thatched shelter, and asked Miyam if they might gather there to explain what had become of the Kinsman, and how Sanctuary had come into existence. Miyam was all too happy to comply, and the soft grass around her home providing adequate seating as they gathered in a circle for Nat to tell the tale.

From the beginning, Nat's tale was intertwined with his life, and there was no shortage of excited interjections as he told of Astéri's presence at his birth and the visions the star had shown him throughout. As he recounted the final vision of the Kinsman, however, all fell silent with interest and solemnity. Nat spared no detail of Gaal's suffering, and his audience winced in pain while he spoke. The story would have been too difficult for Nat to tell, but for the hope of its final chapter.

As Nat completed the account, he connected the first of his visions, that of the Tree Ha Datovara, with the last, explaining that the Tree made desolate in the first transgression of Man was the same made abundant in the affliction of the Kinsman.

He pointed to the Tree, its trunk standing at the center of Sanctuary and concluded, "It was this Tree, the Kinsman's Tree, that I found after leaving you all in Sakkan. Or rather that the Tree called me here."

With the memory, tears welled in Nat's eyes as he told them, "I fell into the waters, and emerged a different Etom. Free of the Stain that had at last shown itself on my skin."

He raised his hand to touch one cheek, then the other, "Here. And here. Completely gone, as you can see. And that's not all. You've seen, or heard, rather, what Sayah and I can do. How is it that an æglet and an Etom can talk to each other? And I believe we've only scratched the surface."

"Let me see if I understand," Dempsey inserted. "You're telling us that you didn't find the Kinsman, but that this, this Tree that He left us can take away the Stain?"

"Yes," Nat affirmed. "Yes. Exactly."

Nida stood at once and asked, "Well, what are we waiting for? We've completed the mission given us before fleeing Endego."

She pointed to the pool and addressed the gathered company, "Here are the waters! What's to keep us from washing in them?"

Dempsey came up behind Nida to grip her shoulders and offer his support, "I, for one, am ready."

Rae, Kehren, and Tram nodded in agreement. Kehren stood to help Rae to her feet then took her place beside Tram's gurney while Dempsey gripped the other side, and the party made their way down to the pool. Unbeknownst to them, a great many Etom eyes followed them across the clearing as several of the escapees watched on.

When their small procession arrived at the edge of the pool, almost everyone stopped along the shore. Everyone except Nida, that is. The etma didn't even break stride, but waded with forceful steps out into water, stopping only when the water had reached her waist. Nat followed her in, then Dempsey, the younger etém arriving at his mother's side as she stared at the Stains that disfigured the backs of her upraised hands. For any self-aware creature, the black stamp of the Stain signaled their eventual death, a manifestation of the disheartening apparition that loomed over them all.

Nida rubbed the back of one hand with the thumb of the other while she mused, "What can wash away my Stain? Nothing . . . nothing."

She became aware that Dempsey and Nat watched her with concern, and tittered, "I'm sorry. I know it's strange, but I feel I must say goodbye. It has become such a part of me that I almost don't know where I stop, and it begins. It's difficult to believe I'll be rid of it at last."

Without further delay, Nida pushed her splayed fingers beneath the surface to submerge her hands. The trio watched with unblinking eyes for any change to the Stain on her hands, but still the inky blemishes remained. After several long moments waiting, Nida retracted her hands in frustration to look them over. No change.

"Nat, what's going on here?" Nida asked, her brow wrinkled in consternation.

She had never known her son to be dishonest and had therefore believed every word of his story this evening.

Now, however, she wondered aloud if Nat might not have been mistaken somehow, "Son, are you certain these waters can remove the Stain?"

The question had already occurred to Nat, and he had fallen into curious thought the moment his mother had removed her still-tainted hands from the water. In his perplexity, he had yet to discover an answer when Nida had spoken, but the interruption was sufficient distraction to cause him to lose his train of thought. In place of his concentration, a rhythmic thrum arose, prompting Nat to seek a response of the Spirit instead, which came in form of images the instant he asked. Images of his collapse into a puddle, and of Sayah's immersion this morning.

"I have it!" he exclaimed. "You have to get all the way in. Your whole self."

Nida was dubious of his direction, but submitted to it nevertheless. She waded a bit deeper, then dunked her entire body under the water, counting to three before arising. She shook the water from her face and her lengthening zalzal with a twist of her head, then wiped the droplets from her eyes to look again at her hands.

Clean. Absolutely clean. The pink skin, once marred by darkness, stood now untouched on the backs of her hands, one of which flew to cover her mouth while she stared at the other in amazement.

"Nat," she whispered. "It's gone. All gone."

Happily, she flipped her hands around to show them to Nat and Dempsey, the latter stunned into silence as the former ran to his mother. Nida turned her hands over, and Nat caressed them with tenderness, then gripped them in his own to splash up and down with her in celebration. Nearby, Dempsey pressed his lips together in determination, then plunged into the water, stiff and straight as a felled tree.

Arising from the flow, the dripping Dempsey called out to Nat and Nida, "Are they gone? Are they gone?"

He cocked his yellow head to present an ear, behind which had resided ugly blotches on either side. But no more.

Nat came close to verify their absence, and in his excitement, hollered with joy into Dempsey's ear, "They're gone, Dempsey! Gone!"

Dempsey recoiled with pain at the shout even as he joined Nat and Nida in celebration. From the water, the three of them waved the others in off the shore. The instant Nida had pronounced herself clean of the Stain, Tram had been trying his best to reach them. Though encumbered by disability, he had clambered headfirst down from the stretcher, his crippled legs striking the earth with a painful thud.

"Tram!" Kehren cried when the sound of his body hitting the ground drew her attention away from those in the water.

"Dad!" Rae shouted, echoing her mother's concern as she and her mother rushed to where Tram clawed with single-minded purpose toward the pool's lapping edge.

"Tram, you're going to hurt yourself!" Kehren warned, but her husband inched forward as if he hadn't heard.

With a prolonged exhale, Kehren arrived at the exasperated realization that nothing she said would dissuade him from the waters. Instead, she gripped Tram beneath an armpit, her daughter followed suit on the other side to carry him with feet dragging awkward ruts in the dirt.

The three already in the water noticed their efforts and came to assist. Before long, Tram more or less floated on his back between them all, his eyes skyward through the canopy as he grunted with urgency.

"Are you ready, Tram?" Dempsey asked.

A furtive nod was Tram's response, and Dempsey nodded to the others before counting down from three to dunk him together, pushing his stiff and useless legs under until the water covered every part of him.

Tram arched his back suddenly, prompting the others to raise him from the waters out of concern. Before they were able, Tram emerged under his own strength, whooping with joy at the restoration of his health and his freedom from the Stain. By now, a small crowd had collected along the edge of the pool to see what they were doing.

Awestruck, one of the spectators, Hezi, pointed at Tram with his cane and hollered to the others gathered, "I know him! He couldn't even talk, let alone walk this morning, but now . . .just look at him!"

The crowd grew, and from it came questions about what had just occurred. Nida pressed a gentle hand against Nat's back to compel him forward, but he turned around instead.

"What is it, Mom?" he asked.

"I think you should talk to them, Nat. Don't you?" she replied.

"What do I say?" he inquired, uncertain.

"I think you'll know what to say," Nida encouraged, "Tell them your story. The short version."

"Do you really think they want to hear it?" Nat asked.

"I think this is something that's meant to be shared, if you take my meaning," she replied, then turned him by the shoulders to face the crowd. "Go! You can do this."

Nat complied, raising a hand to hail the throng as he approached them, his mother watching with pride as he waded from the waters. Nida was correct. Nat knew what to say to the crowd, but only because he began praying with fervency since his first step toward the audience. At what seemed a whim, he stooped to draw from the spring with cupped hands, drinking deep before moving on.

As he stepped onto the shore, the Spirit whispered to him the first words, which now he spoke aloud, "How many of you are Eben'kayah?"

Hands shot up over the heads of those assembled, joined by a smattering throughout of "I am!" "Me too!" and "Same here!" Nat nodded with satisfaction. The answers confirmed his suspicion that most in the crowd were Eben'kayah and had served a second purpose in reminding these of their identity.

Their proclamation was a statement of faith, and provided a starting point from which he began, "It's good that you know who you are. It's good for me to know as well, since it means that you also seek the Kinsman. And I want *you* to know something, too – I have seen Him."

A collective gasp shuddered through the crowd to be replaced almost at once with conflicted murmurs. With peripheral awareness, Nat noticed Iver and his group watching from a distance, then returned his full attention to the throng before him.

He allowed the crowd a moment to react before continuing, "I realize it's hard to believe. I can hardly believe it myself, but here we are, and by the time I'm finished, you'll see that may be proof enough to convince you what I'm saying is true."

It was though a spring welled up within Nat as words poured forth from him, "Since birth, my life has been marked by visitation from the Malakím, one Malakím in particular, in fact. This messenger of Elyon, Astéri, has shown me much over the years: the planting of the Tree Ha Kayim and the Tree Ha Datovara, the moment of our separation from the Tree Ha Kayim and of the Tree Ha Datovara's ruin, and, most importantly, the fate of Kinsman.

"It may surprise you to know that this Tree under which we take our shelter tonight *is* the Tree Ha Datovara, revived at great cost to Elyon and to His Son, the Kinsman. Yes, His Son, and worthy of that title in every way."

Never had Nat spoken with such maturity, and though it frightened him somewhat, he nevertheless surrendered and continued, "When Astéri first showed me the Kinsman, whose name is Gaal, He rode in a cage as prisoner of the Nihúkolem's minions, Men who serve the Empire of Chōl. I didn't know what to make of the Kinsman as a captive, but then He looked at me, and when He saw me, I knew – He was captive only to the will of Elyon, a will He shared with His Father."

Without forethought, Nat drew forth snippets of the Eben'kayah's prophecies to proclaim, "Indeed, it was the will of His Father to crush Him, and crushed He was under the hands of Men, as I witnessed that dark night. We stand now on ground soaked in the Kinsman's blood, His grief poured out so the will of Elyon would prosper. And what was that will? That we might all be free of our guilty Stain."

"He was crushed for *our* iniquities, upon Him was the chastisement that brought us peace, and by His stripes we are healed. From what I've heard, many of you saw me at death's door this morning, and many of you know my friend, Tram, who could neither speak nor walk until minutes ago. Look now! We are healed, but even that is not the greatest gift of the Kinsman.

"After afflicting the Kinsman to the point of death, the Nihúkolem ordered Gaal's execution, and to this once-barren Tree, they nailed His hands and feet. As He hung here, suspended between life and death, He begged His Father to forgive His executioners. He poured out His soul to death and was numbered with the transgressors. Since the Sunder, we have each carried the Stain, and every one of us has gone astray, turning to his own way.

"The Lord Elyon has laid on Him the iniquity of us all, and our Stain has now passed away along with the Kinsman, who perished on the lifeless husk of the Tree Ha Datovara. But that was not the end of Him. After the Nihúkolem and their lackeys departed, leaving Gaal to hang on the Tree as an example to their enemies, something unbelievable happened – before our eyes, the Kinsman returned to life."

A fresh spate of speculation emanated from the crowd, and one unseen listener exclaimed, "Impossible!"

Nat waited for them to quiet, then spoke in a low voice, "You can believe what you will, but how else do you explain this place? Look at the Tree! It returned to life with the Kinsman, as did the surrounding land. Is it normal for a stream to spring from a Tree? Look at me, and Tram! I was almost dead, and he was crippled by Scarsburrow's experiments. Yet here I stand, alive, and he's standing. Period. I'll show you one more thing, and if you still need more proof, then you won't believe no matter what you see."

He called his mother and Dempsey to him and they plodded to shore, where they took their places behind Nat as he began again, "Does anyone here remember where my Mother's Stains were? Or Dempsey's?"

Kaasi stepped forward from the crowd to offer, "Dempsey's are behind his ears. I noticed them when we took down the guards outside the clinic."

An elderly etma Nat didn't know called in a tremulous voice, "Nida's Stains are on her hands. The backs of them, if memory serves."

Nat stood aside, and nodded to Dempsey and his mother, who felt a bit silly as they stepped forward to present themselves to the assembly. Dempsey turned his head to either side to reveal the unblemished, yellow skin behind his ears while Nida held her hands up, flipping them back and forth to show both sides were clean.

Appreciative "oohs" and "aahs" sounded throughout the crowd, its members leaning forward in collective interest to observe the phenomenon. It was a matter of seconds before they had their first volunteer.

Hezi limped forward on his cane, asking in a loud voice, "I believe ya. What does a fella need to do to get rid of this?"

Hezi lifted the pant leg covering his lame appendage to reveal a thick vein of ebony twisting around the limb like a constrictor squeezing the life from it. It wouldn't be long before the Stain took its use altogether, the Blight encrusting it any day.

Given what he knew about the power of the Tree, Nat instructed with confidence, "All you have to do is get in the water. *All* the way in."

"Do you mind holding this for me?" Hezi asked, extending his cane to Dempsey. "I guess I won't be needing it anymore."

Dempsey took the cane gladly, and agreed, "I believe you're right, Hezi. Will you need any help into the water?

"I think I can manage there, youngster," Hezi replied with a sly wink.

The elderly etém stepped down into the water, limping his way out to a reasonable depth with the vast majority of the crowd on his heels. Nat was overwhelmed at the response but was happy to see so many longing for freedom from the Stain.

With puzzlement, Nat noted that almost all who did not enter the water had identified themselves as Eben'kayah earlier. With looks of disappointment, these Etom meandered toward Iver's group to loiter near the hedge in unhappy community. Nat continued to watch the new converts to Iver's faction as they gestured toward the pool in apparent explanation. Iver nodded and smiled, a smug sneer in reaction to those let down in the aftermath of Nat's address that said, "Well, what did you expect, you fools?"

Iver narrowing eyes caught Nat watching again, and this time he lifted his chin in salute, spreading his hands, palms up, over his new recruits as though to taunt Nat with them. At first, Nat thought it strange for Iver to provoke him with the fact that he and his skeptical few were proud to miss out on something so amazing. Nat's sentiment turned at once to sorrow, however, as he realized that in their proud cynicism, Iver's sect might never enjoy freedom from the life-stealing Stain. A wry smile on his face, Nat turned sad, concerned eyes on Iver, and waved to the bitter, orange etém.

The care on Nat's face must have surprised Iver, because his expression shifted for an instant to shocked confusion before devolving into an angry scowl. Iver broke eye contact with Nat and began shouting at the others, waving them together in assembly around his agitated form. Nat had seen enough for the moment, and returned his attention to the splashing, happy throng in the pool behind him.

Bounding Nat's way was a happy sight he'd not seen in while, and he braced himself in anticipation of Rae's affectionate tackle. Rae collided with Nat in her typical fashion, wrapping eager arms around her best friend, whose eyes bulged as he struggled for breath in her embrace.

"I've wanted so badly to hug you like this!" Rae squealed.

It struck Nat at last that Rae was moving as if uninjured. As if healed and whole.

"Rae . . .you're not . . .hurt . . .anymore," he wheezed.

Rae released him from her pale pink coils, and slapped him on the back as she answered, "Of course not, silly! What? Did you think I would miss out on this chance? After all we've been through to get here?"

"That would have been pretty stupid," he admitted.

"So now you're calling me stupid?" Rae asked, her eyes widening with mock indignation.

"No," Nat returned, defending himself with upraised arms. "No!"

Rae clutched his arm with fond attachment and rested her head against his shoulder as she relented, "Nat, I'm just pulling your leg."

With an impish grin and a waggle of her eyebrows, she teased him, "Or your *arm*."

Nat laughed, "Now, that *joke* was stupid."

Rae squinched her eyes in happy agreement, then her smile grew gentle as she cajoled him, "That was a pretty great speech you gave. I couldn't hear all of it, but what I could was . . .was . . .impressive."

The uninhibited Rae blushed, her cheeks turning a rosy red before she turned away from Nat in a moment of uncharacteristic shyness. Nat cocked his head with confused naïveté, uncertain at Rae's behavior.

"Rae, are you alright?" he asked, oblivious.

Rae grimaced, then collected herself to answer, "Yes, Nat. I'm fine."

The crimson flush had receded from her face, but she held herself in atypical reserve while the clueless Nat accepted her answer without question.

She sighed, and proposed, "What do you say we go and see how all the others are doing?"

"Sure!" he replied at once, his broad smile beaming. "But can we bring my friends? I've been *dying* for you to meet them."

Reminded of the morning's peril, he added, "No pun intended."

"Too soon, Nat. Too soon," Rae rebuked with counterfeit dismay. "But, yeah! Let's bring your friends."

Miyam, Sayah, and Astéri had returned to Miyam's shelter once the crowd had begun to gather on the shore, certain their presence would be a distraction. Nat and Rae found Miyam and Sayah in restful repose while Astéri bobbled nearby, humming a quiet, mellow tune and glowing a soft blue. They were enjoying the relative quiet that came with distance from the others, though a shared excitement percolated beneath their exteriors over the many entering into the new life the Kinsman had promised.

"Hello!" Nat called, prompting æglet and Sprig to swivel their heads toward him in a lazy arc.

"Oh, hey!" Miyam replied, arising as she saw Nat's guest.

Sayah, too, stood, and bowed his head in respect at Rae's arrival while Astéri floated to their side.

"I would like to introduce you to my very best friend in the world, Rae," Nat proclaimed.

Rae offered a pink hand in greeting, which Miyam clasped between her leafy ones with care as she spoke, "It's very nice to meet you, Rae. My name is Miyam. Welcome to Sanctuary."

"Thank you," Rae replied, then extended a less-certain hand toward Sayah.

The æglet stared down at Rae's hand, and offered a fluffy wingtip in response before venturing, "Nice to meet you, Rae. Again. But for the first time, now that we can understand each other."

Rae accepted Sayah's stunted wing and was reminded of all the æglet had done for the Etom since they had left Sakkan, "It's nice to meet you, too, Sayah. Again, and for the first time. Thank you for all your help with our escape. I don't believe we would have made it here if not for you."

Rae looked over at Nat, the memory of his limp and deathly form appearing in her mind before she returned her tear-stained gaze back to Sayah continue, "And Nat would probably have died. Thank you."

With bashful reluctance, Sayah accepted her gratitude, "You-you're welcome."

Astéri flitted over to Rae with a chime, shining a warm green.

Nat told Rae, "That's Astéri. He already knows you from Endego, but you probably can't understand him. He takes some getting used to."

"What do you mean, Nat?" Rae asked, confused. "He said 'hello,' and that his name is Astéri Ha'vi . . . Ha'vi . . . what was it again, Astéri?"

Astéri Ha'vimminkhulud, the star responded with a merry tinkle and variegated splash of sparks as he spun. *So nice to be able to converse with someone right off. You may call me Astéri, like Nat said.*

Nat, mystified at Rae's instant comprehension, nonetheless addressed the group, "We were hoping you might come down with us to the water. We thought you might like to see how many have decided to join us in the Vine today. Almost all the Etom we rescued from Sakkan!"

"The Vine?" Rae asked, with a wrinkle of her nose. "What is that?"

"Maybe we can explain it to everyone at once?" Miyam interjected as Nat prepared a response. "I'm sure others will be curious, and they need training in the Way as well."

"How does that sound, Rae?" Nat asked. "Can you wait a minute for an answer?"

"Okaaaaay," Rae said, a bit disappointed. "I *guess* I can wait, but let's go now, then!"

Nat and the others complied with good humor, the cheerful, eclectic band making its way down to the water's edge, where many of the drenched Etom gathered, shivering. Miyam's nurturing heart sympathized with the cold Etom, and she asked Sayah to help them dry off while she, Nat, and Rae set about making a fire some ways from the shore.

Sayah stepped forward and spread his lengthy wings before the dripping Etom, hollering, "Hold still! I'm going to dry you off!"

Most of the wet Etom had winced protectively when Sayah stepped forward, bracing themselves and turning their heads away. Their instinctive reaction was beneficial when the æglet began flapping his wings together in a frenzy to stir up a brisk wind and dry the Etom off. It was chilly, but the Etom set their minds on the crackling promise of the fire blazing behind Sayah while enduring the stiff gusts. The Etom were at worst damp when a winded Sayah ceased to beat the air a few minutes later, and clustered around the cheery fire to warm themselves.

Satisfied to see everyone present who had been in the pool, Nat began to speak, "I know today has been strange, and it may become stranger still. But first, I want to introduce you to a friend of mine, and a friend of the Tree."

Miyam shuffled up to Nat's side and offered a quick wave to the crowd before he continued, "This is Miyam, and she is a Sprig, the first being I encountered here after I, too, bathed in these waters. She has helped me a lot, and I think she can help you, too. Please hear her out."

"I will try to keep this short," Miyam began. "I know it's getting late, and that this day has been eventful. What I would like to explain is how the Kinsman has created something new and restored something ancient and broken in His work upon this Tree.

"As you can see, the Kinsman has revived the Tree Ha Datovara, which stands before you, full of life and power. Inasmuch as the Stain bent and twisted the Tree and this world by the curse it carries, His blood has straightened and beautified the Tree by the Spirit it carries. As for the restoration of the world, that remains to be seen, and rests in large part on your decisions.

"Invisible to natural eyes is the harmonious connection He has also restored between those who have accepted His gift of life. This connection is akin to that which all creatures possessed before the Sunder, before Nature was separated from the presence and the rule of Lord Elyon.

"This connection is called the Vine, and each of you is as a branch upon its length, empowered by the Spirit and made fruitful as you abide in Him. And if you continue to abide in the Spirit and bear fruit, then nothing can separate you from Him. No matter where you go in this world, your connection to the Vine will remain.

"Your friend, Nat, has learned much of this already, and it was by his persistence in the Vine that he successfully guided you from Sakkan. But now I will share something new, even to him – something I've only hinted at before. The Vine unites us to the Tree, of that there is no doubt, but also unites us *in* the Tree, and the restoration of our world depends on us continuing in unity, in truth, and in love.

"And here is yet another mystery – that the Kinsman known as Gaal proclaimed Himself Elyon's Son, one in nature with the Creator, and present with Elyon in shared, brilliant sovereignty, their glory, before the creation of the world. It was by the Kinsman that Elyon created everything, the Son as rays shining forth from the bright cloud of the Creator's glory into the void to bring order to it. It is this oneness shared between Father, Son, and Spirit that Gaal called us to aspire to when He yet walked these lands, and this unity that will return life to our world."

The crowd around Miyam remained still and quiet during her sermon, their attention affixed to her words. Regardless of their interest, many now yawned, exhausted from the day, and the Sprig recognized just how tired they must be. With the realization, Miyam decided to bring her speech to an end. She had said enough, and now the Etom needed rest.

"Well, it looks like you all are ready for some sleep," she concluded. "Why don't we pick this up again later?"

Tired murmurs of agreement from the crowd preceded its dissolution, the various, weary Etom heading to where they had set camp earlier. Having warmed themselves before the fire, the Etom found the temperate bower was warm and pleasant enough to sleep in without additional shelter. All throughout the clearing, Etom lay down to happy, contented sleep in the security of Sanctuary.

Along the hedge wall, however, Iver and his contrary band still roved, seeking an exit in peaky restlessness. Nat, Nida, and their friends convened around Miyam's shelter to watch Iver and his group's efforts in disbelief.

Nida spoke with quiet clarity, "I don't know why anyone would want to leave this place. I have never experienced such peace."

"Neither have I," Dempsey agreed, "but maybe Iver and his ilk aren't looking for peace. Some folks have another end in mind."

"They won't be permitted to harm anyone here, even themselves," Miyam asserted. "They'll wear themselves out in time."

She turned her gaze to the Etom and æglet gathered near her home, and suggested, "You all should get some rest as well. You will be safe. Will the grass here be soft enough for you to sleep?"

Her guests nodded agreement, their yawns likewise affirming their accordance. It wasn't long before the small and gentle snores of the Etom surrounded Miyam where she lay in her thatched abode. The Sprig smiled with relaxed confidence that the Spirit's plan was proceeding with success and fell asleep at once.

Chapter Fourteen

The Harvest of Many

Morning wasn't long in arriving, the nocturnal glow of the bower transitioning to diurnal brilliance to signal the day had begun. Nat stirred beneath the intense light, his trembling eyelids awash in it as his upturned face also grew warmer. With a flutter, his eyes flew open, the golden orbs sparkling in dazzling reflection of the Sanctuary sun, and he lay still under the boughs, taking stock of the morning.

The Tree swayed in soft counterpoint to a gentle breeze, and Nat thought again how vital it seemed, as if it might move of its own accord. Or perhaps it moved under direction of the wind . . .but there was nothing abnormal about that, was there?

He noticed something that shook him from introspection, perhaps something he just hadn't noticed before. From the Tree's extended branches hung a number of fruit, each akin to an acorn in form, and none much larger than a walnut. None save one, which dangled from a precarious and twisting stem near the end of a lengthy branch, its amplitude great in the stir of the wind.

Curious, Nat stood to rouse the others, only to find the area deserted and himself alone. He looked around the bower for them and located no one except Iver and his skeptics strewn along the hedge wall, where they had at last succumbed to sleep the night before.

"Wha—?" the question froze on his tongue, interrupted by a soft thud nearby.

Nat tracked the sound to a tumbling form that soon came to a halt not far from where he stood. After a moment, he recognized Hezi as the figure that had flopped to a stop, and with quick steps went to investigate. Before he could get to the elderly etém, Nat heard another of the strange thumps, and spun in time to spy another Etom in somersault. Then another. And another.

Looking up, Nat observed a downpour of the fruit he'd seen hanging from the Tree and watched on in bemused amazement as even now Dempsey spilled from one of the nutty chrysalises when it struck the ground. It was a hail of Etom! Nat saw his mother bounce along the turf at a distance, and Rae closer by. None appeared hurt in the fall, and Nat recalled with familiarity his own plunging descent. With a gasp of revelation, Nat spun to where he'd earlier spotted the largest of the fruit.

"Sayah!" he shouted, just in time to witness the fall of his encapsulated friend.

The impact forced a surprised squawk from the æglet, who sprung up once in downy revolution, then lay spread-ægle on the grassy forest floor.

The fallen fruit stood in wonder after various degrees of reorientation with terra firma, and Nat couldn't help but snort laughter as he wondered if he had shared the dizzied expression common on the Etom faces. Sayah was an altogether different matter, his æglet form unconstrained to the diminutive economy of Etom-kind. He struggled first to right himself, and succeeding, strode toward Nat with awkward, cross-legged steps.

After almost stumbling at several points, the æglet at last managed to straighten his gait to walk a proper path to Nat. Sayah reached Nat just before Rae, Dempsey, and Nida did, a number of the other Etom clustering about him to form a loose ring.

"What was that all about?" Dempsey asked with bald curiosity.

"Vine, branches, fruit?" Nat shrugged. "Who knows?"

Everyone present was grateful that Miyam was on hand, and she stepped in to provide a brief, if not puzzling explanation, "If you are grafted into the Vine, you are a new creation. The old has passed away, and look! The new has come."

The blank stares that greeted her statement clued Miyam into the amassing confusion among her audience, and so she changed tactics, "You are all familiar with the cocoons of butterflies, right?"

Murmurs of agreement encouraged Miyam to continue, "Just as a larva enters a cocoon for a time to emerge a butterfly, each of you in resting in the Vine for the first time have likewise taken to a chrysalis of sorts to emerge a new creature.

"The only outward sign of your transformation was the removal of the Stain, but the internal reorganization of your being has begun. And that is where the real work will take place as you abide in the Vine, growing and maturing in the nurture of the Spirit."

"Miyam, does that mean that everyone here can learn Resonance?" Nat inquired.

"Yes, it does, Nat," she answered. "However, Resonance is a gift that may manifest in two distinct ways, the first of which you are familiar with. This first form of Resonance is a gift to all in the Vine to assist each one in discerning the will of the Spirit and in detecting general spiritual threats.

"The other . . .well, that's a bit more complicated, and I'd only feel comfortable discussing it after these here have grasped general practice in the first mode of Resonance. Also, the second mode is only granted to those the Spirit wills. Not everyone in the Vine may receive this gift of, shall we say, Enhanced Resonance?"

Though everyone but Nat was lost in the discussion, what Miyam said piqued Nat's interest further, and he asked, "How can I find out if I have it?"

"Astéri and I will do our best to train you and your friends, but you would do well not to focus too much on acquiring the *gifts* of the Spirit," Miyam warned. "Instead, your focus should instead be on bearing the *fruit* of the Spirit, which are love, joy, peace, patience, kindness, goodness, faithfulness, gentleness, and self-control. The gifts of the Spirit are for the good of the Vine, and you will only know how best to use your gifts as you first bear the fruit of the Spirit."

"Wait," Nat interjected, "Now you've lost me as well. Did you say there are more gifts than Resonance? And now fruits?"

"Yes, and I can see that I've said a bit too much," Miyam countered. "It's overwhelming, I know, and you already have some knowledge of the Spirit, Nat."

She raised an upturned palm to point at the crowd behind him, "Just imagine how confused these folks behind you are. Maybe we should just start with Resonance?"

Nat nodded, a tad disappointed, but understanding that the others needed training as well. Besides, it *was* overwhelming as Miyam had said, and perhaps he'd learn something new about the Spirit in the process.

Most of their day was spent in reviewing each one's moment of immersion in the spring waters, and in meditation on what they knew of Kinsman Gaal and Lord Elyon. The exercise served to familiarize the Etom with the divine nature of Father and Son, so they might recognize their essence when the Spirit asserted Himself through the Vine.

It was a challenging process at first, the overall size of the group an impediment to instruction, but after Miyam's brief, general explanation of the drill, followed by several failed attempts as a collective, they decided to split up. Nat would take half and Miyam half, then would devote individual attention to each Etom in hopes of improving results.

Miyam and her bunch began moving off as Nat broadcast to his pupils, "Alright! Everyone keep working at it until I come around to you. I'll spend time with each of you before we're done today, and the better you're prepared for me, the more progress you'll make."

Nat looked over his first student, Hezi, who smiled with neither guile nor many teeth as Nat began, "Well, Hezi, are you ready?"

The elderly etém replied with an enthusiasm that belied his age, snapping off a smart salute as he answered, "Sir! Yes, sir!"

Nat chuckled, and instructed, "First, you need to find that memory of when you first went under the water to remove the Stain. In that moment, you connected to the Vine by the Spirit, and should recall the Spirit's presence, His voice."

"Ah, yes," Hezi smiled ever broader with eyes closed, "I remember. How could I forget? I'd been waiting my whole life for it."

"Good," Nat said, "Focus on that memory, and on what you experienced. The Spirit was there, and He spoke to you. Remember what it's like to be with Him, to hear Him."

"I think I have it," Hezi whispered.

"Ok, now the goal is to stay in harmony with the Spirit," Nat explained. "You should begin to sense that harmony in how you align yourself with Him, and that's Resonance."

"He is good," Hezi announced, eyes yet closed and smile on his face. "So very good."

Satisfied at Hezi's progress, Nat encouraged him to continue as long as he was able, and then to rest. Moving with slow deliberation among the Etom, Nat directed their attunement, some with difficulty, others with great ease, but always he persisted until his pupil had achieved simple Resonance in the Spirit.

A short while later, when Nat was perhaps halfway through his instruction, Hezi approached him and asked, "Nat, I have to thank you for your help. I think I understand the way of this Resonance. Well, at least the bit you taught me. I was wondering if you might want some help with these others?"

Nat blinked, blindsided by his own lack of consideration, then accepted Hezi's offer, "Yes. Please, Hezi. Why don't you show me how with Kaasi here?"

Nat had just come alongside the burly etém to explain the process, but now turned the instruction over to Hezi, who did an excellent job of instructing Kaasi. As Kaasi continued in the exercise on his own, a satisfied Nat guided Hezi to another pupil. He left Hezi behind with the new student and moved on to the next himself, reminding himself to look out for other adepts who might be able to assist in training.

Nat found a number of apt pupils throughout the group, though he soon discovered that it took more than aptitude in Resonance to be able to teach it. Only a select few of those he identified were able to transmit their knowledge to others with success.

Odd, Nat thought, *I see no difference in how they explain it. I wonder...*

As he continued to facilitate the training, Nat's contemplation fell along the wayside, a partial and open-ended thought all but forgotten. With the other trainers at his side, Nat soon had his entire group trained, and looked over to see Miyam still engaged in instruction. Without hesitation, Nat invited all his trainers to join him in offering his assistance to Miyam.

Miyam was surprised to see that Nat and his students had finished, but nonetheless accepted the help. As Nat's crew of instructors spread out, he explained what he had discovered to Miyam. Miyam was struck by the obviousness of Nat's method, and with an open palm smacked her forehead to produce a wooden 'thok.'

"How come I didn't think of that?" she exclaimed, then her eyes went wide, and she grabbed Nat's shoulders with fervent hands to answer, "Of course! Cultivation!"

"Cultivation?" Nat asked with a sidelong glance, his head turned aside from Miyam's all-too-close and eager face.

"YES!!!" she shouted with manic glee and released him to cover his obliterated ear and wince with a pain that closed an eye and contorted the side of his face. "Cultivation, Nat! It's another gift of the Spirit."

Nat recovered his faculties and with renewed interest inquired, "Another gift? How does it work?"

"It's meant to prepare and instruct others in the Vine by the Spirit," Miyam answered, the excited light still in her eyes.

"I think I understand," Nat said with a thoughtful frown. "A lot of Etom picked up Resonance right away, but only a few of them could teach it. I asked only these to help me and left the others to continue in their training."

"Exactly, Nat," Miyam returned, "that's how the gifts of the Spirit work. They are not a measure of natural ability but are given to those in the Vine for the strengthening of it. With practice, someone can improve the use of a gift, but it operates exclusively by the power of the Spirit to do His will."

"Whoa," Nat reacted, "I wonder if we'll start to see more of the gifts crop up on their own."

Miyam looked askance at Nat with speculative eyes, wondering if a different gift altogether might be in operation through the young etém.

Perhaps, she considered. *I'll have to talk it over with Astéri. He may be able to illuminate Elyon's purposes for Nat.*

Sayah was among Miyam's group, and had developed an instantaneous, yet fleeting recognition of Resonance. It frustrated the æglet that the sensation seemed to skitter out of reach as he strove to focus on the Spirit. Nat noticed the scowl on his friend's face and excused himself from his conversation with Miyam to see if he might help.

"What's the matter, Sayah," Nat asked with concern. "You seem upset."

"That's just it!" Sayah replied, his annoyance clear in the tone of his voice. "I don't know what I'm doing wrong. I sense the Spirit, I *know* I do, but then He just…disappears."

"Can you tell me what's going through your mind while you're doing the exercise?" Nat inquired.

"Sure," Sayah answered. "I'm just standing here, thinking about everything we saw together, the Kinsman, you know, and remembering what happened here yesterday. I start to feel what you told us about, and He's so *real*, it seems He's right here speaking to me. But, then, these thoughts come into my mind – images, feelings, stuff from my past – and it's like the Spirit slips away."

"I know it's personal," Nat ventured with delicacy, "but would you tell me what these thoughts are, exactly?"

Embarrassed, Sayah hemmed and hawed before at last deciding to tell his friend, "It's about my family, especially my sister, and about me. Ægles are these great hunters, and what use to them am I? I can't even fly yet, and my sister, Gael has been flying over a week now. She's pretty much always been better than me at everything, and she lets me know it every chance she gets, constantly lording it over me.

"Not that my parents are much better. It seems like all they do is tell Gael how great she is and ignore me. Every day, they leave me all alone in the nest to go on their hunts, and every day, I get scraps when they come back. I'm a beggar. No, worse than a beggar, since I should be so much more."

With bitterness of heart, Sayah finished his diatribe, his head hung low and eyes downcast as Nat absorbed what the æglet had told him. It was heartbreaking to know that someone he had come to value so much as a friend had no value for himself. Great tears slipped from Nat's eyes and rolled down his cornflower cheeks, his little hand reaching out to lay on Sayah's hard, yellow beak.

They did nothing there. No talk. No movement. And all the while something unseen passed between them – a consoling comfort and a salve for Sayah's deep loneliness in Nat's presence at the æglet's side.

Sayah at last lifted his head to look at his Etom friend, this tiny snack of a thing who had discovered the secret of cheering him up. Nat looked back, his bright disposition shining through golden eyes. Eyes not unlike Sayah's own.

With a hitching breath, loaded with emotion, Sayah heard the sudden notice come, *this one is your brother, part of the family you have never known.*

Unbidden arose the resonant thrum of the Spirit's song, a tune complete within each phrase, yet with promise there is ever more locked within the melody. Sayah fell into the unlearned mode, a gift of presence to neighbor and then to overshadow Nat in its salience. To say the Spirit loomed was unjust to the sense of it, for no foreboding accompanied His presence, only overwhelming comfort and joy in the two creatures' shared and expanding understanding of Him.

Together, came His voice. *Only together can you approach a knowledge of My fullness, and by your unity, you will proclaim the good news of the Tree. Freedom from the Stain. Power in the Kinsman's Name. And Kinship in His suffering.*

With golden eyes wide open, Nat and Sayah were transfixed as, unaware and all around, Etom passed them by. The Spirit held them in His power, His presence conveying as much by way of emphasis as had the clarity of His statement. The impression of His glory made the words unforgettable in a way otherwise impossible.

Relinquished from the Spirit's supernatural embrace, etém and æglet breathless stared, recognizing in their common gaze the imprint of His nature. What had just occurred, they would doubtless share, for they sensed the message and experience were invaluable to those in the Vine. Likewise, the Spirit had sealed their improbable brotherhood, and the pair, of one mind, prayed the same for all.

Sayah and Nat soon discovered that everyone engaged in the endeavor of learning Resonance had achieved at least a passing familiarity with the Spirit. The day was almost gone, and though hunger beckoned, the group clustered around Miyam and Nat for release from training.

As Miyam prepared to excuse the gathered company, a strange impulse seized Nat, and he interrupted her to whisper, "Hey, what do you think of trying something new? I believe it's from the Spirit."

"What is it?" she asked, curious.

"I'd like to get everyone down in the water together," he answered.

A knowing smile on her face, Miyam nodded, "I think I know where you're going with this, and I think it's a *great* idea!"

Miyam's eyes flashed with excitement, and she turned to address the assembly, "Hey everybody! Nat has a great idea he thinks is from the Spirit. Are you all willing to try it?"

"Sure!" hollered back Hezi, the rest of the throng echoing his enthusiastic agreement.

"Ok, then!" Miyam countered. "Everyone back into the water! Nat will share the rest once we're there."

Several Etom shrugged and began wading out into the pool, the vast majority lingering a moment before following suit. Within a minute or two, the entire group was in the water, including Sayah. Nat walked out into the water with Miyam close behind and asked the Kinship to form a circle.

While the others moved into a rough, circular shape, Nat called out, "Once you've found your place, take the hand of a neighbor on each side."

Sayah extended his wingtips for the Etom on either side to grasp, and soon the circle was complete. Nat looked around at his fellows in the Vine and smiled, looking to the Tree in awe of the Kinsman's accomplishment.

Nat spoke, "If we could close our eyes and bow our heads to focus on the Spirit, I would like to say a few words."

All around the circle, the Etom responded at once to lower their heads. Sayah, too, craned his great neck as each one humbled himself, and Nat perceived a growing swell of Resonance amidst the gathering.

Eyes closed, and face raised heavenward, Nat began, "Our Lord Elyon out of His love for all, has sent His Only Son so that we might believe in Him, and be cleansed of the Stain that caused all creation to perish. By the Spirit of our Lord, we have received life new and abundant, which the Kinsman Gaal purchased with His blood. And we are grateful for this. Grateful for what He has done and continues to do."

The thrum of Resonance increased until Nat detected the water around him quivering as if in anticipation, and across the water, a voice arose in spontaneous song. It was an ancient song of the Eben'kayah, and Nat recognized Dempsey's voice, clear in the silence of the bower, as he sang the verse,

"Lord, You have been our abode in all generations.
Before You brought the mountains forth,
or ever You had formed the earth and the world,
You are from everlasting to everlasting."

As Dempsey sang, the others took up the song, which was the oldest of hymns among the Eben'kayah, and together they worshipped. Concerned his æglet friend might feel left out, Nat looked to Sayah, who stood enraptured in the song, his beak lifted high and wings draped in open surrender.

Dempsey led the crowd through the hymn, the effervescent sense of the Spirit growing as they finished the song,

"Reveal Your work unto Your servants,
and Your glory unto our children.
And let Your beauty rest upon us:
and establish the work of our hands.

In place of silence as their voices fell, a rumbling met their ears, the waters around them now bubbling as those inside a boiling pot. A spout of water spurted up next to Nat, and he shouted in delighted surprise, then all around them the effervescing water erupted in dozens of miniature geysers to shower them all.

Great joyous guffaws and cheerful giggles likewise erupted from the assembly. Some turned to play in the spouts as they sprung up, while others stood still with faces upraised to bask in showers of falling droplets. Nat raised his hands as well as his countenance, staring up into the crystalline mist as he was able, and what he saw gripped him.

Over their celebration, a multi-colored halo hung, a rainbow of promise for Lord Elyon's adopted children, His Kin made so through the Kinsman. In his deepest being, Nat sensed the Spirit speak the promise that where Lord Elyon's children gathered to worship in Spirit and in Truth, they stood in His very throne room, a forebrightening of their eventual destiny with Him.

Even after the Kinship had departed the waters to dry off, they remained in the afterglow of the Spirit's glory for a good while, the brilliance carrying them onward through the evening. Their fellowship had grown in depth, and all milled together in their newfound sense of family, of unity. Relationships grew, and the community of the Vine was strengthened as they exchanged much of their lives and shared their wonder at the broad horizons that Elyon spread before them.

Toward the evening's end, however, a downcast Sayah approached Nat and the rest of Company Jasper, his eyes forlorn and head hung low.

Nat recognized his friend's distress, and asked, "What's the matter, Sayah? What's wrong?"

Sayah looked toward the top of the Tree, where stood his home upon its crown, and said, "It's been five days since I left home. My family must be wondering where I've gone."

In truth, Sayah doubted they much cared, but felt he ought to return to the nest so at least they'd know he was alive. If it weren't for that, he'd be happy to stay with Nat and the rest of the Kinship.

"Do you have to go back?" Nat asked with disappointment.

"I should really let them know I'm alright," Sayah answered. "I would like to stay the night with you all and go back in the morning after my family has left to hunt."

Nida came close and laid a hand on his wing, "As a mother, I would like to know if my son were safe. I'm sure you're doing the right thing, Sayah."

"Yeah!" shouted Rae, "and when you're ready, you can come join us in Endego. Right?"

She looked around at the faces of her friends and family as smiles spread across them, and Kehren stepped in to answer, "I think that's a fantastic idea, Rae. Would you like to come live with us in Endego, Sayah? I'm sure we could find you somewhere to nest. Plenty of trees there."

Sayah blushed as ægles do, hiding his face beneath a wing, then peeking out replied, "I would like that. Very much."

Jumping up and down at Sayah's response, Nat and Rae both shouted, "Hooray!"

Though not looking forward to his separation from the others, Sayah at least now had the hope and promise of their reunion. He took heart, and warmed anew to the fellowship, determined to make the most of the time that they remained together. Their stories passed long into the night as they sat around the fire, and at last they fell asleep in the gentle peace of that sacred place.

The morning came, and most slept late, except for Iver and his ilk, who yet tested the boundaries of Sanctuary with restless fervor. When at last Sayah awoke with a stretch and a yawn, he discovered he was last to wake. The others had all arisen and stood nearby in a quiet cluster, discussing something in hushed tones.

Nat spotted Sayah stretching and greeted him, "Sayah! You're finally up! Come have some breakfast."

Sayah had taken a deep liking to the rhema and craved it now almost more than meat. He filled himself now with the peculiar bread, unsure when he might taste it again. As he ate, Nat shared his plans with Sayah.

"We were just talking about heading back to Endego, and think we'll probably leave later today," Nat explained. "Once we've got everyone settled there, I plan on coming back for you. Do you think you can wait a while?"

Sayah was determined to endure without complaint, and answered with a brave, "Yes. As long as I need to."

"I'll try not to leave you waiting too long," Nat vowed, his expression doleful.

Sayah passed the rest of the early morning soaking in the company of his Etom family, happy to have these last moments together with them. In the back of his mind, however, the sober thought remained that they would soon be parted.

The camp was astir with activity as the Etom prepared to leave. Even the unenthusiastic Iver and his little band began taking on signs of life and discontinued their search for escape from Sanctuary at the promise that they would soon depart.

Once everything was packed, Nat called the Kinship down into the waters once more to worship. Once again, they experienced the presence of the Spirit, though in place of effervescent, joyous showers, a shining, white cloud of comfort and peace rested over them. In this way, the Spirit gave assurance of His blessing on their journey home, and even Sayah sensed his decision to return home was the right one.

Oh! How they might have stayed there the whole day, but after long minutes that felt like hours, Nat detected the gentle press of the Spirit to leave. It was time.

As Sayah said his goodbyes, he recognized a new tenderness within himself, a fresh and vital pain unfamiliar before this time. It hurt to reflect on his absence from the company of his kind. His kind. That was new, too. His identification with these tiny creatures, the Etom, and with Miyam, a Sprig, and even with Astéri, a Malakím, with whom he had not Kinship, but a holy affiliation because of their alliance in Lord Elyon. No longer an æglet first was he, and he mused on the implications in the periphery of his mind while embracing the many who gathered to see him off.

Sayah released Nida and Dempsey from the envelopment of his wings, and looked to Nat, who had waited patiently to be last to bid his friend farewell. Great, shining tears stood out in eyes of the singular, golden shade they shared as though a hint from Lord Elyon Himself of the bond of brotherhood that would form between them. The etém threw his tiny, blue face against Sayah's dark, downy trunk and he wrapped his little arms as far around the æglet as he could. With gentle deliberation, Sayah gathered Nat beneath his wings, and the assembly gathered around them to lay tender hands on Sayah and pray.

Courage and strength filled Sayah under the affectionate ministrations of these wee vessels as they poured out by the Spirit the power that flowed through them. And over them sang and shone Astéri, who gloried in the simple care given to this tendril of the Vine who soon might feel quite alone.

From the huddle around Sayah, Miyam called out, "Though we may seem far from one another, we are always connected by the Vine, so long as we abide in Him. As was commanded in the record of the Eben'kayah, 'Love the Lord Elyon with all your heart, with all your soul, with all your mind, and with all your strength.' Do this, and you will not fail to 'Love one another as you love yourselves.' This is the ever-living legacy of the Kinsman, our love and unity in Him."

At her words, a hidden gloom over the Kinship lifted, and all raised their heads with smiles bright as they recognized this truth reverberating within them. The shadow of anticipated longing passed, and each one dedicated himself to support their friends from afar by prayers in the Spirit. Miyam had spoken with precision the encouragement they all needed, that even she needed at the prospect of remaining in Sanctuary while so many of her loved ones ventured out into the danger of the wilds.

Their farewells spoken, Nat stepped back from Sayah, and from the æglet's shoulder Astéri whistled a question, *You ready, Sayah?*

Sayah nodded in silence, his head bowed in submission as slowly they began to rise toward his nest. The Etom below waved, whistled, and cheered, and Nat rushed forward to lift a hand high, his brow furrowed in sincerity.

"We *will* see you again, Sayah!" Nat pledged. "I won't forget my promise!"

Soon those on the forest floor passed from view as Sayah and Astéri ascended through the screening branches and leaves of the Tree. A chill wind struck the æglet before they arose through the canopy, and he noticed a transformation in his surroundings.

It appeared that autumn had begun to set in over the past six days, and the umber brush of the season had passed lightly over the forest. Myriad leaves had an earthen cast to their hue, a subtle, yet definite signal that fall was coming. Sayah had heard from Mother and Father tales of these changes, ushered in by cool weather.

As Sayah expected, his family was nowhere in sight, and Astéri set him down with gentle care in the great nest, the raptor's feathery fluff twitching in the breeze.

Dipping low in a shade of violet-grey, Astéri hummed a solemn song, *I wish you the very best, Sayah. Truly, I do. You are a changed æglet, and we're all the better for it. Nat is a good friend, and true. He will do all in his power to come back for you.*

"I know it," Sayah returned, and cracked a wry smile. "You're a good friend, too, Astéri, if not a tad strange."

I think I'll take that as a compliment, Astéri retorted in mock offense, and brightened at the æglet's humor. *Now, dear friend, I must be off. Great dealings are in the works.*

"Goodbye, Astéri," Sayah replied, his voice quiet, and then his sparkling companion was speeding off back toward Sanctuary.

It was strange that the Tree conformed from the outside to the seasonal changes, and it appeared as the others to be preparing for the fall. Sayah knew otherwise, however. Down within the bower, the Tree's leaves would never turn, nor would it cease to bear fruit in the everlasting season of its harvest.

Chapter Fifteen
The Journey Home

It was difficult, the choice to leave Sanctuary, but even more difficult was the moment of their departure. Their farewells to Miyam and Astéri were no less tearful than those they had shared with Sayah, though they were all buoyed in the promise that Miyam had earlier spoken. They found hope also in her assurance they would see her soon, and she told them to look out for her arrival in Endego.

Difficult, too, was leaving behind such an assurance as the safe boundaries provided, and their departure served to wrest a measure of unhealthy comfort from their souls. The comfort they carried in the Vine, and in their fellowship with one another was nonetheless constant as the procession of Etom looked to the broadening horizons that peeked through the thick forest. Beneath the visible firmament stood a far-off hope unknown to most, supported by the pillars of testimony Company Jasper had erected in preceding days.

At a distance lay Endego, the village of their former home, besieged by Nihúkolem, but at last word still unspoiled in their rasping grasp. What Nat and company did not yet comprehend was whether or not it remained thus, and so receptive to their return. But the mission of the Eben'kayah pressed on them, the importance of their discoveries in Sanctuary settling on their collective shoulders as a mantle of responsibility and authority to carry the truths they had learned to those they had left behind.

Company Jasper had grown, and there was no distinction of care between its original members and those they had collected in Sakkan, save for that of common experience among the core group. But even that distinction began to dissolve in the tales shared over the bonfires of the night, the history of the exiles from Endego comingling with that of their new siblings in the Vine. It was odd, the intimacy comparted to the fellowship, though it was an intimacy that grew in profundity and intensity with the passage of time.

Any more, the original members of the Company did not hold themselves apart, which they had at first, before their transformation by the Spirit had begun in earnest. If by happenstance they elected to gather, it was not out of some overweening preference for one another's company, but out of a sense of mutual memory that precluded the need for many words. As hard as the outward journey had proven, their return seemed light by comparison.

Gone were lingering doubts as to their direction, their destination, or their success in locating the Kinsman. They knew their orientation and their destination, Endego. And, most importantly, they knew the Kinsman, had tasted of His goodness, and were eager to share Him with the Eben'kayah of Endego.

Also on their minds was an urgency to recall those others sent forth in pursuit of the Kinsman. There was no telling the dangers their friends from Endego had encountered on their search of the land. They had agreed not to despair of it, for they had no way of knowing, regardless. Better to save their energies for a speedy return, and for the work that doubtless awaited them upon their arrival.

Though a speedy return was preferable to all, it soon became apparent to the well-conditioned Etom of Endego that speedy was a relative term. The many prisoners of Sakkan were in various states of fitness, and most often through no fault of their own. Their detainments in the clinic had been of differing lengths, and the dank, sterile cells created an environment contrary to well-being. With nothing to do but sit in darkness most days, most had atrophied, and some had succumbed to Scarsburrow's more aggressive "treatments," which accounted for their numerous incapacities upon escape.

A major factor in ameliorating the prisoners' debilitation was the removal of the Stain, and those now free of it demonstrated marked improvement in resilience and mobility as their days in the wild increased. Though the journey began with a furtive sluggishness punctuated by numerous breaks and pauses for refreshment, these grew more and more infrequent to accelerate the band's overall pace.

Instead of disharmony, this phenomenon produced wonder among the younger, stronger Etom, who watched on as aging or once-crippled

Etom pushed on with a joyous determination that belied their years. Likewise, these that grew stronger with each day perceived with appreciation the patience and graciousness extended them throughout the process of their strengthening. Even among the Eben'kayah of Endego, Company Jasper had never seen the like.

Nevertheless, not all participated in this productive interplay, and it wasn't difficult to determine which of their number were dissatisfied with the increasing pace. Iver and his crew ever malingered toward the rear of their formation, complaining of the food, the weather, the abundance of light, the lack of light, the distance, the destination, and so on, and on . . .and on. It seemed complaint was their language, and they spoke it with a disheartening fluency sure to dampen the spirits of any in their vicinity.

In fact, the majority of the Kinship took to rotating from the rear to the front of the column in shifts throughout the day. The negativity of Iver and his cohorts was so burdensome that the others deemed it necessary to alternate shouldering the load.

Thus, every Etom had his or her turn near the accursed cluster of dissonant voices, and each sighed with relief when time came to distance themselves. Every Etom but for one, Kabir, who marched along between Iver's bunch and the rest of the Etom. Day in and day out, Kabir was constant in his self-assigned duty until one night, Dempsey brought it up in conversation around the campfire.

All but the pair of them had gone off to bed when Dempsey asked, "Kabir, how do you do it, all day, every day?"

A shocked expression on his face, Kabir look up from his roasted dinner skewer, and responded, "Do what now?"

"You know," Dempsey began, "How can you stand it – listening to Iver and his friends? It would drive me crazy."

"It's *because* it's so difficult to listen to them that I listen," Kabir returned. "I listen because I know they think that no one hears them."

Dempsey looked at Kabir with appreciation, and asked, "And what have you heard, Kabir?"

"As I said before, they think no one hears them. The complaints are a mask for many, concealing their greatest concern: That they have no place among us. That they will have no place among us when we arrive. They have said as much from time to time, but whether or not it's spoken aloud, I hear it in almost every word. And they're right."

"They're right?" Dempsey retorted in confusion. "In what way?"

"Don't tell me you don't see the rift opening between *us* and *them*," Kabir reproached. "Not one of them is in the Vine, and we all know it. That's the main thing. We need to take their complaints seriously.

"What you might not realize is that however difficult this journey is for our weakest member, it is more difficult for even the strongest of theirs. Our people in the Vine are getting stronger every day, while Iver and his group are just barely making it through each day. They trudge along, suffering, and loudly at that, but they haven't quit. Yet."

"Are they thinking about quitting?" Dempsey asked with some alarm.

If Iver's group deserted, they would put themselves in danger, and might present a security risk to the rest.

"They are," Kabir responded. "I've only heard a few whispers here and there, but that means they are talking about it, although it doesn't seem like what they actually *want* to do."

Dempsey polished off his dinner and threw the greasy skewer into the flames before he inquired, "Do you think it would help if we went to them? Tried to figure out what they want?"

Kabir shook his head, as he advised, "For whatever reason, Iver despises us, even as he recognizes the benefit of staying with us. I think going to him would cause him to lose face in front of his people. No. My advice is to slow our pace a bit and offer more frequent breaks. Don't explain the changes to anyone you don't have to. If Iver found out, it would be a blow to his pride."

Dempsey nodded as he absorbed the information, then he thanked Kabir for the advice, and headed off to sleep. In the morning, he gathered Nat and Nida to discuss in private what he had learned. They agreed to slow down, fearful of losing Iver and his grumbly band to the wilderness. The changes caused a few confused murmurs along the line, since now most everyone was keeping pace with ease, but in general, the Etom accepted the deceleration.

At day's end, Dempsey conferred again with Kabir, who laughed when Dempsey asked if the complaints had stopped.

"Oh no! Never!" Kabir chuckled. "I doubt they'll *ever* stop complaining. But *how* they are complaining, and what they're complaining *about*, those are different. To these Etom, complaint is a pastime, but they seem happier now. Not so bitter. I think it is working."

"Good, good," Dempsey returned. "I suppose that's the best we could expect. And, Kabir, thank you for your help. I'm sure we'll need more of it when we get to Endego."

With a quick nod, Kabir assured Dempsey he'd be available to assist when they arrived at last, and Dempsey hurried forward to take his place along the line. The rest of the day, and, indeed, the remainder of their journey to Endego, Iver's crew was more tolerable, and the entire camp's morale improved as they pushed on toward Endego.

For the returning Etom of Endego, the trip didn't seem very long contrasted against the meandering search they'd made before detouring to Sakkan. Their route now was direct and efficient, with concession made only for breaks, during which the more industrious and energetic among them took to the surrounding environs to scour them for food. These short, scavenging forays along their path were instrumental in maintaining an overall quicker pace.

Before Dempsey and the others had agreed to more frequent breaks to accommodate Iver and friends, they had often called an end to the daily march before the sun had gone down to allow time to scavenge prior to nightfall. Since they began collecting food during breaks, supplies were often sufficient to forego any foraging at the end of the day, thus permitting a longer daily march. They were making good time, and with each passing day, it seemed their surroundings took on an increasingly familiar cast.

They had been on the journey for a bit over a month when Rae shouted from the front, "Look there! It's the Anvil!"

Rae's parents, Dempsey, Nida, and Nat rushed up from their positions along the line to look where Rae pointed. Through the tall, yet dwindling screen of autumn straw that stood before them, the singular, rocky shape of the landmark was visible. The six of the them remained at the front, pressing forward with anticipation until the village grove of Endego also became distinct beyond the shelf of stone.

The other Etom were likewise agitated with a curious excitement most common among children during a long trip and bunched up behind the others at the front as they bustled for a view of their new home. At the head of the cluster, Nat and Dempsey parted the dry stalks and let the others push out onto the gentle rise that overlooked Endego. They didn't know if the village was safe yet, but the sun was low in the horizon such that it might blind any observers.

After giving their eager band a long moment to take in the view, Nat, Nida, and Dempsey herded everyone back under cover to discuss their approach. The sun was setting fast, and it was decided that any attempt to reconnoiter the village would naturally occur at night. Nida and Dempsey were the best candidates for the task, and the pair made preparations for the incursion in the dwindling twilight.

Nida and Dempsey's mission was twofold: survey Endego to identify any potential enemy positions and make contact with the Eben'kayah. The former would offer insight regarding the safest route by which to smuggle their guests into Endego, and the latter would serve to recruit help in securing lodging and provisions for them. They were also eager to report the mission a success so the Eben'kayah remaining in Endego could call the others back. That is, if any Eben'kayah still remained.

These thoughts in their minds, Dempsey and Nida stood back from the edge of their cover in the high and brittle yellow grasses, each taking a full and forceful breath and exhaling before looking to one another for confirmation they were ready to start. In unison, they reached out to clasp hands for Dempsey to lead them in a prayer for protection. Their synchronous movements provoked in Dempsey a recollection of the night he'd brought Nida and Nat to his empty home, and he wondered if she might now be open to his advances. Well, after they settled back in at home.

His focus returned as Nida stepped forth into the night, and in silence he rebuked himself for letting distraction cause him to abdicate the lead. If anyone should first present themselves as a target of the enemy, it should be him. Feeling a bit silly, he nevertheless skipped in silent stutter-step to put himself ahead of Nida by a narrow margin.

Nida sensed Dempsey's inelegant advance, and smirked, aware he did so out of concern for her, not of some childish need to go first. It was most probably for the best, anyhow, as he had proven on a number of occasions to be the most competent of trailblazers among them, capable of sussing out a path both considerate of the party's abilities and efficient while maintaining stealth. It was a peculiar skill, but one he nonetheless seemed to have mastered.

Nida, on the other hand, found that her confidence in his single-minded focus on guiding them forward freed up her awareness to scan the surrounding area for anything dangerous or important. Theirs was a curious complement, the pairing of abilities and temperaments that made more of their combination than of their disparate elements. Unaware of Dempsey's earlier woolgathering, she too returned to that moment of tender confession, and hoped they found the home awaiting them would accommodate their romance.

Dempsey led them on a sinuous circuit of Endego, their cautious sweep of the village entrapping nostalgic memory alongside present observation to evoke a poignant doubling within their consciousness: The darkened arch of the Bunker's entryway as a thousand days collecting Nat from school, the slipping, silver ribbon of the Üntfither a hundred clandestine journeys in the coracle.

Remembrance would have been distracting but for the contrast with their dark reality, in which no windows glowed with the homey light of lamp and hearth. It was deathly still, and it seemed none moved about Endego but them. Neither Nida nor Dempsey dared speak a word for fear of breaking the fragile tranquility, its glazed frailty attenuated by the slightest disturbance.

They wound their way throughout the village, avoiding the temple until they had come all the way round the southern end of Endego, and passed by Dempsey's home, an indistinct, crouching form in the murk, before striking straight for the olive tree.

The still darkness deepened to an oppressive weight, which worked against the clarity of their minds like silent, jet-black waves wearing away at their composure. A sense of foreboding filled Dempsey as he rushed now into the inky void toward the temple. And ran face-first into a thick and bark-encrusted branch.

Dempsey would have struck the ground but for Nida, who flailed her hands to catch him when he fell back against her. He spat grit from his mouth with quiet care, and reached out, feeling for the woody obstacle in his path. He found what felt like a sizable bough and followed its length by touch in the general direction of the temple. Nida kept one hand on his shoulder and ran the other along the rough bark of the branch, curious what it might mean.

They cut sharply in the direction of the temple as Dempsey traced the branch. He wasn't sure why it lay along the ground, blocking the most direct route, but was happy to have something to orient them in the dense murk. Any moment, they should come upon the roots of the olive tree, twisting up from the earth to meet the stout trunk.

A clod of dirt fell on Nida, showering them both upon impact with her forehead. Dempsey raised a hand overhead to defend against further such missiles, and his splayed fingers encountered a dangling mass of fibers. He yanked his hand back, bringing with it another spray of grains as primal fears arose within him alongside the spectre of that fateful night with Nat in the spider's web.

But these were no sticky gossamer strands. Dempsey's rationality returned, and he reached again to investigate. As he suspected from his first contact, the rough fibers were covered with earth, and thicker than a spider's web. He reached around for Nida's hand and together they explored the dirty mass draped above. They were tree roots.

As if by some conspiracy among the heavens, the clouds obscuring the moon since nightfall parted at that moment to illuminate the devastation they had yet to perceive. The olive tree lay uprooted, and a near-sundered branch twisted back along the ground to form the guide they had followed. In horrified disregard for their exposure, Dempsey and Nida skirted the prone, lifeless form with slow steps until they stared down into the pit its roots had once occupied.

The homes that had surrounded the tree had also been demolished, and even their foundations removed in the upheaval. And still the pair circled the desolation, unable to take their grim and curious eyes away from it until they fell upon yet another catastrophic novelty.

Where the temple had once stood, a darkened pit remained. The Nihúkolem had been thorough and had chased every facet of the underground tunnels to its end, tearing out the substructure that had once protected and concealed so much life. So much potential. And there they fell together to their knees, hand in hand as they huddled on their faces in silent, mournful tears, two lone and living stones under the moonlight.

Chapter Sixteen
The Welcome of Strangers

Dempsey and Nida's sorrowful commiseration came to an end, their tears poured out on beloved earth where once had stood a home truer than any they had ever known. For all the havoc they had wreaked, no current sign of the Nihúkolem remained. They had changed the contour of the once-beautiful clearing to calamitous effect, and the pair of Etom couldn't imagine how it might be restored.

The only fortuitous element of their situation being the apparent absence of the Nihúkolem, Dempsey and Nida suspected they would have no difficulty smuggling their friends into town. However, their plan had involved at minimum a temporary resettlement of Sakkan's refugees to the temple's underground network, likely to the Forge, where they could have carved out some kind of living space. Now, it seemed that this important component of their plan was lost to them, and they would need to figure out an alternative before bringing the throng into Endego.

"PSSST!" a hidden hiss from near the Üntfither drew Nida and Dempsey's elevated attention at once.

Fearful of betrayal, but not perceiving another viable recourse, the pair arose to their feet and walked with caution toward the sound. Out of the shadows swung a lamp, three times toward the stream, then three times toward them, a reassuring and familiar signal of the Eben'kayah. With growing confidence, Dempsey and Nida quickened their pace, eager to discover the identity of the mysterious stranger and get out of sight. Their grief at the temple's destruction had rendered them reckless, overwhelming their survival instincts in the moment. But now sensibility returned, and they took comfort as they stepped into the shadow of a weeping willow.

"Dempsey! Nida! Is that you?" a recognizable voice inquired with disbelief. "It's me. Shoym!"

Relief flooded Nida and Dempsey's souls when Shoym identified himself. It was good to know they had found a true friend, and good to know he remained well in spite of the Nihúkolem's rampage.

"Shoym!" Nida squealed from behind restrained tears of joy, and she wrapped her arms around his paternal neck with affection.

Nida relented, and Dempsey took Shoym's hand and shoulder in a firm grip, "It is *good* to see you, dear friend."

Shoym received their warm salutations with pleasure but held a finger to his lips as he beckoned them farther back into gloom. Without hesitation, they followed him, flitting from deeper to deepest shade back through the village until they arrived again at the Bunker.

When they had passed the old shell earlier, Dempsey and Nida hadn't given it a second glance, though now that they considered the options available in Endego, it seemed an obvious alternate to the temple: large, hardened, and with a well-concealed interior. Shoym led them under the sloping entryway to knock in staccato code against the school's great doors. At once, the door opened, a sliver gaping on oblivion darkness deeper even than that outside greeted them. Shoym waved them in, turned around to cast a furtive glance about the deserted village, then slipped inside to bolt the door.

In the relative safety of the Bunker, Dempsey and Nida followed Shoym toward the far end of the cavernous space where low, warm light beckoned. In the center of one of the depressed pods once used for instruction, the beleaguered Eben'kayah had built a fire, and around it hunched a number of figures that Nida and Dempsey recognized as they neared.

Along the far perimeter of the fire, stood Agatous, the Stain upon her purple forehead having spread its deadly fingers down across her cheeks. The Chief Counciletma seemed diminished somehow, her shoulders narrower and the light dimmer in her eyes.

That light flared, however, when she spotted the new arrivals, and she stood more erect as questions, like so many loosed arrows, flew from her lips, "Dempsey? Nida? Is that really you? Did you find Him?"

As she began to speak, Agatous rushed to them, and her trembling hand now gripped Dempsey's sleeve in hopeful apprehension to accompany the interrogation. The Eben'kayah that stayed back in Endego had suffered long under the Nihúkolem's persecution, hiding and scrounging for their survival. Now, the potential realization of their sustaining hope stood before them, and Agatous shook with anticipation.

Nida stepped forward to take Agatous by the arm, and reassured the older etma, "Lady Agatous, yes, it is us. We're so glad we found you. We have news of the Kinsman, if you will allow us."

"Of course. Of course, dear," Agatous replied. "Why don't you tell all of us about it?"

Agatous returned to far side of the fire to take her seat and gestured for the others to join them around the fire.

"Shoym!" she called, as Nida and Dempsey took a seat. "Shoym, you'll want to hear this, too!"

From the dim shadows at the front of the Bunker, where he conferred with the guard at the door, Shoym scurried their way, puffing, "I'm on my way. Please don't start without me. I don't want to miss a thing!"

Once everyone had settled in their places, Nida and Dempsey took turns reporting everything they had learned. They related the arduous journey northward, Rae's injury, their detour to Sakkan, and their captivity therein. Shoym, Agatous, and the others listened with unbroken attention to their trials. Then, with joy, they shared their liberation from Sakkan and their cleansing from the Stain, showing bare and healthy skin where once inky blemishes had stood. The Eben'kayah of Endego gathered around them as they did, with curious wonder examining Dempsey and Nida's unspoiled forms.

"How?" Agatous asked. "How did He accomplish this?"

Remembering what Nat had told them about the Kinsman and His death upon the Tree Ha Datovara, they related with imperfect clarity his tale: that the Kinsman was beaten and scourged before the forces of the Empire nailed Him to the Tree. That He had perished, and then rose again, likewise restoring the Tree to new life. That from the Tree had sprung a fount of living water that ran through the now-enlivened land of Sanctuary, and that it was in these waters they had bathed to remove the Stain and receive healing in their bodies.

Shoym was awestruck, and responded to their claims, "Incredible! Could it be that the promises of the Kinsman have come true?"

"Not *all* the promises, friend Shoym," a voice called from the encirclement of Etom.

The dry and bitter tone identified the speaker, Alcarid, and Nida looked to him with interest as he continued, "What of the prophecy of our deliverance from the Empire of Chōl? That the Kinsman would free us from their yoke, and rule us ever after? I've seen no proof of such deliverance, nor that the Man Nat identified as the Kinsman was indeed Him."

Alcarid rose and turned to face those around them as he continued, "Are we gathered here free? I, for one, do not know if I can trust the word of one small etém, no matter how beloved he is among us."

Dempsey bristled, "Is not our unblemished skin proof enough? What other power but that of the Kinsman might remove the Stain, the scourge of our world since ages past?"

It was with defeated resignation that Alcarid replied, "Dear Master Dempsey, I have no doubt that you believe what you have told us, and that Nat believes what he claims to have seen, but we have endured here not in hope of a good soak in some mystic waters, but in the hope that you might return with means of defeating the Nihúkolem. That you might return with a King. Instead, you return with unverifiable fables imagined in a dream while we starve in this hole!"

"Silence, Alcarid!" Agatous rebuked. "What happened to us, to the temple, was not their fault. And they are the first and only company to return with any kind of favorable report. Do you think they would have come back on the basis of wishful thinking? There must be something to what they've told us. It *does* appear their Stain is gone, after all."

Alcarid relented, muttering concession to Agatous' authority, if not her reasoning. Nida pitied the elderly etém, aware that the difficulties of the past months had hardened him in ways with which she was familiar, having been tempted by them herself. To go from such a community broad and deep as the Eben'kayah to this deprived existence must have just been too great a change and too rapid for Alcarid to weather. He had succumbed to despair, and though he persevered outwardly, his heart within him had failed. What a desperate trap he found himself in, and none more aware of his ensnarement than he.

Nida whispered a prayer to Elyon on the old etém's behalf. Perhaps their mission would take on a different form than anticipated, and she considered how they might benefit these Eben'kayah who had stayed behind. But first, they needed to make a complete assessment of their situation.

"Lady Agatous, if I may, I have some questions," Nida implored.

Agatous acquiesced, and Nida continued, "How many of our number remain here in Endego?"

Agatous gave a weary sigh and looked away wearing a somber frown, so Shoym responded in her stead, "This is all that is left of us. Fewer than a dozen in total. Eight, to be precise."

Nida now understood why Agatous had hesitated to answer. Though the contingent of the Eben'kayah left to facilitate communication and maintain an operational hub for the twelve companies that had set out was not large, its original complement had been twenty. They had lost over half to the Nihúkolem and had witnessed the destruction of the Eben'kayah temple and the many homes surrounding the olive tree. Their sadness was a burden that Nida now shared as the realization sunk in.

"And how is it that you've not been discovered here in the Bunker? Where do you go during school?" Nida asked.

Agatous responded, "Endego has been under curfew since the Nihúkolem destroyed the temple. The Empire closed the school when they set curfew. In a way, it was fortunate, they did, since we had nowhere else to go. Etom are only allowed outside for a couple hours each day. They are all prisoners in their own homes."

Nida pressed on, determined to formulate a course of action, "And supplies? What's left of them?"

She suspected from Alcarid's earlier diatribe the answer she received from Shoym, "We've hardly a thing left. The Nihúkolem came quickly and plundered everything in minutes. That's when we lost most of our folks. What we have now, we scavenge outside the village, though that holds its own dangers ..."

Nida seized on his final statement, "Why? Is something out there? We have Etom out there!"

"Foxes," Alcarid intoned. "Foxes, small and swift, wandering the grasses at all hours."

The sudden danger to the Etom outside Endego drove Nida to act, and she sized up the gloomy space before barking, "What is the safest route out of the village? Can one of you guide us? We *must* bring them here. Now!"

Shoym volunteered himself as guide but looked to Agatous for final approval before rousing himself to action. Lady Agatous agreed over Alcarid's numerous protestations, ignoring his sour predictions of calamity should they welcome such a great many strangers into the Bunker.

They departed the armored shelter of the Bunker, Shoym guiding them toward the edge of the grove while taking great pains to avoid nearing any homes along the way. It wasn't far, but the few homes that stood in their path elicited wide detours around them. From their old friend's behavior, Dempsey and Nida concluded that he feared contact with any of the Etom of Endego outside the fellowship of the Eben'kayah and wondered why.

Their musings would need to await an answer, for soon they had passed outside the borders of the village, and Shoym was waving them close to whisper, "Where are they?"

Dempsey pointed to the northeast, to the rise where they had left their companions.

"Alright," Shoym said, steeling himself. "Follow me. Quietly."

They crept along the town-ward edge of the tall stalks without entering the grass, where Shoym knew foxes prowled in search of prey. The ears of foxes are well-adapted to capture the slightest sound, and they track their quarry in the grass by the faint swish of their passage. It was an effective method of hunting among dense foliage that otherwise obscured vision. Thus, it was best to stay outside the grass altogether.

Without incident, Shoym led them to where Dempsey and Nida had parted company with the rest, and the trio was just about to breach the perimeter of the underbrush when a nearby voice rasped, "Who goes there?"

They three Etom froze, and the one who confronted them stepped forth from the shadows, a spear tip leveled at their unmoving forms. Dempsey and Nida recognized Kaasi at the same instant he did them, and he lowered the spear to wave them back behind the cover of the underbrush. They snuck to the edge of the camp, which they had struck just far enough back in the grass to screen them from sight should someone be on the lookout from the village.

The arrhythmic overlap of soft snores emanated from sleeping Etom as Dempsey began, "Kaasi, very carefully and very quietly, we need to wake everyone in the camp and prepare them to move into the village. Right away. We have just learned the Empire is employing foxes to patrol the grasslands around Endego. We may all be in danger."

"Should we warn the other sentries?" Kaasi asked. "They could help us rouse the camp, and they will need to know what we are doing, or they may raise the alarm."

"Good point," Dempsey agreed. "Where are they?"

"There are three others stationed around the camp, and another on patrol near the center," Kaasi answered. "I'll circle around to the west, and you to the east. Once you've informed the sentry to the east, you could head into camp to catch the one on patrol there. I'll get the last one on the north end, and we'll have the camp ready to go in no time."

"It's a good plan," Dempsey affirmed. "Let's go."

Before long, they had recruited all guards on watch, and began awakening the others, whose groggy faces soon surrounded Nida, Dempsey, Kaasi, and Shoym in the center of camp. Nat, Rae, Kehren, and Tram waved to Shoym in quiet, happy reunion, then turned their full attention to Nida as she explained their current predicament in hushed tones.

"Our good friend, Shoym, here," Nida raised an open hand to point Shoym out, then continued, "has informed us that the Empire has recruited several skulks of foxes to patrol the outer perimeter of Endego. As some may already know, foxes have excellent hearing, which means even this conversation increases our risk of detection.

"Shoym has offered to lead us back into Endego, where shelter awaits us. Since the amount of noise we make in our passage might reveal us to the predators, we must ask that everyone bring only the most essential of belongings with you. And last, we request that you all prepare yourselves for departure right now. Our best chance of entering the village undetected is under the cover of night. Please get ready and return here as soon as you are able."

There were no objections to Nida's request, not even from Iver's camp, which surprised her and Dempsey. Perhaps they had decided that their de facto leadership had their best interests in mind. Regardless of speculation, the result was cooperation, for which they were grateful.

In a matter of minutes, the entire company was assembled once more, and stood at attention in the somber silence. Shoym nodded to Nida and Dempsey, who waved the Etom forward behind the older etém as he set out for the village.

Shoym took them on an altogether different route than the one by which they had exited the village, arcing to the southeast to enter the village from its east side. Soon, they encountered the trail by which they had skirted Cliphook Lane the night of their escape, and then the lane itself as their guided incursion took them westward.

Nat noted the forlorn expressions on Rae, Tram, and Kehren's faces as they passed a bit north of their estate, between their home and Rosco's. Shoym led them up to the Altfither, which ran through Rae's familial plot, and stepped quietly into the stream, wading with slow, deliberate steps through it.

As Shoym gestured for them to follow, Dempsey saw the wisdom that Shoym employed in leading them thus and smiled. His clever old friend had brought them the long way around to throw any potential pursuers off their trail, and their scent would disappear in the water. A fox's sense of smell wasn't great in the first place, and any that followed would find it difficult to pick the scent up on the other side of the stream.

With quiet caution, the sneaking Etom swished across the stream, careful not to splash for the attention it might draw. Shoym continued to lead them with the same heightened discretion that he had used in their outward trip and gave any homes in their path at wide berth. Their route took them past Nida and Nat's, but even their small and seemingly-empty home he avoided.

At last, they arrived at the door of the Bunker, and Shoym rapped again the perfunctory coded knock on its thick, wooden surface. The door cracked open, then swung wide when the guard identified Shoym, who compelled everyone into the dark space with urgency.

"Welcome," came Agatous' steady voice from the far end of the hall. "I am Agatous, the leader of the Eben'kayah of Endego, such as we are."

She approached them, examining the ragged band as she resumed, "Please make yourselves at home here, and rest the night in peace and safety. We have many rules here that you will come to learn, but for now, you need only follow two.

"The first is that we must all keep quiet. While these walls keep much of the sound from escaping, they do not contain it all. You may speak, but shouts and cries may yet be heard outside, and our primary advantage here is that we have managed to remain undiscovered.

"Second, and much like the first in that we don't wish to be detected by any outside, only those with permission to do so may leave. If you agree to follow these rules, then we invite you into the shelter of the Bunker."

Murmurs of agreement rippled through the throng, and many of the Etom liberated from Sakkan came forward to introduce themselves to Shoym and Agatous. Even Iver took the opportunity to shake Agatous' hand, his lackeys standing in a bland cluster behind him until he'd expressed gratitude for their asylum. Dempsey watched Iver with skepticism, not sure what to make of the glad-handing malcontent.

A large, amiable hand slapped his back, and Kabir confided, "If you're wondering what he's up to, I'm not sure yet. But he *is* up to something."

"What makes you say that?" Dempsey asked. "Did something happen?"

Kabir crossed his arms and turned his back on Iver's conversation with Agatous, arching his brows as he answered, "No. But that's just the thing. *Nothing* is happening. Since this morning, not a peep out of Iver or his group. No complaints. No grumbling. I'm telling you, they have something planned."

"They must be on to you," Dempsey deduced. "What else could it be? And it couldn't have been too hard to figure out that someone was listening after we changed our routine. You were the only one always at the back of the line."

"I think you're right," Kabir agreed, "but I don't like this silence. Something is up, and we need to find out what it is."

"Do you know anyone else who can help us?" Dempsey inquired. "Someone who could get close without making them suspicious?"

Kabir shook his head in obvious frustration, and replied, "No, they've kept to themselves since we arrived at Sanctuary, and doubly so since they refused the Kinsman's springs. And, honestly, that distinction is what seems to drive Etom to Iver's side. I don't think they would accept anyone new since we're all in the Vine. And they are not."

Dempsey decided to work the equation from the other side, and assured Kabir, "Iver seems especially interested in Endego's Eben'kayah leadership. Whatever they are after, it looks like they will need support. I'll be certain to warn Shoym and Agatous about him and his group. That should at least buy us some time."

"It's something, at least," Kabir conceded. "I'll keep my eyes open."

"That gives me another idea, Kabir. Something I think you could help with," Dempsey proposed. "Maybe we need to expand our network of eyes and ears. Keep better track of Iver and his friends. What do you think?"

"Like spies?" Kabir asked with some concern. "I don't like the idea of spying on our own people, even if it's Iver."

Dempsey's cheeks puffed as he blew out a conflicted breath in advance of his answer, "Listen, I don't love the idea either, but we had better figure something out. How about we think on it a while? Maybe we can come up with a better solution. We need to know if Iver has something nasty planned, and the sooner, the better."

"That, at least, we can agree on," Kabir responded.

The two etém parted ways to find a place to rest in the Bunker's dim, yet warm expanse. Within minutes, they joined the other Etom in their first sheltered slumber in a good while, and their sleep was sweet.

Chapter Seventeen
The Cold Vantage

While Sayah awaited his family's return to the aerie, he spent the rest of the day strengthening himself in the Spirit through prayer and grateful meditation on the blessing of his Kinship in the Vine. He thought also on what he should tell his family, certain they would have a great many questions as to his whereabouts and activities. The æglet rehearsed a lie or two in his mind, but the Spirit shivered with displeasure at the prospect.

"What should I tell them, then?" he spoke aloud in mild frustration.

The answer cropped up at once among the thoughts in his mind, an honest upstart standing tall over its lowly, deceptive neighbors. Tell them nothing, or as little as possible. A refusal to answer was as honest as he might dare be. Anything beyond that might give away too much and endanger his friends.

Sayah knew his parents were no friends of the Empire, but they were Chōl's subjects nonetheless. They had warned Gael and Sayah of the Empire's dark emissaries, the Nihúkolem, and that many of their kind were in its service. If pressed, Sayah knew that Father and Mother would submit to forced conscription into the Empire's ranks of scouts and informants.

Sayah considered the kestrels that had threatened their escape from Sakkan and wondered how many would have rather stayed home in their own hunting grounds. A new and foreign sentiment followed the thought, a sympathy that at first shocked the æglet when he recognized the kestrels as more than enemies. The Spirit had begun a strange work in Sayah, and the æglet welcomed most of it, but compassion would make any conflict or hunting difficult. The æglet tried not to think much about it yet offered up a prayer for understanding to quell his anxiety over navigating such complexity.

A nearby, skyward shriek caught Sayah's attention just in time for him to whirl and face Gael's onslaught as she bore down on him, catching Sayah over his wings to pin him against the floor of the nest. Sayah was familiar with the routine, and with dry comedy could think of no more suitable welcome home.

Sayah accepted his place on his back and looked up into Gael's crazed eyes as she hissed, "Why, hello there, Sayah. Where. have. you. been?"

With each word, she pecked at him in punctuation, then desisted to rant, "Mother has been worried sick, and Father...well, Father has given you up for dead."

Gael lowered her beak to beside Sayah's head, and whispered, "But not me, brother dearest. I *knew* you were still out there. Somewhere. And I heard some interesting rumors around the forest over the past several days. *Very* interesting rumors."

The fresh stink of raw flesh billowed around Sayah's head as she spoke, a perfumed and humid cloud that almost made him retch. It had been days since he'd slain anything to eat and discovered his appetites had changed in significant ways.

Gael interrupted his reflections, lifting herself up to look him over before she asked with bewildered curiosity, "Something's different about you. Isn't it?"

Her question sparked a reaction in Sayah and illuminated within him something unnoticed that he'd acquired over the past few days – courage. He wasn't afraid of Gael anymore. Not one bit. She had at last recognized his lack of trepidation at her assault, his pure and fearless gaze under domination garnering her haughty attention. As Sayah likewise identified his own bravery, his beak cracked in an involuntary grin, which widened into a smile while Gael sputtered.

"Wha—what is that? Why are you smiling?" she spat in vexation.

Unable to control himself, a great guffaw flew from Sayah's beak, then another. Gael's head twitched about as she looked down at her brother in confusion. Soon great peals of uncontainable, unconstrained laughter burst from Sayah, and he threw his head back without concern. Gael might tear his throat out, but what did it matter? He refused to live in fear anymore and would rather die free of its shackles than endure another instant of intimidation.

Gael's agitation only increased as Sayah bellowed and shook with laughter under her steely talons, and she soon stepped off his prostrate form. From close by, she peered at him askance, uncertain what to make of his abnormal behavior. Deep inside her, the caged bloodthirst fell still and silent, unable to answer Sayah's sudden change.

Gael turned her back on Sayah, whose laughter had subsided, then looked back over a feathered shoulder at him, and with a sniff strode to the edge of the nest to brood over the forest. It was almost nightfall as Sayah rolled to his side and sat up to wipe joyful tears from his eyes with the fuzzy edge of a wing. He felt at once liberated and empowered and was pleased in a peripheral sense that Gael had stopped.

Though Mother's keening cry drew Sayah's gaze, Gael didn't turn from her dark meditation even when Mother dumped her catch with careless abandon and flew to Sayah in a loud rush.

Mother's flapping wings stirred up a maelstrom of dust and bracken from the nest, and she cried, "Sayah! You're home!"

Sayah had arisen at the first sign of Mother and stood now with wings low and extended to either side. His shoulders lifted in a gentle shrug and a sheepish smile adorned his young, homely face as Mother folded him in her great wings, crushing him to her breast with ferocity.

"Where have you been?" she scolded. "How dare you make me worry like that!"

Sayah maintained his silence and embraced her in return, certain that the less he said, the better. Father's presence was felt more than heard, his silent glide down to the aerie terminating in a single, quiet snap of the wings to produce a powerful gust and bring him to a stop.

Opening her wings, Mother presented Sayah to Father and reproached him, "See? I told you he was still alive. A mother always knows."

Father furrowed his brow and opened his beak in reprisal, then thought better and clicked his beak shut. Instead, Father's eyes bored into his son, who had turned to face him. Father's stare was penetrating, but not malevolent, though Sayah sensed the intensity of Father's interest contained in it. Perhaps Father, too, had heard rumors?

"Hello, Father," Sayah offered, at last.

Sayah's expression still held no fear, only the deference appropriate of offspring to a parent.

Father stared a little longer, then straightened and answered, "Hello, Sayah. It's good to see you well. You look stronger than before."

With a smart, respectful nod, Father ended the brief conversation, his immediate satisfaction apparent in terse approval of Sayah. Father picked up his quarry in his beak and retired to an open edge of the nest to dine, his sharp gaze questing outward between bites.

Sayah's heart soared at his Father's words, which were tantamount to an ode of praise from the taciturn ægle. That nod, too. Never from Father had the æglet sensed anything approaching the respect paid him in that simple gesture. If Sayah had blinked, he would have missed it, and he was grateful that he hadn't. Forever the memory would live emblazoned in his mind as the first moment Father acknowledged his potential, his worth, his very being.

It seemed that Gael, too, had noticed Father's praise. From her perch along the edge of the nest, she cocked an eye of malice at Sayah. Accustomed to her ill will, Sayah returned her glance with none of his own, and, smiling, raised a wing to wave at her. A sour glint crossed her eye, and she turned her dour head back toward the forest, the hackles on her neck standing up for Sayah to see.

That, too, was food for Sayah's thoughts, and not once had he seen Gael respond to him with raised hackles. So self-assured was Gael in her dominance of him, that she never perceived him a sufficient challenge for such a display, which was reserved for true threats. Sayah mulled over this metamorphosis of his family dynamic, and decided he rather enjoyed being taken seriously for a change. The Spirit sounded a warning not to get comfortable with the sensation, and a chastened Sayah heeded His wisdom.

After all, Sayah pondered, *it seems such a terrible burden for Gael to always seek the praise and approval of others. She must be miserable.*

And there it was again, the insight given to pity those who might murder him. It was disconcerting and unnatural, but somehow *right*, and Sayah accepted it with thanksgiving as another blessing of the Spirit.

Mother clamored for his attention, concerned that he'd not eaten well in his absence. She tossed him a small weasel from the clutch of prey she'd brought back from the hunt. Mother explained that she'd brought Sayah something each night he'd been absent in hopes that he might return. In her waning hope, she almost hadn't today, but now was glad she had.

It warmed Sayah to know that even his somewhat distant parents expressed their care in his absence, and accepted the meal with gratitude, but for one minor hitch. As he leaned over the long and furry carcass, ready to tear into the still-warm remains, Sayah swooned. The sight of blood, in small droplets on the weasel's fur, and the faint smell thereof made Sayah gag. He didn't vomit. He only almost did.

Sayah turned his head away from the meal, and Mother, noticing his reluctance, asked, "Is something wrong, Sayah?"

Sayah didn't know how to answer, though he had suspicions, none of which he wanted to share with his family.

Instead, he answered, "I'm not hungry right now. Would it be alright if I ate later?"

"Sure!" Mother replied. "Just make sure you don't starve yourself. A growing æglet such as yourself needs to eat."

Sayah nodded, hoping to try again later, but concerned he might not succeed. He retired to huddle near the edge of the nest where he would be out of the wind. Any fears he harbored that Gael might attack him while he slept were gone, and he lay down in warm security to sleep.

While it was still dark the following morning, Sayah arose before the rest of his family. He approached the untouched remains of the weasel that Mother had given him the night before and tried again to eat. Once more, his gorge arose, and he wondered why. Without a clear and immediate answer, however, he decided the best course of action would be to get rid of the carcass.

Fighting his impulse to throw up, Sayah, gripped the weasel's tail in his beak, and quietly inched out of the nest and onto the spreading branches of the Tree. He couldn't just throw the corpse from the nest to have it land in the bower below. He decided that Miyam with her prohibition on hunting would be displeased if it started raining dead weasels in Sanctuary, and thus, he crept to the far end of a branch to toss the body as far as he could.

Sayah felt the branch sway and quiver beneath his weight and that of the weasel, and decided he was far enough out that he could pitch the body past the Sanctuary hedge below. He turned his back toward the outer edge of the Tree and passed the weasel from his beak to one of his talons with care. Sayah seized the branch beneath him with the other claw, his talons digging into the bark for stability. Looking past his shoulder, Sayah raised the claw holding the prey in front of him, cocked in anticipation of his cast. He swung his foot, corpse and all, back behind him as hard as he was able, pitching the stiffening body in a long arc.

Sayah was surprised at his own strength as the weasel flew well past the perimeter of Sanctuary to crash through the canopy with the soft, distant snap of small branches. Satisfied at disposing of the body, and feeling a little guilty at the deception, Sayah looked around to see if he'd been detected. All else was quiet and still from what he could tell, and none stirred in the nest.

Sayah took great pains to return to the nest with as little noise as possible, and was already over the wicker edge when Gael's voice drawled with veiled venom, "And what are you up to so early in the morning?"

Indignation overrode Sayah's initial startlement at her voice, and he rebutted, "Mind your own business, Gael. I don't have to answer your questions."

There, he thought, *I don't* have to *lie.*

Gael's hackles flew up again, and she looked to start toward him from her place, but she reconsidered, scanning the area for clues as to

Sayah's activities. A small, bloody stain marked where the weasel had once lay, and Gael's eyes narrowed at its absence.

"Did you finally finish your dinner, then?" she inquired with suspicion.

Sayah's heart leapt at the question, but his expression remained impassive as he repeated, "Like I said. What I do is none of *your* business, Gael."

A wild, foolish impulse to prod her drove him to add, "I know I didn't stutter, and I've said it twice now. Perhaps your memory is failing?"

That was enough, Gael was up and halfway to him when Father's voice broke in, bringing her advance to a halt, "Now that's enough from both of you. Can't your parents get a moment's rest without you bickering? Gael, at least Sayah was quiet enough he didn't wake us. Leave. him. alone."

Father's great eyes gleamed from atop his neck, which stood tall and erect, outlined against the pre-dawn gloom. The æglets perceived the menace in his voice and his body language, and even Gael wasn't quite ready to challenge Father, despite her high opinion of herself. She muttered agreement and skulked back to where she lay to nestle down into what warmth remained there.

Sayah concealed the grin that threatened to reveal his pleasure at the turn of events, and he rasped a respectful, "Yes, Father!" on his way back to his sleeping area. His reckless head whirled in the fleeting darkness, and he reconsidered his foolishness in provoking Gael. The Spirit concurred, and Sayah wondered at his Comforter's constant presence.

Maybe I can get some answers about my sudden change in appetite? Sayah thought.

Clear to his mind came a memory of his first sips of water from the Tree's streams and of the rhema he'd consumed each day following his immersion in the springs. Before he'd washed in the waters, the rhema had revolted him, much like the weasel had earlier. Once he'd bathed in and partaken of the Tree's waters, however, the rhema had appealed to him. He'd eaten it and been satisfied, its sweet savor filling him with strength and a longing for more.

Sayah realized that the rhema hadn't just sated his appetite for flesh but had *replaced* the bloodlust that had once driven him to kill and to eat his quarry. It would seem the changes the Spirit had worked in him ran deeper than Sayah had at first thought. But if he couldn't eat the meat that Mother brought him, then what *could* he eat? The question remained unanswered for the moment, and though his stomach rumbled, Sayah didn't sense a pressing need to eat as he neared the shallow indentation he hoped remained warm.

In the depression, a single wafer of the rhema lay. Sayah hadn't noticed it when he left to dispose of the carcass and knew he hadn't brought any up with him from Sanctuary. He glanced left and right for any sign of Astéri and found none. Still, it wouldn't do for Gael or his parents to discover it, and Sayah didn't have anywhere to hide it, so he did the obvious – he ate it. The sweet, crisp flake soon dissolved on Sayah's tongue, and he settled in to doze until the others awoke to the hunt.

Mother and Father soon arose to the breaking day, prompting Gael to do the same, and she cast Sayah sullen glances while she and the older ægles prepared to leave on their hunt. Concerned for his friends' safety on their journey to Endego, Sayah hoped his family's flight would take them any direction but southward today. It wouldn't do if the ægles spotted the column of Etom as they traversed the woodlands on the way to Endego. The raptors would make short work of Sayah's friends, and bring talons full of them, dead or alive, back to the nest with the expectation that Sayah, too, would partake. Sayah shivered at the thought, and the feathers all over his body stood out, giving the underdeveloped æglet a strange, fluffy appearance.

Mother noticed Sayah's disquiet, and asked, "Will you be alright today while we hunt?"

"Yeah. I'll be fine," Sayah replied.

"One day soon, I'll expect a full report from you on where you were and what you were doing while you were gone," Mother insisted. "You'll want to be ready, because on that day, I won't take 'no' for an answer. Do you understand?"

Sayah nodded and followed the trio to the edge of the nest where they perched in preparation to leave. Without a word of farewell, Sayah's family launched into flight, and arced their way eastward, spreading out to sweep sky and earth for any sign of prey. Sayah exhaled with relief that they appeared to be hunting to the east for the day and sought some means of distraction to relieve his boredom while he awaited his family's return.

With the Spirit's guidance, Sayah meditated on the truths he'd learned in Sanctuary and on his adventures with Nat. His memory served him well, and soon he sensed his attunement to the Spirit in Resonance with His presence.

It was similar to when he had learned to distinguish Father's cry from the various tweets, chirps, and calls issuing from forest and sky around the aerie. As a wee æglet chick, Sayah had learned to focus on what he knew of Father's voice and screen out the various distractions around him.

Now, Sayah "listened" along those same guidelines for the Spirit's "voice," his inner being homing in based on previous, unmistakable experiences with the Spirit and the Kinsman, while forcing distraction from his mind. With practice, Sayah learned he could sense the Spirit more readily as he became more familiar with His essence, though the occasional wayward thought or external stimulus intruded beyond his tolerance to ignore it.

Thus occupied, Sayah passed a good many hours in meditation and prayer as he learned to discern the Spirit's voice, and nary a thought of hunger entered his mind until at last his stomach no longer rumbled but roared. The resolute pinch of hunger pangs seized Sayah to the point of interference with his task, and he opened his eyes to scan the horizon with sporadic twitches of his gaze.

As he looked about him, an odd light outlined the landscape in intermittent flashes. Spots swam in the narrow bands of light that limned the scenery, and its color varied according to its surroundings. From time to time, a dark smudge would soar across his vision, and Sayah wondered if he was quite well.

He closed his eyes and with the edge of each wing, rubbed his eyelids, hoping to extinguish the aberrant light he'd seen. To his distress, closing his eyes had the opposite effect, and with great clarity, the strange cords of light yet stood in sharp relief behind the once-comforting darkness of his shuttered lids.

He cried out in frustration and tucked his head beneath a sparse wing in attempt to hide from his startling vision. While it didn't cease all at once, the strange, luminescent network subsided over ample moments until disappearing altogether. Sayah raised his harried head, pleased to find the world once more aright in his eyes. He turned to the east, looking in the direction his family had flown this morning, and perceived the trio in hurried flight his way.

It's unusual that they're back so early in the day, he thought. *I wonder if everything's alright.*

All three ægles shrieked their approach and flew straight at the nest instead of circling as usual to slow for landing. Father flew at the head of a tight, triangular formation, Mother and Gael on either side. While they were yet a good way off, Sayah's uncanny eyes caught the fury on Father's face, and the worry on Mother's. Gael met Sayah's gaze with sinister glee, and for the first time since his return home, Sayah felt fear.

The æglet stood surrendered in the center of the nest, a lone figure awaiting sentencing for his crimes. Father snapped his wings open for a sudden stop as soon as he reached the nest, momentum carrying his bulk to crash into Sayah and pin the æglet down.

Standing over his son, Father roared, "WHAT HAVE YOU DONE?!?"

Mother and Gael likewise dropped into the nest, opening their wings at the final moment to drag themselves to a stop.

From around Father's heaving form, Mother peered down at Sayah, and spoke, her anxiety apparent with every word, "Sayah, we've just come from Sakkan. A contingent of kestrels intercepted us over the village because they were looking for an æglet. An æglet who doesn't fly."

Sayah had stiffened at the mention of Sakkan, and spotted Gael's sneering smirk beside Father's furious grimace.

Sayah guessed, *I wouldn't be surprised if it was Gael's idea to go to Sakkan today.*

"Well?!?" Father barked. "Is there something you want to tell us?"

Even in the tumult of the situation, Sayah was able to sense the Spirit tugging for attention.

Really? Right now? Sayah thought, at first exasperated, but then submitting to the call.

Sayah closed his eyes and sought the Spirit's wisdom, higher than his own, and perhaps his only chance. Fear was swept away, awash in peace as the Spirit lent Sayah His understanding.

Sayah's eyes, shining and clear, opened to look back at Father and answer, "I think it's best if I don't tell you anything. No doubt the Empire will be very interested to learn what may or *may not* have happened in Sakkan. You wouldn't want the Nihúkolem to come *here* would you? From what I've learned, not many survive their interrogations…intact."

Sayah watched his words penetrate each member of his audience: Mother's anxiety increased, Father's fury turned to worry, and Gael's conceited mask fell away to reveal the insecurity there.

Once comprehension had sunk in sufficiently, Sayah proposed, "Perhaps it would be best if you just…let me go? I could leave and never come back, and I wouldn't tell anyone that you're my family. If I go now, I could get far enough away that the Empire might not catch up with me."

He'd had momentum in unbalancing them all, and Father in particular, until his final statement.

With a sudden snap, Father locked eyes on Sayah, his grimace deep and bitter as he spoke, "Far enough away? Might not catch up with you? Son, you don't seem to understand. The Empire is *everywhere*. There is nowhere you can run, nowhere far enough away to escape the Empire of Chōl. No. I have others plans for you."

"Son, none of us said a word to the kestrels when they asked us about you," Mother began, "but we've been conscripted into the search. For *you*! And for a bunch of miserable Etom! How could you risk our family for these strangers? They're not even your own *kind*!"

The Æglet's Answer

Conscious that Mother was growing louder, Father interrupted, "We can't hide you here with all manner of eyes on the aerie. We're taking you far away to some relatives up north. If you're discovered there, just lie and say they found you wandering out that way. It's the least you can do for your family."

Gael cleared her throat for Father's attention and inclined her head toward the westering sun as a reminder the hour grew late. She'd not said a word since landing, and that unpleasant smile had crept its way across her face again.

At Gael's prompting, Father arose and turned his back to Sayah, calling over his shoulder as he stooped, "Hurry! You must get on my back. We leave now!"

Stunned at the suddenness of their departure, yet nevertheless compliant, Sayah arose and leapt to Father's broad back, wrapping his meager wings best he could around the stiff neck.

"Hold tight!" Father shouted, and raced to the edge of the nest, pushing off hard with his feet as he fought for immediate altitude.

It was an awkward launch that was absent Father's usual, effortless grace, and relied on brute power to climb under Sayah's added weight and the restriction the æglet's form imposed on the action of Father's wings. Regardless, they ascended in steady increments with each of Father's arduous wingbeats until they met a powerful updraft that carried them to heights Sayah had only dreamed of reaching, Mother and Gael followed close behind.

To say Sayah enjoyed his first flight would misrepresent the experience. It was dizzying wonder and heartbreaking loss all at once as Sayah's excitement crescendoed in the majesty of flight, only to crash when reminded of the purpose of the flight – his exile and further separation from Nat and the Kinship he had come to love. How would they know where to find him? Would he ever see them again?

These questions and more assailed him while Father carried them through the night on unceasing wings, their course taking them ever into the wintry north. Bittersweet, too, was the realization that in all his life, his life-or-death grip around Father's neck was the nearest thing to an embrace that Sayah had ever shared with him. A glance to either side revealed Mother's anxiety remained unchanged, as did Gael's smug, satisfied smile.

The succession of discouragements might have made Sayah altogether despondent if not for the steady reverberation in his soul reminding him the Spirit was with him still, connecting him also to his friends through the Vine. Encouraged, Sayah rested in Resonance for the remainder of their flight.

The air grew colder, and from time to time, they flew through snowy flurries. Soon strange, undulating ribbons of eerie green and purple light arose across the horizon, and Sayah wondered if the earlier phenomenon with his vision was recurring. These were different than the all-encompassing, brilliant web he had seen earlier, and appeared only on the northern horizon.

He ventured a question to Father, "What are those?"

Father bellowed, "The Northern Lights! We're nearly there! No more talking – the air is thin here!"

A dark and crooked shelf of stone loomed beneath the Northern Lights, a high and bitter precipice of stone whose jagged lip sparkled as the ice and frost upon it reflected the shifting, brilliant display. Father aimed well above the cliffs, beating hard against the cold and thinning air for meager gains in altitude, and Sayah felt the pounding of Father's heart as he labored against the constant pull of gravity.

Confused, Sayah wondered why Father struggled to climb so high over the cliffs. The answer came when they were only a short distance from the stony shelf. A terrifying, frozen blast of wind slammed into them from above, driving them almost straight down. It was all Father could do to maintain their forward momentum, and their trajectory angled steeply downward. From Sayah's perch atop Father's back, it seemed they would strike the face of the cliff before reaching the safety of its edge. But Father locked his wings wide open, leaning back hard while tipping his tail feathers upward and spreading them as a fan for maximum resistance. The overall result was a scooping effect that scooted them forward through the frightening wind current.

Sayah looked back to find Gael and Mother performing the same maneuver, though with greater ease, and the trio circled wide to land in a flat, rocky clearing among icy, jagged stones. Great sheets of stone leaned upthrust against one another atop the precipice, and in the shadows of the space beneath their tented forms, Sayah detected movement.

"Sayah," Father growled as he straightened and swatted at Sayah's wings, which yet encircled his neck.

Sayah released his cramped wings, brittle with cold pain, and slid down Father's back to scan the frigid landscape. His attention returned to the gloom of the strange, lean-to caves, haphazard in their natural arrangement, and whence proceeded a troupe of strange, great birds. Their eyes were grave and their necks thick and long as they marched forth on well-feathered legs to greet their visitors. They looked a bit like vultures Sayah had seen from time to time, circling in the distance, but these were larger, and each had a tiny tuft of feathers protruding from beneath his chin like a beard.

From the forefront of the procession the largest, a female, hailed them, "Who goes there?"

"Hollowback!" Father called in response. "Cousin, it's Windspanne. I've brought my family."

Hollowback stepped into the clearing under the shifting lights from the North, and peered at Father before answering with cool detachment, "Windspanne. Yes, I know you. What brings you here, so far from your warm home in the South?"

Though Sayah knew Father's name, he had only ever heard him addressed as Father, and it struck him strange to hear him named aloud.

Father extended a wing toward his family, who stood in a loose cluster nearby, and introduced them, "This is my mate, Stromweise, and the fledgling is my daughter, Gael. The æglet's name is Sayah."

The frozen wind could not have chilled Sayah as deeply as his Father's introduction. Not "his son." Just "the æglet." Such distance Father placed between them. Any tattered remnants of the honor Father had bestowed upon Sayah at his return home slipped away into oblivion on the frigid gusts. Even so, the Spirit salved his wounded soul, beckoning he step away from the yawning void that opened in invitation before him. No! He would not submit to the despondent yearning.

Instead, Sayah leaned in to hear the smattering of conversation drifting on the wind from Father's conspiratorial huddle with Hollowback.

"...hide...Empire...stay here...don't...how long...much food..."

Their discussion concluded, Father returned to where the ægle family waited and addressed Mother, "They said they would take him. He's not very big, so it's not much trouble to feed him, and it's far enough away that it should take the Empire a long time before they come looking here."

Mother lowered her head in resignation, and whispered, "At least he'll be safe. For a while."

Father looked at Sayah, and commanded, "Don't you give our cousins here any more trouble than you already have, Sayah. They are taking a great risk by hiding you here, and you owe them your life."

Contempt in his eyes and dubious derision in his tone, Father added, "Who knows? Maybe you'll learn to make some use of yourself while you're here."

With that, Father lifted a wing to Hollowback in farewell, and then launched from the cliffs, his form dipping hard toward the distant ground as he encountered the forbidding downward current. Mother passed a wing across her son's back, but didn't embrace him, though Sayah saw the bitter agony in her eyes as she turned to leap from the stony heights.

Only Gael remained with Sayah, and broke her smug silence at last, "Well, *Brother*, I couldn't have arranged a more fitting torture myself, though I *did* make sure we ran into those kestrels in Sakkan.

"Enjoy yourself here in the cold. At least the Lights are nice. Try not to freeze to death before I see you again. I'll want to tell you how I picked apart your little Etom friends, bit by bit."

Horrified at Gael's threat, Sayah started toward her in protest, but she had already turned her back to saunter toward the edge.

Before she launched from the icy edge, she called over her shoulder, "Welcome to the Cold Vantage, Sayah! Enjoy your stay!"

Then she was off, her figure blurring, then disappearing as it began to snow.

Chapter Eighteen
Busting the Bunker Mentality

Dempsey awoke to the buzz of activity within the Bunker, and ran a hand through his straggling zalzal, which were both too dirty and too long for comfort. He hoped they could soon find some fresh water and shears for the ragtag group. He imagined they'd all be more welcome in the Bunker and in Endego if they improved their hygiene and grooming, long-neglected in favor of more critical priorities.

A good many Kin yet stretched in their bedrolls, which didn't account for the hushed, yet busy clamor that Dempsey detected. He spotted Alcarid's avocado-colored form in motion across the Bunker . . .with Iver right behind, chattering in the elder etém's ear. Dempsey shook his head in dismayed wonder at the speed with which the disgruntled Iver was ingratiating himself.

Iver was up to no good, and Dempsey would have to get to the bottom of it before long. Dempsey eyes met Kabir's where he sat alone, his oversized form laughable in a child-size seat as he leaned, face in hand and an elbow on one of the student lunch tables. Kabir took the hand away from his face and cocked a subtle, two-fingered salute, then inclined his head and pointed at Iver. His lips pursed, Dempsey nodded that he, too, had noticed, and arose to approach Kabir's awkward sentry perch.

"He's been at it all morning," Kabir murmured as Dempsey sat down across from him. "Up even before me. He was at Alcarid's side first thing. I have to wonder if he even slept."

Dempsey thought it odd that the oft-listless Iver was now so motivated, but was more concerned at the malcontent's motives, *What is he up to?*

"Did you think over our discussion last night?" Dempsey asked.

"I did," Kabir began, "and I can't say I'm any more excited about it now than I was last night, but I don't see how else we can figure out what his plans are."

"How about this?" Dempsey proposed. "What if we keep the number of observers extremely small? Only the most trusted Etom in key places?"

"If we are going to do this, then that seems best," Kabir concurred. "Secrets have a nasty way of getting out, and of spoiling trust when they do."

"Well, I hope we don't have to watch him for long, anyway," Dempsey returned. "If we don't figure out his plans soon, we might be too late. You see how quickly he's moving."

Kabir inquired, "So who do we trust?"

"Nida, Tram, and Kehren are obvious choices, but maybe *too* obvious. Iver might expect them to be watching," Dempsey surmised. "How about Kaasi and Muta? You've spent some time with them. What do you think?"

"I've trusted them with my life more than once now," Kabir replied. "They are like brothers to me, and they know how to be discreet."

"So those two for sure, then," Dempsey confirmed. "With you and I, that makes seven. Any others?"

Kabir, his lips askew in thought, gave a slow, doubtful shake of his head and offered, "I don't know. Hezi? He's all in for the Kinsman, and Nat or Rae might be able to handle it."

Dempsey thought about it, then objected, "I don't question Hezi's loyalty, but he lacks a necessary measure of caution. And I don't think we should involve the children. They are capable kids, but it could be dangerous."

"I see your point," Kabir conceded. "I think the seven of us ought to be able to keep tabs on Iver and his group, but are you going to talk to Agatous? We need to warn her about Iver."

"I think I'll take Nida with me to speak with Agatous," Dempsey affirmed. "Agatous trusts us both, and we'll need her to handle Alcarid. He seems to be getting pretty cozy with Iver."

Dempsey stood to go, then leaned down to tell Kabir in a low voice, "I'll get Nida, Tram, and Kehren on board, then go see Agatous. Can you talk to Kaasi and Muta?"

"You got it," Kabir answered, standing to find his recruits. "I'll see you later."

Dempsey and Kabir each went their separate ways, and as he departed Kabir's company, Dempsey chuckled – a bath and a trim didn't seem very important anymore. Again. He found Tram and Kehren seated on the floor with Nat and Rae, who laughed as they indulged one another in that secret language only true friends speak. Tram and Kehren watched them in relaxed amusement, and the domestic scene struck Dempsey as one uncommon to their recent lives.

Dempsey sidled up next Tram and Kehren, crouching down to join the couple, who offered distracted greetings when he said, "hello."

"I'm guessing you're not here for breakfast," Tram stated, matter-of-fact.

A knowing look passed between Tram and Kehren as Dempsey confirmed, "You are correct, my friend. I'm not hungry right now. I'm a little too busy trying to figure out what Iver and his faction are doing."

Kehren stepped in, "We noticed, too. He's been a busy little bee today."

"So, you've been watching him as well," Dempsey replied. "Well, that should make this a tad easier."

"What do you need?" Tram asked without reservation.

Dempsey's eyes flickered toward Nat and Rae to ensure they were still focused on their play, and answered, "We need to keep an eye on Iver and his people, and we need to be careful about it. It won't do if we're detected. We should have some help, but I don't want to say who just yet."

The question on his face, Tram looked to Kehren, who gave a short nod of assent, though her weary displeasure was evident. Dempsey understood. They had been on mission for many months, and it wore at the soul.

"Look. I wouldn't ask unless I thought it was absolutely necessary. I trust you both like family, and right now our greater family may be at risk," Dempsey pleaded.

"I know," Kehren answered. "We have a responsibility, and we love all these new Etom, strangely enough. We'll do it."

"What do you want us to do?" Tram asked.

"Just keep doing what you've already been doing this morning," Dempsey answered. "If you see anything you think I ought to know, tell me. If I need anything else from you, I'll let you know. Otherwise, I'm grabbing Nida on my way to warn Agatous."

"Oh!" Kehren exclaimed, "She's probably already with Agatous. She headed there a few minutes ago."

"Perfect. I'll get going then," Dempsey declared as he stood to leave. "Thank you both. I'll catch up with you later."

Dempsey ruffled Nat's zalzal and patted Rae on the head as he left, wishing them both a good day, and then headed for the back of the Bunker, where they had met with Agatous the night before. On the way, he passed close by Alcarid and Iver, who shot Dempsey a contemptuous sidelong glance that Dempsey pretended to ignore.

It was difficult in places to see across the Bunker, which was now crowded with the many Etom delivered from Sakkan. As Dempsey slipped past the press of bodies, the way before him began to clear, and he soon caught sight of Nida and Agatous in conversation around the fire pit at the end of the large chamber.

Moving with determined strides, Dempsey was at Nida's side in seconds, and heard a snippet of their discussion as Agatous concluded, " . . .heard from six other companies that they are already on their way back. We should see them over the next few weeks."

Nida was at the same time excited and alarmed, "It will be great to see so many of our old friends, but where is everyone supposed to stay?"

"We will have to work that out," Agatous admitted, "but isn't it best for us all to be together again? Especially with the news you brought back of the Kinsman?"

"Yes, I supposed it is," Nida conceded, then turned her attention to Dempsey, whose eagerness was apparent as he waited. "What's going on, Dempsey?"

Dempsey requested, "Agatous, do you mind if I borrow Nida for a moment? I'll need to speak with you after, if you can spare the time."

"Of course," Agatous answered, while Dempsey took Nida aside to explain the situation with Iver.

Seconds later, they were back with Agatous, and were just about to warn her when Shoym arrived. With a quick glance to one another, Dempsey and Nida decided they ought to bring their trusted friend into their confidence as well. With a rapid-fire back and forth between them, Dempsey and Nida described Iver's behavior since they had left Sakkan and warned the two Eben'kayah leaders that Iver must be serving his own agenda in getting so close to Alcarid. They left it in Agatous and Shoym's hands how they might handle Alcarid, but in no uncertain terms indicated Iver's ill intent.

"You say you have people watching Iver already?" Agatous inquired.

"Yes," Dempsey responded. "We are quietly assembling a team now. Would you like us to keep you informed?"

"Definitely," Agatous agreed. "If this Etom is a traitor, then we need to determine his designs at once and put a stop to them. My primary concern is that he or one of his group might move to alert the Empire of our presence here."

"If that happens, we need to be ready," Shoym concurred, "I'll make sure my people at the door are on the lookout."

"And may I suggest that none of them be allowed outdoors or on any security details until we know what's going on?" Dempsey advised.

"Certainly not!" Shoym blurted. "Only the most trusted and capable among us are permitted those privileges and duties."

"Speaking of going outside," Nida began, "how are we going to keep feeding everyone here if we can't hardly go outdoors?"

"An *excellent* question, Mistress Nida," Alcarid asserted as he drew near with Iver close behind, their arrival surprising them all, though none of their faces registered alarm.

Alcarid complimented Nida, "I have always appreciated your practical mind."

"It's a question we must answer if any of us are to survive," he continued with conviction, then turned a pointed gaze on Agatous. "How, indeed?"

Agatous, her smile thin, but accommodating, answered, "We have just begun to address that very question, as you well heard, Alcarid. Perhaps you might join us for the discussion? We will have need of your insight to determine a solution."

"Why, of course, Chief Counciletma Agatous!" Alcarid returned with mock sincerity. "It would be my pleasure!"

Oh dear! Nida thought, *He's already worse than he was last night.*

Her eyes flickered to where Iver stood, impassive, behind Alcarid, and concluded, *It must be Iver's influence. I wonder what in the world he's been telling Alcarid?*

Alcarid moved to join their gathering around the ring, and Iver intended to follow, but Shoym blocked him with an extended arm, "My apologies, but this meeting is for the Eben'kayah of Endego only. I'm sure you understand."

The disappointed rage that flashed across Iver's face showed that he, in fact, did not understand. Then his face was once more serene and eyes dull, though the heated flush of his anger had yet to drain altogether from his countenance.

"It's fine, Iver," Alcarid reassured. "I'm certain we'll continue our discussion later."

"Very well," Iver managed with a saccharine smile. "I look forward it."

Turning on his heel, Iver stalked away. Dempsey watched him until he lost track in the milling crowd, but not before he determined the unhappy etém was headed back to his sullen followers clustered along the wall.

Dempsey's eyes darted about until he spotted Muta not far from the bunch. The large etém spied Dempsey and offered a near-imperceptible nod before returning to his surveillance of Iver and his crew. Satisfied,

Dempsey brought his focus to bear on the meeting, which was still in the preliminary stages.

He caught the tail end of Nida speaking, "...which is why I say our capacity for scavenging has increased with our numbers, we just need to train properly and establish protocols."

"It's very risky," Agatous rejoined. "The more Etom we send out, the greater our chance of discovery."

"While I agree that the risks are high, we mustn't allow that to discourage us," Alcarid asserted. "If we don't do something to augment our stores, there won't be any Etom left to be discovered. We'll starve to death. And we've yet to mention waste disposal, bathing, washing...the list goes on."

Thinking aloud, Shoym spoke up, "If we could begin to move out from the Bunker in all directions, just a bit at a time, and perhaps establish a system of warning? Something to tell us when a threat was near?"

"A large part of the problem is the other Etom in Endego," shared Agatous. "They've been coerced into informing on any activities the Empire deems illegal. If an Etom is caught outside except for the few hours mid-day it's allowed, then they are subject to arrest.

"Neighbors, acquaintances, family – anyone in the area when the violation occurred are also interrogated to determine why these Etom didn't inform on the violator. If they don't answer to the Empire's satisfaction, they too, are arrested.

"This makes for a population very motivated to keep everyone else in line, and the Etom of Endego are constantly watching one another, making *our* movements very difficult as well."

"That's why we only go out at night," Shoym explained. "The darkness helps us stay out of sight while most Etom are asleep anyhow. The foxes don't come into the village often, as that might cause a panic, but they prevent folks from leaving to seek freedom elsewhere.

"Also, and we don't know how exactly, the foxes have a way of calling for the Nihúkolem. The Nihúkolem themselves do not often appear in the village, but we know they have their ways of watching, and the foxes are just one of those ways."

Dempsey thought back to the atmosphere of Sakkan – the hushed, rigid conduct of the Etom there and the sense of constant watchfulness. It was oppressive, and he hated to think it, too, had come to pass in Endego, where they had for the most part enjoyed the liberty of being left alone.

The presence of the Eben'kayah had changed that, however, when they became a lightning rod for the Empire's attention. Especially since the appearance of the Kinsman, who had posed a serious enough threat to the Empire that the Nihúkolem were dispatched to suppress any talk of His coming.

But why? Dempsey thought. *Does the Empire fear the Kinsman that much? No! Not just the Kinsman Himself. The Empire doesn't want anyone to hear about Him, even after executing Him. Maybe that's the point of keeping everyone isolated in their homes.*

Distracted by his own thoughts, Dempsey had failed to follow the discussion, and he again came in as Nida spoke, "But who are the best candidates for such a scouting mission?"

Shoym replied, "Well, only two of us who stayed behind are skilled or fit enough to venture outside. I'm one of them, and it's a stretch for me."

Dempsey jumped in as Shoym finished, "I know this might seem off the topic, but has anyone reached out to the other Etom in Endego? I know it's dangerous, but maybe there's support there."

"I should think not!" Alcarid objected. "That's far too risky to attempt, and with too few benefits."

Dempsey leveled a sober stare at Alcarid and asked, "Would you consider greater freedom of movement throughout the grove and the potential restoration of our community of little benefit, Alcarid? Don't you see that if we recruit these others to resist the Empire, they won't inform on us if they spot us, and may even join us as Eben'kayah?"

Eyes shining with excitement, Nida and Shoym nodded in agreement, but Agatous balked, "How do you propose to accomplish that, Dempsey? Every instance of contact with an outsider may result in capture. Every Eben'kayah captured might give up our location under interrogation or torture. And who would be willing to attempt it, given these risks?"

"It seems we ought to consider the risk of *not* doing as Dempsey proposed," Nida interjected. "We have several dozen Eben'kayah on recall whose homes were demolished along with the temple. We are nearly at capacity here in the Bunker and have an unsustainable need for resources as it is. What happens when all these others return? What if, like us, they bring others with them? Where will everyone stay? What will everyone eat?"

Alcarid's head looked like it might explode, and his cheeks went dark with blood as he responded, "I still don't see how what you're proposing will help with the housing issues you bring up, and we don't anticipate the others bringing back a great lot of hangers-on as you have. You yourselves have created the scarcity by which you argue a disastrous point!

"We were doing fine until you showed up with your, your . . .refugees and your fanciful tales! We had plenty of room for all of *our* Eben'kayah and plans for how to feed them *without* risking ruin. Now we're stuck taking care of these strangers, and our own have no place when they get back. It's not fair, and it's not right!"

Agatous had been content to allow Alcarid his outburst, but now cautioned, "Alcarid, that's quite enough. I believe you've made your position perfectly clear."

As if a spring bubbling up from within, the Spirit arose within Nida and in a quiet voice, she began, "I see now what's happened since we left. You've forgotten what it was to *be* the Eben'kayah, but now I will remind you.

"When I first met all of you, I had no one but the Lord Elyon to support me, and that was sufficient. But the Kinsman has revealed that was not Elyon's ultimate plan for any of us. We're meant to be together. To grow together. To love *together*.

"And that is who the Eben'kayah of Endego were to me. The first to see me and my son not as a burden, but as a blessing. Each Eben'kayah is a vast resource and each must decide if he will give of himself to help others. Or not.

"It saddens me to see that you, Alcarid, have elected for the latter, rather than the former. Did not Elyon provide for me and my son through every season before we met you? Did He not draw us to the Eben'kayah, and all the Eben'kayah together? And did He not promise us the Kinsman to free us from the Stain and from the chains of oppression that the Empire has laid on us?

"It seems that you've allowed these trials to destroy your faith in Him rather than strengthen it, and I pity you. I pray that Elyon restores you to the loving soul I once knew, Alcarid. The etém who appeared so calculating on the outside, but whose tender heart beat for the ones he loved."

The color drained from Alcarid's face, and tears rolled from his eyes as he lamented, "Mistress Nida, you cut me with your words, but you are right. I have given up. After all the pain and loss of these past months, I don't have the strength to make room in my heart for these, too."

He waved an arm over the mass that milled about the Bunker, and meanwhile Nida approached him to lay an arm across his shoulder and a hand upon his heart, saying, "Do you think you might have room for just One more? Please just let the Kinsman in. He's waiting for you."

Once Nida overcame Alcarid's objections, they had agreed to assume the risks of connecting with the other Etom of Endego, and the scouting program pushed forward at a rapid pace. It felt a bit like the old days in the Forge as the original members of Company Jasper took assessment of the refugees of Sakkan. They had a few Etom in mind already, those who'd proven able and quick to learn while on the journey to Endego.

These they took aside and drilled on various skills with the limited space and resources available inside the Bunker. Depending on their aptitude when performing the drills, they culled even more from the group, leaving just a handful of recruits. Those culled they asked Shoym to take aside and prepare instead for sentry duty outside the Bunker.

While these might not be the best equipped for the task of scouting, most had basic competencies that they could put to use watching for danger outside.

Given their prior commitment to watching Iver, Muta, Kaasi, and Kabir were included in the initial group, but excused themselves from the running with less than spectacular showings during their assessments. They hoped they weren't too obvious in their intentional failures, but it would have been even more so if they hadn't been considered in the first place.

All the while, Iver watched on in frustration. None of his group was considered for training due to lack of ability or motivation while on the trail, though that was not the only reason. In addition, Iver found it ever more difficult to get close to Alcarid or any other leadership in the Bunker. Dempsey warned them to put the disgruntled etém off with subtle care, and even Alcarid complied after his conversation with Nida.

It only took a day or two to prepare the selected bunch for a dry run outside the Bunker. In the wee hours of the morning, they ventured outside into the ebon shadows of the grove, Shoym in the lead and Dempsey at the back. Shoym led for the simple reason that he'd grown quite familiar with the altered reality of navigating Endego under Chōl's martial edict, and now guided them on a circuitous course to where the temple and olive tree once stood.

From the west, they rounded a clump of willow trees, keeping their distance from the homes beneath them, which stood dark. They might appear empty, Shoym had warned, but he was almost certain they were occupied, since no one had been allowed to leave Endego unless the Nihúkolem had carried them off. Through the dwindling underbrush, Dempsey spotted Potter's Arch, the old bridge that had once seemed a friendly link over the Üntfither to the temple and all the promise it once held.

Shoym halted the stealth parade with an upraised fist and scanned up and down the length of the stream's far side. The moonlight was dim, but sufficient to see from where they crouched in the grass that over the past few days, the Nihúkolem had dragged what remained of the olive tree away. All that remained of tree, temple, and homes was a deep concavity so untouched by the meager light that it appeared full of hopeless darkness.

Their position was only a short distance south of Galfgallan Road, and Shoym was preparing to signal the troop onward when a distant glow on the boulevard stopped him. The luminescence was dissimilar to that of a torch or a lamp, and had a curious, golden-green cast that Shoym didn't recognize. He hesitated, watching to see what the road carried their way.

To the contrary, Dempsey found the light familiar, though at first, he couldn't place the source. A brown and leafy figure perhaps twice the height of an adult Etom glided down the road toward them, bathed in the strange glow. Dempsey noticed Shoym's anxious eyes fixed on him and raised a patient hand to signal they should wait.

What is it? Dempsey speculated, *Perhaps a Malakím we've not met before? No, there's something about it. I feel like I know this creature.*

Breathless moments passed as the Etom hid, still and silent, and then speculation gave way to recognition when the figure had come close enough for Dempsey to get a clear look at its face.

Miyam! Dempsey realized in shock. *What is she doing here?*

Catching Shoym's attention, Dempsey signaled that he would like to go alone to get closer and was obliged without complaint. Dempsey crept past the huddled Etom with care, hurrying to intercept Miyam best he could without making too much noise. The Sprig reached Shirkrose Lane and turned south on the lane, toward the demolished clearing.

Dempsey changed course to catch up, crossing Potter's Arch with careful, low steps. It was a slow chase, and Dempsey was too far behind Miyam to reach her before she arrived at the edge of the pit.

Concerned the Sprig had not seen the chasm, Dempsey nearly cried out to warn her, but stifled the alarm when she glided down into its depths without stopping. Rushing to the edge in a silent frenzy, Dempsey looked down into the pit to find his friend, and what he saw astonished him.

Miyam's light began to fill the dark hole as she proceeded to its deepest depths, where the olive tree's roots were once established.

Taking her place at the lowest point, Miyam turned around, and Dempsey saw her face, serene and with eyes closed while she appeared to settle down into the rich soil.

All was still at first, and then the Sprig began to grow. Miyam's trunk lengthened and broadened as she sprouted up with slow deliberation, the earth rising beneath her in a mound and small clods cascading down the ever-steepening slope. Dempsey stood away from the edge of the chasm, for its edges had grown unstable at the nearby disturbance.

In amazement from afar, Shoym had witnessed the radiant form grow since it became visible from where he and the others waited. Mesmerized, he had led the others closer, unwilling to miss the event, regardless of peril.

Before long, he arrived at Dempsey's side, and asked, "What is this, Dempsey?"

Dempsey could scarcely manage, "A friend," and then fell silent beneath the vital brilliance of Miyam's spreading boughs.

While they were more than qualified to accompany Dempsey and Shoym, Nat and Nida had remained at the Bunker to ensure those assigned to guard duty knew their duties well. The role of sentry involved some climbing, and because of their proficiency therein, Nat and Nida had assumed the responsibility of training the guards.

From a high branch of the old oak tree, Nat and Nida looked around Endego for any sign of the Nihúkolem or their informers. The village was quiet, and though they couldn't see much of the clearing where the temple once stood, glimpses were visible from where they perched. All of the sudden, a light bloomed in the distant clearing, and intensified with each passing second. Nida and Nat looked at one another and, without a word, scrambled down the tree.

With a quick notice to the guard behind the Bunker's door, they lit out toward the strange glow, which was soon visible, even from the ground. There was no way the other Etom of Endego wouldn't notice it, and they wondered what fool would draw so much attention to himself with the Nihúkolem and their lackeys around.

It wasn't long before open shades revealed the vague outline of curious Etom staring from their homes, confirming Nat and Nida's earlier surmise. In normal circumstances, the pair might have been more concerned at being spotted, but the citizens of Endego were otherwise occupied, and dark clothing and masks obscured Nat and Nida's identities besides. They threw caution to the wind and sprinted down Galfgallan Road toward the brilliant disturbance.

Nat and Nida turned at Shirkrose Lane, eyes sharp for their first glance of what might be causing the commotion. When at last they had a clear view of the clearing, the scene they found was somewhat familiar. In place of the olive tree stood another tree that even now was growing to fill the void the olive had left. Its branches stretched forth, casting the tree's peculiar radiance, which covered the clearing with a mellow light that grew in brightness along with the tree. Mother and son recognized Dempsey, Shoym, and their group not far from the tree, and rushed to join them.

"What's happening?" Nida asked, the question flying from her mouth.

"I don't know if you'd believe me," Dempsey whispered in wonder, his gaze fixed on the spectacle.

"After all we've seen lately, you know better than that, Dempsey," Nida insisted, an eager Nat alongside.

Dempsey's wide eyes met hers at last, and he declared, "It's Miyam. This tree...it's Miyam!"

A sympathetic shock blossomed within Nida and Nat to accompany their comprehension of Dempsey's words, and the desire in each for further conversation ceased. In wonderment, they stood side by side while they watched, and from the homes around them issued the besieged Etom of Endego in timid trickles.

No fear showed on any face alight with the daybright glow beneath the tree, and the Etom gathered with increasing boldness to surround the strange phenomenon outside the ringed depression that remained of the once-lifeless hole. The tree seemed to reach its apex, though its trunk yet thickened and its boughs extended. At last, the tree ceased to grow, and swayed softly in the breeze, a patient presence in a moment gravid with anticipation.

Among those Etom in the Vine present, the Spirit hummed in happy harmony, a reverberant trembling attuned to the growth of the tree before them. The Resonance grew until almost intolerable, an ebb and flow of intensity building toward some unknown purpose.

In a shocking wave, power flew forth from them to meet the crux of the tree's lowest branches, where a spring erupted. The crystal waters of Sanctuary spilled down the gnarled trunk to fill the space beneath that had once signified destruction to encircle the tree in a shimmering moat.

At some indeterminate point, Miyam's face, surrendered and serene, had disappeared into the knotted bark. She had submitted her being to the will of Elyon, the Father, and had become a seed of the Kinsman's redemption planted in a world awash in the Stain.

Muttering to himself, Nat repeated her earlier words in Sanctuary, "'…we may be expanding soon.' So, this is what she meant."

"What was that, son?" Nida asked, her eyes bright and attentive in the Sanctuary glory.

"It's just something Miyam told me before we left the Kinsman's Tree," Nat answered, tears of grief and joy comingling as they ran down his face. "She said, 'we may be expanding soon,' and I didn't understand it then. But I do now."

He sobbed at the loss of his friend yet smiled with joy at what she had delivered to their land, "She laid herself down for Endego, our home, just as the Kinsman did for the world. There is no greater love."

"But she's still alive, isn't she?" Nida inquired with concern.

"Yes. Very much so," Nat replied. "Probably more so than any of us will be in this life. But don't you see? She has abandoned herself in replication of the Kinsman's Tree to give Sanctuary to us all."

At the Spirit's prompting, Nida gathered their Kin aside to discuss what they should do with the Etom of Endego assembled there. From what Nida could see, Miyam had stopped growing, but a familiar hedge began sprouting up about the clearing to encircle them all. While Nida addressed the Kinship, the others continued to watch the wild growth in amazement.

"Well, we've definitely been spotted," she began. "What do you suppose we should do about these others?"

Nat piped up, "When I first met her, Miyam told me that no one could enter Sanctuary unless the Lord Elyon drew them."

Something puzzled Nida, however, so she asked Nat his opinion, "Don't you think it might get confusing? This isn't *the* Sanctuary, so then what do we call *this* place?"

"Well, it *is* Sanctuary," Nat mused, "so maybe we could just call it Sanctuary Endego?"

Nat's suggestion seemed appropriate: Miyam's similarity to the Kinsman's Tree was striking, and the springs flowed as clear and pure as their distant source.

"If He drew them here, then I have to wonder why," Dempsey returned.

"What other reason could there be?" Nida queried. "He wants them to join us in the Vine."

"But is it possible?" Dempsey asked. "We don't know how it works. What if this is just a symbol? What if the waters here don't cleanse the Stain?"

"I know how we can find out," Nat offered.

"How, Nat?" Nida asked with interest.

"Do you remember what happened when all of us stood in the pool before the Tree?" he returned. "Both times, the Spirit interacted with us, with the Tree and with the waters."

"You're saying . . .?" Nida stopped herself, then declared. "Let's do it. Why not? Worst thing is that we might look a bit silly."

"Do we need the others from the Bunker?" Dempsey wondered.

Nat shook his head, and replied, "I think if just two, or even three of us are gathered, the Spirit will be there."

The other Kin waited in contented silence for the trio to finish their discussion and responded in the affirmative to their proposal. They were all eager to share what they had learned, what they had *become*, with the Etom of Endego. Without delay, they walked toward the water's edge, shedding their stealthy disguises as they went.

Before they had reached the expanding pool, Shoym ran up beside them, calling out, "What are you doing? You will be recognized! And you're not getting *in*, are you?"

Nida nodded gently, and explained, "Dear Master Shoym, you've known us all for quite a while now, and we hope you'll believe this truth: The Kinsman has removed our Stain and made our souls brand new.

"It's our belief that this tree is planted here to do the same for all of you. We who have already washed in the water and joined ourselves to the Kinsman wish to confirm that today salvation has come to Endego as well. Bear with us just a while, friend, and we will know for sure. We hope you'll be the first here to join us in fulfillment of the Kinsman's promise."

Shoym gave an anxious nod and backed away to join the rest as they watched his friends wade into the shallow pool. Once in the water, they joined hands to form a circle, and without prompting sought the Spirit's Resonance within.

From all corners of the darkened grove came Etom to see the radiant scene, and many from the Bunker soon arrived, though covered in disguise. The Kin who came along with them at once joined the others in the pool. For the time being, the hedge admitted everyone, and before long, almost all the Etom in Endego ringed the shining tree. And in the distance, the barking voices of many foxes approached from all sides.

Meanwhile in the pool, the Kinship tarried in expectant wonder, the susurration of whispered prayers falling from their lips. Until at last the waters shook, and beneath their feet, a trembling began. The Spirit came to give them blessing in fire from above, and the Kinship watched in wonder as upon each head alit a cloven tongue of flame. At once, Nat turned to those who stood along the shore, and nearing them, boomed in a voice that did not seem his own.

"Dear Etom of Endego!" he began, "Listen to me now! As you know, the first of Men failed in their devotion to the Creator, Lord Elyon, and ate of that fruit forbidden them. We have since suffered the consequence of their failure in the Stain that haunts us all."

"What you may not know is that Elyon promised us One who would deliver us from the curse of the Stain, a Kinsman who would redeem us. I saw the Kinsman at His death, a death upon the same tree that ruined us all – the Tree Ha Datovara. The Nihúkolem enlisted Men to nail the Kinsman to that tree and mocked Him as a counterfeit while He suffered torture on our behalf."

Recalling now the Kinsman's speech, the etém spoke his creed, "Even still, He asked of Elyon, 'Forgive them; for they know not what they do,' and cried out to Lord Elyon before he died, 'Father, into your hands I commit my spirit.'"

A discontented murmur arose along the banks among the Eben'kayah there, and Nat recognized a skeptical voice. It was Iver! The disgruntled Etom must have followed Nat and Nida here, and had dragged his fractious faction along as well.

Iver called out, "Do you expect us to believe this Kinsman was Elyon's Son? And that a just and holy Creator would forgive the ones who slew His Son?"

As one, the interested faces of the other Etom there turned to Nat, who answered, "I do, and I believe He answered the Kinsman's prayers, for when the executioners had gone, something unheard of happened – the Kinsman returned to life."

Riveted, the Etom pivoted again in unison toward the Eben'kayah's murmurs, which exploded into furor as Iver called for order and responded to Nat's claim, "Quiet! Quiet! So now you've seen the Son of the Creator murdered and then resurrected? Where is your proof, you silly dreamer?"

Nat placed an open hand on his own chest and waved the other over the Kinship in the water, replying, "*We* are that proof, as is what occurred here tonight."

Nat turned to address the crowd, scanning their faces as he continued, "And if that evidence is not sufficient, then we invite each of you to taste for yourselves and see. These who stand before you in the waters have been cleansed of the Stain and have joined the Kinsman in the family of Lord Elyon by the power of His blood. We are partakers of His Holy Spirit, by Whom He has breathed new life into us, and we ask you now – will you join us?"

"I will!"

Through the tense crowd of Eben'kayah along the shore, Shoym broke, nearly bowling several Etom over. He strode past Nat, who smiled at him and nodded, happy to see the elder etém join their number. Shoym returned the gesture, and continued to where Nida, Dempsey and the others yet stood.

"I'm ready," Shoym declared to Dempsey and Nida, who stood side by side before him. "What do I need to do?"

Dempsey suggested, "I think you ought to point out your Stain to everyone, so they'll see for themselves when it is gone."

Shoym turned and pointed to the murky blemish that spread between his eyes and saturated the growing bags beneath his eyes, "So there will be no doubt afterward, see here my Stain, which has grown here since my youth! I believe these good Etom, and I believe in the Kinsman's promises."

He turned back to face Nida and Dempsey, and asked, eager to continue, "What now?"

Nida nodded to Dempsey, who stood beside his old friend, and then she instructed, "You already believe. Now, you must immerse yourself completely in the waters here. Dempsey will help you, and when you come up, the Stain will be gone. Simple as that. Are you ready?"

Shoym covered his nose with one hand and braced himself before nodding.

Dempsey put a hand on Shoym's back between his shoulders, and called out, "In the name of the Father, and the Son, and the Holy Spirit!" then leaned Shoym back to lower him into the water.

Chapter Nineteen
The Æglet's Answer

Sayah stood alone in the stony clearing, exposed to the unforgiving wind of the Cold Vantage as Hollowback approached. She did not speak with cruelty. She did not speak with care.

It was in sober monotone that she addressed the æglet, "You must sleep as we do, among the rocks. Come. Or you will die."

Sayah took just one last look in hopes he'd spot his family, but even his fine ægle's eyes could not penetrate the blasting, snowy blizzard that now stood between him and his kin. In sorrow, he turned to follow Hollowback, who stared with stern impatience at him from the edge of the clearing.

She guided him to some tented rocks, and ordered, "Get inside. Do not come out until the sun is up, or you will freeze to death. You were not meant for such cold."

Without waiting for response, Hollowback shuffled onward to her own place of rest, and Sayah stepped into the shadowy shelter. He nestled as far back as possible without touching the frigid stone walls and found the chill wind did not much reach into the tiny cavern. He passed the night in shivering sleep, and no dreams came to haunt him.

The first shaft of sunlight awoke Sayah in his cave. He stood to stretch the cold and brittle pain from his body, unaccustomed to rest on such an unyielding surface. Stepping out into the blinding rays, he half-expected warmth, but his first contact with the morning air disabused him of the notion.

The air was cold. Very cold. It was colder than the night before, and Sayah nearly stepped back inside. Nevertheless, where the sun struck his dark and downy fluff, a soft heat began to grow, convincing him to stay outside. Sure enough, over time the temperature rose, and, with wings spread and face upturned into the sun, Sayah basked in the radiant heat.

To the Spirit, Sayah spoke his gratitude. The warmth assured him that Elyon would not let him die here. Sayah sensed he still had much to do, and the hope of seeing Nat and the others galvanized his resolution. Then his stomach rumbled, gnawing at the painful emptiness. He hadn't eaten for almost two days.

At the Spirit's prompting, Sayah looked down between his feet, where lay a single flake of the rhema. Again, he wondered whence it came, but this time dispelled the notion that Astéri or another of Elyon's agents might have brought it. It hadn't been there when Sayah had left the nook. Only the Spirit Himself could have provided it. As at home before, he snapped up the wafer at once. Although it did not much fill his belly, the morsel of honey-sweet bread filled his being with strength.

Sayah looked about for his hosts, and spied a number of the great, bearded vultures streaming from their separate coves in regular, measured steps toward the precipice. Hollowback was first out, and led the others, who funneled into a single file line from all directions without a break or stutter in their coordinated pace.

Hollowback reached the edge of the cliff, and turned sharply to the west, away from Sayah's nesting cave. The procession followed until all the vultures walked along the edge, then stopped. With a squawk, Hollowback signaled the rest, and turned to face outward. The other vultures likewise spun until they all faced out to line the edge. With another squawk, Hollowback dropped off the cliff, her wings furled, and in succession, the others followed suit until the vulture closest to Sayah took the plunge.

Sayah expected the blasting wall of wind to force the vultures first downward before they recovered beyond its powerful current. Instead, the vultures all zipped westward, flung upon the wind, and Sayah concluded that the stream must have changed directions since last night.

Interested, the æglet approached the edge with caution, and looked for his cousins. To the west, and well below his perch, Sayah located them fanning out in all directions in search of food. Far below that, Sayah caught a view of the landscape, diminished in scale by great distance, and realized for the first time just how high up they were.

Looking out to the south, Sayah found his view obscured by a vast sheet of clouds beneath his position. Holes in the clouds gave Sayah glimpses of the land below, a grey and barren place that looked as though it supported little life. He couldn't even watch the vultures once they had dipped below the cloud line, and with such dismal prospects to entertain himself, he sought the Spirit's guidance for something to do.

Boredom can be a fantastic motivator, as Sayah soon discovered. At least at home, he'd had the vibrant forest and teeming sky to watch and pass the time. It wasn't very exciting to watch the vultures "hunt" since they only went after carcasses for food. Over and over again, the vultures would pick the bones out of dead beasts below, ignoring the meat from some twisted, backwards sensibility. Flying high, they would drop the bones on the rocks until they broke open to reveal the marrow that the vultures favored. It was a tedious practice that Sayah didn't care to watch.

Hunger, too, was motivational, though in supernatural inversion to Sayah's intuition. His first day atop the Cold Vantage, Sayah learned more about the powerful current of wind that had nearly prevented his delivery the night before. His vulture cousins called this phenomenon the Windwall, and Sayah also discovered that its direction changed every few hours. In the first hours of the day, the Windwall blew to the west, stopped for a short while altogether, then blew upward, and then to the east. From nightfall to daybreak, it blasted straight down the face of the sheer precipice.

The vultures took advantage of the Windwall cycle, scavenging down below until the upward stage, then riding the powerful updraft to the Cold Vantage. The vultures were not as powerful flyers as ægles, so a vulture caught down below after the upward portion of cycle would have to remain below until the next day. This could be dangerous for the vultures, so they were very careful to avoid such a circumstance.

In any case, that first day Hollowback circled down over Sayah with a sizeable leg of lamb in her talons.

She dropped it on the stony shelf in front of him, and stated, "Eat. I will have the bone when you are done."

She had left him at once to join a close cluster of her kind in terse conversation, and Sayah had just stared at the bleeding stump, trying to decide what he would do with it. No matter how he tried to approach it, the flesh that would have once tempted him no longer held any appeal. Indeed, the more he attempted to consume it, the greater his repulsion until at last he almost vomited.

It was no good. Sayah could no longer eat meat, and Hollowback soon ceased to bring him meals when she noticed he did not eat them, though she warned the æglet that he would die without food. Instead, he looked for the smidge of rhema set outside his domicile each day. The daily bread did not satisfy the hunger of his body, yet his spirit soared every time at its savor, and Sayah soon learned that the growing hunger, coupled with the rhema's nourishment, lent him a quickening sensitivity to the Spirit.

Thus, Sayah took to meditation and prayer to break both the monotony and his lengthening fast. With time, he discovered that communing with the Spirit was more satisfying than a full belly. And while Sayah did not hear His voice in the audible sense, the Spirit guided Sayah's inner æglet through thought, image, emotion, and impression to express Himself. Where the Spirit led, Sayah did his best to follow.

Over many chill and starving days, the æglet discovered that the Spirit had distinct likes and dislikes, as well as preferences and proclivities that Sayah began to identify with increasing readiness as he became acquainted with Him. In the barrenness of the world around him, Sayah discovered a richness to his inner world that he never would have fathomed before, and the Spirit became his refuge from the cold and from hunger.

Regardless, not all was well within the æglet, and in moments of weakness, his thoughts darkened beneath a growing cloud of despondency. To Sayah, the dejection was a familiar companion that had shackled him since birth. His escape from the oppressive gloom had been brief, the span of days since meeting Nat, but the fog had returned to engulf him once more. Enfolded in the dark wings of his family's rejection and his abject worthlessness, the æglet had never felt the more a shadow, and in the darkness Sayah's thoughts flitted in futility.

Into this obscurity, the Spirit shone as Polaris, the North Star by which Sayah might orient himself. Simultaneously, the Spirit's pure light illuminated what displeased Him in Sayah's character, and Sayah stood convicted of every frail crime of corruption, the glare softened only by the understanding that the Kinsman stood condemned in his place.

In this furnace of soul-shattering reflection he was broken and, between the murky press and the bracing light, ground down to sand. Then, sifted into the awaiting crucible to be fired and melted, he was reformed. It was then that Sayah learned the Spirit did not always intervene to comfort, but rather to exhort the æglet to endure, to persevere through the seeming malediction.

With increasing clarity Sayah sensed an internal dichotomy, a war between two selves in which his sifted self was refined and separated. The Stain within him had gone deep, but this went deeper, to the core of who Sayah was. Since he hatched, the æglet's eyes were ever tinged with darkness until Sayah passed beneath the waters to remove the Stain. At that moment came old Sayah's death, or rather the beginning thereof, and another Sayah had arisen into new life. The Stain was gone, but that weary, lifeless creature yet remained with evil sentiment etched upon its deathly nature.

The Sayah of new birth found himself at odds with what he'd once been, and recognized the distinct natures were incompatible. His first clue had been his changing appetites, though he saw now his tendency toward hope as another, and contrary to who he'd once been. Desperation, too, arose, compelling now a fateful choice: death or transformation. Or, rather to let the dead within him rule, carrying his passive soul onward to death, or submit to the Spirit of Life and surrender all he was to the change he sensed was already underway.

Sayah's winter war raged through the weeks until a month had passed, and then some. Still he elected to eat only the rhema that appeared each morning. The life or death nature of his struggle had come into sharp resolution, and the æglet determined to lose no ground to his old and bloodthirsty being. So it was, on the eve of his fortieth day without food, that he at last conquered the gloomy beast.

When the darkness came that day, it was no longer a cloud, but a mere membrane, stripped of most its power. Sayah perceived the weakness, yet remained cautious, aware of careless folly. Indeed, it was well that he was wary, for at once hunger wracked his body with such pain and frailty that Sayah collapsed onto the stony ground.

His mind filled with images of tender flesh, and blood still warm within delicate bodies. His dormant cravings arose, impassioned by the prurient promise, which in the same instant screamed its doubts of Sayah's survival. Sayah nevertheless sought the Spirit's strength and found confidence in Elyon's daily provision of the rhema, which had long sustained him.

The pain and hunger desisted, and the vision faded from the æglet's mind. At once, his limbs were strengthened, and he arose from his cold repose, invigorated beyond any prior reckoning. A haughty voice, scarce-perceived, sung the æglet a ballad to himself, a song of praise foretelling how Sayah would surpass Gael to rule all ægles as a prince of the air. An unhealthy impulse seized him, and compelled him to leap from the precipitous edge, all the while promising Elyon would prevent him any harm. At the last second, Sayah stopped himself, and peeked over the verge, dizzy with a vertigo derived from heights both material and egotistical.

Sayah raised once more his trust in Lord Elyon to shield himself from the dark thrust, both direct and sinister, and blunted the dual-pronged attack. While Sayah believed that Elyon was more than able to protect him, the æglet would not presume to risk himself out of an inflated sense of importance to Elyon's plans but might rather at the Spirit's direction. To pursue the former was to tempt Lord Elyon. Likewise, Sayah knew his purpose now lay in following the Spirit, not in chasing the same self-exultant glory as Gael was wont to do.

The brittle black ceded at last to the radiant mirror of the Spirit's light that Sayah had become. The darkness evanesced in full while Sayah looked toward the heavens, directly into the sun, his eyes pouring joyful tears of thanksgiving to run down his diminished form. Although conscious of future battles, the æglet stood today in victory, and marked it as the day he'd lost his former self to the Spirit to claim instead a regenerate existence. The battle won, Sayah recognized his deep exhaustion, and retired to rest in his stony alcove. The Spirit granted the æglet sleep so sweet that Sayah did not wake until late the following day.

When at last Sayah awoke, he dragged his weary form from the cove to consume his bit of rhema. While he chewed, he determined it was midmorning by the sun's position in the sky, and with bleary eyes shuffled to the cliff's edge. The still phase of the Windwall was nearly over, and Sayah blinked in the still, dry air as he looked out over the land.

And then it happened again – the shift in vision that cast everything in brilliant, colorful outline. Well, not everything. His vision stuttered and flashed while resolving in greater detail, but even as it did, Sayah's sharp eyes caught blurs of darkness streaking about in the distance. So dark were these that Sayah could not quite call them black, though he knew no other approximate hue. They were the negation of light, and its complete absence was as antithetical in essence as in description.

Far to the South, a dark spire stood, stretching high into the sky beyond the limits of Sayah's powerful sight. From all directions, many similar black threads converged on the column, and Sayah thought he saw vague dark forms streaming toward the spire.

What is this? Sayah thought, his question a silent prayer to the Spirit.

Only once before, when in Sanctuary with Nat, had Sayah heard the Spirit speak with such clarity as it did now, and it at first alarmed him, *Sayah, the time has come for you to act. The column you see is a signal of the Nihúkolem and of their masters, the Shedím. Servants of Chōl have activated this Dark Beacon near Endego to summon the Nihúkolem against your Kin there. You must help them.*

Sayah balked with uncertainty, and asked, *How can I help them? I'm stuck here. The best I might do is pray.*

And that is better than most, came the response, *but not what I ask of you now.*

Sayah, do you trust Me?

I do, Sayah answered at once.

Do you love Me more than you fear death?

Sayah hesitated at the implications, but responded nonetheless, *I do. You know that I do.*

Then you know now what I ask of you, the Spirit replied, then spoke no more.

Sayah stood along the edge in breathless silence, the gentle upward breeze stirring his spotty fluff as he looked into the distance with eyes uncloaked. There stood the far-off challenge, a dark and insolent tower to rally the assault against his Kin. And him, unfledged on a distant cliff at the northern edge of the habitable world. He may as well have been on the moon.

Oh well, he thought. *Whether to the moon or just a mile, it's all the same to Lord Elyon.*

The updraft came on now stronger, gusting in infrequent billows at the lofty border marking the end of Sayah's fears and the beginning of his true faith.

His vision returned to normal as he closed his eyes and with folded wings, whispered aloud his prayer, "Father, whether in this life or the next . . . catch me."

In final answer, the æglet turned his back to the edge and pushed off, leaping out into the unsteady, upward breeze.

Chapter Twenty
The Dark Beacon

From across the Üntfither, a great many unblinking vulpine eyes glinted in the strange, arboreal glow while their owners debated what course they ought to pursue. The Nihúkolem's mandate to the foxes was to patrol Endego's perimeter and to return any they caught attempting escape to their doorsteps – dead or alive. Whether the foxes delivered the offending Etom intact or not, the practice was a terrifying preventive, and the foxes had rarely caught anyone outside after the first few brave souls had failed to reach freedom.

To intervene in the peculiar scenario before them now would exceed that mandate, but the leader of the foxes, a stately old silver fellow named Blithewit, reasoned that at minimum they ought to report these happenings to the Nihúkolem. Otherwise, the foxes themselves might fall under suspicion of complicity. It was interesting, however, this circumstance. Of that, there was no uncertainty, and even as Blithewit dispatched a messenger to summon the dark hosts, a curious doubt arose in his mind.

A speedy vixen raced away to activate the Dark Beacon, the mysterious device the Nihúkolem had left behind to call them to Endego at need. In the meantime, Blithewit was rather enjoying the spectacle. From his vantage, he spied the ring of Etom encircling the moat that poured from the odd spring in the upstart tree.

That tree – it was the source of this . . .peculiarity. And Blithewit knew with certainty there had been none only hours before. After dragging away the remnants of the olive tree and temple there, the Nihúkolem had demanded a daily report on the site in addition to the foxes' general report on the grove. Blithewit himself had come to look over the demolished clearing to ensure nothing was afoot with the group that called itself "the Eben'kayah."

Blithewit had long heard rumors of the Eben'kayah, most of which he'd discounted as irrelevant. Over the past two years, however, the Servants of Chōl had received numerous briefs on the group, most concerned with identifying and suppressing them wherever they were found. Knowledge of Gan and of the Sunder remained common among creatures of all kinds, but these Eben'kayah claimed to special knowledge of the Creator and His promises to deliver the world from the Stain. Blithewit ranked high enough as an officer in the Nihúkolem Scoutmaster's division that he'd heard varied accounts of the one called the Kinsman, and that he'd been sighted in the land. Until today, Blithewit had given no credence to the whispers of the Kinsman's miracles, but now reconsidered. Where the shining tree stood, and waters pooled had once been the gathering place of the Eben'kayah of Endego. To Blithewit, it seemed more than mere coincidence.

Outside the village, a grating rumble arose from the direction of their dens, pitching low at first, then rising to a shriek. Blithewit shivered at the sound, which hurt his sensitive ears and those of his team. He recalled hearing it the first and only other time in training, where instructed as a soldier of the Empire in how to activate the Dark Beacon.

It had been creepy then, and was creepy now, especially with Blithewit's awareness of how the grim unit functioned. He shivered again with sympathy, regretful he'd sent one so young to signal the Nihúkolem. With high probability, he predicted the vixen would be shaken by the experience for weeks to come, if not longer.

While the foxes kept a stock of fresh, caged quarry in their dens as emergency rations, they kept other prey on hand in a separate den where they stored the Dark Beacon. When the time came, these would be fed into the beacon's grisly chamber, an oddly clean and sterile-looking space in the midst of the beacon's dark, cylindrical form.

If an escapee from Sakkan had seen the Dark Beacon, they might have thought it a replica of Scarsburrow's clinic in miniature. But this had enough room for only an Etom or two, a frequent enough, though not exclusive, guest of its smooth, stainless interior, and possessed a single sliding door from which one was unlikely to exit. For the beacon ran on blood and flesh. And perhaps its victims' short-lived screams of terror.

Its operator had to stand by to ensure the machine was fed each time the tiny hatch opened of its own accord to reveal the shiny walls, disquieting in their perpetual spotlessness. Once the hungry relic was sated, its door shut tight as a clamping jaw to begin its disturbing transmission.

Even now, the shriek climbed until it surpassed the highest frequency audible to the Etom, who cringed in confusion beneath the tree until the beacon disappeared from their hearing. The Etom looked around, relieved, while Blithewit and the other foxes endured the beacon's ultrasonic range, which the foxes found uncomfortable, debilitating even. For several excruciating moments more, the foxes hunkered down, lying flat with paws over their ears. This was contrary to their Imperial training, which insisted they remain alert and vigilant regardless of circumstance. Notwithstanding, Blithewit did not begrudge his subordinates their protective instinct and even joined them in their meager respite from the sonic assault.

At last, the beacon's scream surpassed even the foxes' range of hearing, and with relief they lifted their heads to look about. From what the technical officer had told him, Blithewit understood the beacon to project a beam that only the Nihúkolem could see for miles around, day or night.

Blithewit knew most Men and Beasts loathed their service to the Empire, but none had been able to stand against its might since its inception, and none believed they could now. The Nihúkolem that ruled them from the dark, invulnerable clouds were too powerful, and the aging silver fox suspected a deeper, unseen darkness commanded the Nihúkolem behind the scenes.

The conquered Men and Beasts of the world had pieced together some of the hidden history that followed the Battle of Za'aq Ha Dam, the subjugate soldiers sharing in close conversation what they knew of that day. Parác and Mūk-Mudón had both been Warlords of renown before the battle, and well-known to all sapient beings of the land. All had waited with bated breath to learn who would emerge the victor, aware they would owe such a one their fealty in the aftermath.

Thus, it followed naturally that many had backed one or the other in the contest, if only in amicable speculation of the result, and of those a number had even staked money on their chosen champion. A much younger fox then, Blithewit recalled a certain festival atmosphere on the day that freedom failed. He himself had rooted for the eventual winner, Mūk-Mudón, who seemed the more magnanimous of the two, a daring, charismatic leader who was easier to love by far than the stern and brooding Parác. In addition, before the Empire's advent, those lands under the Western Sorrel enjoyed greater liberty and lower taxes than those under Parác's dominion.

To Blithewit, the Warlord of the West presented the overall greater chance at a good life for him and his pack and was his instinctive choice. None, however, had anticipated the oppression that swept the world in the wake of the battle, for the Empire of Chōl in its employment of the Nihúkolem surpassed any level of control the world had seen before. Terrifying in their hyper-animate lifelessness, the Nihúkolem had seized every land at once, leaving those who survived to wonder what had happened. Over time, the survivors came to see the shadows of Men and Beasts amidst the swirling, black dust, and to hear the echo of their voices in frightening interaction with those possessed by a cruel and malign will.

That Mūk-Mudón led the Nihúkolem was no secret. Indeed, the tale was scattered abroad that the Western Sorrel spoke as ever he had, his amiable, cheery voice sounding from the ebon silhouette of his form, the sweeping, horned helm still apparent even in its gloom to distinguish him from others. Yes, he spoke in friendly tone, even as he dismembered the disobedient, or tortured secrets from the mute. The bleak expanse between Mūk-Mudón's speech and his actions inspired ever-growing terror among the conquered, who soon discovered their new ruler possessed neither natural affection nor humanity to which they might appeal.

A few brave souls had investigated Za'aq Ha Dam in secret to seek evidence of the dark holocaust that had transformed heroes into monsters and found only the battered armaments of the great armies, most empty of their hosts and scattered upon the vast plain. Concluding some great evil had befallen those who had waged war there, the band of explorers left almost at once, but Nimrod, a Man more foolhardy than courageous, had left their company in search of a worthy artifact. Amidst the armor and weapons was a small clearing, and in its center Parác's decapitated body with several more armaments about it.

One object stood out among them, a bright helmet adorned with antlers, the helm of the Western Sorrel. Now this was a treasure! At once, Nimrod snatched up the prize, and in his most imprudent act, placed it on his head. It was well-crafted, and fit Nimrod comfortably despite the weight of its adornments. He placed a fist against his hip and a foot upon Parác, with mock authority commanding to action the husks that littered the landscape.

Nimrod expected no response but the whistle of the forlorn wind, but from inside the helm came a tittering, unintelligible reply. He froze, then spun around, looking for the speaker. Dim nonsense again rang out within a helmet now become a grim bell tolling out in haunted call to madness. Nimrod gripped the horns as handles, pulling to no avail with all his might to remove the afflicting armor. There would be no such escape.

Panic struck Nimrod when he sensed insanity's creep, and he ran as though his feet might carry him from the threat that encroached within his mind. In aimless retreat, he fled across the battlefield, but no distance was sufficient to evade the madness that gripped him. At the edge of the field, Nimrod's foot met the bowstring of a forsaken bow, and thus entangled, he fell headlong amongst the martial refuse there.

A short while later, Nimrod arose, the helm yet in place upon his beleaguered brow. The fall had snapped off most the antlers on one side of the helmet, leaving a scant, jagged remnant though the other side remained intact. Nimrod arose a different man, head inclined, and shoulder slumped to one side under the helm's imbalanced weight. A crazed and crooked grin sat hard and brittle on his lips as he looked around through bulged and unblinking eyes. Nimrod's gaze met the bow that had ensnared him, and he crouched down to collect the weapon and a nearby quiver of arrows from beneath a shirt of mail.

His expression remote and eyes untouched by the strange, frozen smile, he looked out into the blowing dust, and growled, "To the hunt, then."

Nimrod, his frame lopsided under the tottering helmet, lurched away on errant paths to pass for a time into vague rumor.

The others of Nimrod's band returned to civilization with tales of a graveyard battlefield bereft of bodies. From those whose guessing was best originated an uncomplicated theory, fair in its accuracy though lacking in detail. Tales of Mūk-Mudón's inexplicable powers had spread far and wide before the battle, and with the disappearance of both his and Parác's forces, these few postulated that Mūk-Mudón's abilities had backfired in spectacular fashion to transform both armies.

The theory was sound but lacked one critical detail – the involvement of the Shedím, those vainglorious Malakím formerly of Lord Elyon's service. Unbeknownst to the subjects of the Empire, Helél stood behind the puppet ruler Mūk-Mudón, issuing orders in persistent rebellion against the Creator. Helél remained bent on tormenting those the Creator loved, and on destroying those whose souls he failed to oppress. His malevolent presence ever lurked near Mūk-Mudón, a distinct yet invisible force to which living creatures' hearts alluded in fear. They sensed the unseen cloud of cold horror behind Mūk-Mudón but did not perceive its genuine source.

Blithewit shuddered in remembrance of the only time he'd stood in Mūk-Mudón's presence and recollected his soul's revulsion in proximity of the chief Nihúkolem. From where he surveilled the Etom, the fox watched them return to what looked like ceremonial bathing in the water that surrounded the tree's glowing trunk. Blithewit stood to look over the heads of the Etom who had yet to enter the pool, hoping for a clearer look at what the tiny creatures were up to.

A growing number stood within the pool behind a trio of Etom Blithewit hadn't seen in Endego before: one a grown etma with distinct black markings, another an etém juvenile, and the third an adult etém. As the fox watched, another Etom entered the waters, wading forward in apparent shyness. The newcomer was a grandmotherly etma who rolled up her sleeves as she approached the trio. She and the adult etém spoke for a moment before she raised her arms into the air to show the ugly Stains running down both her forearms to the crowd gathered on the shore. The adult etém cradled the elderly etma's neck in one hand and placed a hand on her back while his etma partner gripped one of the newcomer's hands.

The aging etma covered her face, and the wind carried the etém's raised voice to where Blithewit watched, "In the name of the Father, and the Son, and the Holy Spirit!"

The pair of Etom lowered the grandmotherly etma back into the water, immersing her entire body for just a second, then raising her up out of the water to stand. The jubilant etma raised her hands high in the air for a second time, though this time she displayed forearms without spot or blemish. Every Etom in the water celebrated, and the younger etém of the trio embraced her as a grandson might.

Wait! Blithewit thought, filled with burgeoning curiosity. *Did they just wash away the* Stain?

Thoughts collided in Blithewit's mind while he considered the ramifications of what he was witnessing and Etom after Etom joined the spotless throng. After a while, however, no more Etom joined them in the pool, and seemed to jeer the others from the edge. The indistinct scorn perplexed the fox, who'd had to restrain himself from running to join the Etom in the water. The cloying Stain that covered the brush of his tail grew heavier each day, and he feared the murky ooze that would soon mat the fur there as the Blight set in. He might pay any price to avoid that fate, but the approach of the vixen he'd sent to activate the Dark Beacon drew his attention instead.

"I have activated the beacon, as you commanded," reported the vixen, refusing to meet his eyes.

Blithewit felt for the young fox but could not afford to show any emotion to his subordinate. Instead, he commended her on a job well done, and ordered her to the rear watch, where she might recuperate away from her peers. The vixen still appeared troubled but was grateful for the opportunity to be alone.

Blithewit grimaced as she left, and mused, *It's a nasty business, working for the Empire.*

It was not the last time the thought would cross his mind.

Dempsey, Nida, and Nat grew more encouraged with each Etom that joined them in the waters, and they welcomed each new member of their Kinship with joy. A good many Etom of Endego never before associated with the Eben'kayah had entered the pool, and Dempsey figured they wouldn't have much trouble establishing contacts among these to help the Kinship.

At last, only those unwilling to entrust themselves to the work of the Kinsman to be cleansed stood along the edge of the pool. The three of them thought these doubters would leave, but instead, with Iver in the lead, they continued to mock those in the water. Why not let them be?

The questions would have to wait, for the Dark Beacon had done its work, calling forth the nearest Nihúkolem to investigate the disturbance in Endego. This, the shadow of a grizzly, did not hesitate to approach those Etom, scornful or no, who stood under the tree, which cast light beneath its branches instead of shade. The Nihúkolem gathered momentum in its charge, crossing the Üntfither at increasing velocity until it met the vital light.

As if colliding with a solid wall, the Nihúkolem burst into a grainy cloud of soot against the light that blanketed the clearing. The Etom noticed the Nihúkolem at the last instant before it struck the radiant barrier, and even Iver and his surly crew flinched back from the explosion of black dust. Nat knew from experience that it wouldn't be long before their enemy collected itself for another offensive. In wild tangent, he noticed some of the grit had fallen into the Üntfither and wondered whether the water might be safe to drink afterwards.

Nat forced the irrelevant distraction from his mind and shouted to his mother and Dempsey, "Do you think there will be more?"

"Yes!" Dempsey responded.

Nida concurred, "I'm guessing that awful noise earlier is what calls them."

Nat looked around at the Etom with them, and asked, "What do we do?"

Dempsey and Nida stared at one another, uncertain until Shoym's voice broke in, "If there are to be more Nihúkolem, then I'd wager we're safest here."

He pointed to the coalescing shambles that yet limped outside the clearing, "You saw what happened to that one. There's nowhere else I'd rather be if it's an all-out assault."

Nida inquired, "If this is the safest place in Endego, then oughtn't we bring the others from the Bunker?"

"That's a great idea, Mom!" Nat answered.

The young etém turned about to holler at the rest of the Etom there, "Now who's going to go get them?"

Feeling mischievous, Nat picked on his favorite antagonist, pointing a sharp stare at Iver, who looked every which way but at Nat until at last he broke down, "What?!? *I'm* not going out there! Get yourself another martyr."

Even many of those yet outside the Kinship backing away from Iver, hoping to disassociate themselves from his cowardice. From Iver's band stepped forth a single etém, Ënar, who had been with them since Sakkan.

Ënar stood out as the only Etom Nat had ever seen with skin black as midnight, though his eyes shone with resolute fire when he spoke, "I will bring the others here."

Nat and the others recognized Ënar's courage at once, and they approved him for the mission. Ënar looked back at Iver to level a withering, contemptuous gaze at the fuming orange etém.

From the water's edge, Ënar called to Nat, "And I *will* hear more on this Kinsman when I return!"

Then the brave fellow dashed from the shore for the northern edge of the clearing, his speedy form disappearing at once into the shadows. Iver, meanwhile, blushed the color of brick fired by fury as he glowered and skulked away from the other Etom to sulk alone just inside the perimeter of showering light.

With a lucid mind, Nat realized the inconsistency of Iver's position in that while he was openly disdainful of the Kinsman's Tree, he was more than happy to partake of its protective benefits. Nat also recognized it wasn't only Iver who did so, but a host of Etom who yet lingered on the shore, hesitant to entrust themselves to the Kinsman's work, even though they'd witnessed the removal of the Stain from so many. He wondered if they might never believe, if they did not already with what they'd seen.

Outside the daylit clearing, Blithewit gaped at the shattered form of the Nihúkolem that struggled to pull itself together. His prior passing interest in the tree had grown to captivate his complete attention. Even as a pitch-black Etom broke away from the rest to sprint into the darkness, Blithewit's eyes stayed fixed on the trio who seemed to lead those in the water.

A nearby subordinate whispered to his preoccupied commander, "What should we do, sir? Shall we give chase?"

In a distracted voice, Blithewit murmured, "No. No. Let him go."

A wild thought arose within Blithewit's mind, sprouting potent and tall as the brilliant tree before him, and before he knew what he was doing, the old fox was creeping toward the light.

"Sir!" his subordinate barked with concern. "Sir! What are you doing? You saw what happened to the Nihúkolem!"

But Blithewit, hypnotized by the beauty of the form that stood now in heart and mind, walked tall and fearless, no longer concerned with concealing himself as he muttered, "Just a bit closer. I just need to see it."

The panicked underling roused the rest of vulpine cohort for help, and their many fox heads sprung up in answer just as the vixen Blithewit had ordered to the rear arrived with news that she'd spotted more Nihúkolem entering Endego.

The vixen's report died on whiskered lips when the she spied Blithewit approaching the clearing, and in confusion asked, "Wha – What is the commander doing? Is he going in?"

When only mute and dumfounded stares met her in response, the vixen decided *she* would support Blithewit on his mission, whatever it may be. The commander was stern and reserved, but his care for those under his command was apparent. He was a good fox, and the vixen resolved not to let him go alone into peril. Ignoring the blubbering protests of the others, after Blithewit she bounded, a sleek and stealthy dart flying low over the ground.

With an agile hop Blithewit crossed the Üntfither, peripherally aware of the grizzly's floundering form, which grew and stabilized with each passing second. And there it was, the streaming light that painted the brittle autumn foliage in sunny yellow tinged with fresh, leafy green. That light, it reminded him of his first spring, the world around the kit vital and full of promise. It seemed spring was never again so vibrant, nor was the promise fulfilled, the disappointment quenching the hopeful flame of his young soul with each passing year.

But now, glum embers sprung aflame as Blithewit reached forth a timid paw, wincing from anticipated shock. So great was his desire to pass into the light, that he was willing to incur harm. None came, and he strode beneath the brilliant canopy toward the three Etom he'd watched from outer darkness. A worried yelp from behind made Blithewit turn to his subordinate, who stood just outside the luminescence.

With another yip, she asked in bewilderment, "Sir, what are your orders? What is the mission?"

"I have no further orders for you," he answered, looking around the clearing and up into the tree, "and my mission is here. I *have* to know what this is."

He turned again to his task, and the vixen barked again, "But . . . sir!"

With tender eyes, he glanced back at the vixen, and called her by name, "Whisperweave, if you will, come. We can take this adventure together."

Whisperweave looked down at the ground with a contemplative scowl, then back to Blithewit, who waited, patient, but ready to proceed.

With a decisive leap, she sprung into the radiance, her orange pelt ablaze in the effulgence as she joined Blithewit to approach the Etom.

None of the Etom noticed Blithewit and his companion at first, but it wasn't long before someone raised the alarm. The Kinship had come out of the pool to dry off while they planned their next move. They all anticipated more Nihúkolem at any second and were busy discussing what they ought to do when a shout alerted them. Nida, Dempsey, Nat, and Shoym looked up from their conversation, startled see a pair of foxes strolling right for them.

Uncertain he'd be able to much protect his friends, Dempsey nevertheless moved to stand between the foxes and the other three Etom, and Nida confronted them with a shout, "You there! What is your business here?"

More Etom gathered around as the silver fox inclined his head in deference and spoke, "I beg your pardon, my Etom friends. I didn't mean to frighten you."

He looked up at the tree behind them with a wondrous sparkle in his eyes and explained, "I just couldn't stay away."

The wonder did not leave his expression as he looked to them, "I saw you in the water, and watched what happened to the Nihúkolem, and thought you might be able to tell me what's going on here."

"How do we know you're not a spy sent by the Empire?" Dempsey asked, narrowing suspicious eyes.

"Fair question," the fox responded. "I don't think I can offer you much proof, but perhaps an introduction will help. My name is Blithewit, and I command the foxes that surround Endego."

The Etom started with surprise, but Blithewit continued, "I have been an unwilling servant of the Empire for a great many years, as are many. Like most subjects of the Empire, I lived without hope of freedom, since I saw no means of defeating the Nihúkolem. Until tonight.

"When I saw that the Nihúkolem earlier did not prevail against the light of this place, that hope returned. More than that, though, something deeper beckons me to this tree."

The mesmerized twinkle brightened in the fox's eyes, and he fought for words, "I can't describe it, but I sense a beauty here. Something full of life."

Blithewit dropped his head in surrender to the indescribable and gasped with welling tears, "You can see it too, can't you? Can anyone tell me what it is? I feel I might die if I don't know!"

Unable to restrain her compassion, Nida went to the old fox, reaching up to cup his nose in gentle hands, and spoke, "Yes, dear fox. We do know. We know Him very well."

For the remainder of Blithewit's days, the following minutes were etched in glowing gold among his memories as the very best of his life. The group of tiny Etom led him down to the sweet waters, and only too happily did he drink. And roll. And splash. And frolic like a pup, prancing with snowy, white-tipped tail held high behind him, free of the weight and blemish of the Stain.

Loyal Whisperweave was quick to grasp why Blithewit was drawn to the tree but was hesitant to follow him into the pool until she looked out to where they'd left the others. The pinpoint flash of the foxes' eyes, a galaxy of waning red stars against the field of night, reminded the vixen of their hopeless enslavement to the Empire. Snatched from her family as a cub, bitten and beaten into submission, and forced to serve far away from any home she'd known, Whisperweave was beyond fed up.

Upon her back the Empire had lain its final straw this very evening in form of the Dark Beacon. The vixen understood the law of the hunt as a universal truth of their world and had always honored her prey with grateful comprehension it might be her own neck next under tooth and claw.

The Dark Beacon, however, revealed the twisted perspective of its creators, a paradigm of mechanical slaughter that repulsed her even as she fed the device its victims. She'd known what the caged quarry were for but had failed to recognize her complicity in their doom until ordered to carry each warm and wriggling body to it. Their cries still echoed in her ears in tongues she did not know, but nevertheless had understood.

Like most of Chōl's denizens, her contact with the Nihúkolem was minimal, and she was happy it was so. With readiness, she had joined the consensus that more than any other thing, the shadowy creatures disgusted the living soul. Yet, there she had been, feeding victim after victim into the perverse machine to call the Nihúkolem near.

She had almost blamed Blithewit for the atrocity but relented at once. He was just another cog, like herself, in the greater machine of the Empire's oppression, and she knew him to fight for what honor he might scrape together for himself and for his troops in a landscape devoid of it. The Empire was just too powerful to resist, and she had resigned herself to the fate she shared with those she'd tossed into the beacon – just another bit of fuel to propel the grinding black beast onward.

No! Whisperweave contended, returning from the dark reverie to scowl out into the dying starlight of her compatriots' eyes. *I'd rather die fighting!*

And it seemed now, at last, they might have a chance. Reflection wasn't long in bringing her down to the edge of the pool. She had heard the strange blue etém child with golden eyes tell Blithewit what he'd seen of the Kinsman, a figure who had ever stood far off from Whisperweave, more remote than legend in her mind. He was an impossibility, the Son of the Creator, and why should *He* care?

But the results were unmistakable and undeniable. She'd not seen her commander so much as crack a smile before, and here he played like a pup. And the Stain. It was gone. What was *that* all about? She sensed the ache of her own brutality in her paws, and with chagrin thought it probable her part in activating the beacon had pushed her past the threshold into the realm of the Marked.

Doubt wracked Whisperweave as she stepped down into the water, her eyes squeezed shut in distress. What if it didn't work for creatures like her, guilty of such bloodshed that she might awaken Marked in the morning? The wee pink etma with black markings watched her from the shore and waved at the vixen when she opened worried eyes.

"Hi there!" the etma called. "Everything OK?"

"I don—I don't know how," Whisperweave whimpered. "What do I do?"

"I'm Nida! Mind if I come to you?"

"Please," the vixen answered, and muttered when the etma was close. "I'm Whisperweave."

The etma stroked Whisperweave's foreleg above the water line, and repeated with appreciation, "Whisperweave . . .that's a beautiful name. You have a beautiful coat as well, Whisperweave. Did you know that?"

"Noooo," the vixen warbled, uncertain why she suddenly trembled beneath the ministrations of this tiny creature.

A great tear rolled off Whisperweave's furry cheek to meet the water with a splash. With perfect, circular symmetry, ripples spread out along the surface, and the fox stared into the diminishing epicenter, transfixed.

"I imagine you've had no mother to care for you, then," Nida continued, leaning against the vixen's foreleg to wrap a stubby arm around it. "You are quite the lovely young vixen, and if you were my daughter, I'd tell you every day."

"I – I don't understand," Whisperweave wept.

"Shhh shhh shhh," Nida hushed her. "This is who our Father is, and if you'd like Him to be yours, too, then you know all that you need to. Just wash in the water, and let the Kinsman do the rest."

Nida let go of Whisperweave, who crouched down on all fours, dipping her snout and what she could of her lower body in the pool. The shallow water covered everything but the top of her head, shoulders, haunches, and back. In a stiff, unpracticed motion, the vixen rolled over in the pool to wet herself. Nida clapped and whistled first but was soon joined by the crowd of Etom who had gathered on the shore. Blithewit, too, was there, and he offered Whisperweave a gentle, happy nod to acknowledge the moment.

Whisperweave *felt* different, that much was true, and she realized the ache in her paws was gone. With it went the shame and guilt of her role in actuating the Dark Beacon, and her inner being stood resolute against participating in anything like it again, even on pain of death. It was a conviction that would soon be tested, for even now, the Nihúkolem converged on Endego.

Chapter Twenty-One
Sanctuary Siege

Ënar led the Etom who had remained in the Bunker back to Sanctuary Endego without incident. Alcarid, Agatous, and the sentries were all who had stayed behind, and their arrival now signaled a complete evacuation of the Bunker. Agatous and Alcarid had been hesitant to leave at first, but Ënar's concise recounting of recent events in the village had convinced them. That, and his forceful insistence that a large force of Nihúkolem was on the way. To Ënar, it was foregone conclusion that the Nihúkolem would destroy the Bunker and anyone within it with ease, and his imposing presence made him a difficult etém to argue with. In the end, they had packed their scant belongings and left without further debate, Ënar guiding them with patient confidence, even slowing the pace to accommodate the two elderly Eben'kayah at the front of their short column.

Thus, Agatous and Alcarid entered Sanctuary Endego, marveling at the transformation of their former home and place of worship. The pair hadn't been outside much over the past several months, and even the light of the place was difficult to bear, although it was a welcome affliction after so long in hiding.

Without so much as a greeting, Ënar waved a hand back toward those in tow as he addressed Dempsey in passing, "Here are your Etom."

Ënar did not break stride but continued on to where Nat stood along the water's edge, calling, "You! Young one! I must speak with you."

The juggernaut advance of the strange etém took Nat aback at first, but then he recalled what Ënar had said before leaving – he had wanted to know more about the Kinsman. Nat relaxed before the aggressive Ënar, prepared to share the good news of Gaal's sacrifice with him. It turned out to be a short conversation, as were most with Ënar, who sought clarification and further explanation of just a few points before deciding to join himself to the Vine.

Ënar's jet black body showed no visible evidence of the Stain, however, and Nat wondered if Agatous and Alcarid might believe without the proof of the Stain's removal. He need not have worried, though, for such was the softening of Ënar's brusque manner in the aftermath that his peaceful smile was sufficient, at least for Agatous.

Her humble conversion likewise brought Alcarid into the Kinship, his recalcitrant pride melting away along with the ever-present and spreading stigma on Agatous' forehead. In tears, he refused to wait, and tore open his robes to reveal the Blight over his heart before plunging into the pool.

The others awaited Alcarid's emergence with bated breath, uncertain if the waters would remove a Stain gone to Blight. Alcarid arose, and the Kinship at first sighed with disappointment when they saw the sickly, orange crust yet affixed to his chest. Led by the Spirit, Nat held up a hand to examine the sore, plucking away at the upper edge with his fingers once Alcarid had consented.

Finding a small gap, Nat asked Alcarid, "Does it hurt when I pull at it?"

Alcarid shook his head, so in a single, sweeping motion, Nat peeled away the scabrous Blight to reveal healthy flesh beneath. Removed from its host, the parasitic growth crumbled between Nat's fingers, falling into the water to dissolve there.

The sentries who had stayed behind with Agatous and Alcarid were already Kin, but the addition of these three was cause enough for celebration. Merry with the unexpected triumph of the day, the Kinship gathered before the tree, and Dempsey once again led an old hymn of the Eben'kayah. This time, the Spirit demonstrated His delight without visible fanfare, but within each one exhorted them to confidence in the will of Elyon. The Kinship of the Vine discovered their souls buttressed with certainty and strength. In advance of oncoming conflict, they were nevertheless assured of victory and set a few to watch and pray while the rest fell to peaceful sleep.

The call to action that the Dark Beacon signified among the Nihúkolem had gained special urgency upon the unequivocal failure of the grizzly. The eerie link they shared had informed each of the great bear's defeat at once, and Mūk-Mudón had dispatched a member of his personal cadre to command the Empire's forces in Endego.

It was unprecedented, this resistance, but the Nihúkolem did not yet comprehend the power they faced. If they had, their initial response might not have been so tepid. Regardless, the forces that began to mass along Endego's outskirts were substantial, though unprepared in their overbearing complacency to meet the threat.

At last, their general arrived, the commander of the Scout Regiment, Imafel, whose slim silhouette yet conveyed a vain and dashing impression of the Man he once was. By wordless order, he commanded his forces to surround the shining tree and await his signal, then demanded a report from the foxes. One such unlucky Beast, the nervous fellow who had tried to stop Blithewit, soon shrank before Imafel in terror as he attempted to explain the events of the evening.

"Ye—yes sir," the fox stammered, "our unit commander appears to have defected."

"Why did you not stop him?" growled Imafel in displeasure.

The years had diminished his charm with the Beasts, replacing affection with a tyranny that was nonetheless effective.

The bumbling fox offered, "After what happened to the Nihúkolem, we believed he would be destroyed upon entering the grove. Besides, another gave chase to stop him. A vixen also under his command."

"And what, pray tell, happened to this vixen? Where is *she* now?" Imafel countered.

The Beast's discomfort grew, and trembling, he replied, "She appears to uh . . . to have . . . uh . . ."

Imafel's patience failed him, and he barked, "Spit it out, soldier!"

"She . . . defected, too?" the fox responded with dubious certainty and a sheepish, wan smile on his pitiable face.

The Beast was uncertain he'd survive this encounter, but still had difficulty explaining just what had occurred with his commander and Whisperweave. It hadn't made sense to the servile creature. It still didn't.

Imafel roared, swinging a leg into the fox's huddled form, which arced into a pile of leaves crowded beneath a nearby tree. Thankful that the leaves had broken his fall, and that Imafel did not pursue to finish him off, the fox presumed his dismissal and limped away to lick his wounds.

Imafel brooded in silence, aware Mūk-Mudón, too, had heard the account, and cursed the inseverable connection that allowed his old friend a portal into his senses. At least his thoughts remained his own. For now. But what else might Mūk-Mudón's dark master concoct? He, Belláphorus, and Cloust had stood at the Western Sorrel's side the instant the mysterious being pressed them all into what seemed interminable servitude, and over time they had learned little more of Mūk-Mudón's patron devil.

Since their first day as Nihúkolem, Mūk-Mudón alone reserved the right of full control over the link between them, and he alone was able to shutter his senses away from all others. As his generals, however, Belláphorus, Imafel, and Cloust were given similar privileges, closing their beings to all Nihúkolem except one another and, of course, Mūk-Mudón. When they did so, the three generals recognized the blindness of their subordinates was reciprocal. The other Nihúkolem could no longer sense them, and neither could the generals sense their subordinates. It was a blind spot that would prove useful.

The first time their leader disappeared from the inner experience they shared, his generals detected his absence at once. The three wondered if he might share the blind spot they discovered in their own consciousness when employing the privilege of privacy with their underlings.

Neither spoke to the other in advance, but the instant Belláphorus first ventured a minor infraction, the other two stood at the ready to join the experiment. Each transgressed in small ways to test their hypothesis, and after many such trials, their confidence grew until the theory was a near-certainty.

Once the generals determined the possibility of interaction outside Mūk-Mudón's observation, they awaited the opportunity to utilize what they had learned. It wasn't long before they felt their leader's looming presence disappear from the hive-like, mental continuum of the Nihúkolem, and likewise slipped away at once to convene.

With a certain giddiness at the once-common and human quality of discriminate fellowship, Belláphorus, Imafel, and Cloust savored discussion away from prying eyes and listening ears. In a strange twist, the distance that had grown between them in years leading up to the fateful Battle of Za'aq Ha Dam began to diminish. Their conspiracy was not against Mūk-Mudón, for their loyalty to him remained. Instead, they hoped to learn more about the powerful being responsible for their transformation and enslavement.

Sharing their thoughts over several such careful convocations, the three generals soon deduced the purpose of Mūk-Mudón's privacy was likely for dark communion with the strange creature. What else might their leader have to conceal? And just who and what was this being? They pieced together from their broader history of the world and from that more personal to arrive at the conclusion it was one of the Shedím, and likely *the* infamous Shedím of old, Helél.

It had been Cloust, intuitive Cloust, who had uttered the profane truth that their old friend had sold himself and their armies into service to the Shedím. The silence that followed the pronouncement betrayed the others' somber agreement. Oh! How Belláphorus had raged against Mūk-Mudón's foolish ambition and against the secret chains that link by link had gripped them all.

It was everything that Imafel felt, though lacking in special disappointment that the grim metamorphosis had stolen too his looks. Imafel had barked in bitter laughter at how ridiculous the petty loss seemed in the darkness that embraced them, smothering their souls in an existence more dead than alive. And how now to remove these chains? For they felt it better to jettison their forms altogether in death than to haunt the world in perpetual slavery to the Shedím.

Not willing that they all risk censure, bold Belláphorus insisted that he alone present to Mūk-Mudón the possibility of release from this bondage. What is it they must do to negotiate their own deaths? It had been a tense conversation, and Belláphorus had stated it was his private concern. It was his and his alone, though all four had been present in their shared psychic space away from the subordinate Nihúkolem.

At first, Mūk-Mudón had reacted in selfish caprice, unwilling to lose his oldest friend when he would remain tethered to the mortal plane. Mūk-Mudón fell silent, and the others waited long minutes for his final word.

And you two? Imafel? Cloust? Mūk-Mudón had inquired with weary sadness. *Do you share this desire to desert me? To join Belláphorus when we could reign together, immortal?*

Imafel and Cloust had responded in the affirmative, to which Mūk-Mudón had reacted without emotion, *I will see what can be done.*

With no further word, Mūk-Mudón had departed their company at once to seal himself away. The others had continued together in cautious conversation, awaiting his return. It was not long before Mūk-Mudón rejoined them.

Good news, friends! Mūk-Mudón announced with hollow enthusiasm. *I have discovered the author of your bondage! Only if we find and destroy him will you be free.*

Who is it? Cloust had ventured.

Mūk-Mudón offered backhanded praise, *Cloust! Dear Cloust! Right to the point, as usual. If you have one, that is.*

The one we seek holds the keys to your chains. I trust you all will join me in the search? Spare no effort! He should be found in a backwater near the center of our glorious Empire, where the people may call him . . .the Kinsman.

The reaction of the three generals was at first one of confusion at Mūk-Mudón's irrationality. They knew Helél had been the one to remake them into Nihúkolem, and their memories yet recounted to them the scene – Mūk-Mudón standing over Parác's decapitated form, his rival's head tucked beneath an arm while the world slowed.

But a curious thing happened. As it had before. As it had the first time on a fated hunt long ago. With practiced skill, Mūk-Mudón's will rewrote their recollection in accordance with the lie he'd told his generals. Not that Mūk-Mudón had any choice in the matter. He was Helél's – heart, soul, mind, and strength – until the devil had his due.

Decades had passed, and still Belláphorus, Imafel, and Cloust wandered the world at the Shedím's command, ever watchful for any sign of the Kinsman. And here he had at last arrived, and the Nihúkolem had put him down like the bleating sheep he was. But the promised release had not come. Instead, the wily Mūk-Mudón had blamed a hidden vestige of the Kinsman's power to string his three generals further along on the empty hope their captivity would end when they had also eradicated the Kinsman's legacy.

It was insufferable, and after all these years seeking release from their bondage, it seemed there would be none. That is, until the Dark Beacon had gone up, Mūk-Mudón identifying the unusual phenomenon in Endego as the very power they sought to destroy. Imafel had been quick to volunteer himself in service of its destruction, eager to be rid of this repellent light that vexed their kind. He cursed it in frustration, but to no avail. Besides, the current situation demanded action, not pathetic rumination over his present predicament.

Now decided, Imafel evanesced, leaving a puff of swirling, black dust behind as he sped in dissolute form to join his troops at the front. The general dropped in behind the foxes yet arrayed west of the Üntfither, their prone forms snapping to attention at Imafel's appearance. The foxes reported the arrival of several more Etom in the last while, and that most of the small creatures appeared to have gone to sleep.

The light dazzled Imafel, who was unable to distinguish with clarity what lay beyond its rays. The general could not focus on the variegated forms of the Etom that swam beneath the shroud of golden-green light. It frustrated him that these dust-licking runts should slumber, untroubled and in the open, though the weight of Chōl's mighty hammer bore down on them. It frustrated Imafel almost as much as the light he believed empowered his oppression, and the combination infuriated the world-weary Nihúkolem.

Spurred into a rage, Imafel commanded all Nihúkolem to full assault, determined to retake the village in a single action. From all corners, the ebon forms of Beasts and Men rushed forth, distinct from shadow only as a darker shade surrounding the shining tree in a ring of closing, impenetrable gloom.

A century of darkness detonated against the radiant wall in a curious inversion of fireworks, the black forms splashing in rapid succession against the border of the daybright bower. So secure were the Etom beneath the tree that the vigilance of those on watch had failed. In safety steeped, their eyelids drooped, until at last they had succumbed to sleep.

Though outside Sanctuary Endego, the battle raged, within resounded only scanty pops for each deafening crash as Nihúkolem dashed against the brilliant barricade. Enough of these, and Nat awoke, and looked out with shock at the shower of black smoke cascading outside the bower. He raised the alarm, and roused the others, and they stood together in surprise that with ease the light repulsed the Empire's most powerful soldiers.

The Spirit spoke, and the Kinship responded, wading out into the waters to worship with songs of gratitude for the provision of this, their Kinsman's Tree, and for the great protection of Lord Elyon. Outside the bower, the bright barrier resonated with their song to amplify the sound throughout the village and down the countryside, rousing creatures from their slumber. All around the clearing, the shining barricade pulsed, expanding beyond the borders of the boughs as Imafel and his remaining troops fled, terrified they'd been unable to overcome the light.

The rout of the Nihúkolem put the Kinship further at their ease as, afterwards, they examined Endego under noonday brightness, the tree's rays stretching deep into the village to illuminate the grove. In hushed, reverent tones, they marveled together at what Lord Elyón had done in defeating their enemies, and animate shadows played without as the piercing rays withdrew to illuminate only the bower once again.

Though the battle had brought the Kinship wide awake, quickening their spirits to alert readiness, Nida and Dempsey saw now the haggard faces of their Kin as a sign further rest was needed. It was not difficult to convince everyone to sleep again, for their confidence in the protection of Elyon was further bolstered by the night's events. They set again the watch, warning these to awaken their relief if they might fall asleep, then all the rest settled in for sweet slumber.

Well, almost all the rest. But for the four sentries posted at the compass points of the bower, only one Etom, of deep orange color, remained awake. Iver watched until opportunity arose, the eastern guard yawning as he trudged back toward the cluster of sleeping Etom near the pool. While the drowsy guard attempted to rouse his relief, Iver slipped from the clearing to hide in the shadows outside. He was tired as well, but he forced himself onward in bitter resolve until he found a hollow in the roots of a tree as far from the glowing bower as he could manage, then collapsed into exhausted, fitful sleep.

Though he had flown as quickly as he was able, Imafel had not succeeded in escaping the shattering light. Even now, his form remained scattered across the ground, the dark bonds that held his grains together somehow loosened, enfeebled in a manner before inconceivable. He had tried to gather himself at once, but found the effort required was beyond his ability. He'd only been able to move a single grain at a time, ponderous as it lurched along to join a meager pile. It wasn't long before he retired from the project in hopes that he'd regain his strength in time. Besides, he sensed the remote summons of Mūk-Mudón compelling him to report what had happened, though even that connection seemed somewhat vague and dissolute in the aftermath of the radiant explosion. Nevertheless, Imafel managed to force his consciousness into the closed company of Mūk-Mudón, Belláphorus, and Cloust to debrief them on the battle.

Battle. A word strange to Imafel even as he uttered it. Its meaning had grown distant and unfamiliar over a passage of years in which the Nihúkolem had met no challenge warranting its use. But it was so. And it had been a battle lost, nonetheless. A defeat, another word not quite so unfamiliar, though reserved until this day for their opponents. Mūk-Mudón was displeased, to say the least, yet at first covered it with a tense jocularity as he reacted to Imafel's report.

Pull yourself together, Imafel! Mūk-Mudón chuckled with warmth before his tone grew icy cold. *But really, Imafel, how could you have let this happen?*

Imafel didn't excuse or defend himself, but offered, *You have not seen this light, milord. Would that you had, I don't know that even your might would have penetrated its power. Over a hundred Nihúkolem burst into a billion pieces on contact with it, myself included. And afterward, we are unable to recompose ourselves, as though the power that holds our forms together has been weakened.*

Impossible! Mūk-Mudón exclaimed.

As you say, milord, Imafel placated, *seemingly impossible, but nevertheless true. My bits lie strewn about Endego as we speak, and I was nearly unable to join our convocation here for lack of strength.*

You're saying this light saps us of our power? Cloust inquired. *Interesting.*

Belláphorus listened in silence, though Imafel knew his friend considered the matter with care.

Mūk-Mudón barked, *And what of the foxes? Your interrogation revealed that two of their number, one of them their commander, defected? Do you have reason to doubt the report?*

None at all, Imafel answered. *You know well my way with Beasts, and this one was too terrified to be anything but truthful.*

Belláphorus spoke at last, *These two, they entered the clearing? Unharmed?*

Imafel saw where Belláphorus was heading, and replied, *Yes, as far as we know.*

I believe we possess the key to victory, milord, Belláphorus offered. *We must conscript every available subject of the Empire in the assault on Endego. The Nihúkolem will command from the rear, but these others shall win the day.*

Nat awoke to a brilliant morning, the excited calls of Etom resounding in his ears. He stirred and shifted, then pushed off the ground with a crackle to prop himself up. Wait! A crackle? Nat looked around the clearing, where spread a blanket of puffy white wafers he recognized from Sanctuary.

"Rhema!" he shouted, gripping the flaky morsel he'd put his hand through.

Rae arose from her slumber nearby to see what was the matter and reacted in a near-identical manner to the rhema that covered the bower floor. She and Nat didn't have an opportunity to discuss the strange bread, however. Clusters of Etom and a pair of foxes hung encapsulated from the tree's branches overhead. Without warning, they came raining down to bounce along the ground. Nat and Rae saw Shoym's bounding form roll past, followed not long thereafter by Agatous, Alcarid, and Ënar.

Though a bit dazed, they and all the others added to the Vine the day before were fine, and they stared amazed at the transformation of their landscape beneath the snowy sheet of rhema. Its appearance was unexpected, even to those who had partaken in Sanctuary, and they did their best to explain this, yet another example of Lord Elyon's provision.

Before long, all those in the Vine had collected a share of the wafers for the day and settled down to munch on a morsel for breakfast. A sip of pure water from the pool was a wonderful complement to wash the rhema down, and the eyes of all Kin brightened with new life afterward.

Those few Etom who remained undecided on the Kinsman eyed the food with distrust and were unwilling to consume either the rhema or the water. Nat noticed the phenomena and concluded that perhaps it was best they did not partake if they neither believed nor understood yet what the Kinsman had done for them.

Regardless, these Etom yet remained in Sanctuary Endego for the moment while they whispered in secretive discussion of their chances outside the bower now the Nihúkolem had attacked. Nat understood how conflicted they must feel, trapped between warring factions, and wondered if there might be something they could do.

Approaching his mother, Dempsey, and the remaining Eben'kayah Council where they had gathered, Nat waved at the isolated huddle and asked, "How can we help these Etom who don't believe? I'm sure they'd rather not stay here, but most don't have anywhere else to go. Only one or two of them have homes in Endego."

"I can't imagine anyone wants to leave here while we're still under threat from the Empire," Agatous responded.

Nida jumped in, "I think I see what Nat's getting at, though. They might not want to be associated with us now we're the open enemies of Chōl."

"If they wish to leave, then they best do it now before the Empire identifies them," Alcarid suggested.

Nat noticed Shoym muttering to himself as he looked around, "I wonder..."

Dempsey responded to Alcarid, "But where would they go? They probably wouldn't last long in the wilderness."

In a seeming daze, Shoym wandered away from the conversation, ignoring Alcarid's calls for him to come back. After a few attempts, Alcarid desisted, and the discussion continued without much progress. After a while, they stood silent but for the occasional suggestion, none of which was viable, until Shoym returned with several Etom.

They were all Etom of Endego, and new members of the Kinship. Shoym explained that none of them were interested in returning to their homes until the conflict with the Empire was decided, believing themselves best protected in the bower. As such, their homes would stand empty for the time being, and available to those Etom who wanted to leave Sanctuary Endego. With humility, these Kin offered their homes and their belongings to house the unbelieving refugees of Sakkan.

When Shoym informed the Etom who desired to depart that some of Endego's Kin were offering them their homes until peace was established, they were shocked at the unselfish sacrifice of the Kinship.

Incredulous, they accepted the offer, thanking Shoym and the small attachment of the Etom who elected to share with them.

Provided with directions and keys to their temporary lodgings, the unbelieving Etom set out from Sanctuary Endego. It was at this time that Nat realized Iver was missing from the outgoing contingent, and he couldn't find the surly orange Etom anywhere in the bower.

In all their excitement over the rhema and their preoccupation with the impending battle, no one had been paying attention, neither could anyone provide information on where Iver had gone. Because Iver had not been seen, even by the sentries, since the dark pre-dawn hours when they had all gone back to sleep, Nat concluded he must have snuck off before sunrise. Nat hoped that Iver had simply left and didn't harbor any malevolent plans for the Kinship.

In anticipation of inevitable conflict, the entire Kinship gathered near the edge of the pool to discuss preparations. Although any of their number had the right to speak, only a few felt inclined to do so.

The conversation began with Ënar, who at once recommended, "We ought to gather or improvise some weapons."

"Do we really think that necessary, given the Nihúkolem weren't able to penetrate Sanctuary Endego?" Agatous rebutted.

Alcarid concurred with Ënar, "I say, 'better safe than sorry.'"

Nida joined in, "I believe in the power of the Kinsman. However…"

With a gentle, firm voice, Blithewit interrupted, "If I may?"

Surprised at the fox's participation, Nida conceded, "Of course, friend fox."

"As you well know, the Nihúkolem are not the only troops under the Empire's command," Blithewit began. "Whisperweave and I are only two of a great number of Beasts and Men at their disposal, and we met no resistance but the trembling of our own hearts at the edge of Sanctuary Endego."

Emboldened at Blithewit's mention of her by name, Whisperweave also chimed in, "Blithewit is correct. Even if you only account for the foxes in the area, that's several dozen enemies whom the wonderful light of this place will not stop."

"I, too, agree," Shoym interjected.

Dempsey responded, "We had a number of weapon caches around the village before we left on expedition. Perhaps some of them are still intact?"

"If we proceed, that would be the first place to look," Agatous answered. "My only concern is that don't depend too heavily on these arms. I don't wish to take the provision of the Lord Elyon for granted."

"I understand and agree. We wouldn't want anyone to do that," Nida returned.

Dempsey followed up, "Elyon forbid! Nevertheless, we should take every advantage we can get as His provision."

Nat offered, "If we receive with thanksgiving and in submission to the Spirit, then who is to say it's not His will that we should arm ourselves?"

The pale blue etém, though young, was well-regarded among all the Kinship, and a ripple of consent passed through the assembly. Without further objection or delay, they agreed to prepare for battle thus.

"And let us not forget these new recruits of Endego," Alcarid reminded. "Do any of you residents of the grove possess weapons?"

The Empire forbade its citizens to arm themselves, so it was with hesitant, sidelong glances that the Etom of Endego admitted they had weapons stored at or near their homes.

"Good!" Shoym exclaimed, pulling out a worn map of the village and a short stub of pencil. "Would you all join me over here to tell me precisely where they are?"

A fair number of the congregation broke away to meet with Shoym while Nida and Dempsey conferred with Agatous and Alcarid to eliminate any compromised caches from their search. Nida and Dempsey returned to the larger group to begin organizing small parties for forays from the clearing, and Shoym soon brought back his contingent with a satisfied look on his ashy grey face and a well-marked map in hand.

Nida and Dempsey worked with Shoym to compose the groups with care, combining the natives of Endego with skilled and powerful Etom less familiar with the village. Escapees from Sakkan, such as Kabir, Kaasi, Muta, and Ënar were strong enough to serve as something of a combat escort to the residents of Endego, as were Blithewit and Whisperweave. The foxes were only too happy to serve outside the bower, which was a wonderful place, but lacking in the open space they were accustomed to. Besides, who knew how long it might be before they were free to leave again once battle had been rejoined?

A third contingent developed among the Kinship when Hezi approached Nida and Dempsey with a proposal.

"Ya know, I was thinkin,'" the old, sprightly etém began, "someone ought to stay here, and keep praying and such. Don'tcha think?"

The idea was sound, but took Dempsey and Nida by surprise at first, although they gave their full attention to Hezi as he continued, "Well, ya see, we don't know everything the Empire's gonna throw at us, but we know the Spirit can handle it, whatever it is.

"We also know we have some power here at the foot of the tree, and we ought to use it, too. I betcha the oldest and youngest of us Kin are of most use here anyhow. Whaddaya think?"

Dempsey and Nida looked at one another with amused grins, and agreed, asking Hezi to take charge of collecting Kin for the "special operations" division. Excited his proposal had been well-received, Hezi whooped with joy and began hollering for the attention of those nearby as he took to his new duties.

Dempsey let slip a snort of laughter, eliciting one from Nida as well. Efforts on either of their parts to restrain the sporadic, chuckling interchange failed, and they soon burst into great, uninhibited guffaws. Neither had laughed so hard in a long while, and with tears in their eyes, they soon realized they laughed for laughter's sake alone. It was a sudden, poignant reminder of times long-past: the dance at the temple, training in the Forge, talking over their future in Dempsey's empty home. As they fell silent, the moment became difficult, almost awkward, and they looked into one another's eyes with wistfulness.

Dempsey averted his gaze, not willing to make Nida the first to look away, and they looked down at the ground until both spoke at the same time. The resultant mishmash was unintelligible to either one, and they each exclaimed, "What?" afterward.

Words tumbling from his mouth in a tight jumble, Dempsey asked, "Maybe-we-should-just?"

He hooked his thumb and jerked his head toward the scouting parties that milled close by, and Nida blinked with relief, replying, "Oh, yeah ...yes. Yes. Let's go."

It was apparent that Dempsey hadn't forgotten his feelings for her, and neither had Nida discarded hers for him. They had just been ...mothballed, shelved like the wedding dress she'd repurposed for the dance so long ago. She only hoped Elyon had plans to tailor their sentiments to fit whatever life might look like ...after. In any case, she didn't have time to dwell on it now, and she hurried to join Dempsey in preparing to leave Sanctuary Endego with the others.

Lack of romance notwithstanding, she considered, *we* do *make a great team.*

Nida and Dempsey weren't long in coordinating with Shoym to assign regions of the village to each of the teams. They gave strict warning to everyone that speed was essential – there was no telling when Imperial forces might return. With a quick goodbye, they set out, eager to return with a trove of weapons for defense of Sanctuary Endego.

Though Hezi gathered a good many Etom to pray, including Rae, Nat, for his part, withdrew to a solitary place to pray alone. He sought a clarity of guidance he knew would be difficult to find among the distraction of any but the Spirit's presence. Nat climbed high into the tree's branches, and the bizarre thought arose that it might tickle Miyam that he walked amidst the leafy boughs. It was obvious he needed look no further than himself for distraction, but he pressed on regardless, limbs enlivened by the exercise and heart eager to attain the tree's utmost heights.

At last Nat's head broke through the canopy, and he pulled his wee form atop the tree's crown to look out over Endego. At night, the tree stood out for the obvious reason that it shone, but in the bleak, deep-autumn daylight it stood out as the only tree in leaf. All others within view were barren but for a few distant spruces.

Nat perched in the swaying fingers of the tree, and gazed all around, reflecting on the beauty of Creation as he did. He closed his eyes and sought the Spirit, the cool breeze dancing about him while he prayed. He might have come looking for guidance, but the Spirit did not offer it at first. Instead, Nat sensed the peace and comfort of familiarity with the Spirit, and in His goodness breathed deep.

At last, the Spirit urged Nat to look northward, to the sky. Without a second thought, Nat responded, uncertain what to expect as he swiveled in obedience. The sky stretched a clear and steely grey-blue across the northern horizon, mere wisps of cloud visible in the distance. Nothing broke its heavenly continuity at first, and Nat wondered what the Spirit meant to show him.

Look again, the Spirit spoke, and Nat complied, narrowing his eyes.

There, he thought, spying a dark, broken line of faint figures spanning a good portion of the sky.

"What is that?" he wondered aloud.

It was too late for geese to migrate, and these birds did not fly in the geese's characteristic chevron formation. The Spirit impressed an image of the kestrels that had pursued them west of Sakkan upon his mind, and Nat squinted in alarm to confirm the impression, lamenting Sayah's absence now more than ever. The æglet's eyesight was much sharper and had far greater range than his and would have been certain to tell Nat what he was desperate now to know.

While Nat's vision lacked the accuracy of Sayah's, he could soon make out in sufficient detail the forms closing on Endego from the north with frightening speed. He was sure they were raptors, one of which became clear first as the largest of their number – a great ægle with a cowl of white and dark wings extended wide, began the descent to the village.

Nat was well aware of an ægle's visual acuity from his time spent with Sayah, and, wondering if he'd already been spotted, debated whether or not to slip beneath the tree's leafy cover to hide. Hesitant, he stared instead as the birds approached, estimating perhaps a dozen ægles and twenty or so smaller birds that he now recognized as kestrels.

Or so Nat thought, frozen but for the movement of his eyes as he watched one kestrel in particular with curiosity. This one was a bit larger, its plumage darker, and its profile resembling that of the larger ægles.

It is *an ægle,* Nat noted with interest. *Maybe it's just younger than the rest?*

Even though the raptors had yet to reach the edge of the village, they were close enough that Nat detected the young ægle's head tilted in his direction. The raptor locked eyes with Nat, whose interest turned to alarm as the ægle altered course in his direction with a piercing shriek. Nat had seen enough and dove under the canopy to begin a hurried climb down the tree to warn the others. The Empire's forces had arrived.

Gael dove at the blue Etom that stared up at them from the crown of the leafy tree, her wings aflutter in frustration as she broke off her attack. She was zealous for blood, and the novelty of Etom flesh intrigued her hungry mind. These were their targets, according to the kestrel that had conscripted their service to the Empire, and Gael was likewise eager for glory, certain she'd rise through the ranks if given ample opportunity for bloodshed.

The fledgling grumbled as Father called her back to their loose formation and reminded her that their first priority was reconnaissance. She fell back in as the kestrels led them to land at a nearby staging area outside the village. Though any of the ægles could eat the strongest of the kestrels for breakfast, the ranking officer on this mission was regardless one of the smaller raptors. The ægles would have to submit to the military hierarchy and follow instructions . . . for now. Gael longed to be unleashed on the Etom and hoped for combat once they had assessed the enemy's strength.

Strength! she scoffed.

Gael thought the term ill-applied to Etom, though rumors indicated the lowly beings had managed to repel a hundred Nihúkolem. But rumors were often false, and Gael couldn't see how the Etom might have managed it. In any case, their unit was first to the battlefield following the Nihúkolem's purported defeat. If anyone was to have a chance at first blood, it should be them.

Nat began shouting from the treetop down as he descended in haphazard form, "They're here! The Empire is here!"

More than a few times, the etém almost fell to his death in his rushed descent, but each time he caught himself, determined to help the Kinship fend off the threat. Nida had just returned with the stash of weapons they'd found and recognized her son's voice drifting down. She looked up into the tree, locating his small, cornflower form clambering down the trunk. He was in a reckless hurry, and his shouts were urgent.

She caught a single word on a favorable gust of wind, "...Empire!"

Looking around the bower, she saw most of their scouting parties had returned, though not all, and called those present together to determine what arms the Kinship possessed. While the others gathered all the weapons, Nida spotted Rae, and shouted for the rosy pink etma's attention.

Startled, Rae turned and asked, "Yeah? What's going on?"

Nida pointed to Nat's crawling figure, and instructed, "Nat's shouting something about the Empire, and he almost fell a second ago. You know him. He doesn't slip like that, and he's in an awful hurry. I need you to keep an eye on him, and an ear out for what he's shouting. If it's important, I need to know right away, OK?"

Rae nodded, her brow furrowed with care, and answered, "Yeah. Sure, Nida. I mean, yes, ma'am!"

The young etma spun to leave on her errand, but turned back to ask Nida, fear in her eyes, "Do you really think they're here already?"

Nida pursed her lips to contain the anguish she felt for these young ones, and gave a short nod, turning away before the tears welling in her eyes could spill forth. No use crying. Time for war.

Sayah tumbled uncontrollably in the gusty updraft, catching sporadic glimpses of the faraway land below approaching faster and faster as he fell. While remote introspection informed him that he might soon meet his doom, he was not anxious. Rather, he held his peace with confidence the Spirit had directed his departure from the Cold Vantage. The æglet's unfledged feathers slowed his descent, if only by a meager amount, and the unsteady billowing of the Windwall at times decelerated his descent further. It was possible the updraft would engage in full before Sayah reached the bottom and slow the æglet enough to survive. With the Spirit, anything was possible.

At the mere internal mention of the Spirit, Sayah's sense of Resonance kicked in, so attuned was he to the Spirit in his quickened state. At the Spirit's urging, Sayah spread his scrawny wings, made more so by the prolonged fast, and attempted to stabilize himself. It took a moment, but he soon halted the dizzying somersault, engaging the untested instincts for flight that he nevertheless possessed to render himself upright with long, thin wings extended to catch what wind they might. Sayah decelerated still more, but the ground was much closer now. The inexperienced æglet suspected he yet fell far too fast to prevent his death.

The Spirit brought to mind a memory of Father spiraling down over the nest with a heavy catch in his claws, and Sayah did his best to emulate the recollection. Dipping one wing and raising the other a bit, the æglet soon achieved the familiar form, slowing his descent yet more as he circulated downward. With relief, Sayah chuckled that he might have doubted the Spirit intended his survival. And then the Spirit spoke.

Faster, Sayah! Tighter!

At first the æglet couldn't believe what he'd heard, but then shook his dark and fluffy head clear and surrendered, *Well, I knew what I might be in for from the start. What difference does it make now?*

In obedience, Sayah tucked his talons close and angled his wings to steepen his descent, accelerating at once into an unstoppable, downward corkscrew. Sayah's downy fluff fluttered hard in the violent airflow, and the æglet marveled that his fuzzy feathers did not detach until, at the tip of his upheld wing, one did. At once, the Spirit resonated with a powerful, trembling force, and deep inside Sayah's frame, a sudden pressure swelled. Sayah's feathers began to fly off with increasing frequency, as within him an eruption seemed imminent. The æglet's body shook from the Spirit's quickening vibrations as Sayah awaited an uncertain fate.

All at once, the pressure shifted, moving out along Sayah limbs to fill his bones, and then spread across his tense and bunching skin. In a single florid burst, pure white feathers sprouted from his body, transforming the æglet in an instant for full-fledged flight. Sayah, shocked at his own sudden metamorphosis, leveled out and cupped wings and tail in an instinctive braking action. His descent came to a near-complete halt, then reversed in the upward Windwall current as it at last engaged.

Sayah kept his wings spread for purchase in the powerful and sustained blast of wind that carried him up, up, up as quick as he had ever fallen. As the snowy white æglet soared, so too did his heart, which leapt with joyful gratitude at what the Spirit had accomplished. It was a miracle, and Sayah recognized his transformation as having begun long ago at the Kinsman's Tree. An æglet no more, the fledgling had become a vessel of Elyon's glory, and he was honored at the distinction.

Below, Sayah saw the vultures likewise begin their ascent on the Windwall flow and glanced up to discover he had almost regained the Cold Vantage. But the fledgling did not cease to climb when he reached the stony crest. No, he let the current carry him well beyond the heights, and looked northward, past the vantage, where ice and snow together ruled the landscape to sparkle bright in the midday sun. The unrelenting reflection of the sun's light on the world's white and icy cap would have blinded any other creature, but Sayah reveled in its brilliance and likewise shone as he spread his wings at the apex of his climb.

Sayah felt he'd summited the sky as he folded radiant wings, rolling back into a dive. Sayah's beak curved into a mischievous grin when his gaze fell on bunches of bearded vultures forming far below once they'd exited the Windwall updraft to settle on the Cold Vantage. Seeking maximum velocity, Sayah tucked wings, tail, and talons and stretched his neck long to become a snowy bolt of lightning flashing down on the raptors that milled along the precipice.

With wry humor, Sayah spotted Hollowback nearing his cove in apparent search of him. He hoped she'd think it a happy surprise to find him in the sky, and for the first time in life, he pitched a true ægle's cry. Every head atop the cold and stony crest turned Sayah's way as he bore down on them in full hunter's dive. Unsure of his abilities, however, Sayah pulled back earlier than he thought necessary, and it was well he did. Such was his speed that even at full extension of wing, tail, and feather, the wind of his passage skimmed the vultures' heads when he buzzed past them on his way to the Windwall.

The vultures' expressions of surprise remained indelibly burned on Sayah's memory for many years, even though his sharp eyes only had an instant to record the moment as he shot past them. Then he struck the Windwall, which almost flipped him back onto the cliff with its force. Despite the near setback, he recovered at once, diving forward into the perpendicular wind without concern for how much altitude he might gain. His objective was beyond the shearing force, and the Spirit gave witness to his determination not to let anything impede him.

With a flurry of powerful wings, the fledgling broke through the Windwall's southward edge to soar forth on the momentum of his efforts. Excitement filled his soul, even as he experienced the physical exhaustion of flight when heretofore he'd not. Sayah looked out in the general direction he'd established earlier using augmented vision, and knew the distance was great. He would need the Spirit's guidance if he hoped to help the Kinship.

Sayah closed his golden eyes in prayer, looking now with spiritual eyes for assistance from the Spirit, who responded with great pleasure to reveal again the supernature of the world. Even through shuttered lids, Sayah saw the world unveiled, and would have set out at once but for the Spirit's voice.

Wait. Rest in Me, and I will give you strength.

So Sayah rested on the breeze, awaiting the promise of new strength. Soon, the weariness drifted from his fledgling limbs, and it seemed all heaviness left his frame. He lost awareness of the passage of time and became uncertain if he slept or not.

With a gentle, yet sudden voice, the Spirit roused him, *Sayah. It is time.*

Sayah's eyes flipped open, steely and bright, as he fixed them on the dark nexus he detected on the southern horizon. His body felt imbued with metaphysical strength when he adjusted course to target the darkness.

Good, the Spirit affirmed. *Now make yourself ready for the wind at your back. Like your dive over the Cold Vantage. I will tell you when.*

At that, Sayah stretched out his wings, the Spirit supercharging his form with light in anticipation of high-speed flight. The coiling tension built around Sayah until almost intolerable, and he likened it to the energy preceding his earlier transformation, though it differed in subtle ways.

The word came, *Go!*

Sayah snapped his wings back to aid in the propulsion, but he was already well on his way, carried along on the mighty wind that for safety behooved him to adopt a streamlined pose as forewarned. Sayah became an arrow in flight, set ablaze with white flame that burned a trail across the sky as he traveled at a speed that rivaled the light that empowered him.

The Æglet's Answer

The kestrels and ægles fluttered down outside a large assembly of foxes, who licked their chops with restrained hunger, aware that on pain of death they mustn't indulge the instinct compelling them to pounce on the raptors. They *were* all on the same side after all. A disdainful Gael followed stoic Father and Mother through the foxes in a tottering procession behind the kestrels to the command center. So arrogant was the fledgling that she imagined herself a match for a fox, though reality would doubtless dictate otherwise.

The command center was a broad, square tent of ornate work, its flaps open toward Endego and the dim glow of oil lanterns illuminating the interior. The kestrel in command ordered her unit to fall in before the tent, which they did in spectacular fashion to form three staggered rows while the second in command called them to attention at the front. Gael eschewed such discipline, thinking it beneath her prowess, but was impressed nonetheless at their obvious rigor.

The kestrel commander invited Father, Mother, and Gael to accompany her into the tent, and Father told the remaining ægles to wait outside. In a much less impressive display by comparison to the kestrels, the independent ægles dawdled about, though their eyes remained attentive as they waited.

The trio of ægles trailed behind the kestrel as she entered the command center. Gael didn't know quite what to expect but imagined a Nihúkolem of some sort awaited them inside. They were the ones really in charge, after all. In the center of the tent lay a mound of black sand, a few grains at a time slipping upward in slow reversal of gravity to heighten the pile. A voice rasped within their minds, emanating from the grit to surprise a frown out of Gael, though the other raptors remained impassive.

I see our airborne troops have arrived, Imafel mused to himself, then addressed the raptors. *Well, are you prepared for your orders?*

The kestrel snapped to attention, "Sir! Yes, sir!"

Father and Mother inclined their heads in compliance, though their unblinking eyes never left the uncanny mound, and Gael shook her head in confusion before imitating the martial posture of the kestrel. She intended to impress this Nihúkolem, if possible.

Very well, Imafel continued. *You are to provide a count of enemy units and weapons by kind. Accuracy is important when measuring the strength of an enemy force.*

Also, and this is critical, you must send one of your troops to pass beneath the boughs of this strange tree. There may be risk to life and limb for the one who flies this mission, as the tree possesses a mysterious force. It is responsible for my current state of discomposure, though we suspect it will have no effect on those who are not Nihúkolem.

Sensing an opportunity, Gael dashed forward, drawing scathing stares from the other raptors, and implored in feigned servility, "Sir, if I may have the hon—"

What is this impertinent thing *that addresses me thus?* Imafel interrupted.

The kestrel sidestepped in front of Gael, extending a wing to push the foolish fledgling back a step as she apologized, "I beg your pardon, Lord Imafel. She is but a youthful ægle, eager to serve you and the Empire. She meant nothing by it."

Then she must learn the significance of her pledge to the Empire, whether offered in haste or not, Imafel responded. *She wishes to fly this mission? Then she shall, and perhaps she will survive her own ambitions. That is all. Dismissed.*

In a rare show of emotion, Mother and Father shook their heads, their eyes full of disappointed regret as they turned to leave. Gael had a veiled understanding of her own mortality, cloaked in excessive regard for herself. Nevertheless, her parents had pinned hopes of family honor on her in place of Sayah because she had proven so strong. In this moment, however, they wondered if they hadn't selected the wrong child, and Mother rested in the fact that Sayah yet awaited them in the relative safety of the Cold Vantage. Perhaps if Gael got herself killed, they might discover their continued legacy in Sayah.

The Æglet's Answer

The Kinship's scouts had left in the early morning to collect weapons from around the village, and all but the group escorted by Blithewit and Whisperweave had returned by noon. It was well that it was so, for Nat's report did not bode well for the Kin. The predatory birds that he had spotted overhead would present special difficulty in defending against them.

An Etom with a spear or blade *might* have a chance, but it was unlikely, and they had collected only a few bows and crossbows from the village. Also unlikely was any significant penetration of the birds' plumage, which further reduced the effectiveness of even the ranged weapons. They needed a solid plan but didn't know if they had time for one.

The Kinship gathered around the outspoken few to listen for the wisdom of the ragtag council, consisting of Agatous, Alcarid, Shoym, Dempsey, Nida, Ënar, and Nat. Wisdom was not immediately forthcoming, and the council at the center of the scrum stood downcast as they considered their options. One ray of hope was they had two foxes at their side, and the Beasts were more than a match for either kestrel or ægle one on one.

At a loss for any feasible plan that might be to their advantage, Nat proposed they go before the tree to pray. Perhaps the Spirit would deliver up an answer to their predicament. But it was not to be so, for on their way down into pool, the loud screech of an incoming ægle interrupted their journey. Nat recognized the fledgling that had tried to attack him earlier, swooping low to circle the bower. Fixed to one spot, he turned to watch the ægle's passage as the rest of the Etom scattered to all points of the clearing, some wading through the pool in hopes of escaping up the tree.

Gael likewise recognized the tiny pale blue Etom that followed her with golden eyes, eyes that reminded her of Sayah. A fury arose within her at the similarity, and she banked tighter to angle around a leafless tree north of the clearing, determined to complete her mission and pick up a tasty little snack in the process. And here it was, her shining, heroic moment to prove her worth to the Nihúkolem, waiting just beneath the branches of the tall and leafy tree.

Gael dove hard for the Etom, ignoring altogether Imafel's warning about the strange force that had disassembled so many Nihúkolem overnight. In the daylight, the border was near-invisible, though the quality of light under the tree was somehow warmer, richer than that outside.

Gael crossed the light-bound barrier, and at once time seemed to stand still within her, aware a gaze even more piercing than Father's had fallen on her. Father's fierce eyes still cowed the fledgling, though in Gael's brash estimation, the disparity between them shrank day by day. She fostered the knowledge that one day, perhaps soon, she would surpass him, and gloried in the coming day of her ascension.

This was different, and the pressure of these hidden oculi revealed a presence so peerless in power that no number of days, years, or millennia seemed sufficient that Gael might match it. She faltered on the wing, disturbed at a prospect her conceited mind had never considered – the existence of One whom she could never hope to challenge. The consideration tore the veil over her eyes away, to reveal the truth that creation ever spoke of the Creator and Judge of all creatures. And Gael was terrified.

As a flash, the realization blinded Gael for an instant, and she missed her swipe at the unmoving Etom, twisting in unsteady flight as she recovered for another pass. The sense of righteous judgement hanging overhead made the bloodthirsty beast within Gael howl with rage, beating the bony bars of her ribcage for release. Shaken, she swept past the strange tree, and with baleful eyes askance upon its vital frame, she hated it for the supremacy of the unassailable force it conducted.

Though fear and hatred distracted the ægle, Gael managed to hook around the tree, sighting the lone Etom in the clearing. On her first pass, she had thought him frozen in terror, but in his countenance, her ægle's eyes with pristine clarity read now a different tale. The small, blue figure stood with hands upraised as in surrender, and tranquil face upturned to reflect the golden light mirrored in his eyes. Gael watched in growing confusion as her unconcerned target's tiny fingers grasped the air as if for hands to lift him, his face now beaming and beatific with joy as favor showered him.

With a gasp, and for the first time, Gael recognized love, the beauty thereof wracking a tear from one eye. She clamped the weeping eye's lid shut, driven in pursuit of success as she bore down on the Etom. Her focus singular and trajectory true, Gael was certain to savor the disconcerting creature this time.

With relish, the Spirit whispered to Nat, *Look up! For your deliverance draws near!*

The etém shifted his gaze toward the fierce and fledgling ægle that intended his doom, its talons spread sharp for him and wings flung wide with feathers billowing in the braking air. Almost too fast for his eyes to see, a blazing, white missile intercepted the murderous ægle to blindside Nat's attacker, whose dark form crumpled beneath the force of the impact. Nat's wide, shocked eyes followed the trail of white flame to a roiling cloud of dust where, covered in snowy feathers, what appeared to be another ægle stood over Nat's attacker.

Wings pinned beneath the talons of the pure white ægle, whose eyes burned with a pure white fire, the prostate Gael squawked, "Who *are* you?"

Placing his beak beside Gael's ear, the luminous ægle spoke, "Hello, *Sister.*"

"No!" Gael gasped. "I don't believe it!"

Though Sayah intended Gael no further harm, his sister trembled, then convulsed with mad laughter as the incomprehensibility of her defeat shook her to her core. So, judgement had come after all. And in the form of her once-feeble brother, unrecognizable now in the power he manifested.

Gael bucked beneath Sayah, shaking her head side to side in baffled negation, and eyes wild as she shrieked, "No! No! No! Never! Never! Never!"

Sayah gazed down at Gael with pity as she lifted her head from the ground to scream in his face, "NEVEEER!!!"

Gael was a defeated creature, and Sayah no longer feared she might harm Nat as he stepped off her. Once released, Gael sprang up, spinning around to face Sayah, then backing away with cagey, slinking steps.

With malice, she glanced at Nat, who stood behind Sayah's shining form, and Sayah warned, "Gael!"

Gael's eyes pinned as, shaking, she forced her gaze back to Sayah, and with a sneer, growled, "*Brother.*"

Without another glance, Gael turned tailfeathers and fled into the sky, clawing the air for altitude with great, desperate wingbeats. Sayah turned to follow Gael's course, offering his profile to Nat for the first time. Curious to learn more of his rescuer, Nat approached, sensing something familiar about the ægle as he came close.

"Sayah?" Nat asked, incredulous.

The snowy ægle straightened, his pose dignified as his faraway gaze yet blazed with white fire to obscure his eyes.

In somber response, the ægle intoned, "The one you knew as Sayah is no more. Only I remain."

At first, Nat was alarmed and saddened at the loss of his friend to . . .whatever this transformation had produced. Nat knew it had to have been a work of the Spirit, but he was nonetheless distraught as he inched nearer to ask if the ægle formerly known as Sayah still remembered his old friend, Nat.

With a sudden, sidelong dip of the head in Nat's direction, the ægle winked, the fire fading from his gaze as he did.

A mischievous grin snuck along the curve of yellow beak as the ægle asked, "I had you going for a second there, didn't I?"

"Sayah!" Nat exclaimed, running to embrace his friend.

Sayah enfolded Nat in his broad wings as the other Etom crept from their hiding places to marvel at their much-changed ally. It wasn't long before introductions were made all around, and ægle, fox, and Etom-kind celebrated the unexpected victory. It was a small triumph, but it proved they might just have the means to fight this battle . . .and win.

The Æglet's Answer

Just before sunset, Sayah invited Nat and Rae on a short flight. Nida and Kehren bit back their objections as Nat and Rae clambered onto the crouching Sayah's broad, white back. Within seconds, they were aloft, soaring past the treetops. Sayah turned toward the setting sun, and soon they saw the enemy encamped, a great host of Beast and Men trampling down the nearby grassland as they prepared for war.

"Look at that," Rae said with apprehension.

Nat replied, "Regardless of the size of the army gathered against us, Elyon has a plan for our victory."

"True!" Sayah interjected, craning his head back to speak. "And whether the Tree protects us or not, we must be ready to fight to the last."

Nat, Sayah, and Rae's minds whirred, and their hearts burned as they considered how they might attain victory against such a great army. As the sun winked below the eastern horizon, a single ray lingered, a finger of light pointing to a distant land to the northeast, past Sakkan. As one, the trio wondered if this might be where their next adventure would take them, and in response, the Spirit resonated confirmation.

Epilogue

Iver awoke, shivering in the cold of the late-autumn air, aware in some vague sense that a shadow passed by overhead. He was in an unfamiliar part of Endego, east of the clearing where that hateful tree stood. Long shadows told him it was late, and he became distressed that he had slept so long. Any longer out here in the chill weather, and he might freeze to death.

With a groan, Iver arose, the frail ache of bone-deep cold having stiffened his joints. He was careful to look around before leaving his shadowy nook, desiring contact with neither the fools he'd left nor the puppets of the Empire. All seemed quiet and still, and he saw no homes nearby, so he risked leaving his cold shelter in search of someplace warmer.

Heading west with caution, the orange Etom encountered an old path, overgrown, yet still visible, and decided to follow it. A short while later, the path turned northward, and Iver spied the hulking shadow of a large manor at the path's end. He crouched down to assess his options as he looked the mansion over.

It was obvious it had once been a great estate with gardeners to tend its spreading lawn and now-decrepit hedges, which now ran broken and crooked about the grounds. Iver saw no light in the manor's many windows, nor did any smoke escape its chimneys. It appeared deserted.

Desperate for shelter, Iver decided that the old mansion presented as good a chance as any other, and so crept along behind the hedges to get closer to the entrance. The home stood broadside to the path, and its numerous dark windows overlooked the lawn. Iver hoped to pass to the end of the manor undetected, where he might crawl past windows to gain access through the wide front doors. Not that he was above breaking a window to save his own skin. He just thought he would be less likely to draw attention if he needn't do so.

Iver was successful in reaching the eastern end of the house without being accosted and thought himself unobserved as he darted low between the windows across the front of the manor. He tiptoed up the steps to the double doors at the front, and hesitated to try the knob, uncertain now the moment of truth had arrived. Just as he reached for the doorknob, the creaking door opened inward onto darkness.

A voice that creaked more loudly than the door had called to him from the gloom, "Come in. Do, please, come in."

Iver glanced around to either side before staring, undecided, into the gloom. At last, with a deep breath, he plunged into the darkness.

Iver closed the door behind him but kept a hand on the knob should he desire a sudden exit.

Again, the voice groaned, "Welcome, stranger. What brings you here of a chill, autumn evening?

"P-P-Please," Iver in a stammer his pride attributed to the cold, "perhaps a light?"

"But of course," came the squeaking response.

The light of a long match flared, leaving spots in Iver's eyes as his host lit a handheld lamp. His eyes were still adjusting to the light as its bearer held the lamp at waist level, the mellow flame revealing only the lower portion of a face. Iver restrained a horrified howl at the Blight-encrusted chin and mouth that greeted his eyes as even now, the scabrous lips cracked into a grin.

With a dignified etiquette that belied her appearance, Iver's hostess offered hospitality, "Now, now, there. You look about to freeze to death. My name is Pikrïa, and I am the lady of this manor. Why don't you join me while I build us a fire in the study, and you can tell me your name? I so long for a little company, and I'd very much like to hear about the happenings in Endego."

Pikrïa turned from Iver, ostensibly to build a fire, and was already shuffling away, along with the comfort of the lamp and the promise of a warm fire. Iver deliberated a split second, then decided to take the risk, and hurried to join Pikrïa in the study.

Look for
Keys to the Captive Heart, Book 3 of *The Kinsman's Tree Series*
Available Now

Author Biography

Timothy Michael Hurst continues to pursue God's call and is working hard to finish *The Kinsman's Tree* series by the end of 2019. He holds a bachelor's degree in Foreign Languages and Literature from the University of New Mexico, and currently resides in New Mexico with his wife and four children.

In the author's own words:

"I am a writer who believes that the life lived best is lived in service to God and that only under the guidance and power of the Holy Spirit one might produce a worthwhile work. I seek to craft entertaining, enriching, and inspiring tales that glorify the Lord in confidence that the Holy Spirit will use them to change lives and draw people closer to Jesus Christ.

In simply offering myself in surrender to the Spirit, I have discovered the satisfaction of worshiping the Lord as an instrument of the writing process. I believe my experience be confirmation of God's calling on my life and pray that each and every person is as deeply transformed in reading these stories as I was in writing them. To Him alone be the glory."

—Timothy Michael Hurst

Made in the USA
Lexington, KY
20 November 2019

57376533R00192